*A Costume Ball in an Italian Villa . . .
A Timeless Dance of Desire*

Pandora was in the masked man's arms, whirling in a waltz before she could say a word. . . . She stared up at him, at the almost-black eyes glittering at her through the slits in his satin mask. Something stirred inside her. Suddenly the villa was thrown into darkness. The moment of unmasking. The moment of the kiss.

He held her face between his warm palms. His lips captured hers, and even before the lights came on, she knew . . .

"Ward," she whispered, staring up at him as the room flooded with lamplight. "What on earth are you doing here?"

Forever, For Love

Becky Lee Weyrich

POCKET BOOKS

New York   London   Toronto   Sydney   Tokyo

An *Original* Publication of POCKET BOOKS

 POCKET BOOKS, a division of Simon & Schuster Inc.
1230 Avenue of the Americas, New York, NY 10020

ISBN: 0-671-66047-0

First Pocket Books printing September 1989

10 9 8 7 6 5 4 3 2 1

POCKET and colophon are trademarks of
Simon & Schuster Inc.

Printed in the U.S.A.

For a special friend, my aunt,
Vesta Dickerson

Acknowledgments

My thanks to several friends who helped at various stages with this novel—Nancy Knight for suggesting my trip to Galveston, Sandra Chastain for sending me Patricia Rae's *Storm Tide,* Eugenia Riley for acting as my Texas connection and putting me in touch with Mr. Bob Nesbitt of Galveston, who sent me a copy of his intriguing book, *Bob's Galveston Reader.*

And, as always, many thanks to my husband, Hank—my research assistant, driver, and patient companion in this life and perhaps . . .

Forever,
For Love

Pandora's Box Recovered!

A dramatic postscript was added this week to the Historical Preservation Society's rescue of the fabulous Gabriel Castle on Broadway. Saved from the wrecker's ball by an anonymous eleventh-hour donation last year, the great pink marble palace stands as a reminder of the Oleander City's glory days, a monument to the Sherwood and Gabriel families, and a tribute to architect Nicholas J. Clayton's fine talents.

A spokesman for the Castle Museum said at a press conference today: "We have made quite a find. In response to our plea for the return of original furnishings that were auctioned several years ago, a distant relation of the Gabriel family wrote the museum from New Orleans that she was sending us a lady's writing desk. In transit, the piece was damaged slightly, revealing a secret drawer which contained Pandora's Box. The mahogany box, over a hundred years old, is believed to have been owned at one time by Jean Laffite. In later years, Ward Gabriel presented it to Pandora Sherwood.

"Besides some fifty or so letters, clippings, and mementos from Galveston's golden years, the box contains two coins of Spanish silver, a lock of hair tied in ribbon, a shell on which has been painted a single rose, and a pair of antique opal earrings. We hope these items will shed new light on the Sherwood-Gabriel family history, so that we may offer our museum visitors an even more complete exhibit."

Prologue

August 27, 1886
Galveston, Texas

Ten-year-old Pandora Sherwood huddled in the linen sheets of the strange bed, clutching her pair of white angora kittens tight against the frocked bodice of her nightgown. At this terrifying moment, the wriggling, blue-eyed fur balls seemed her only links to the past. All else had been swept away a week ago this very night.

When the fierce tropical cyclone roared in over Matagorda Bay, her parents, her friends, her home, the whole town of Indianola vanished on the crest of the storm tide. As if by some whim of destiny, Pandora, her kittens, and her young maidservant, Cassandra, had floated to safety on a deep bureau drawer.

But why had she been spared? Pandora wondered. To come here to live with strangers, in a strange house, on a strange island? To quake with fear each time the wind blew or the thunder rumbled in the distance? At times like this, in the darkest, loneliest part of the night, Pandora almost wished she had drowned with her mother and father.

Why hadn't her parents listened to her? She had warned them of her terrible dream two nights before the storm. But they had dismissed the dream along with all her other premonitions as no more than childish fantasy. They had refused to leave their home, and they had died.

The full moon, sailing high above Galveston on a sea of storm-tossed clouds, shed eerie patterns of silver and black on the silent landscape below.

Shadows cast by the lacy wrought-iron trim of the balconies played over the white-painted brick of the Sherwood mansion on Broadway, giving the effect of some grotesque magic lantern show. The whole world seemed distorted, twisted, unreal. And Pandora, wide awake, all alone, and terrified in the bedroom on the second floor of the big, white house, felt herself an integral part of that unreality.

Pandora was aware of the night air pressing in through her open window. It felt as warm and sticky as blood—the blood of the woman who came in her dreams.

She tossed restlessly on the bed, fighting the heat, the humidity, and her own subconscious. The dream would come again tonight. She tried to avoid imprisoning sleep. But it was no use. Her lids grew heavy. Once she nodded off, she was powerless over the midnight visitations that had plagued her since earliest childhood.

Suddenly, the sound of bells could be heard over the distant pulse of the Gulf, filling the quite night. It seemed as if every church bell in the city was clanging a desperate warning . . . a warning to Pandora alone. This was the way it always began.

Even when sleep finally overtook her, Pandora tried to shut out the sound, pulling the pillow over her head, hoping to escape the visions sure to come. The effort proved useless. The toll of the bells was the prologue to the usual grisly nocturnal drama. The nightmare would come as surely as the storm that it presaged.

An instant later, all was total, deafening silence once more. Pandora tensed and moaned softly, waiting for *him* to appear. Perhaps she would see his face this time. But would she recognize him?

The sound of his boots came to her clearly. Heavy boots,

pacing the hallway outside her door. Then his husky voice, calling, "Darling! Darling, where are you? Hurry, the ship's waiting. We haven't much time left."

Pandora was certain the man called out to her. She tried desperately to answer him each time she heard his voice. But her attempts to speak brought only frustration and silent weeping as she slept.

Pandora had mentioned this night visitor to her aunt. But Tabitha Sherwood had only laughed and said, "Well, the bounder's back, is he? That's the ghost of Jean Laffite you heard, my dear. He's haunted this house since the day it was built. Some say he buried treasure on this site and comes back in search of it. I've never heard him myself, mind you, but I *know* he's here."

As certain as her aunt was that the ghost was a part of her house, Pandora was just as convinced that he was her own personal property. She'd heard him many times at her parents' home in Indianola, before their deaths in the storm, before she came to live with her father's brother and his wife and their little daughter, Angelica.

As the man's voice faded from her dream, another took its place, a child's voice reciting a singsong nursery rhyme. Pandora relaxed slightly. She knew this apparition. The sad little girl had come a thousand times before, slipping down the chimney or in through a window when no one was watching. She would sit for a time and play cat's cradle at the hearth, twining the silken thread round and round her chubby fingers. Lovely, dark-haired, sad-eyed Jeannette. Pandora had no idea how she knew the girl's name. But it seemed to belong to her.

When Pandora was very young, she had tried to tell her parents about this girl who came to her in the night.

Her father, with a hopeful look in his green eyes, had said to his wife, "You see, my dear, our Pandora's as normal as can be. She even has a make-believe friend like all children her age."

Pandora's mother had said nothing. She had turned away, tight-lipped and grim, as if she had heard not a word that either her husband or her daughter had spoken. At her mother's reaction, Pandora had sighed and shrugged and vowed never to mention Jeannette to anyone, not ever again.

Soon Jeannette began to fade. "Don't go!" Pandora pleaded in her sleep. But it was no use. Already the little girl on the hearth was losing substance. Pandora could see through her—the painted tiles around the fireplace, the brass tongs and shovel, the last glowing embers in the grate. Then, like a puff of smoke blown by a strong wind, Jeannette vanished completely.

When she disappeared, so did the bed, the fireplace, the very room where Pandora slept. Suddenly, she found herself high in the air, hovering over Galveston. Miraculously, she had a gull's eye view of the island. She could see all from east to west, from the Gulf of Mexico to Galveston Bay. Yet everything looked so different. There were no houses on Broadway, no Broadway, in fact. No fluttering palms or fragrant oleanders. The whole place was barren of trees, save for a grove of three small oaks, struggling to sustain their foothold in the sand.

Soon she began to descend, her eyes focusing on a single scene being played out on the beach. A tall, handsome man with dark, shoulder-length hair was hurrying a woman toward a waiting boat. His arm embraced her shoulders protectively. He wore heavy boots. She was barefoot. When they reached the hot sand of the beach, he swept her up into his arms to carry her the rest of the way. For a moment, he stood motionless, leaning down to press his lips against hers in a long, deep kiss that sent a shiver of pleasure and pain through Pandora. A kiss of farewell, perhaps?

Then he turned, and they both gazed back at a great red mansion in the distance. Pandora saw tears on the ebony-haired woman's face and she realized that she was crying, too.

"It's over, darling," the man said in a voice husky with emotion. "But we'll find another place to be together."

The woman leaned her head against his shoulder, clinging to him desperately. "It makes no difference, my love. We'll *always* be together now. Nothing else matters."

Suddenly, Pandora spotted something that neither the man nor the woman could see—a movement in the grove of oaks. The gleam of a pistol barrel. She tried frantically to call out to them, to warn them. But they ignored her cries.

"I love you, darling," the man whispered to the woman in his arms. "I'll love you until the day I die."

"Our love will last longer than that," the woman assured him. "We'll love each other through all eternity."

And then it happened. The sharp report of a pistol, followed so quickly by a blossom of red blooming at the woman's breast. The man cried out in anguish and disbelief.

His lover lay dead in his arms.

Desperate now, Pandora felt herself reaching out, trying to wipe away the blood, trying to soothe the grieving man. But even as she drew near, the scene faded, dissolving to blackness before her eyes.

Out of this total void came the nightmare's final evil, a scene so terrible that Pandora felt herself trembling in anticipation even before it materialized.

The black nothingness before her closed eyes turned into monstrous waves, driven by cyclone winds. In the midst of the terrible tempest, Pandora saw herself, naked, clinging to a bit of flotsam for her very life. Her bright copper-colored hair flew in the wind and she writhed and screamed in agony as cold rain pelted her body. Time and again, the huge waves slammed against her, trying to sweep her away. She coughed and gasped, half drowned in the deluge. She could feel herself weakening. She could not hold out much longer against the killer storm.

Ahead of her, she saw long black fingers reaching out for her, ready to tear away her life-saving grip. Then, as she watched, she spied a thin, silver thread spiraling to her, a lifeline from a figure far below. As she drew nearer, she spied a ghostly woman with ebony hair and a bloodless white face.

"Come, share my love and my grave," the woman instructed.

The waves quieted, the wind died, the blackness gave way to a bright, blinding light.

Pandora's nightmare was over . . . *for now*.

Part
I

Chapter One

September 15, 1893
Galveston, Texas

Ward Gabriel stood at the window of his beach cottage, nervously running his fingers through his unruly shock of black hair. His mood was as turbulent as the sea outside. A muscle twitched at one side of his square jaw and his slate-gray eyes reflected the Gulf's restlessness. Something more than foul weather was brewing, but he wasn't sure what. Maybe part of his uneasy feeling had to do with the flame-haired beauty who was celebrating her birthday tonight.

He had declined the Sherwoods' invitation to the elegant soirée. He'd used work as his excuse and, since Horace Sherwood was his employer, there had been no questions asked. That was good, he told himself. He would have been hard pressed to explain his real reasons for excusing himself from the festivities. He wasn't sure he understood them himself.

He had wanted to be there for Pandora's birthday celebration. He'd been looking forward to it. For years he'd watched with rapt attention as Pandora grew and changed—

from an adventurous child to a mischievous, pre-teen pixie
to a charmingly flirtatious coquette. Now here was the
moment he had waited for so long—the night that Pandora
Sherwood would become a woman. An exciting thought!
He'd even decided on a very special gift for her.

But then Mr. Sherwood had confided in him. "There'll be
a surprise in store for our guests. Since Pandora's turning
eighteen, I've decided to announce her engagement to
young Dr. Saenger at her birthday ball." Ward had been too
stunned to reply.

It had come as a shock to hear that Pandora planned to
marry . . . *ever*. Somehow he had pictured her racing her
matched team of white horses up and down Galveston's
streets forever, leading the town's dandies on a merry chase
for years to come, and trucking off to Europe whenever the
spirit moved her. He couldn't picture her catering to a
husband, managing a house, raising a passel of kids. Pandora wasn't the type. She wasn't like ordinary women. She
needed excitement in her life, adventure, fun . . . passion.

But now she was going to be wed. He had known for
years that Pandora's parents desired this match. It had even
been mentioned in her father's will. The wealthy Sherwoods
had feared their daughter might fall prey to some fortune-
hunting cad. Jacob Saenger was both brilliant and stable,
the perfect man to manage Pandora and her money. Still,
Ward had never believed that Pandora would accept such a
loveless match.

"Pandora *married?*" He couldn't imagine it.

What had shocked Ward most was his own gut reaction
to the news. He'd felt cheated and angry, and it didn't make
a particle of sense. Why, he was allowing himself to pout
like a rejected lover! Nothing could be farther from the
truth.

He was fond of Pandora. He'd always liked her. Well,
almost always. He frowned, remembering. From their first
meeting, when she was only eleven and literally fell into his
life out of an oak tree, she had seemed more adult than child
to him. And even then, as angry as he'd been, he had taken
to her. Since that initial, explosive meeting, when he'd
caught her spying on him and a lady friend, she had intrigued

him. She was different, a little wild at times, with a quick temper and a strange, faraway look in those wise, green eyes. Ward felt as if she knew some secret that no one else in the world would ever be allowed to share. Perhaps it was her sense of mystery that so attracted him.

Although Ward had often wondered what made her so different, so *exotic*—yes, that was the word—he'd never thought of her in a romantic context. He was much too old for her—almost thirty to her eighteen. And the life he led, traveling the world as mercantile tycoon Horace Sherwood's chief purchasing agent, left little time for settling down. Not that he'd ever seriously thought of it, mind you.

Still, he mused, his heavy brows drawing together in a frown, *she could have waited and given me a chance!* He'd thought for a long time now—never seriously, of course—that it might be interesting to give her a whirl, provide her with a few thrills before she settled down to wifing and mothering. He'd told her five years ago, when she'd asked why he'd never married, that he was waiting for her to grow up. He realized now he'd been only half-joking.

Yes, the news of Pandora's engagement had hit him hard, there was no denying it. Perhaps he'd reached that time in life when his mortality was beginning to make itself felt. After all, if a man never married, never fathered children, what did he leave behind on earth to show that he'd ever lived and loved and toiled—that he'd ever even existed?

Or perhaps the very opposite was true, he and Pandora were two of a kind—both free spirits, meant to blow with the wind. If she could get entangled in the web of matrimony, then he could be none too safe himself. Maybe for the first time in his life he was experiencing real fear. Whatever the cause, he had no longing to be present when the end of Pandora's freedom was announced.

Ward turned away from the window and the thundering waves of the Gulf. He'd said he would work tonight and so he would!

Setting his coffee mug down on the cluttered oak desk, he opened a thick ledger and stared hard at the neatly penned entries. The lines of figures danced before his eyes and his mind wandered, straying to the white mansion on Broadway. His hand moved from the page to touch the antique box he'd meant to give Pandora tonight. The hand-rubbed mahogany felt smooth and soft to his touch—as alive as a woman's warm flesh.

Abruptly, Ward slammed the ledger shut and stood up. He wandered back to the window that overlooked the storm-tossed beach. There seemed no logical explanation for his black mood, and no help for it.

Perhaps he'd been too long without a woman. For a moment he'd thought of paying a visit to Abbie Allen's sporting house on Postoffice Street. Abbie's girls were always happy to see him and more than willing to provide him with an hour's entertainment. He flopped back down in his deep leather chair with a weary sigh. No, that wasn't the answer.

Without giving any thought to what he was doing, he reached for Pandora's box and opened it, fingering the objects inside, wondering who had put them there and what mysteries lay locked in their past.

A few blocks away, the Sherwood mansion glowed that night, and all up and down Broadway the sweet strains of a string quartet filled the warm night air. Carriages arrived in an endless flow of polished wood and gilt trim, their smartly groomed teams prancing in high spirits that befit the occasion.

Pandora's engagement to Jacob Saenger was an ill-kept secret thanks to her aunt and uncle, Tabitha and Horace Sherwood. The *crème de la crème* of Galveston society arrived, glittering with their best jewels and twittering with the juiciest gossip of the year. It wasn't every day that the only son of a middle-class German family managed a match with a beautiful heiress. Nor did it often happen that a strange, wild girl like Pandora Sherwood was able to find a respectable man to marry—fortune or no fortune!

Old Proteus, the Sherwoods' butler, heard it all as he helped the gusts down from their carriages, then led them along the full length of red carpet, rolled out from the front door of the Italianate mansion to the road to protect the ladies' gowns.

"My dear," Mrs. Landes whispered to Mrs. Rosenberg, "I never thought she'd marry. Such an eccentric girl! Lovely, but so *different*."

"Different matters not at all, my friend, when there's a fortune involved. You know her father was in *railroads* and left her everything. Jacob Saenger will never have to tend another patient once they're husband and wife. He'll be moving up in the world, no doubt about it."

"Do you suppose they'll *dare* have a family? After all, the children might turn out as odd as she."

"Ladies, ladies, please!" Mr. Landes interrupted with a reproving glance at his wife. "No more of this. They'll hear you. Jacob's a fine young man and Pandora will make him a lovely, sweet wife. Let's leave it at that, shall we?"

The women fell silent, but exchanged meaningful looks. Both of them had sons who had proposed to Pandora Sherwood. Both mothers had held out high hopes. But both sons had been summarily dismissed by the flighty young woman. She hadn't good sense, in their opinion.

In spite of their bruised egos, the two rejected mothers smiled graciously as they entered the gleaming mansion to greet their hostess, Mrs. Tabitha Sherwood. After all, good manners counted for everything, especially here in cultured Galveston—the New York of the West.

Pandora paced her room, her panic rising with each passing moment. Aunt Tabitha had demanded that she stay put until the right moment. "Once all the guests have arrived, you'll make your grand entrance down the stairway, my dear. Oh, I can see it now! Every woman at the party will be green with envy at the first glimpse of that Worth gown. And as for the young men, well, they'll all be wishing they were in Jacob's shoes. Everyone who matters in Galveston will realize at last how wrong they've been about you. If you are different from their daughters, that difference is definitely to your advantage."

With a slightly indignant sniff, Tabitha had left Pandora alone to await her cue.

Pandora wished her aunt had not made that final remark. She detested being looked upon as different. Granted, she had some strange power that other people did not possess, but did she have to be constantly reminded of it? To cover her "queerness," as most people referred to her unnatural abilities, she put on an eccentric facade. If they wanted to whisper about her, she would give them plenty of juicy gossip for their rumor mill—her extravagant wardrobe, her unchaperoned trips, her many casual suitors, her shocking paintings, and her seeming disregard for what anyone might say about her. The only problem was she'd been caught up in her own act for so long that now she hardly knew any longer where the pretend Pandora left off and the real Pandora began.

"What does it matter?" she said with a sudden, angry flutter of her fan. "I am who I am and there is no help for it."

She tilted her head to one side and thought about it for a moment, then spoke again to her image in the mirror. "Actually, I like myself quite well, thank you. Never mind what anyone else might think."

At least her aunt and uncle accepted her "oddity." They took great pleasure in having her demonstrate her second sight for their friends as if she were some sideshow entertainer. Her own mother and father, on the other hand, had tried to hide her gifts away, to *protect* her, they'd always said. She'd even been somewhat isolated from playmates until after her parents' death. When at age ten, she came to live with her aunt and uncle and her younger cousin, Angelica, in Galveston where she'd been born, everything changed.

"Eighteen years ago this very night," Pandora said aloud, staring out the window at the palm fronds tossing in the blustery wind. The feel of an approaching storm sent a shiver through her.

Her birth had coincided with an awesome West Indian hurricane that struck the island, battering it viciously. Her mother was visiting her in-laws when Pandora chose to arrive ahead of schedule. Lucretia Pennington Sherwood had thought she had plenty of time before she was due. But

16

the storm, old Dr. Saenger said, brought on her labor prematurely. So Pandora had entered this life—scrawny, sickly, and perpetually shrieking—six weeks before her appointed debut.

Oddly enough, Pandora remembered every detail of the night of her birth. She even remembered the discussion between her mother and old Dr. Saenger, Jacob's father, only moments after she was born. She recalled her mother's tearful gratitude and the physician saying in a soothing, teasing tone: "I've a fine strong boy for this pretty girl of yours once they're of an age to wed." Pandora always figured that it was Dr. Saenger who put the idea in her mother's head. A good idea, she reminded herself. She was happy to comply with her parents' wishes in this instance. They hadn't often agreed on things. Her parents had always dismissed her dreams, her visions, and these memories of her birth, saying that she had only heard them speak so often of that night that it *seemed* an actual recollection. Still . . . Pandora wondered. Remembering one's birth hardly seemed stranger than being able to see into the future. And that she did regularly.

A sharp rap at the door brought Pandora out of her reverie. "Come in," she called.

Angelica stood before her a moment later—a girl of sixteen with long silver-blonde hair and pale blue eyes large, lovely, and mesmerizing. Her cousin's fragile beauty never failed to shock Pandora. Angelica's features were finely cast, classically sculpted. And her fair coloring gave her an ethereal look. Pandora liked to think of herself as attractive. But when her younger cousin was near, she realized that her own mouth and eyes were too large, her lips too full, and her nose a fair copy of those patrician ladies in Roman sculptures. As for her coloring, she seemed to have been baptized in a brilliant rainbow. Her hair blazed as red as a sunset over the Gulf. Her green eyes were an odd, light shade that reflected the colors around her. On stormy days they were gray-green, while in bright blue weather they turned turquoise and in full sun they paled to the color of tender spring grass.

In artists' terms, Angelica mirrored some pale, cool

beauty from Botticelli's brush, while Pandora saw herself more in the image of Edouard Manet's much-maligned *Olympia*. She even shared the nude model's faithful, dark-skinned servant and her love of cats.

Pandora smiled at these self-deprecating thoughts. Angelica looked too unhappy to be envied. The girl's hostility was a palpable force in the room. Angelica's jealousy had been clear from the moment Pandora came to live in the Sherwood home. Pandora tried everything, but she could not win her younger cousin's trust and affection.

"Angelica, you look gorgeous! That gown is simply perfect for you."

The slender blonde tilted her head back at a defiant angle and stared at Pandora, unsmiling. "Well, it isn't from the House of Worth, but I suppose it will serve well enough for the evening. After all, it's only a birthday party."

Pandora had pleaded with her aunt to order both their gowns from Paris, knowing what Angelica's reaction would be. But Tabitha had replied, "Go to all that expense for a child? My dear, your tastes are far too extravagant. Besides, you'll want to outshine Angelica at your party. She'll look dazzling no matter what she wears. But you must work at it, dear."

Pandora avoided her cousin's accusing gaze and asked, "Is Aunt Tabitha ready for me to come down?"

Angelica shoved one of Pandora's six white cats out of the slipper chair and sat down, being careful not to muss the peach lace ruffles of her skirt. "I think this whole business of a *grand entrance* is silly."

"I couldn't agree more. But you know your mother when she sets her mind to something," Pandora replied. Then with a twinkle in her eyes, she added, "I'm half-tempted to sneak out the back way and let *you* come down the stairs while I slip in through the servants' passage. Wouldn't *that* frost the cake?"

Angelica stared in silence at her cousin. Finally, she said, "I can't believe you really intend to marry Jacob."

Pandora turned back from the window in surprise. "Angelica, what are you saying? Everyone has known for years that Jacob and I would marry eventually. You know it's what my parents wanted for me. Why, I've never given any other man a serious thought. Of course, it won't be right away. Jacob has to establish his practice here in Galveston and I still plan to go to Europe to continue my art studies for a few months. And I'll buy my trousseau while I'm in Paris. When I return, we'll both be ready."

"And where will you live?" Angelica persisted. "In his father's old house over on Avenue O? That will be quite a comedown for you after having been raised in a mansion on Broadway. Honestly, Pandora, I don't see how you can even consider it."

Pandora laughed. "Angelica, when you care for a person enough to marry, it doesn't matter where you live. You're young yet . . ."

Her voice trailed off as a strange dizziness descended over her. An instant later, Pandora seemed to be far away, in a strange time and place. She tried to come back, but she seemed trapped. She heard herself saying the same words she had just spoken to Angelica: "It matters little where I live as long as I'm with the man I love. I know it's hard for you to understand. You're young yet, Isabel."

Gone was Pandora's gown from Worth, replaced by a long, full skirt of scarlet and a loose-fitting peasant blouse. Her only bit of finery was a pair of golden earrings set with brilliantly sparkling stones. The girl with her was dressed in similar fashion. Pandora's feet were bare, the sand warm beneath them. The brisk Gulf breeze whipped her long, ebony hair. She was holding a baby in her arms, her own child she was sure, although she had no idea how she knew that or who the father might be. But, obviously, the black-haired woman loved him very much.

They were standing on a sandy path that wound through a jumbled maze of huts and hovels. The sun was beating down on them. The girl with her was tall and slender, not blonde like Angelica, but dark of hair and eye. She glanced beyond the village, toward the water. Tall ships lay at anchor—not the steam-driven vessels of Pandora's day, but sailing schooners, flying the flags of many nations.

Slowly, the scene began to fade. Pandora blinked rapidly,

trying to clear her vision. Angelica still sat pouting before her.

"You'll understand when you're a few years older," Pandora said gently, willing the dizziness away, "when you fall in love."

Angelica—or was it Isabel? The strange girl from her vision was in Pandora's room now, still dressed in the ragged costume from moments before. Whoever she was, she flounced up from the chair where Angelica had been sitting and turned angrily toward the door.

"Don't treat me like a child, madame! I am a *woman*. You don't really know anything about me. Perhaps I'm already in love!" Isabel's angry expression turned to a malicious smile as she added, "Or perhaps you *do* know that I am in love and that you can do *nothing* about it."

The words stung, causing pain in the deepest part of Pandora's heart. She tightened her hold on the child as if to protect it from the other woman's harshness. But her arms closed on empty air. The baby had vanished.

Pandora put a hand to her forehead and closed her eyes for a moment. All traces of the vision vanished.

Fighting waves of confusion beyond her understanding, Pandora reached out for the bedpost to steady herself. This was not the first time she had experienced such a vision. But never before had it seemed so real, so threatening. What could it mean?

She was still struggling to regain her poise when her aunt called from the hallway, "It's time, Pandora!"

Taking several deep breaths to steel herself, Pandora started for the door. Jacob would be downstairs waiting. Perhaps what she felt for him was not the giddy sort of love she heard other girls talk about, but she admired and respected her future husband. He was a kind and caring man, a man who would protect her from the harshness of the world. Her parents had chosen well for her. With that thought in mind, she could face any threat—real or imagined.

Dr. Jacob Saenger felt uncomfortable in his newly acquired evening clothes and out of place among the first families of Galveston. He stood patiently at the base of the tall, curving staircase, waiting for the first glimpse of the woman who would soon be his wife.

Only for Pandora would I endure this, he thought with a wry smile.

All around him, the Sherwoods' guests mingled in their usual cliques. The pecking order never changed. On the surface they put on an appearance of friendliness with one another, but the railroad people stayed with the railroad people while the merchants moved within their own circle. And the elite members of the Galveston Wharf Company— the Octopus of the Gulf—made up a totally private and exclusive group, their conversations centering around shipping, tariffs, and port fees.

So where in all this did the son of their good German doctor fit? *He didn't!* And Jacob Saenger knew it. As a physician, he was little more to them than any other paid servant. But his marriage to Pandora would change all that, elevating his position in society. For her and for what this marriage would mean to him, Jacob could make small talk while he sipped imported champagne instead of the whiskey he favored. He could smile when required, nod at the right moment, and even pretend to be enjoying himself.

"Jacob, there you are!"

The familiar chime of a feminine voice made him turn. He smiled genuinely into Angelica's silvery-blue eyes and let out a sigh of relief. He didn't have to pretend with Pandora's young cousin.

"Ah, it's an angel of mercy come to rescue me. And not a moment too soon." Jacob led Angelica away from the crowd, to a relatively quiet corner of the parlor.

"You aren't enjoying yourself, Jacob?" Angelica frowned, not at Jacob, for him. He was clearly miserable at the moment.

"You know me, Angel. I'm not much use at a party."

She bestowed a dazzling smile on him and leaned close to whisper, "I like it when you call me that, Jacob. You're the only one who ever does."

He gazed down at his soon-to-be-cousin and smiled warmly. She looked like an angel tonight, all wrapped in peach-colored lace the same shade as the glow of her cheeks. Overnight, it seemed, she was becoming a woman.

"Ah, I'm a lucky man," Jacob quipped.

"Lucky?" Angelica put on a pretty pout, sure that he referred to his coming marriage to Pandora.

He laughed at her injured expression. "Yes, you little charmer. Lucky that I'll be out of harm's way by the time you're of courting age." He waved his arm in an expansive gesture. "I'd be willing to bet that before you settle down, you'll have broken every heart in Galveston. But I'll be safely married by then."

Angelica lowered her dark gold lashes and gave him a seductive smile. "Stop it, Jacob! You'll have me blushing soon."

He touched her cheek in nothing more than a playful, friendly gesture. "There's not a lady at this party who can wear a blush so becomingly, Angel."

She covered his hand with hers, holding it to her face. "Oh, Jacob . . ."

Just then the music swelled and all eyes turned toward the staircase. Without a word, Jacob moved away from Angelica and shouldered his way through the crowd to the foot of the stairs. He held his breath, waiting.

Suddenly, there she was. To Jacob it seemed that everyone else at the party vanished in an instant. He saw only the statuesque figure poised at the head of the stairs. Pandora had never looked lovelier. Her fiery hair was parted in the middle and drawn back and up in soft waves, ornamented with twists of pearls that ended in a coil atop her head. Her gown of *ciel-bleu* damask was richly trimmed in embroidered lace. Festoons of pink pearls and glittering crystals trailed down the narrow-waisted skirt, ending where the train swept out to trail majestically behind her.

She looked like a queen. Jacob had difficulty equating this vision with the down-to-earth woman who would soon be his wife. For an instant, he told himself he was making a terrible mistake. She was too grand to be a mere doctor's wife. How could he ever live up to such a woman? But he quickly brushed all doubts aside as their eyes met and she smiled. A moment later, she started down to him.

Pandora was still feeling a bit unsteady after her recent vision, but the second her eyes lit on Jacob, she began to relax. As soon as they were alone, she would tell him what had happened with Angelica. He wouldn't understand any more than she did, but she could talk to him about these things. He had a way of making her feel better simply by listening.

She had come down this staircase a thousand times in the past, but tonight the walk seemed longer. She smiled to herself, remembering how in younger years she'd seldom *walked* down the stairs at all. The wide, smooth banister was an excellent slide. Poor Aunt Tabitha was mortified the first time she caught her niece in mid-flight.

Childish pranks were behind her now. Pandora would no more think of sliding down a banister than she would consider performing her mental "parlor tricks" for the guests this evening. She was a young lady now, about to become the wife of a respected doctor. She knew Jacob expected her to make the transition gracefully.

Pandora held out a gloved hand and slipped it smoothly into the warmth of Jacob's palm. He looked solemn, but she noted with relief that there was no disapproval in his tawny brown eyes. She thought that he might think the gown too extravagant or her hairstyle too extreme. The heat of his gaze sent a jolt through her. There was no mistaking his look of raw desire. In that instant, it struck her that Jacob would soon demand more from her than an occasional chaste kiss. Her face flamed at the thought.

"My dear, you are magnificent," he whispered, bowing rather stiffly as he brought her gloved hand to his lips.

She leaned toward him, about to whisper that she needed to talk to him privately, when the band struck up a lively rendition of "Happy Birthday" and the guests crowded round, singing and raising their champagne glasses in a toast to the lady of the hour.

Soon Proteus, assisted by two other servants, wheeled in a six-tier birthday cake, festooned with sugared pink rosebuds and crystalized violets. Pandora blew out the candles to thunderous applause. The moment the cake-cutting ceremony was done, the string quartet began the birthday waltz.

"Shall we, my dear?" Jacob asked formally, offering his betrothed his hand.

"By all means," Pandora replied.

None of the guests joined in. Pandora and Jacob had the entire floor of the Gold Room to themselves. Jacob might not be of much use at parties, as he'd told Angelica earlier, but on a dance floor he could do no wrong. He swept Pandora round and round, making her head spin and her train swing in a graceful arc from her wrist.

When the piece was nearing its finish, Horace Sherwood raised his arms, signaling for attention. All heads turned to him.

"Friends, we've all wished Pandora proper health and prosperity in honor of her special day. But tonight there is another reason for your congratulations. It is with a great deal of pleasure this evening that I announce my niece's engagement to Dr. Jacob Saenger."

A round of applause filled the Gold Room. When the noise quieted, Mr. Sherwood invited all the guests to join him in a toast to the engaged couple. The music ended and the tinkle of crystal goblets took its place.

Pandora finished the waltz, breathless and beaming. If Jacob made love half as well as he danced, she was bound to be a happy woman. She laughed gaily at the thought.

"What do you find so amusing?" Jacob asked.

Pandora felt herself actually blushing, something she never did. "I'll tell you on our wedding night," she whispered back to him.

He shook his head. "Ah, so many secrets. I hardly know how we'll fit them all into that one night."

Pandora answered shyly, "We don't have to, Jacob. We'll have a whole lifetime together."

Suddenly, inexplicably, her words brought a deep sadness over Pandora. Her smile faded and she gripped Jacob's arm.

"What's wrong, Pandora? Are you ill?" Unconscious of his automatic reaction, Jacob gently gripped her wrist between his thumb and forefinger, testing her racing pulse.

"I'm fine, Jacob. It's only . . ."

"What, my dear?"

"I only wish we were getting married right away. I suddenly don't feel right about waiting."

"Pandora, we've discussed all this before," Jacob reminded her. "I thought you wanted it this way. It will be good for you to have one last vacation before you're tied down as a doctor's wife. And in the next few months I can establish myself and move into my new office. By the time we're wed, everything will be in order." He paused for a moment, looking uncertain before he went on. "I've had a letter from Dr. Pinel in Paris. He's agreed to see you. I think it would be wise."

Pandora ignored Jacob's statement concerning the French specialist and remarked instead on his earlier statements. "I know we planned it this way, Jacob. This feeling, it's just something that came over me moments ago. I suppose it's all the excitement tonight. And the storm. You know how the weather affects me."

"Relax, my dear. No hurricane flags have been hoisted. This is just an early nor'easter."

"I know, Jacob, thanks for reassuring me."

Just when Pandora was about to tell him of her earlier vision, they were swept apart—Pandora to the dance floor on the arm of one of her uncle's friends and Jacob to the far side of the parlor where Mrs. Landes wanted to discuss her latest malady.

For the rest of the evening, they only glimpsed each other across the crowded room. Whenever Pandora spotted Jacob, Angelica was with him. That was a relief. At least he wasn't being bored to death by patients seeking free advice. Pandora made a mental note to thank her cousin later.

But her cousin's gratitude was hardly what Angelica was seeking. So what if Pandora had the gown from Worth and the spotlight and all the attention tonight. Angelica smiled. For the moment at least, *she* had Jacob.

"You're going to be awfully lonely while Pandora's in Europe, Jacob," Angelica said while her cousin's fiance whirled her about the dance floor. "If you ever want company, someone to talk to, please feel free to call on me. After all, Pandora and I are just like sisters. I'm sure she wouldn't mind."

Jacob smiled at the lovely young woman in his arms. She was as sweet as she was beautiful. Most girls in her position would have felt envy and resentment, but not Angelica. He would, indeed, take her up on her offer. The months that Pandora would be away were sure to drag for him, and Pandora couldn't object to his taking her young cousin to the theater or out for a drive now and again.

"That's nice of you, Angelica."

She smiled, the picture of innocence and youth. "Nice has nothing to do with it, Jacob. I'm very fond of you. I always have been. I'm glad you're going to be part of this family soon."

Jacob was touched. "Those feelings are returned, I assure you, Angel."

Moments after the quiet conversation between Jacob and Angelica on the dance floor, Pandora finally extracted herself from her guests long enough to make her way to her fiance's side. She slipped her arm through his, successfully dismissing Angelica without a word.

"Do you think we can slip away soon?" Pandora asked. "I'd like to ride down to the beach. The waves sound monstrous."

Jacob frowned. How like Pandora to want to sneak away from her own party to go to the beach. He'd never understood the strange attraction storms held for her. He knew foul weather terrified her. She'd lost both her parents in a hurricane and very nearly lost her own life. Still, the roaring surf and high winds also held a strange appeal, drawing her like a moth to the flame.

"Pandora, I don't see any way that we can slip out with no one noticing. After all, you're the guest of honor."

"Oh, please, Jacob," she begged. "I've had enough

congratulations to last me a lifetime. My head is pounding.
I need some fresh air. You wander over to the side entrance.
I'll go out the back and meet you in the garden."

Jacob shook his head, shocked that she would suggest
such a scheme. "Certainly not, Pandora. Besides, it's time
for me to meet with your uncle in the library for the
traditional father-son chat."

With or without Jacob, Pandora needed some air. She
worked her way toward the back of the house. She was
nearly at the door separating the dining room from the
butler's pantry when she heard her aunt announce, "Angelica's had a fine idea. Pandora, where are you? Since this is
such a special night in your life, we want you to look into
the future and tell us what you see."

Pandora tried to dart into the butler's pantry, but she
wasn't quick enough. Aunt Tabitha spotted her.

"Oh, there you are! Come now, dear. We're all dying to
know your future."

Pandora was led, against her will, through the dining room
and back into the Gold Room. Finally, feeling foolish and
trapped, she stood upon the musicians' stage with all the
guests looking on. Only Jacob and her uncle were missing,
sequestered in the library over brandy and man-talk. Pandora was glad. She didn't want her fiancé to witness this
embarrassing scene.

"Now, close your eyes, dear, and concentrate. Tell us all
what you see in the future for yourself and Jacob," Tabitha
instructed.

"Yes, Pandora," Angelica added, "tell us *everything*."

The last thing Pandora saw before she closed her own
eyes—wanting to be done with this parlor game as quickly
as possible—was Angelica's smiling face. Her expression
sent a shiver through Pandora's whole body, chilling her
very soul.

She closed her eyes quickly to escape her cousin's
haughty gaze. Usually, when Pandora willed it so, she could
summon her visions of the future instantly. She fully expected to see an older version of herself and Jacob with
silver frosting his sandy-brown hair. She would not have
been surprised to see several children playing about a

white frame house with gingerbread trim. Any or all of these visions would have been pleasing, satisfying, acceptable.

What she saw instead struck terror in her heart. Pandora began to gasp for breath. She went hot all over, then cold. The very walls of the room seemed to be pressing in on her. She had to get out!

"Please," she whispered, "oh, please, no . . ."

A moment later, she fled, shoving startled guests out of her way. She ran toward the back of the house, sobbing Jacob's name, but he was nowhere to be seen.

"Oh, dear." Tabitha Sherwood fumbled for words, distraught that her guests were now whispering about Pandora's odd behavior. "Just let her go," she told them. "Jacob's the only one who can soothe her when she's this upset. It's bridal jitters, you know. All young women have these spells."

The guests refilled their glasses and milled about, gossiping quietly about the strange girl and her soon-to-be-long-suffering husband.

Even as her aunt was making excuses for her, Pandora burst into the stable. "Hitch my team!" she shrieked at old Tombee the stableboy.

Frightened by her harsh tone and tears, Tombee quickly followed her orders.

In no time, Pandora was in her surrey, racing through the rain toward the sound of the surf as if the devil himself were chasing her. As she drew ever nearer, the pounding of the angry waves seemed to merge with the thundering beat of her heart. She felt as if her life depended upon getting away, reaching the beach.

She never remembered actually arriving. Nor could she recall hitching her team or climbing down from the surrey. Somewhere along the way, she lost both her satin slippers. It didn't matter.

Only when she was on the beach, with the cool, wet sand beneath her feet, tasting the salt spray and feeling the pounding pulse of the waves, did she come back to her senses. For a time she stood at the high water line, her arms flung wide, her hair whipping her tear-stained cheeks. She swayed with the wind, celebrating her feeling of freedom.

Then, in a moment of sheer desperation, she sank to the sand, sobbing her heart out.

Chapter Two

Ward Gabriel pulled on his oiled cape against the rain. He'd made up his mind at last. Since he wasn't getting any work done, he might as well go to Abbie Allen's. He'd grown more restless and more convinced that what he really needed was a woman. He wanted someone warm and willing to hold, to fondle, someone to ease the ache from deep in his gut.

Switching off the electric light over his desk, he plunged the room into darkness except for the glow of the embers on the hearth. He headed for the door, ready to leave, when something outside the window caught his eye, making him pause and turn for a closer look.

The stormy beach was bathed in shifting patterns of black and silver as heavy, low-flying clouds allowed the moon to shine through from time to time. At first he thought he'd only glimpsed a moving shadow. But then the moon streamed through once again and he saw her distinctly—there was a woman out on the beach.

He was too surprised to react immediately. He stood watching as she swayed in an odd sort of dance, the wind whipping her clothes to tatters that flailed wildly about her.

It was near midnight, high tide, and storming. The woman was all alone. That suggested one thing—suicide. More than one hapless human had become disenchanted with life and ended it all by taking a midnight stroll into the Gulf of Mexico. Only last week a man had put an end to his earthly troubles in this manner. His body had washed up three days later.

"Well, not on my stretch of beach," Ward raged.

Running for the door, he flew down the long flight of stairs, then felt his boots bite into the soft sand. "Wait!" he yelled. But the wind tossed his words back into his face.

She moved closer to the water, tempting it to claim her. His heart was thundering in his chest as he fought the sifting sand and the fierce wind to reach her before she could reach the waves. Then, just as it seemed that she would sink into the water and out of sight, Ward saw her crumple to the sand in a faint.

"Drunk!" he muttered under his breath. Disgusted that she'd put him through such torment, he almost turned back. Let her sleep it off where she was. But he was here now, he might as well get her in out of the storm, he reasoned.

With a huff of annoyance he bent over the limp figure and scooped her up into his arms. To his surprise, he realized that she was no homeless drifter off the docks—the sort who usually did themselves in out of sheer hopelessness. On the contrary, even in the darkness he could see that she was expensively dressed. The crystals on her gown gleamed in the moonlight and the long train was heavy with sea water and sand.

To his surprise, she was not dead weight as he'd expected. The moment he picked her up, she slipped her arms around his neck. When he looked down, he could see that her eyes were wide open and staring into his.

"It must have been some damn party," he commented in a gruff voice.

"It was, but you missed it, Ward Gabriel."

Ward stopped in his tracks, staring down at the woman in

his arms, but unable to see her face clearly. The clouds had put out the moon's light again. Still, he knew that deep, throaty voice. He knew it well.

Then in a flash, it came to him. "Pandora? What the hell are you doing out here?"

"It's my birthday, remember?" She laughed softly, humorlessly. "I can do whatever I like."

"I doubt your uncle or your fiancé would agree."

Pandora shivered against him. She was wet and cold and the blowing sand felt like tiny needles pricking her arms, shoulders, and face. She could think of nothing except how good it would feel to be warm and dry again, and how safe she felt in Ward Gabriel's arms.

"You knew about my engagement. That's why you didn't come tonight," she accused.

Ward bristled. "That had nothing to do with it. I had to work."

"Whatever you say." Pandora was suddenly weary, emotionally exhausted. She leaned her head down on Ward's broad shoulder and closed her eyes.

"I'll have you inside in a minute. Just hang on, Pandora."

She did exactly that, feeling a strange warmth flood through her as she clung to his neck and breathed in his musky male scent.

Pandora roused herself only when Ward carried her into his cozy cottage. A low fire of driftwood glowed on the hearth, the flames rainbow colors from the sea salt in the wood. He set her down and she hurried over to warm herself.

She'd never seen Ward's house before. While he put on a fresh pot of coffee, her gaze went exploring. The whole place looked like a beachcomber's hut. The mantel over the fireplace was a heavy driftwood log, probably a part of some long-sunk sailing vessel. Arranged there in no special order around a ship's clock were seashells, old bottles of amber and green glass, and beautifully colored corals. On a far wall, the sun-bleached jawbone of a shark gaped widely at her, its silvery black teeth razor-sharp and gleaming in the firelight. The furniture was of simple design, probably made by some local craftsman. Bright Mexican serapes and Navajo rugs thrown here and there added splashes of color to the room. In a curio case near the windows, more shells were displayed along with several antique coins—doubloons and pieces of eight. No curtains covered the windows, only a drape of fishnet, hung with corks and colored glass floats. A beachcomber's clutter of treasures, to be sure, she told herself. But the paintings on his walls were valuable and framed in ornate gilt.

Ward Gabriel obviously was a collector of eclectic tastes. Pandora found that appealing. She felt suddenly very much at home here and, as always, perfectly comfortable with Ward himself. It almost seemed she had known him forever. Since that hot day at the grove when she'd interrupted his tryst, they'd been a part of each other's lives. Ward was different from anyone else she knew. He never laughed at her bizarre fantasies or seemed shocked by her desire to become an artist. He simply seemed to accept her as she was, no matter what she said or did.

Pandora had been acquainted with Ward Gabriel for years, but she realized now that she knew very little about him. She thought over what she had heard from her aunt and uncle. Ward's parents—both dead now—had come from New England during the Reconstruction years. His father had been a successful shipbuilder in Bath, Maine, but his wife's poor health had forced them to a warmer climate. Mrs. Gabriel had died only hours after giving birth to twin sons. Ward's brother had not survived long enough to be named. Most of Ward's formative years had been spent in the best boarding schools in the East and in Europe. When he returned to Galveston, Ward sold his interest in his father's company, went to work for her uncle, and invested his wealth in some mysterious venture in Mexico.

She once heard Ward tell Uncle Horace, when they were discussing the sale of his father's business, "I'd rather be a first-class passenger on a ship than build one." She also remembered her uncle calling Ward a "soldier of fortune" and a "modern-day pirate, who could turn a deal with a merchant anywhere in the world as quickly and as easily as he could turn a pretty woman's head, with his silver tongue and ready smile."

She'd heard her aunt and the other society matrons describe Ward as "a prime catch." But Ward seemed determined not to be caught. He obviously enjoyed female companionship, but was seldom seen with the same woman twice.

Pandora glanced his way, wondering what it was that Ward Gabriel wanted in a woman that he had yet to find.

"You'd better get out of those wet things," Ward said from across the room. "You'll come down with God-knows-what if you don't."

Pandora stared down at her ruined gown. Aunt Tabitha would be furious, but there was no help for it.

She cast a quizzical glance at Ward. "In the bedroom, behind that curtain," he replied to her unasked question. "There's a heavy robe on a peg by the bed. That should warm you up in no time."

She watched him pouring brandy into their coffee mugs. That, too, she thought, would warm her. She took the thick, white cup from him and went into his bedroom, never worrying for a moment about being alone with a man—a man she really hardly knew—in the middle of the night.

When she returned—stripped to the skin, covered in an oversized robe—Ward was standing by the fireplace, gazing down into the flames. His dark eyes glowed like obsidian.

"Do you suppose it will dry or simply fall apart?" she asked, handing him her dripping garment.

He took the gown from her and looked it over with the practiced eye of a professional importer. "French, isn't it? And quite expensive. Worth?"

She nodded.

"It won't see any more balls, but it should hold together to get you home in decent fashion." He draped it over the back of a chair near the fire, then turned on her. "Pandora, what the hell were you doing out there?"

Pandora looked away quickly. "You sound like an outraged father, Ward. Please don't scold me. I couldn't stay at the party any longer, that's all."

He reached out and touched her hand. "I'm sorry," he said in a softer tone. "I didn't mean to be harsh, but you had no business out there on the beach all alone. Not at this

34

time of night, storm or no storm. Why, anything could have happened to you!''

She looked up again, a half-smile curving her full lips. ''Nothing did, did it?''

''No. But only because I happened along at exactly the right moment. Two minutes later and I would have been gone. I wouldn't have seen you at all.''

''Gone? Wherever were you going at this time of night, Ward?''

He started to tell her that was none of her damn business. For no good reason, he found that he was angry with Pandora Sherwood. How dare she put herself in such danger? She knew better than to come right into his house and sit there beside his fire—all but naked, mind you—looking so soft and feminine and utterly, maddeningly appealing. She needed to be shocked to her senses and he was just the man to do it.

''If you really want to know, before you sidetracked me into my errand of mercy, I was headed for Abbie Allen's.''

Pandora wasn't shocked, but she was embarrassed. She had ruined serious plans. A soft ''Oh!'' escaped her lips as she felt her cheeks flush warmly.

''I could leave now,'' she offered meekly.

''Wearing *that?*'' He tugged gently at the sleeve of the burgundy velvet robe. ''Don't be ridiculous, young lady! Why, I'd be tarred and feathered by the good citizens of Galveston as soon as the sun came up. You'll stay here until your gown dries. And so will I.''

Several long moments of silence followed as they both sipped their brandied coffee and stared into the fire. Finally, Ward said, ''You still haven't told me what you were doing out there tonight. What happened? Why did you leave your party?''

Pandora shook her head. ''I'm not sure I can explain it. I'm still confused.''

''All right. We'll talk about something else.'' Ward broke another long silence, asking, ''Don't you think you'd better call your uncle?''

Pandora bit her lip and stared at the newly installed

telephone on the wall, trying to decide. "What could I tell him?"

Ward shrugged. "If I were in his place, I'd want to know that you're safe, that you'll be home soon. Otherwise, he'll have the sheriff's men and every volunteer fireman in the city out in this storm searching for you. You don't want that, do you?"

Pandora shook her head. Ward was right, of course. She'd better call. As she went to the phone and turned the crank to ring the operator, Ward disappeared through the curtain into the bedroom, allowing her privacy.

The conversation was brief. Uncle Horace was relieved and then furious. He demanded to know where she was. She refused to tell him. He ordered her home. She said she would return when she was ready. Then she hung up.

Ward came back into the room, a worried expression on his face. "You're in deep trouble, I take it?"

Pandora puffed out her cheeks in imitation of her heavy-jowled uncle and in a gruff voice said, "I *demand* you return at once, young lady! If you won't think of your own reputation, consider your poor aunt, your distraught cousin, and Jacob."

"What about Jacob?" Ward interrupted. "What will he think of all this?"

Pandora expelled a long sigh. "He'll be upset with me, but he'll understand. He'll have to. He's the only one who ever does. I certainly don't understand it myself."

Ward could see that she was withdrawing again, growing more depressed by the minute. He cast about for a change of topic.

"Do you remember the first time we met, Pandora?"

She looked at him suspiciously. Was he asking for more mental tricks from her? No. He was only thinking back to that hot summer day at Laffite's Grove several years ago. She grinned at him, looking much like the eleven-year-old imp she'd been at the time.

"How could I ever forget? You were with a beautiful young woman," she recalled with a mischievous grin.

"Ah, yes." Ward leaned back, nodding at the fond memory. "Estelle Armitage. What high hopes I had for that affair."

Pandora laughed. "You mean you had high hopes for that afternoon, Mr. Gabriel. Why else would you have taken your lady fair to such a secluded part of the island?"

"We only wanted a little privacy for our picnic." His tone made him out as the injured party. "How was I to know that there were *spies* lurking about in the oaks?"

Pandora suppressed a smile. Ward obviously had no idea that she had been on the scene for a good while before she climbed up into the oak tree to get a better view. She had seen far more than he knew.

She could still remember the odd warmth that had flooded through her as she sat hidden in tall grass a few paces from the oak grove, watching the lovers. Ward and Miss Armitage had been stretched out on a blanket in the shade of the trees. For a time they talked quietly, laughed softly at private jokes, then Ward leaned over his golden-haired beauty and kissed her—a long, deep kiss that had set Pandora's pulses racing. A moment later, she had watched, wide-eyed, as Ward's large, sturdy hands crept to Estelle's bodice, fumbling at the ribbons there. Even now, a blush stole over Pandora's cheeks as she recalled what he had done next. Freeing the woman's breasts at last, he had leaned down, kissing the rosy nipples until Estelle squirmed beneath him and cried out for mercy. As young as she'd been at the time, Pandora understood that *mercy* was far from what Ward's lady truly desired.

At that point, Pandora had decided to climb one of the three trees in Laffite's Grove so that she might get a better view of the proceedings. After all, this was her introduction to the sensual side of life. She hadn't wanted to miss a thing.

"If that branch hadn't broken . . ." Ward interrupted her thoughts. He was laughing heartily. "Well, I just don't like to imagine what you might have seen."

Pandora offered him a look of sheer innocence. "Why, Ward! You were *only* having a picnic, weren't you?"

"It was a picnic all right. But you spoiled my dessert."

She turned fierce. "I should have told my uncle what you

did. No one else has ever spanked me, before or since, Ward Gabriel!''

"Are you saying you didn't deserve it—spying on us that way?''

"Well, yes, I probably did. But, oh, how I hated you for it!''

Ward's voice dropped nearly to a whisper. "If you hated me, I *feared* you. I had no idea you were Horace Sherwood's niece—the prim and proper young girl I'd heard about who'd just come to live with them. You looked like a wharf urchin—a rough little boy in ragged knee pants and that big floppy hat, and shirtless to boot.''

Pandora dropped her gaze when Ward described the way she'd been dressed. Her shirt had been discarded on a nearby bush. But what really embarrassed her was the fact that when other girls her age had been quickly maturing, the absolute flatness of her chest at the time had convinced Ward that she was a boy.

"I was sure, the moment you told me your name, that my career was finished,'' he said. "Pandora, I've always wondered, why didn't you tell your uncle? I was baffled at the time. I expected to be dismissed that very day and ordered off Galveston Island besides. I've always admired you for keeping silent about the incident.''

Now it was Pandora's turn to laugh. "Well, you needn't have worried. And there's certainly no need to think of my silence as noble. I *couldn't* tell Uncle Horace. You see, he'd forbidden me to go to the grove. If I'd told on you, I probably would have received a second spanking for disobeying his orders. When I first came to live with them, my aunt and uncle tried awfully hard to control me.''

"Obviously, it did no good.''

Pandora giggled. *"Obviously.''*

"You were an outrageous child.''

"And now I am an outrageous adult.''

He smiled at her. "And loving every minute of it, I'll wager.''

She turned pensive. "No, Ward. Not loving it. Simply trying to survive as best I can.''

He stared at her in silence. How could her life be as

complicated as she hinted? She had everything—family, wealth, beauty, intelligence. Why, there wasn't another woman in all Galveston with such true *elan*. But perhaps her elegant swagger only hid deep insecurities. He'd never thought of that possibility before.

Pandora leaned forward and touched his knee with one finger, her eyes glittering with green devilment. "But, Ward," she whispered, "I have to admit to you—*only* to you, because the others must never know—that I do gain a certain satisfaction from watching others watch me. If they didn't provide quite such a wonderful audience—so easily shocked and inflamed—I doubt that my performance would be half as magnificent."

He laughed and gripped her hand. "I guessed that about you some time ago, Pan. I happened to be at a dinner party one evening a couple of years ago when you spied Mrs. Landes staring at you. You immediately sneaked a puff of your uncle's cigar, blowing the smoke directly at her. I thought the poor woman would go into a coma on the spot."

Pandora groaned and clasped her belly. "Oh, I was *so* sick that night! Even now, the smell of cigar smoke turns my stomach. But I had to do something. The woman had been staring at me all evening, waiting for me to perform some outrageous act. The cigar was there and available, and much more suitable, I thought, than dancing barefoot on the dining room table. Poor Mrs. Landes! That was so long ago, but she still looks on me with a jaundiced eye. I'm afraid she'll consider me the enemy forevermore."

They both lapsed into fits of laughter that left them gasping and coughing.

"I'm glad *we* didn't stay enemies," Ward confided.

"How do you know we didn't?" Pandora asked teasingly, her hysterics fading at the warmth of his smile.

"Well, look at you," Ward said, returning her fond gaze. "You're even wearing my clothes now."

Pandora smiled. "Yes, thanks, Ward. You did save me tonight. And, really, I didn't hate you for long. Actually, I had sort of a soft spot for you when I was younger. You know how it is with little girls. They always choose some older, attractive man for their fantasies. You were mine."

Now it was Ward's turn to blush. His tanned skin turned a ruddy hue and he avoided Pandora's large, green eyes.

"I'm flattered, I think. But do I seem *that* old to you?"

"Not anymore," she answered with a soft laugh. "It seems somehow that you got younger while I was growing older. Does that make any sense?"

"Probably not, but I like the sound of it." Ward grew serious. "Pandora, I don't want to press you." He moved closer so that he could look directly into her eyes. "But I wish you'd tell me what's troubling you tonight. I'm a good listener, if you feel like talking about it."

Maybe it was the rich, soothing tone of his voice that persuaded her. Or perhaps it was the brandy that loosened her tongue. At any rate, the words came pouring out.

She told him about the strange vision she'd had of the woman named Isabel. She described the party and the way she'd felt when she first saw Jacob waiting for her at the foot of the stairs, how she knew they were meant to marry, but she wasn't sure she could please him. And, finally, with a deep shudder, she told him what she had seen that so terrified her when her aunt insisted she look into her own future as Jacob Saenger's wife.

"I saw *nothing*, Ward. *Absolutely nothing!* I closed my eyes and willed my mind into the future as I've always done before, but no visions came." In a moment of renewed fear and confusion, she gripped his hand and sobbed, "I don't understand. What can it mean? What's going to happen to me?"

Ward pulled her into his arms and let her cry on his shoulder. Any other time, with any other woman, he would have taken full advantage of the situation. When had female hysterics ever meant anything more to him than a perfect opportunity to move right in? A touch here, a stroke there, a kiss, another, and they always succumbed with willing, trembling pleasure—their sobs quickly turning to sighs.

But somehow it was different with Pandora. He tried to tell himself that it was because her uncle was his employer, because she was engaged to be married, because she was so young. But none of those excuses held up. Pandora was different; Pandora was special. It all boiled down to that. He would not take unfair advantage of her because he *could* not. Somewhere deep down in his jaded, much-scarred heart, there remained a faintly flickering ember of decency. He couldn't decide if he was relieved or disgusted to realize that fact.

Still, he had to admit that the feel of her unbound breasts pressed tightly to his chest stirred up a coursing of blood that no visit to Abbie Allen's could arouse. Pandora Sherwood might be young, but she was all woman—*warm, tempting, passionate woman.*

"Pandora," Ward whispered softly, "listen to me. I'm no doctor and I know nothing of these powers of yours. But I don't think what happened to you tonight is anything to worry about. Nothing works all the time. You simply had a slight lapse of memory in the reverse. It was probably all the excitement, all the people."

Pandora's crying subsided and she drew back, looking up into the warm darkness of Ward's eyes, feeling safe and reassured. "Do you think that could be it?"

He smiled. "I'm sure it is. And certainly it's not worth crying over."

"I thought when I couldn't see the vision, it meant I was going to die," she admitted. Then she clung to Ward more tightly. "I don't want to die," she whispered. "I have too much to live for, Ward."

Ward clenched his teeth as he held her. She was so warm and soft, and her hair smelled of limes and salt sea air. The ache in his groin intensified by the minute until there was no other course but to put her away from him.

Gently, he removed her arms from around his neck, rose, and walked over to his desk. "I have a surprise for you. A birthday present," he said lightly.

"A gift for *me?*" There was a child's delight in her voice.

"Of course for you. I would have brought it to the party, but . . ."

She gave him a sly, amused smile. "But you had to *work.*"

He lowered his dark brows, looking serious and solemn. "Exactly. And don't you dare tell your uncle otherwise, young lady."

He sat down again next to her and placed his special gift in her hands.

"I figured anyone named Pandora should have her own special box."

"Oh, Ward!" She cradled the antique lovingly, smoothing her hands over the rich, age-darkened wood. "It's beautiful."

He nodded and said simply, "Look inside."

Carefully, Pandora turned the old-fashioned lock and lifted the lid. She gasped softly. "Oh . . ." Why was she feeling dizzy? she wondered. She shook her head to clear it. Her hand trembled as she reached inside and drew out the two silver coins.

"They're Spanish," Ward told her, "and quite old. Probably part of some pirate's treasure trove."

Then the gleam of gold caught her eye. She reached into the box and held the trinket up to the light—a single golden earring set with fire opals. The stones seemed to glow with an inner flame, flashing vivid green and orange.

"It's lovely," she said. "But only one?"

Ward shrugged. "That's all that was in the box when I found it. But there's something else. See?"

Ward himself felt in the box and brought out a dark lock of hair tied with a faded scarlet ribbon.

"If we knew who this belonged to, we'd probably know the secret of the box," he told her.

Pandora trembled all over as she reached for the oak-colored curl. It felt warm to the touch. She held it gently, caressing it with one finger.

"Thank you, Ward," she said quietly. "You've given me a real treasure."

He laughed. "You're right about that. I dug this box up when I was ten years old, down at Laffite's Grove. My friends and I used to search for treasure down on the west end of the island when I came home from school on my vacations. I was the only one who ever found any. And now it's yours. Happy birthday, Pandora."

The dizziness was back, accompanied by a warm, tingling feeling in her limbs. Bells rang in Pandora's ears and the whole room seemed wrapped in mist. She felt as if she were drifting away. Then the ship's clock on the mantel called her back, chiming eight bells—midnight.

She leaned toward Ward, still holding her box of treasures close. "Thank you," she whispered. "Thank you for everything."

Pandora closed her eyes and pursed her lips, offering Ward a kiss of gratitude. He hesitated only briefly.

The moment their lips touched, Pandora felt something akin to an electric shock. Jolted, she opened her eyes. The room with its driftwood fire and fishnet curtains had vanished. Ward Gabriel was gone, too, but she was not alone.

She was seated not on the couch, but on a palm log before a blazing bonfire on a wide, white beach. Not Galveston's familiar beach. This was some place she'd never seen before, with strange, twisted cedars and a ragged shoreline. All about the fire, a ragtag lot of men and women sang and danced. Some sort of celebration was in progress.

A tall man with tanned skin and tawny, sun-bleached hair loomed over her, offering his hand and smiling down at her.

"It's time, darling," he said, caressing her with eyes like dark jade.

Pandora slipped her hand into his and rose. He leaned down and kissed her—a long, searching kiss that seemed to set her very soul aflame.

She was barefoot. The sand sighed as she walked through its deep drifts. The man beside her kept his arm protectively about her, his fingers stroking the side of her breast, sending little thrills of pleasure through her.

"I got it, Boss, the broomstick!" cried a dark monkey of a man, waving a broom handle decorated with flowers and ribbons over his head.

The men and women gathered round singing as the dark-skinned dwarf placed the broomstick gently on the sand.

The man beside her spoke in a voice husky with emotion. "I love you," he whispered. "I think I always have. I *know* I always will."

Then, taking her hand in his, the tall, handsome stranger, dressed in tight britches, polished boots, and a scarlet sash, jumped the broomstick, marrying his love in the native fashion.

The scene faded before Pandora's eyes into a dazzling array of colors. She became aware then that Ward Gabriel's lips were still pressed to hers. She knew she should pull away, but she seemed to have lost all will of her own. She closed her eyes again.

In the next instant, the bright kaleidoscope began forming new patterns and she felt the hot colors throbbing through her whole body.

When the swirling shades of red, green, and orange fell into place, she was no longer on the beach, but in a huge, gilt bed. And *he* was beside her—as naked as she, she realized, spotting her own filmy gown of ecru lace on the bedpost and his burgundy robe lying on the floor.

Already they had been involved in their prelude to love-making. She felt the scald of her blood in her veins and the throbbing ache of desire deep within her. Every nerve in her body felt as if it were dancing on the very surface of her flesh. She lay tense—listening to his breathing, waiting for his next move.

Slowly, he drew the cover down over her, exposing her nakedness to his eyes, inch by agonizing inch.

"Just relax, darling," he whispered, and his warm breath passing over her made her nipples harden with need.

He touched her breast—a featherlike stroke that brought a soft moan from her throat. He smiled down at her, leaning ever closer to her lips. When his mouth covered hers, she gave in to him at once, parting a way for the gentle stroking of his tongue.

He tasted of sweet, red wine. Yes, she remembered now! They had shared a glass earlier. He had passed the warm liquid from his own mouth into hers as they kissed. That had been the very start of it all. The awakening of passion and longing and desire.

As his kiss deepened, she clung to him—moving as he moved, willing him with her silent actions to take her as he would. *Now,* her heart sang. *Now, my darling, please.*

He loved her slowly. Trailing his strong, brown fingers down her body until her flesh quivered beneath his touch. His mouth rained kisses down her throat and breasts, and he captured a taut nipple between his warm lips and suckled deeply. She twisted on the bed, her head flailing from side to side. She dug her fingers into his shoulders, feeling the hard muscles tighten beneath her palms. He released her, but it was only a moment's respite. His teeth grazed her other nipple, his tongue lashed it viciously. Fire raged through her body, turning her flesh, it seemed, into a mass of hot, throbbing colors.

Down and down and down his lips trailed until she felt his hot breath upon her thighs. He held her in place with those big, strong hands while his tongue stroked slowly, taking her beyond desire to ecstasy. She no longer existed except for him. She was his to love, to torment, to do with as he would.

He was there above her, easing down gently until flesh met flesh. She felt his hot pulse between her legs. Without fear, she opened to him. His thrust came quickly—a bright burst of pain that instantly turned to excruciating pleasure. She clung to him, knowing that now they were one. And as one, they reached that final, ultimate moment when the heavens opened up to welcome them and the night stars sang and all the colors of the universe glowed in their souls.

After a time, he drew away from her slightly. He kissed her lips with the slow, lazy pleasure of the afterglow of their loving.

"Now, you are truly mine," he whispered. "For now and for all eternity."

Suddenly, Pandora's eyes were wide and staring. She was still in Ward Gabriel's house, still seated on his couch, with her lips still pressed to his. Quickly, with a start, she drew away.

Ward opened his eyes slowly, looking decidedly puzzled as he smiled at her. "Thank you, Pandora. That was sweet."

Sweet? What was he talking about? Her heart was thundering, her whole body ached, and there was a peculiar tenderness between her thighs. There was nothing sweet about his taking advantage of her while she was out of her head. Her head—it throbbed terribly.

"I've got to get home. It's late."

She jumped up from the sofa and looked at the clock. She

froze. It couldn't be! She glanced out the window. Still dark. Then she couldn't have spent the whole night here. And surely she hadn't been here since the night before.

"What's wrong, Pandora? You're as pale as a corpse."

She ignored Ward, but said aloud to herself, "The clock must have stopped."

"No. I heard it strike eight bells only a few minutes ago. It's in fine working order, Pandora."

She turned to stare at Ward, utterly confused. "But it can't be. So much has happened. Everything has changed . . ."

Ward frowned. She was making no sense at all. And she was obviously on the verge of hysterics.

He reached out to touch her arm. "Take it easy, Pandora."

She jerked away from him. "No! Don't touch me. Don't ever touch me again!"

Now he looked angry and his voice when he spoke was cold. "If I remember correctly, *you* kissed *me,* Miss Sherwood. Of course, I didn't exactly fight you off, but it's hardly my style to force little girls."

She was so confused. Her head was spinning. Yes, of course, the kiss had been her idea—in thanks for his gift. But what about all the rest? She covered her chest with her arms. Her breasts were still aching. If it had all simply been one of her visions, she wouldn't feel this way now. Somehow, Ward had managed to take advantage of her. Perhaps he'd put something more than brandy in her coffee. Yes, that had to be it! And then, before she came around, he'd turned the clock back. It was the only explanation.

"Your gown is almost dry. Perhaps you'd better go home now. I'd take you, but I still have plans for what little's left of this evening."

Pandora could tell Ward was angry with her by his tone and his curt dismissal. But all that mattered now was that she get away from him as quickly as possible.

Grabbing her bedraggled gown, she ran into the bedroom. She didn't bother to turn on the overhead electric light as she shed his robe and pulled on her clothes. A few moments later, she was dressed and ready to take her leave of Mr. Ward Gabriel.

She came out of the bedroom and, without a word, made for the door. He stopped her, thrusting the antique box into her hands. "Don't bother to thank me again," he said coldly.

She didn't. She fled into the night as if she were running for her life.

Ward, completely taken aback by her queer behavior, watched from the open door until she disappeared into the darkness.

"Strange girl," he muttered, shaking his head.

He reached for his oilskin cape but stopped, frowning. There was still time to get to Abbie's. How odd. He didn't want to go there now. He didn't *need* to. His body still ached, but now it was a nice, relaxed sort of weariness. He felt as if he'd just had extraordinary sex with a very accomplished lady.

He threw his coat down and settled back on the sofa, gazing at the dying flames. He shook his head in wonder. If a simple kiss from Pandora Sherwood could do *that* for him, what must she be like when it came to serious lovemaking?

Pandora found her team tethered where she had left them. She climbed into the surrey and headed for home at a much slower rate than before.

The chilly wind felt good in her face. She didn't even mind the light rain. At last her head began to clear. What a fool she'd just made of herself. Of course Ward Gabriel had not taken advantage of her! It was her own mind playing pranks again.

When she'd kissed Ward, something about that moment had triggered the vision. She knew from past experience that when she lapsed into one of her dreamlike states, time lost all meaning. She could see a lifetime in a matter of seconds. She saw it was, indeed, only slightly past midnight when she passed the old church clock. Even if Ward had wanted to take advantage of her, he wouldn't have had time. She vowed to seek him out before she left for Europe. She wanted to apologize for her strange behavior tonight and to try to explain as best she could.

By the time she reached the house on Broadway, she felt much calmer. Now, if only she could get past her aunt and uncle without too much explaining. They had given up trying to control her actions long ago. But embarrassing them in front of guests was strictly forbidden.

"Pandora, *darling!*" her aunt sobbed as she spied her niece coming in through the servants' entrance. "Oh, I'm *so* glad you're safe!"

Running to her, her aunt took Pandora in her arms, weeping in relief.

"I'm fine, Aunt Tabitha, just cold and sandy. I went to the beach. It was a silly thing to do and horribly rude of me to dash away from my party like that. Can you ever forgive me?"

"Oh, my dear, of course. You hurry upstairs and I'll have Cassie bring you hot water for a bath. Your uncle and I are just so relieved that you're all right."

Pandora felt guilty for putting her family through all that she had. Still, it was a relief to escape to her room without any big to-do about the whole matter. Aunt Tabitha hadn't even mentioned her ruined gown.

Cassie, Pandora's personal servant, brought hot water and a new cake of French lavender soap. Pandora sent her maid to bed, then shed the damp, clinging gown.

Before she stripped off her underthings, she walked over to the vanity where she had set Ward's gift. She opened the lid and peeked in. What a mysterious collection of objects! She wished she knew who had owned them and how they had come to be in this box. She picked up the earring and turned it this way and that so that the opals caught the light. Somehow the bauble looked familiar to her. But where could she have seen one like it? It was very old and obviously hand-crafted.

She replaced the earring, closed the lid, and began removing the rest of her underclothes as she stood before the vanity mirror.

She felt sore in the oddest places tonight. But then, she'd had quite an unusual evening. She shrugged out of her camisole, relieved to note that her aching breasts bore no telltale bruises. This reaffirmed her belief that Ward Gabriel had left her untouched.

She stepped out of her pantelets and stood up, gasping at her own image on the mirror. Suddenly, the throbbing tenderness she'd noticed earlier pulsed to new life.

All the color drained from her cheeks as she stared, aghast, at the dried blood smearing her inner thighs.

"It really happened!" she gasped.

Chapter Three

Three days later, the foul weather had blown through, leaving a bright Indian summer day in its wake. Pandora kept to her room while the rains continued, pleading a head cold from her midnight stroll on the beach. Actually, the ills she nursed were more mental than physical. She hadn't felt up to seeing anyone, not even Jacob. She still wasn't sure what had happened to her at Ward's cottage. Her problem was hardly the sort of thing one discussed with one's fiancé.

Jacob called several times a day, inquiring after her health, but she had yet to speak with him. By the third day, he would be put off no longer. He telephoned, requesting Tabitha Sherwood to inform Pandora that he would call for her at noon. He planned lunch for them at the Beach Hotel and a long ride afterward.

"Inform Pandora that this time I refuse to be refused," he told her aunt.

So there it was; she would have to face him. But what would she tell him? That she had been unable to conjure up any vision of their married life together, so she'd fled to the beach in the middle of the night, where she'd been rescued by Ward Gabriel, who later in the evening may or may not have stolen her virginity?

She sighed wearily as she pinned her navy straw hat securely in place. The entire tale sounded as phony as a Houston aristocrat to her. Certainly, Jacob would find her story difficult to believe. She would just have to *try* to make him understand. In a few days, she would be sailing for Europe. She couldn't bear to leave with bad feelings between them. Surely, Jacob wouldn't want that either.

Cassie knocked gently at the door. "Miss Pan, Mr. Jacob's downstairs."

Pandora took a deep breath and closed her eyes for a moment, willing the afternoon to go well. "Thank you, Cass," she called back. "Tell him I'll be right down."

The moment Pandora saw Jacob, her heart sank. What a beast she had been! He was always a serious person, but today he looked unusually somber, tired, and perplexed. The dark circles beneath his eyes told her that he had had little sleep since the night of their engagement party.

She went to him at once and kissed his cheek. "Jacob, I'm sorry I've put you through all this."

His words were clipped as he cast a meaningful glance toward her aunt, who was hovering nearby, listening. "We'll talk about it over lunch, Pandora. Shall we go?"

Outside, Jacob helped her into his open buggy without a word. For several blocks they rode without speaking—down Broadway by Ashton Villa, the Italian Renaissance mansion where the Brown family lived, and "Open Gates," the fabulous Sealy estate, built at the exorbitant cost of three hundred thousand dollars, with its gilded ballroom and attic theater. Soon they turned into Tremont Street and headed for the beach.

The silence finally became too much for Pandora to bear. "Jacob, I hope you'll let me explain," she said softly.

"I hope you *can* explain, Pandora! That's exactly the reason I insisted you come out with me today." He turned and searched her face, his own filled with concern. "The other reason I wanted to see you is that I've been so worried about you, Pandora. You obviously weren't yourself the other night.''

She wanted to reach over and cover Jacob's hand with her own, but she dared not. He objected strongly to any public show of affection. "I know that, Jacob. And I'm so sorry I've caused you such anxiety. It isn't fair of me.''

"Fair has nothing to do with it, Pandora. You were out of control when you left the house the other night. I was worried sick about you. I tried to find you, but when I reached the stable, Tombee told me you'd ridden out like a wild woman. He said he thought you'd headed toward the docks.'' He laughed, but there was little humor in it. "I guess I don't know you as well as I thought, Pandora. I figured you'd be at the ruins of Laffite's old mansion. I spent over an hour combing the area around *Maison Rouge,* Water Street, and the wharves. I even stopped by Crazy Nettie's shack. She and her man were there, but she claimed she hadn't seen you.''

"Don't call Daniel Nettie's *man.*" For no reason that she could think of, Jacob's comment made her angry.

"Well, what would you call him?" he demanded. "Her *servant?* I don't believe a word of his wild tales about his being an old family retainer who's stayed with her through thick and thin. The woman's balmy.''

"She is not," Pandora insisted hotly, gripping the edge of the seat and fighting for control. "Nettie's just different from most people. As for her relationship to Daniel, they're friends. They look after each other because no one else cares about them. It's very sad. That's why I try to be nice to her.''

"You're too tender-hearted, Pandora. That old woman is nothing but a liar and a pickpocket. I've seen how she and old Daniel work the sailors when they come off their ships. Why, they both ought to be put away!''

"If Nettie is forced to steal occasionally, it's only to keep the two of them from starving. That's why I try to help her out when I can. But she refuses charity. She's very proud. I admire her for that.''

Jacob realized that Pandora had successfully maneuvered

him off the main subject, luring him into talking about the pair of ancient beggars—Nettie and Daniel—who lived in a lean-to down on the docks near the ruins of Jean Laffite's mansion.

"Never mind them. It's you I'm interested in, Pandora. As I was saying, I searched that whole part of town for you. By the time I gave up and returned to your uncle's, you had called. It seemed obvious that you didn't want to be found just yet, so I honored your wishes. But, as your fiancé, I think I have a right to know where you were and why you left so suddenly."

Pandora stared down at the wide blue and white stripes of her skirt, tracing the distinct pattern with one steady finger. "You deserve to know," she said quietly. "I only hope you'll understand when I tell you."

The horse had been clopping slowly down Tremont Street toward the Beach Hotel. Architect Nicholas Clayton's gaudy, four-story fantasy rose before them, all mauve and greenish-gold, its red and white striped dome gleaming in the noon sun. Although Pandora admired all of Mr. Clayton's other works in Galveston, the Beach Hotel reminded her of something out of the nightmares of a mad Moorish potentate. The massive structure gave her a feeling of foreboding. Still, the Beach Hotel had been *the* place to lunch ever since it opened ten years before, and was Jacob's favorite restaurant.

"Here we are," Pandora said, excusing herself from further explanations for the moment.

Minutes later, they joined the chatty throng on one of the hotel's many wide verandas. Jacob shouldered his way through the crowd to speak with a waiter.

"We'd like a quiet table for two, please, Zeb, near the windows."

The tall black man grinned and nodded. "Yessir, Dr. Saenger, just as soon as I can. May be 'most an hour yet. We got a bunch of folks here today, come out after the rain. Can I bring you and Miss Sherwood something on the veranda while you wait?"

Jacob nodded. "Whiskey for me and a champagne cocktail, Zeb."

Pandora and Jacob settled themselves at a round wicker table. Jacob made sure they were a comfortable distance away from the other luncheon crowd. He wanted privacy.

"We'll have time to talk before we go inside," Jacob said, then waited for Pandora to speak.

Pandora had been dreading this moment for days; now that it had finally arrived, she felt relieved.

"You're right, Jacob, we do have to talk about the other night. First, I've changed my mind about your Parisian physician. I *want* to see him."

Jacob smiled for the first time that day. "I'm so glad, Pandora. I'll make all the arrangements. But what changed your mind?"

She avoided his searching brown eyes as she answered. "The other night, Jacob. I've been very frightened every since. All my life I've lived with these visions, this second sight. But it has never scared me this way before." She clasped her hands nervously. "Oh, Jacob, I'm really afraid I might be losing my mind!"

"Sh-h-h! I won't listen to that, Pandora. You are perfectly fine," he assued her.

Zeb appeared with their drinks, then slipped away silently.

"Really," Jacob continued, "I'm sure there's nothing seriously wrong with you."

She nodded, still unconvinced. "Of course I'm perfectly normal! That's why you've urged me to see Dr. Pinel. Jacob, we both know I have a serious problem. Let's not try to hide the truth from each other any longer."

Jacob paused for a moment, gazing at Pandora. She was such a beautiful woman. This morning the light in her unusual green eyes was shadowed by her troubled expression. He wanted so to chase away her fears. How could he? How would he react if he had to live not only with uncertainties of the present, but with her disturbing visions of the future and the past as well? At best it would be unsettling, at worst terrifying. All he could do to help was listen to Pandora and try to understand and reassure her.

He leaned closer, speaking slowly, distinctly. "The truth

is, my dear, that you are a very gifted woman. Your intelligence is far above the average. You paint, you play the harp and the piano, you can add a column of figures faster than most businessmen, *and* you can sense things ordinary people can't. It's not surprising that sometimes you have difficulty handling it all. Most great men and women in history have been considered a touch strange.''

Pandora giggled in spite of herself. "Oh, Jacob, I do adore your logic! What you're telling me is that I *am* slightly mad, but you are willing to marry me just the same.''

"I said no such thing!" he protested. "I'm only trying to make you understand, Pandora. Dr. Pinel is no ordinary physician. He deals in problems beyond the physical. These dreams or visions of yours, he'll know how to interpret them, and how to make them go away, if that's what you want.''

"Then lead me to him!" Pandora said emphatically. "I've had quite enough of seeing the past and future, thank you! I'd be more than content having to deal only with the present.''

He looked at her oddly. "Some people would pay a fortune for your powers, Pandora.''

"How I wish I could sell them this minute!"

"So, you're saying that what happened at the party had to do with your aunt's insistence that you look ahead, to some point after our marriage.'' He frowned. He'd been afraid of that the moment he'd heard the guests whispering about what had happened. She must have seen something truly tragic happening, just as she had witnessed her parents' death in advance. "Can you tell me what you saw, Pandora?''

She clenched her hands together to stop their trembling, then quickly, before she lost her nerve, she spoke her piece. "There's nothing to tell, Jacob, because I didn't see a thing.''

He frowned, thinking at first that she was refusing to confide in him. Then the real truth struck home. "You mean, you ran away before the vision came?''

She shook her head fiercely, fighting tears. "I tried. I could not see us together as man and wife.''

The deep frown creasing Jacob's forehead belied his comforting words. "That's nothing to be upset about, dear. Surely you can't summon these powers of yours anytime you choose. You shouldn't have let it frighten you."

"But it did, Jacob. Don't you understand?" she cried, even more upset now. "It *terrified* me! What if I couldn't see anything because there was nothing to see? No future for us. You know how much I care for you, how much I've always cared for you. I depend on you, Jacob. We're not *two* people. You and I are like one being. I know what you're thinking before you say it. I know when you're happy, when you're sad. I feel what you feel! Without you, I'd be only half of who I am. Our being together was planned from the beginning of time!"

Jacob smiled gently at her.

"Pandora, you have just described love in its purest form. Do you realize we've never spoken that word to each other?" When she shied away from his direct gaze, Jacob changed the subject. "You shouldn't think I would ever let anything or anyone come between us. Of course we'll be married. We'll have a grand future together."

Before Pandora could respond, Zeb approached and offered a stiff bow. "Dr. Saenger, your table is ready, sir."

As they walked into the crowded dining room, Pandora felt the hair on the back of her neck prickle as if someone were staring at her. She glanced about, but there were so many people. She shrugged off the feeling and allowed Jacob to seat her at their table overlooking the beach. She could pick out the exact spot where she'd stood the night of the party. Willing herself not to, but unable to keep from it, she glanced toward the houses standing on stilts at the edge of the sand. Ward Gabriel's white, frame cottage was the first in her line of vision. Quickly, she turned her eyes away.

"What is it, Pandora? You haven't told me everything about the other night, have you?" Jacob asked suspiciously.

She looked down at her menu and shook her head. "I'm not sure I can, Jacob."

"Pandora, you can tell me *anything*. You know I'll do my best to understand."

"But will your best be good enough?" she whispered.

Her words stunned Jacob. What could possibly have happened to her that night? He had to get her to talk about it, to cleanse her own mind . . . or her *conscience,* he thought with a flash of dread. During lunch at a crowded restaurant was not the time nor the place for such a discussion.

"I'm starved," he said. "Let's forget all this for now and order. What do you feel like, Pandora? Shrimp? Lobster? Oysters?"

Pandora laughed a little too gaily. "If you must know the truth, I feel *exactly* like an oyster today. All rough ugly shell, trying to hide myself from the world. And, I must admit, being an oyster is not a wonderful experience."

Jacob cocked one eyebrow, looking almost amused. "Ah, but, my dear, inside that hoary shell you are as smooth and soft as satin. And anyone who searches deeply will find a pearl gleaming where you've hidden it away."

They did *not* order oysters, but settled for a salad of Gulf shrimp, nestled pink and pretty on a bed of crisp green lettuce. A cool, tall bottle of imported white wine complemented the feast and put Pandora in a mellow mood. By the time they finished, they were making plans for their wedding the following June.

Dare he? Ward Gabriel wondered.

He had spotted Pandora the moment she entered the dining room. How could he miss her? So tall and attractive, wearing that crisp blue and white striped dress that clung so snugly, accentuating every one of the curves he'd become so familiar with while she'd been dressed in nothing but his robe. Her bright hair looked sleek and shiny, not tousled in wild disarray like the other night. The tangled ropes of pearls were gone, replaced by a saucy blue hat that shaded her face just enough to add an extra hint of mystery to the already mysterious young lady.

God, she was a handsome woman! Above and beyond that, he found his attraction to her ran much deeper. They

57

had always shared the secret of that day at Laffite's Grove. Now it seemed to him that they shared a far more precious secret. If only he could figure out exactly what it was.

When she and Saenger came in, Pandora had glanced directly at Ward's table for a moment. He thought she'd seen him. Then he'd realized that the huge potted palm beside his table hid him from her view. All during lunch, he'd had trouble keeping his mind on his companion—a wrought-iron wholesaler from New Orleans.

At last he gave up. "Please excuse me for a moment, Mr. Latrelle. There's someone I must speak to."

The balding businessman only nodded as he continued attacking the mound of Gulf delicacies heaped on his plate.

As Ward approached their table, he heard Pandora's laughter—like the tinkling of wind chimes in some oriental temple. The way she was gazing at Dr. Saenger made him pause for an instant. Perhaps he had better not disturb them. Before he could turn to leave, Jacob spotted him.

"Ah, Ward!" Jacob called, motioning for him to come over. "We missed you at Pandora's birthday party."

Pandora turned and stared, the laughter freezing in her throat as the color drained from her face. Ward Gabriel was the last person on earth she wanted to run into today.

Ward nodded and smiled warmly at Pandora, then offered a congratulatory handshake to Jacob. "You are a lucky man, my friend. Miss Sherwood, I wish you every happiness."

Insufferable cad! Pandora thought, refusing to return Ward's smile. How dare he present himself looking cool and cordial as if nothing had happened that night? She reminded herself, nothing had happened. A simple kiss of gratitude. *Nothing else!* She was determined to believe that despite the evidence to the contrary.

While her mind wandered, Ward and Jacob chatted casually about business. She rejoined them mentally just in time to hear Ward say, "Well, I must get back to my guest now."

Without thinking, Pandora looked quickly toward the table Ward indicated with a wave of his hand, expecting to see some charming female waiting impatiently for his return. She was relieved when she spotted instead a rather portly gentleman seated there. Ward must have noted her reaction, for he said, smiling directly into her eyes, "A business lunch with one of your uncle's contacts from New Orleans. I'm afraid Sherwood and Associates leaves me little time to entertain socially during the week. But perhaps the two of you could join me for dinner at my place sometime soon."

The mention of his cottage set Pandora trembling. "Thank you, Mr. Gabriel, but I'm sorry. I have a lot to do before I leave for Paris next week," she answered curtly.

At that moment, their eyes met. Pandora smelled the driftwood fire, tasted the brandied coffee, and felt Ward's full, warm lips pressed to hers once more.

Ward's dark eyes narrowed and he gave her a queer look—as if he, too, was smelling, tasting, feeling those same things. "Perhaps after your return, then, Miss Sherwood. It will be my pleasure, I assure you."

Jacob, sensing the underlying strain between the two, rose and offered his hand. "Well, we're certainly glad we ran into you, Ward. Aren't we, Pandora?"

He looked to her for an answer, but Pandora could only nod. Her face felt frozen. She could not manage even the barest smile. All she could see was that huge bed with a man's naked body poised over her own. The eyes staring down into hers were not green as she'd thought before, but as black as midnight. As dark and stormy as Ward Gabriel's eyes, which were even now caressing her face and form with more than casual pleasure.

"Again, my best to both of you." Ward gave them a quick bow and strode back to his table.

"Pandora, what was all that about?" Jacob demanded. "Why, you were so rude to him!"

"I'm sorry, Jacob. Could we just go? It's awfully warm and stuffy in here."

Pandora felt much better once they were outside and riding along the beach road. She unpinned her hat, took the combs from her hair, and shook her head, letting the freshening sea breeze have its way with her long, bright tresses.

Jacob looked over at her, his desire swelling to such intensity that it was almost painful. "I love your hair that way." He caught one flaming curl between his fingers and brought it to his lips. "But, Pandora, I have a request concerning the way you wear your hair at our wedding."

"Yes?" She gazed at him intently. Dr. Jacob Saenger had far too much on his mind to concern himself with such trivial matters as ladies' costumes or their coiffures. "What is it, Jacob?"

"At our wedding, I'd like you to wear your hair pinned up, the more intricate the style, the better."

He turned and gave her such a long, probing gaze that it sent a shiver through her. She'd never seen him like this before.

"Whatever you say, Jacob."

"Aren't you going to ask me why?"

"Why?" she asked, hypnotized by the strange look in his eyes.

He leaned close and whispered, "I want hundreds of those lovely, golden hairpins to remove ever so slowly once we're alone on our wedding night. I want to take your hair down, strand by strand. I want to feel it slide through my fingers, over my shoulders, down my bare chest."

Pandora shifted slightly in her seat, uncomfortable with Jacob's boldness. What had gotten into him? She wasn't sure. The change was almost frightening. Jacob was the kindest man she had ever known. Since the first time they met, seven years ago, when he was a shy, awkward teenager and she mere child, he had treated her with formal respect. He rescued her that day, ministering to her badly skinned knee, after she'd tumbled down the rickety stairs at Laffite's ruined mansion, *Maison Rouge*. At that first meeting, he had seemed like a white knight out of a fairy tale. She'd been overwhelmed to find out that her "shy prince" was none other than Jacob Saenger, the boy her parents expected her to marry.

On the rare occasions when Jacob embraced her, Pandora felt utterly safe and protected. True passion was something they had yet to share. They had never discussed their feelings openly. There seemed to be a tacit agreement that any shared intimacy would wait until they were husband and wife.

Pandora blushed slightly and avoided Jacob's direct gaze as she whispered, "I'll have a thousand gold hairpins made to order while I'm in Paris. Just for you . . . for our wedding night."

He stared down at her, his brandy-colored eyes smoldering with a look that unnerved her.

Pandora remained silent for a long time after that exchange. Jacob, pondering his own fantasies, left her to her thoughts. He couldn't know that he had stirred up a hornet's nest inside Pandora's brain.

She closed her eyes, willing herself with all her might to witness the scene Jacob had just described.

Please, dear God, just let me see one hairpin falling to the floor!

Nothing came; it was no use. No scene of a beautiful wedding, no quiet intimacy in their honeymoon suite. Her heart sank. Something—she had no idea what—was terribly wrong!

Suddenly, another sort of fear gripped her. What if their wedding night transpired exactly as Jacob planned? After the hairpins were all plucked away, after the kissing and touching and whispering, Jacob would make love to her for the first time. He was a doctor, sure to know if his bride had been bedded before. As hard as she tried to make herself believe that nothing had happened between herself and Ward, the proof seemed too positive. Not only had she suffered the soreness, the blood, but how would she know what it felt like to reach that perfect moment of lovemaking unless she had actually lived through the experience?

The horse stopped on a lonely stretch of road and Jacob turned to her, ready to hear the rest of Pandora's tale. The moment she'd been dreading had come.

But his mind was on other matters. Aroused by his thoughts of their wedding night, Jacob, in a moment of uncharacteristic impulse, leaned down and pressed his mouth hard against Pandora's. His move surprised her, but she didn't pull away.

This was good! she thought. *This was right!* This was the two of them, sharing what they were born to share. Her pulses quickened and she recognized immediately the ache deep within her.

When Jacob drew away, he stared into her eyes for several moments before he said, "Well, my dear, are you ready to tell me about it?"

Jacob's change of mood shocked Pandora back to reality. She knew she could postpone her full confession no longer. Somehow, without bringing Ward Gabriel's name into the discussion, she had to tell him all and make him understand. She took a deep breath and began.

"You're right, Jacob, I didn't tell you everything that upset me the other night. I did see visions—deeply disturbing visions—but they had nothing to do with the two of us or our marriage. What I saw later concerned two people I don't even know. They seemed to go through some sort of marriage ceremony on a beach. Later, I witnessed their wedding night. I saw every intimate moment of it." She could not bring herself to confess to him that she had actually physically *experienced* the whole thing as well.

Jacob was staring at her as if he wanted to say something. She paused to allow him to speak, but he held his stunned silence.

"That wasn't the first time that evening that my mind traveled back to eavesdrop on strangers' lives. Just before I came down to the party, Angelica and I were in my room. While we were talking, I grew dizzy. Angelica and all our surroundings disappeared. I said something to her. An instant later, I was someone else, repeating the same words to a woman named Isabel. The woman I saw had dark hair and she held a baby in her arms and she was afraid of Isabel. Afraid and jealous of her. What's happening to me, Jacob? Am I going insane?"

Pandora covered her face with her hands and began to cry.

Jacob put his arms around her, trying to comfort her. "Hush now, my dear. It's not so terrible. Let's try to figure it out together. Do you know the woman's name—the woman with the baby?"

Pandora shook her head. "No. But she was the same woman I saw later—with the man on their wedding night."

"Do you have any idea who he might be? Do you know *anything* about either of them or this Isabel?"

This was the question Pandora dreaded most of all. How could she tell Jacob her feelings about these strangers from the past? He would never understand; she didn't understand herself. He would think she had lost her mind.

"No," Pandora answered slowly, "I don't know who the man was. I do know that he and the woman loved each other very much. So much that I could feel it like a tangible force. I became a part of it, or it a part of me." She shook her head. "Oh, Jacob, it's so difficult to explain! When he made love to her, it seemed as if I became that woman. I felt what she was feeling. I knew what she was thinking. Lately, I feel like I'm two different people. I'm so afraid!"

"Please, Pandora, don't be frightened. I wish I could help you. Maybe Dr. Pinel will be able to unravel the mystery." He brightened. "Do you suppose this could all be from some book you read? Or some story you heard as a child? Nettie is always telling you wild tales about Laffite and his pirates. Perhaps she's put the seed for all these imaginings in your head."

Pandora stared at Jacob as if he were the one losing his mind. "You think this phantom lover might be Jean Laffite? Oh, come now, Jacob!"

"I know it sounds farfetched," he admitted. "I suppose I'm grasping at straws, but it would explain everything."

"I'd like to know how."

"Don't you see? Ever since you came to Galveston as a little girl you've been fascinated with the Laffite legends. You used to haunt the grove, looking for his treasure. The site of *Maison Rouge* is still one of your favorite places. You've listened to Crazy Nettie's tales of pirates and brigands and now you've made up your own legends about the man. Maybe your mind is just playing everything back. Like photographs in the mind, taken with one of those new-fangled cameras. I don't think you are actually seeing scenes from the past. I'm convinced it's your vivid imagination at work, Pandora. I'd be willing to wager that Dr. Pinel will tell you the same thing.''

Pandora gazed at Jacob and smiled, trying to make him believe that he had comforted her. He was a dear man. He tried so hard. And she wanted to believe him. Oh, how she wanted to! But Jacob was wrong this time and she knew it.

Chapter Four

The following days went by at whirlwind speed as Pandora made last-minute preparations for her trip to Europe. Accompanied only by her maid, Cassie, she would travel from Galveston to New York on board the Morgan Line's new steam vessel, *El Valle*. She still maintained her parents' suite at the Fifth Avenue Hotel at the junction of Twenty-third Street, Broadway, and Fifth Avenue at Madison Square. She and Cassie would stay there for a few days before leaving on the *SS France* to cross the Atlantic to Le Havre. In less than a month, she would be in Paris, the city of lovers and romance. She tried not to think about her visit with Dr. Pinel, concentrating instead on the thought of renewing her art classes.

This morning, Pandora had too much on her mind to spend long considering the journey ahead. In the course of packing her mistress's fourteen trunks, Cassie discovered that a number of items were missing. Where they had disappeared to, only heaven knew.

A thorough search of Pandora's room finally turned up a cozy nest far back under the armoire, elegantly feathered with lace gloves, embroidered hankies, and shredded silk stockings. Pandora's spoiled kittens protested with hisses and growls as Cassie—down on all fours—dragged the ruined articles into the light.

"Miss Pan," the outraged maid huffed, shooing and swatting at the furry little pests, "I don't know what you're going to do with these naughty cats. Just look at this tangle they made! They every one needs a good paddling!"

Pandora swept around the room, giving her precious pets a ride on the train of her dressing gown. "Don't fuss so, Cassie! They meant no harm. I'll simply drive down to the Emporium and buy what I need. The gloves and stockings were getting too tight anyway." She knelt down and fondled her purring babies. "Oh, I wish I could take all six of you with me!"

"You do that and I'm staying right here in Galveston!" Cassie declared, her hands on her hips and her eyes glaring at the tiny, blue-eyed felons as they tumbled and frolicked over Pandora's skirts, snagging the peacock-colored silk with their claws.

Pandora pooh-poohed Cassie's threat. Then, placing the kittens in their wicker basket, she dressed and headed straight away to Sherwood's Emporium on the Strand to replace the vandalized articles.

The morning was one of those bright, balmy days in late September that set Galvestonians in mind of spring rather than fall. As Pandora—dressed in apple-green the exact shade of her eyes this morning—drove her matched team of white horses along the Strand, heads turned and gentlemen tipped their derbies in salute.

Pandora nodded and smiled, feeling a special elation as her departure drew nearer. She would miss Jacob while she was away. But, once she was gone, every day that passed would bring her nearer to her return and her wedding. She had high hopes that Dr. Phillipe Pinel would be able to cure her of her troubling second sight. When next she drove her fancy surrey down Galveston's palm-lined streets, she would be as normal as anyone else.

Galveston's business district—often called "The Wall Street of the West"—bustled with commerce that morning. Servants scurried from shop to shop, baskets balanced on their heads, as they made the daily purchases for their various households. Businessmen in frock coats moved determinedly along the raised sidewalks or stood in clusters outside the ironwork facades of the buildings, discussing cotton prices, shipping rates, and the new bridge being built to the mainland, which would be the longest wooden structure of its kind in the world.

Pandora halted her team before the glassed-in front of the Emporium. She glanced toward the windows of the three-story building, noting that her uncle's displays ran from A to Z—Austrian blown glass to zinc washtubs. The Sherwood family's "fancy grocery" had grown over the years until it rivaled some of the finest *galeries* in Paris. Starting out small twenty years ago, Horace Sherwood had expanded his business to include additional mercantile stores in Houston, Dallas, and New Orleans. Now he was a wealthy man— almost as rich as Pandora's father had been.

Gathering her skirts about her, she stepped down from her carriage and, mounting the step to the sidewalk, hurried into the store.

"Ah, Pandora, you're out bright and early this morning," her uncle said, greeting her.

"I need a few things, Uncle Horace. Lace gloves, stockings, and handkerchiefs."

"Well, help yourself, my girl. You know where everything is."

The store was busy, the customers adding their scents of orange water and bay rum to the pervasive smells of tobacco, spices, and hemp that always reminded Pandora of her uncle's store. She made her way down the center aisle, past pickle barrels, displays of imported chinaware, buggy whips, basins, and beehives. She had to wait her turn at the glove counter. While she was sorting through the stacks, trying to find the right shade of blue, someone walked up behind her. Another customer, Pandora assumed, not bothering to look.

When a hand touched her arm, she turned to find herself staring up into the storm-gray eyes of Ward Gabriel.

"Good morning, Pandora. I'm glad you stopped in. I was afraid I wouldn't get to see you again before you left for Paris."

Pandora took a deep breath, trying to convince herself that she felt perfectly calm and collected. She must *not* let Ward think anything to the contrary. She realized she had to come to terms right now with the fact that there was no way she could avoid the man. After all, he was a part of her uncle's business. If she wanted to continue shopping at the Emporium, she would have to continue seeing Ward Gabriel.

Regaining some measure of composure, she answered, "I leave the day after tomorrow, Mr. Gabriel."

One dark brow arched upward toward his unruly hairline. "The other night it was *Ward*."

Pandora felt a blush creeping into her cheeks. Why did this man always bring that reaction? She'd never blushed before in her life until the past few days. He was no gentleman, that she was sure of! How dare he mention the other night, right here in her uncle's store where anyone might overhear his words?

"Very well, *Ward*," she said with deadly quiet. "Now, if you'll excuse me, I have several purchases to make."

She turned from him abruptly, but again he touched her arm, this time gripping her elbow with some force. In order not to create a scene, she faced him again.

"Is there something you wanted?" she asked curtly.

His answer was a slow, crooked smile that infuriated her totally.

"Ward, please," she whispered. "People are staring!"

He released her arm, but made no move to leave her. "Your uncle tells me you'll be in New York for a few days before you leave for France."

She nodded.

"That's quite a coincidence. You see, I'll be in the city, too. At exactly the same time."

"How nice for you," she said in a cool, sarcastic tone.

"On the contrary, Pandora. How nice for *you!* Your uncle

thinks it would be a fine idea for the two of us to get together—go to the theater or out to dinner, perhaps. He's uncomfortable with the thought of your being in New York all alone, and he considers me quite the proper escort.''

Pandora could hardly believe her ears. The idea of Ward Gabriel squiring her about the city was outrageous. He had his nerve even suggesting such a thing. She was about to dismiss him totally, sending him on his way in less than friendly terms, when Horace Sherwood came up to them.

"Oh, Ward, I'm so glad you've had a chance to speak with Pandora.'' The heavy-set merchant beamed at his niece. "Well, what do you think, my dear?''

"If you mean about New York, I think that I have my own plans, Uncle Horace. I'm sure in the eyes of most young women Mr. Gabriel would be¹ the ideal escort, but . . .''

Sherwood cut her off. "That's right, my dear. And I'll feel much better about your being in New York if I know Ward is keeping an eye on you. A big city is no place for an unescorted young lady, in my opinion. Jacob heartily agrees.''

"What?" Pandora gasped. Jacob had been her way out of this. She had planned to tell her uncle and Ward that her fiancé was opposed to her being escorted by anyone but himself. Since he could not go to New York with her, she would simply make her way alone, as she always had before.

"I'm sure your fiancé was quite relieved, Pandora,'' Ward added. "I would be, in his place.''

Ward was smiling that maddening smile again. Lord, how she hated it! She had to admit to herself that it was neither Ward Gabriel nor his smile that she hated, but how he made her feel when he looked at her that way. All that had happened the night at his cottage—real or imagined—came flooding back to haunt her.

"Then it's all settled,'' Horace Sherwood said, stroking his gray mutton-chop whiskers. "And a load off my mind, I can tell you!''

Pandora started to object, but decided to hold her peace. Let Ward Gabriel *assume* that she would be at his beck and call in New York. He would find out otherwise once he arrived. Nowhere was it written that she had to obey her uncle's orders or even her fiancé's for that matter. Away from Galveston, she would do exactly as she pleased.

"I'll call at your hotel as soon as I arrive, Pandora. I have some business to attend to for your uncle which should take no more than a day at the most."

Pandora smiled with feigned politeness. "Oh, please, Ward, take all the time you need."

With a swish of green skirt, Pandora turned and hurried out. The other things she needed, she could buy in New York. She planned to have plenty of time for shopping . . . *alone!*

A slow, easy smile curved Ward's lips as he watched Pandora sashay out of the store, her bright hair like a blazing halo in the morning sun.

So, he thought, *you plan to avoid me, eh, Pandora?* He chuckled softly, already figuring how he could break down the wall formed between them the night of her party. She was a tricky one, all right! Well, he had a few tricks up his sleeve too. By the time he finished, she would be putty in his hands.

He frowned suddenly. Pandora's spirit was what he had always admired most about her. He had no desire to break it. Even if she was engaged to be married, he found her desirable just the same. Could the fact that her betrothal to Jacob Saenger put her beyond his reach make him want her more? Very possibly. He knew himself for the rascal he was. He had no plans to disrupt Pandora's wedding. Still, he did want to be with her in New York. He hoped they could become friends—close friends. He had often wondered what it would be like to have such a spirited young wife. If they could be real friends, he would settle for that. He would have to. New York would give him the chance he needed to cement their relationship.

There was something very odd about the way Ward felt toward Pandora Sherwood. He didn't understand it. His feelings toward her were almost protective. He knew that he would do anything for her; he would even lay his life on the line, if it ever came to that. But why? He shook his head.

70

There was no answer to the question. Pandora was special, Pandora was troubled, and, as much as he wanted her, Pandora belonged to another man. Ward was obsessed with her.

Outside the Emporium, there was a regular melee in the middle of the street. Pandora stood on tiptoe and craned her neck to see over the heads of the crowd. All she could make out was a tussle going on and a blur of bright colors.

She heard a familiar voice. "I didn't do it, Mr. Sheriff. How come they always accusing this poor old woman of takin' stuff? Don't throw me in the jail. Please, Mr. Sheriff!"

Pandora, recognizing the woman's voice, shouldered her way through the crowd.

"Come along, Crazy Nettie!" Pandora saw the sheriff trying to haul the woman away. Nettie clung desperately to a lamp post, digging her bare toes into the shells and sand of the street.

"Sheriff," Pandora called. "What seems to be the problem?"

The florid-faced officer turned to her and rolled his eyes. "The usual, Miss Sherwood. Caught her red-handed. Old Nettie helped herself to Mr. Appleton's wallet, but he managed to grab her and I happened to be passing by. We've got the goods on her this time."

The sheriff's attention was on Pandora. The crowd was staring at the sheriff as he spoke; only Pandora saw what Nettie did next. Giving her body a brief, hard shake, the town's antiquated eccentric managed to dislodge the wallet from somewhere inside her clothing. It fell to her feet and she quickly kicked it some distance away.

Nettie flung her arms wide and wailed, "Search me! Go on, I dare you! I got nothing to hide. I'm innocent as a newborn babe, Mr. Sheriff." Her words were followed by her familiar wild cackle, a sound that announced her presence and contributed to her neighbors' belief that she was, indeed, deranged.

Nettie stood, defiantly daring the sheriff to search her. A gentleman in the crowd called out, "Look here. Is this the article in dispute?" He held the leather wallet on high.

"Why, that's mine!" a red-faced Mr. Appleton declared. "Where did you find it, sir? Oh, my apologies, Sheriff. I must have dropped it in my haste."

The crowd began to disperse, grumbling their disappointment that no arrest was necessary.

Pandora hurried over to Nettie, shaking her head, but smiling in spite of herself at the cunning old woman's outlandish garb. Underneath the threadbare uniform coat of a Confederate officer, she was wearing a tattered ballgown of scarlet lace. Her feet were bare; her hands and arms were covered with cheap rings and bracelets. She wore a wide-brimmed straw hat, decorated with flowers, a stuffed bird, seashells, and bits of bright ribbon. Her gray hair straggled down past her knees in ugly tangles. Nettie smiled at Pandora and the old woman's eyes lit up like two star sapphires and her face took on a girlish look that belied her advanced age.

Pandora wanted to scold Nettie firmly. One of these days the crafty old woman wouldn't be so lucky. She *would* wind up in jail! But Nettie's smile chased all thoughts of a rebuke from Pandora's mind.

"Can I give you a lift home, Nettie?" Pandora asked.

Nettie, already headed toward her friend's waiting buggy, cackled again and slung her croaker sack of trashcan-treasures up to the seat.

"Bless you, Missy! It ain't far, I know. But I think I cut my foot on one of them goddamn shells."

Pandora shook her head as she climbed in beside the woman. "Nettie, you really *must* get some shoes. The weather will be turning cold soon. You'll catch pneumonia going barefoot. Perhaps I can find some to fit you."

Nettie scratched her chin and laughed again. "Honey, I got more damn shoes than you could shake a stick at. It ain't I don't got 'em. It's just I don't wear 'em! Take after my mama, I reckon. I seen her wear them fancy slippers of satin to go to balls, but when she was home with only me and pappy and the servants, why she'd as soon take a lickin' as put on her blasted shoes."

Pandora smiled indulgently, making no comment. Nettie had more tales than the law allowed. The old woman claimed to have come to Galveston back in the days when Jean Laffite brought his men from Louisiana to establish new pirating headquarters at what he thought was Campeachy, Mexico. The pirate missed his mark and settled instead on Galveston Island—a wide sandbar back then, inhabited only by snakes, alligators, and a tribe of Karankawa Indians.

Only four years later, the U.S. Navy forced the band of a thousand smugglers and privateers to leave Galveston after they'd fired on an American ship. Nettie claimed her father left her to live with a couple who remained on the island. She'd grown up while Galveston grew, living through the years when the town was wide open. Back then it had been known by the drifters who settled the village in the 1840s as Saccarap, after Saccarappa, Maine. Some of the settlers came, bringing Maine timber with them to build their houses.

Pandora thought for a moment, fixing dates in her mind. Laffite's lawless band had come to Galveston way back in 1817. Why, that would make Nettie nearly eighty, even if she arrived as an infant!

"Nettie, how old are you?" Pandora asked.

With a chortle and a grin, she replied, "Ain't how old you *are,* honey. It's how old you *feel!*" She paused, sighing deeply. "I feel like I'm nigh on to a hundred and twelve-teen today."

"Why? What's wrong, Nettie?"

"It's my boy Dan'l. He's got the miseries. I was hoping to come by some cash money today so I could buy him a bottle of horse liniment for his damn, old creaky joints." She sighed again. "Guess he'll just have to suffer on through without it. I ain't no good at stealin'. Never was!"

Pandora reined in her horses outside Drummond's Drug Store. "Wait here, Nettie. I won't be a moment."

As good as her word, Pandora was back in a flash, carrying a bottle of violet-blue liniment. She held it up for Nettie to inspect. "Is this what Daniel needs?"

The old woman beamed. "Why, if you ain't just a pure angel, honey! That'll set ole Dan'l right in no time. And it makes me feel better already. I been *so* worried about that boy!"

That boy, Pandora knew, was older than Nettie, if the woman's tales held any truth at all. Daniel had been a slave, "snatched from the very jaws of death by my mama, back before I was born, when he was just a tad," claimed Nettie. After this rescue, he was considered to be "Madame's boy" by the family's other servants. So now, Nettie referred to him as her boy. But the bond of loyalty and trust between the pair went much deeper than the relationship of mistress and servant. The two of them had each other and precious little else.

Pandora turned her buggy into Water Street, spying Nettie's two-room shack—the town eye-sore. It was constructed of bits and scraps of wood, tarpaper, tin, and a door with peeling paint that Nettie had found washed up on the beach after the hurricane that killed Pandora's parents. The outside was decorated with handbills, bright splashes of paint, and bits of broken mirror—"To keep the haints away," Nettie had told her.

"Hope he ain't up and died on me while I was gone," Nettie grumbled. "That'd be like him. Always so damn ornery and wantin' to do things his way."

Pandora felt a moment's panic. Then her mind eased. People didn't die of rheumatism, after all. She hurried toward the sagging door.

Nettie touched shoulder. "Best let me go in first," she said. "Could be he ain't up to company just now."

The old woman—liniment in hand—hurried inside alone. When Pandora heard two voices, she felt relieved. Daniel was still with them. Very much with them, as he and Nettie launched into a heated argument. Pandora couldn't tell what they were saying, but their anger was perfectly clear.

Moments later, Nettie hobbled out and slammed the door so hard after her that it almost fell off its rusty hinges.

"Goddamn-old-son-of-a-diseased-nigger-whore!" Nettie swore.

Pandora tried not to look shocked, but Nettie did have a colorful way with words at times.

"You know what he just done?" Nettie shrilled. "He laid into me for stealing. When all I was trying to do was get him some medicine. Damned old black bastard. I shoulda just let him suffer. Serve him right. He don't care nothing about me. Ain't no reason I should give a good goddamn what happens to him!''

Only then did Pandora realize that Nettie was crying. Daniel's scolding wounded her deeply. She felt for the woman. She put her arm around Nettie's quaking shoulders and whispered, "He didn't mean it. Don't cry!"

Nettie jerked away from her and swiped a dirty sleeve across her face. "I *ain't* cryin'! You think I'd waste a tear on that old shiftless, ornery bag of bones? *Hell no!* Come on. Let him stew a while in there. Me and you'll go over to the big house and set a spell."

Pandora knew that by the "big house" Nettie referred to the ruins of Laffite's mansion, *Maison Rouge*. Now, only the stone steps and a pile of rubble remained. According to legend, the house was a magnificent showplace in its day, the only real house on the island during that time. All of Laffite's men lived in shacks, rough lean-tos not much different from Nettie's jerry-built house. For no reason anyone knew, Laffite's house had been painted bright red. Some said the Devil himself did it to get even with Jean Laffite.

"You see the Boss made a bargain with Old Nick hisself," Nettie had told her long ago. "He said he'd build him the most wonderful house. But in payment, he demanded the soul of the first living being he saw after it was finished. Next morning ole sneaky Laffite, he threw out a mangy dog to the Devil. Satan got him back though, painted that house bright red like a target. Them Navy ships way out in the Gulf could spot that place, plain as could be."

Whatever the truth about *Maison Rouge*, the ruins fascinated Pandora. She had been drawn to the site from the time she first came to Galveston. Somehow its mystery lived for her as a tangible force in her life.

As the two women drew near the house and walked over to the old ballast stone steps, Pandora felt a rush of sensations. Voices came alive in her head. A man and a woman were arguing. A baby was crying.

"I won't leave here!" the woman sobbed. "You can't

75

make me! I know where I belong. My place is here with *you!*"

Covering her ears with both hands, Pandora sank to the mossy steps. She closed her eyes, willing the voices away. They faded, but in their place she heard cannon fire, then the roar of a storm—the howling wind and crashing waves, followed by screams and hysterical sobs. Pandora felt the cold rain slashing her face, tearing the clothes from her body. In her arms, the baby was howling, terrified by the mother's fear.

When she began to come out of it, Nettie was shaking her. "You all right?"

Pandora opened her eyes. The sun was shining brightly. The air was calm, still, warm. Ships rode safely at anchor in the harbor before them. There was no storm . . . no baby! Only the worn stone steps, a lizard lounging in the sun nearby, and Nettie sitting beside her, holding her hand.

"Lord, Lord, them was some times, back then." Without preamble, Nettie launched into another of her tales. "Why, back in 1818, they was a tropical cyclone come through this place like you wouldn't believe. Lasted two whole damn days, it did, with winds so fierce it like to blew us clean to hell. When it hit the island, it sounded just like cannons shooting off from out in the Gulf." Nettie paused and shook her head. "By God, I can *still* hear it!"

So can I! thought Pandora, wondering if the old woman were a mind reader who could sense her thoughts.

"When it was all over, there wasn't but half a dozen houses left standing. *Maison Rouge* rode it out, but most wasn't so lucky. The Gulf waters got *so* high." She raised her hand to indicate the level. "Come right over the men's damn boot tops. Three ships was lost with all hands. A fourth got blowed clear up onto dry land over to Virginia Point. She was some goddamn monster storm, she was!"

"Nettie, you must have been very young at the time," Pandora said. "How can you remember it all so vividly?"

For a long time, the old woman searched Pandora's face, her own unsmiling. Pandora became almost mesmerized by Nettie's wide, blue-black eyes.

When Nettie finally answered, her voice was no more

than a whisper. "Don't know how I can remember so much. Ain't sure how you can either. But you do, don't you?"

Pandora sat there, stunned, for several moments. Her heart was racing and perspiration beaded her brow. Finally, Nettie looked away, releasing Pandora from the strange paralysis.

"I'd better be getting home, Nettie. I have a lot of packing to do." Pandora rose quickly. "I hope Daniel gets better."

"Don't worry none about Dan'l. He ain't gonna die, less he just uglies away one of these days. Besides, that boy claims he got something yet left to do 'fore he lies down for good." Nettie leaned close to Pandora and whispered, "He swears he was told all about this years ago, but he won't say what it is. Not even to me. He's stubborn enough, though, so I reckon he'll wait around a while yet."

"Nettie, I'll be gone several months. Is there anything you need before I leave?" The old woman refused her help, as she always did.

On her way home, Pandora wondered why she felt so responsible for Nettie and Daniel. She had from the moment she met them one long, hot day in her eleventh summer when she'd been exploring *Maison Rouge*. She could still remember how she'd felt as she crept down the narrow cellar stairs, pretending she was one of Jean Laffite's spies, just home from a mission. Imagine her shock when she saw a dim light flickering in the low-ceilinged cellar. After her initial scare, she moved on down to find two figures hunched over a hole they were diggin in the dirt floor.

"Belay that!" she'd ordered, slipping back into her role as one of Laffite's henchmen once she saw that the two figures were flesh and blood instead of pirates' ghosts. "What do you think you're doing in the Boss's house? He'll have you both keel-hauled for trying to steal his treasure."

Nettie had turned and gasped at the sight of her, then gripped Daniel's arm. Pandora still wasn't sure what Nettie had said to the man, but it had sounded like, "She's come back."

Pandora had been certain at the time that she'd misunderstood. She had never visited the cellar before, so how on earth could she "come back"?

"You better answer me or else!" Pandora had warned, warming to her role as keeper of *Maison Rouge*.

"I lost something my mama give me a long time ago," Nettie'd answered. "I thought it might of got buried down here. That's all."

Fired by the lure of a treasure hunt, Pandora joined the excavation. They'd unearthed nothing, but had spent a most enjoyable afternoon together, swapping tales and lies.

It was Cassie who found Pandora that day. She'd come marching down the stairs, looking like the admiral of an invading Navy.

"Miss Pan, what am I going to do with you? Just look, that new dress is ruint! Your uncle sent me to find you and find you I have. How am I going to keep you for getting a switching this time? Mercy, child, I just don't know!"

Nettie had thrown herself protectively in front of Pandora, shrieking, "Ain't no one gonna lay a hand to this girl, less it's over my dead body!"

Ignoring Cassie's protests, Nettie hauled Pandora off to her shack, cleaned her up and mended her torn skirt.

"There," Nettie told her, beaming with motherly pride. "Now you're good as new, honey!"

Pandora had been horrified to see the way her two new friends lived. There was not a morsel of food in the shack.

"Why don't you and Daniel come home with me to supper?" Pandora invited.

Nettie had cackled at the thought. "I don't think your aunt and uncle would take too damn kindly to that, Missy."

After a moment's thought, Pandora had been forced to agree. Later that evening, after the Sherwood family finished dinner, Pandora slipped out of the mansion on Broadway, bearing a veritable feast to the shack on the waterfront. She had set the tray beside their door, knocked, then run away.

Later, Nettie told Pandora all about their feast and how much she and Daniel had enjoyed the roast beef, potatoes, carrots, and fresh bread.

"Ain't et like that since I was a little biddy thing!"

Then Nettie had pressed a gift into Pandora's palm. A

shining shell, all rainbow colors, with a delicate rose painted on its smooth surface.

Pandora stepped from her carriage and climbed the steps of her uncle's beautiful home.

Just as she walked in the front door, Jacob telephoned. She could tell by the grim tone of his voice that all was not well.

"We have to talk, Pandora."

"Of course, Jacob. What is it?"

"I don't want to discuss it over the phone. May I come to the house? *Now?*"

"Certainly, Jacob, but I don't understand. I thought you had patients to see this afternoon."

"I do. However, this is far more important. I'll be there shortly."

He started to hang up, but Pandora stopped him. "Jacob, can't you give me a hint about what's on your mind?"

"Ward Gabriel!" he answered curtly, then abruptly rang off.

Pandora felt her blood turn cold. Guilt washed over her in waves. She tried to fight it. After all, she had no reason to feel guilty. There was absolutely nothing between her and Ward. She was determined to believe that nothing other than an innocent kiss had passed between them the night at his cottage. But the tone of Jacob's voice when he spoke Ward's name filled her with dread.

True to his word, Jacob arrived in barely fifteen minutes. Pandora was watching for him and met him at the front door. Taking her hand, he led her out onto the front veranda.

"Let's talk in the garden where we won't be overheard."

Pandora nodded and followed quickly along. "Whatever you say, Jacob."

She glanced about. The garden was such a lovely spot this afternoon, with pink oleanders scenting the air and begonias ringing the bubbling fountain like green and white lace at the edge of a full, blue skirt. It seemed a shame to waste all this peace and calm on a lovers' quarrel.

She sat down in a white wrought-iron lawn seat and patted the place beside her. "Please sit here, Jacob. And try to calm down. Whatever's the problem, I'm sure we can work it out.''

He sat, but he looked far from calm. "I told you the problem, Pandora. It's Ward Gabriel! How could you possibly agree to allow him to squire you around New York? You know the man's reputation as well as I do. He has more lady friends than the law allows. . . . Why, I heard just the other day that—"

"Stop it, Jacob!" Pandora cut in. "You're making no sense at all. Surely you know better than to think that it was *my* idea to see Mr. Gabriel."

Jacob expelled a long breath. "Well, I'll admit, it didn't sound like something you'd arrange, but what was I to think? I ran into Ward earlier today. He seemed to assume I knew all about this, so I didn't let on that it came as a total shock. He said it was all settled—that he would take care of you while you were in New York, so I shouldn't worry. *Not worry?* Ha! That's really a laugh! I'd as soon entrust you to some pirate—Bluebeard or Jean Laffite himself!"

Suddenly, it all became very clear in Pandora's mind. "Uncle Horace!"

"What does your uncle have to do with any of this? I don't understand."

Pandora turned toward Jacob, a sense of outrage coursing through her. "Well, I do! He set it all up."

She went on to tell Jacob about her chance meeting with Ward at the Emporium earlier in the day. "Uncle Horace told us both that he had your full approval. So, you see, *he* set us all up—you, me, and Ward. Ward may be a ladies' man, but I don't think he's the type who would stoop to trifling with an engaged woman. At least, not unless he had her fiancé's permission, which Uncle Horace assured him he had."

"Oh, Pandora!" Jacob pulled her into his arms and held her tightly, almost desperately. "I have to confess, I'm a very jealous man. Can you forgive me, my dear?"

Suddenly, the sun became warmer, the oleander perfume sweeter, the bubbling of the fountain turned to the tinkle of crystal chimes. Jacob was not a demonstrative person. Often, Pandora found herself longing to be held just as he was holding her now. Surely, once they were married, he would shed his cool reserve. She longed so to be truly loved, but she dared not voice her desires to her fiancé. Right now, she wished with all her might that their wedding were this very day. How she would live through the next months alone, she couldn't begin to imagine.

Pandora pulled away. "Jacob, let's get married right now!" she said breathlessly.

Gazing into her sparkling green eyes, he was sorely tempted. But his calm, serious nature forbade such a hasty change of plans.

"We can't, Pandora. You know that. Why, you're all set to leave for Europe day after tomorrow. What kind of a honeymoon would that be, with me here and you in Paris?"

"I don't have to go," she insisted. "I'll stay here with you as your wife."

Jacob smiled and sighed. "It's tempting, my dear." Then his smile turned to a frown. "But what about your appointment with Dr. Pinel? You really should see him."

Some of Pandora's enthusiasm cooled. "You're right. I did promise." Then she brightened. "You could come with me to Paris, Jacob. Use Cassie's ticket. The trip would be a wonderful honeymoon."

He shook his head slowly. "Pandora, you've lived your entire life on a whim. I love that about you. You do whatever you please, whenever you please. But I can't live that way. I have responsibilities to my patients. I can't just pack my bags and run off to Europe. If I did, we'd have nothing to come back to. Don't you understand?"

Pandora felt tears very near the surface. The idea had been so thrilling. She hated to admit that Jacob was right, but he was. It made no sense to rush to the altar now, without proper preparations. Nor would it be wise for her to postpone her trip.

"I understand," she said softly. "Still, it was an exciting thought."

He kissed her again, lightly this time. "The thought of marrying you has excited me for as long as I can remember, Pandora. It won't be long. You'll see."

Suddenly, the initial reason for their discussion came

back to mind. "As for Ward Gabriel, you needn't worry, Jacob. I told him and Uncle Horace that I would see him while I'm in New York. Actually, I planned to give instructions to the desk clerk that I was not in if he called."

Jacob ran a finger down inside his tight collar and a sheepish look came over his distinguished face. "Pandora, I don't really mind if you want to go to dinner with him or to the theater. What bothered me was that I thought the whole thing had been your idea—that you'd rushed ahead with plans before even consulting me. As your fiancé, I do feel I have certain rights. But your uncle is correct. You shouldn't be gadding about New York all alone."

"Jacob! Since when have I ever been known to *gad about?*" She drew back, suddenly angry.

Another man might have laughed at her reaction, but Jacob Saenger turned deadly serious. "Always, I'm afraid."

Pandora felt a stab of guilt. He was right, of course. She defied convention at every turn, never "giving a good damn," as Nettie would have said, about what people might think. As Jacob's wife, she would have to mend her ways and settle down. She was about to promise to do just that when Jacob spoke up.

"I have a proposition for you," he said. "We'll trade off so neither of us will have to feel lonely while we're apart. You have my permission to go out with Ward Gabriel in New York, if I may, with your blessing, call on Angelica occasionally."

Pandora stared at him for a time and then began giggling. "Oh, Jacob, that's priceless! You want to see *Angelica?*"

"Well, it's not that I want to so much, but she's your cousin and she can be entertaining company. I'll be lonesome, too, you know."

She stared at him, trying to look as serious as he. "Jacob, it's good that you're a doctor. You'd make no businessman at all. That's no proper deal! I get a man you've styled a seducer of women—a rogue, a pirate—while you get a mere child in the bargain."

"Who would you have me see while you're gone—Abbie Allen?"

Pandora drew back at the name as if Jacob had struck her. *"By no means!* If you would like to take my little cousin out while I'm away, you have my whole-hearted approval." Suddenly, her bright smile faded. "But as for Ward Gabriel," she murmured, "I don't know. I just don't know . . ."

Chapter Five

New York was rainy, windy, and gray the day Pandora arrived. The heavy skies reflected her mood during the journey from Galveston. No matter how hard she tried, she couldn't shake the depression that had gripped her as she'd seen her island home and Jacob disappearing from view.

Pandora had stood on the deck of the *El Valle*, feeling lonely and depressed that morning. She knew she cared for Jacob Saenger. She realized she would miss him while she was gone. She had not expected such a dismal, heartrending misery to overtake her as she watched his tall figure on the dock growing smaller and more distant. Never in her life had she experienced such an empty feeling, such an all-consuming pain. It had seemed as if the ship, slipping slowly away from Galveston, was carrying her into another life.

And now, as her rented carriage—its isinglass curtains closed against the foul weather—swayed along New York City's Broadway, her spirits grew no lighter.

"When we get to the hotel," Cassie said, "I'm going to

find where they sell Dr. Rose's Celery Malt Compound and buy a whole case full. I never seen you so jumpy and out of sorts, Miss Pan.''

Pandora, who was usually too excited to hold still at her first glimpse of this great city, smiled weakly at the older woman. "If it will help, I'll *drink* a case of it, Cass. I can't figure what's come over me since we left home."

"I reckon it's love, pure and simple," Cassie replied, patting her charge's hand solicitously. "I remember once when I got struck down by the very same ailment. Thought for sure I'd die of it."

Pandora turned to Cassie, concerned with something other than her own misery for the first time in over a week. "*You* were in love, Cass?"

Cassie stiffened and sniffed. "You got no cause to say it like *that*, Miss Pan. I can fall for a good-looking, sweet-talking man easy as the next woman. And, mercy me, my Elmo was one *sweet* talker!"

"Elmo?" Pandora sifted through her memories, trying to recall Cassie's beau. "I don't remember any man by that name."

"You wouldn't, Miss Pan. You was no more than a baby at the time. I'd just turned fifteen. Elmo came through Indianola with a medicine show. He played the fiddle fit to kill while that sporting man, Curly Jim, sold his snake oil to the folks. I reckon my Elmo learnt all his slick talk from that medicine man. They was something, the two of them in their fancy duds, in that bright yeller wagon. I could almost believe that that nasty-tasting concoction they sold could grow hair, cure what ailed you, or make a man fall in love." She paused and sighed deeply. "I reckon I should have paid my two bits for a bottle of it to use on Elmo."

"Then nothing came of your romance?" Pandora was feeling depressed again.

Cassie shook her head, and Pandora could have sworn she wiped a tear from the corner of her eye. "No, child. Nothing came of it. But, I tell you, that flashy city boy sure taught this country girl what lovin' was all about!"

Pandora gasped softly. "You mean . . .?"

"That's right, Miss Pan! I ain't never told another soul

and I ain't sure why I'm telling you now. Me and Elmo loved us up a storm right out there in your papa's hayloft one starry June evening with the full moon peeking through the cracks in the roof." Cassie, tears dribbling down her dark cheeks, looked away. "And—Praise God!—it was beautiful! So beautiful it was almost holy!"

"What happened to Elmo?" Pandora asked gently.

"Next morning, Curly Jim up and left, and my Elmo with him. It fairly broke my heart. I never saw hide nor hair of him from that day to this. But I got my memories. Oh, yes! I got those to treasure of a dark and lonely night."

Cassie's tale, sad as it was, worked better than celery tonic on Pandora's nervous system. Suddenly, she forgot all about her own state of melancholia and began to think of her companion. She gazed out the window, trying to figure a way to lighten the mood.

"Oh, look! We're almost to the hotel, Cass. I can see the tower of Madison Square Garden in the distance. It's all lit up. I can almost make out the figure of Diana on top." Pandora leaned toward her servant and whispered, "They say she's as naked as a jaybird these days—lost every last shred of her drape in a thunderstorm!"

Cassie chuckled. "Lord, Lord, who'd of ever thought that me of all people would be seeing these sights one day. And traipsing off to Paris, France, at the drop of a hat. You ought to have one of those high-toned ladies' maids along with you, Miss Pan. Me? I'm just a past-my-prime mammy trying to keep up."

Pandora knew that what Cassie said was true. But the very fact that her friend was no proper chaperone made her the best companion of all. What fun was travel if you had some sour-faced guardian watching your every move?

"Hush that, Cassandra!" Pandora ordered. "You're not old enough to be put out to pasture yet. What are you now? Thirty-three? When I'm in my thirties, I plan to be going strong—in *every* way. And you should be, too. I'd be willing to wager that some sweet-talking Frenchman—who'll put your Elmo to shame—takes a shine to you the minute we arrive in Paris." Pandora turned a mischievous look on her servant. "You have to promise me right this minute, Cass, that you won't run off and get married. Why, I'd be helpless without you!''

Cassie giggled like a schoolgirl. "I promise, Miss Pan. But, lordy-mercy, I sure would be tickled pink if you was right!''

Moments later, they were helped out of their carriage by the uniformed doorman at the Fifth Avenue Hotel. He held umbrellas for both women as he ushered them up the steps to the lobby.

"Thank you . . ." Pandora paused, forgetting the man's name, although she remembered his face.

"It's George, Miss Sherwood," the beaming man filled in quickly. "We're honored to have you back with us.''

The desk clerk was all smiles as well. Pandora made no attempt to remember his name. She had never seen him before.

"Ah, Miss Sherwood!" the bespectacled man enthused. "So nice to have you staying with us for a few days. Your trunks have arrived already. I hope you'll find everything in the suite to your liking. And you might be interested in this." The clerk shoved a copy of the *Times* across the desk to Pandora as she signed the register.

"Oh, tonight's paper. Yes, thank you," she said, handing the complimentary copy to Cassie.

"If there's anything you need, don't hesitate to ring the desk, Miss Sherwood.''

She glanced quickly at the desk clerk's nameplate. "Thank you, Leon.''

A bellman showed the two women up to the suite, and unlocked the room, throwing open the door with a flourish. Pandora gasped. The whole chamber was filled with flowers—red, yellow, and white roses, irises, mums, and hot-house violets. Her first shock gave way to sentimentality. Tears brimmed in her eyes. Jacob had felt as badly at seeing her leave as she had at having to go. To make up for it, he'd spent a fortune on flowers. How sweet!

She tipped the bellhop quickly, then went to look at the card on the yellow roses—her favorites. A frown shadowed her face as she read: "Welcome to New York, Pandora.

Your presence here will turn the autumn gloom into the warm sunshine of spring. Fondest regards, Ward Gabriel."

Pandora hurried from one bouquet to the next. All of them, every last one was from Ward. Her heart sank. But then she went back to smell the yellow roses. She caressed the velvet-soft petals. She should have guessed, she told herself. She was *glad* they were from Ward instead of Jacob. Her fiancé, with his budding practice, could ill afford such extravagance. He was saving his money so that they could build a home of their own once they were married.

"*Miss Pan!*" Cassie gasped suddenly. "You got to read this."

Pandora turned to see the other woman holding the copy of the *Times* the desk clerk had given her.

"I never!" Cassie breathed, chuckling as she handed the paper to her mistress.

"What is it?"

"Read it, Miss Pan."

Her green eyes grew wide as she glanced at the page Cassie indicated. She scanned the lines quickly.

Welcome to Miss Pandora Sherwood

Welcome, Dear Lady, thrice welcome to town.
I've flowers and candy and imported French wine
To show you how grateful I am for your time.
We'll dine and we'll dance and we'll do things up
    right,
Until the wee hours when stars fill the night,
And your green eyes a-glitter with stars from the
    heart,
Will reflect all my feelings, my joy till we part.
And then, Southern Princess, you'll sail o'er the sea,
While I live on for now with your fond memory.
So, welcome, Dear Lady, thrice welcome to you.
I'll call on the morrow and see you at two!
                                        W. G.

Pandora, her cheeks flaming, continued to stare at the paper. She hardly knew how to feel. What a crazy thing for

Ward to do! First the flowers and now *this!* Whatever could she expect next?

"He's a *terrible* poet!" she said as much to herself as to Cass.

"But you like what he wrote just the same, don't you, Miss Pan?" Cassie chuckled and started unpacking. "I can see it plain as day!"

Ignoring Cassie's remark, Pandora reread Ward's schoolboy verse. She knew that fashionable gentlemen often wrote witty poetry dedicated to attractive ladies they admired, but never before had anyone honored her in such a wonderfully silly way. A blush of sheer pleasure warmed her face. She looked up, gazing again at the profusion of flowers. Suddenly, she realized that the depression she'd suffered since leaving Galveston was completely gone. She felt lighthearted, excited, and ready for anything. Gone too were all her misgivings about seeing Ward while she was in the city. She'd always loved New York and she meant to enjoy every minute of her stay here. She knew that Ward Gabriel would add a pleasant dimension to her next few days.

Was it Ward's bouquets . . . his quaint poetic tribute that had worked this magic? *Surely not!* Pandora told herself. But she did have to admit that she found it exciting to receive such lavish, outrageous attention from as charming and sophisticated a man as Ward Gabriel.

The next day was as blustery as the one before it, so Pandora dressed warmly in a new coat of soft wool and pearl-gray velvet. The lovely ensemble from Paris was trimmed in black Persian lamb at the neck and wrists, with strings of jet bead fringe festooning both front and back. The little capote nestled atop her bright hair was fashioned of gold braid and black lace, ornamented with a large dragon-fly, its delicate wings of gleaming blue and gold.

She was totally pleased with the effect. In Galveston, the costume would have been a bit too showy. But it would be perfect for a chill, rainy day in New York, even if her escort did show up in the usual, dreary business suit.

True to his word, Ward Gabriel called for Pandora at precisely two.

To her delight and surprise, when Cassie went to the door to let him in, Ward stood before them looking dapper and suave in a long sealskin coat and a black top hat. Pandora could hardly hide her pleasure. All heads were sure to turn as the fashionable pair paraded along Fifth Avenue.

"Well, ladies, I must say this is a pleasure!" He handed each of them a box of chocolates wrapped in shiny foil, then offered a sweeping bow. Pandora returned an exaggerated curtsy, while Cassie giggled with delight and a touch of embarrassment.

"Lord, Mr. Gabriel, if you ain't one to turn a girl's head! No man ever brought *me* chocolates before."

He gave her a bemused smile. "Then, Cassandra, it is high time."

At a slight nod of dismissal from Pandora, Cassie scurried out of the room, leaving the two of them alone.

Ward turned serious. "I wasn't sure you would see me. I figured when you agreed to this in Galveston it was for your uncle's benefit . . . and to get rid of me as quickly as possible."

Pandora felt a moment's panic. How could he read her so well? Finally, she decided honesty to be her best course.

"You are very intuitive, Ward. That was exactly my plan."

"What changed your mind?" His dark eyes glittered merrily at this cat-and-mouse game.

Pandora held herself as straight as the patrician lady she was trying to appear and did her best to assume a haughty expression. "Well, it certainly wasn't your poor attempt at a love sonnet. And it was hardly your extravagant display of floral excess. Ward Gabriel, do you realize how many of the world's starving you could have fed with all these bouquets?"

He belted out a laugh. "My dear Pandora, I know very few people—even starving ones—who would relish a banquet of roses for supper!"

Her anger flared. He was making fun of her.

"Be that as it may, Ward, you went overboard! As for my reasons for seeing you, it was Jacob's idea."

One dark brow arched and his smile changed to an

expression of surprise. "The man has more faith in you than I imagined. Surely, he can't trust me all that well after the night of your birthday party and what happened at my house."

Suddenly, Pandora felt hot all over. She snapped at him, *"Nothing* happened at your house!" Avoiding his gaze, she added, "Besides, Jacob doesn't know I was there that night."

Now Ward was grinning malevolently at her. "If nothing happened, then why didn't you tell Jacob you were there?"

Why was he doing this to her? "Can't we forget that night?" she begged.

Ward took her hand and kissed the back of her glove gently. "We can stop talking about it, if that's what you want. However, I doubt that I will ever forget it."

His words sent a strange shiver through her. For a fleeting instant, she saw herself again, standing naked before her vanity mirror with blood on her thighs. The horror of that moment renewed itself, sending a chill through her. She *must* find out for sure exactly what happened that night before she and Jacob married. Pandora made up her mind in a flash. She would see a doctor in Paris. An examination would reveal the truth of the matter.

"Pandora, I'm sorry." Ward sounded truly sincere. "I won't mention it again . . . *ever*. I want you to enjoy your stay in New York. And I think it's high time we began this adventure." He offered his arm and a warm, pleading smile. "Shall we, Miss Sherwood?"

After only a moment's hesitation, she took his arm and smiled up into his dazzling, dark eyes. "Indeed, Mr. Gabriel, lead the way."

By the time they arrived downstairs, the sun was peeking through the clouds and the rain had stopped.

"What first, Pandora? Madison Square Garden? Trinity Church? The Statue of Liberty? Or shall we take a hansom cab up Fifth Avenue and have high tea with the Vanderbilt clan?"

Pandora laughed at his exuberance. "My parents were on quite good terms with the Roosevelts and the Clintons, but I'm afraid I've never been introduced to the Vanderbilts.

New money, you know!'' Then turning serious, she said, ''You know what I'd really like to do?''

''You have only to name it.''

''I'd like to walk through Madison Park. I played there as a child. My mother used to take me on sunny days, but I haven't been back in years. Somehow, I could never bring myself to go there alone.''

The six-acre expanse of green, with its shady walks, marble statuary, and comfortable benches, lay directly across Fifth Avenue from the hotel. Pandora entered the place, feeling a rush of nostalgia. It seemed that nothing had changed since she last walked this very path over ten years before. She led Ward to the imposing statue of Admiral Farragut.

''This was new the last time I was here. Let's see, that must have been 1881,'' she told him, staring up at a cluster of pigeons seated on the Civil War hero's broad shoulders. ''Augustus Saint-Gaudens did the statue and Stanford White the base.''

Ward shuddered slightly. ''It looks like a tomb. I hope he's not buried there.''

Pandora laughed at his reaction. ''I don't think so. But he might be. Actually this whole park was originally the city's first cemetery for paupers.''

Ward gave another shiver, thinking that at this very moment he might be standing atop the remains of some poor, destitute Dutchman.

''How do you know so much about this place, Pandora?'' He took her arm, gently leading her out of the park that seemed to him to be haunted by Pandora's memories and the ghosts of New Amsterdam's poor.

''My mother came from New York. She was born and raised in a house on Twentieth Street. She always loved to roam the city. She took me almost everywhere.''

''You were a lucky child. I never knew my mother.''

''I'm sorry, Ward,'' Pandora said gently.

''Enough sad talk!'' he boomed, smiling broadly again. ''We are supposed to be having a grand outing. I say it's time we got on with it.''

"Oh, yes!" Pandora enthused. "I want to see it all! We'll cover every step from the Bowery to the Bronx!"

Ward had to laugh at her passion. He only wished he could stir her to such heights of enthusiasm. He guessed that only his floral and poetic bribes and Jacob Saenger's permission had given him access to this special woman. He supposed he'd have to be satisfied with escorting her for the short time he had. He wasn't about to stoop to stealing another's fiancé. He had given himself several stern lectures already on that subject.

Jacob, my boy, he thought with a wry smile, *unfortunately for me, you can rest easy!*

The sun went behind the clouds and a chill wind whipped about them. Pandora leaned close to Ward. "Br-r-r! I'm cold. Let's get inside. There's a nice tavern in the hotel. I can show you the paintings of Franconi's Hippodrome, the circus that once stood where the hotel is now."

Ward steered her instead toward Broadway. "I have a far more exotic idea. Have you ever been to the Hoffman House, Pandora?"

She stopped dead in her tracks and stared up at him. "The Hoffman House? Ward, you can't be serious!"

His eyes twinkled with merriment, going almost black with some change of emotions. "They have a painting, too."

"So I've heard!" Pandora answered curtly. Then she glanced right and left, grinned up at him, and whispered, "But I've never seen it. Do we dare?"

"My dear young woman! These are the 1890s! If you can't have a respectable glass of mulled wine in a respectable tavern with an even more respectable escort, then I simply don't know what this country's coming to. Let's go!"

Eyes cut surreptitiously to examine the handsome young couple as they entered the popular watering hole on Broadway. Even at this early hour, the Hoffman House was crowded—mostly with men, but a few women were sprinkled about in the taproom. Women of Abbie Allen's ilk, Pandora was sure.

Ward led Pandora to a dark back corner. Ordinarily, she would have objected, but not here. She wanted to be a discreet distance from the bar and the infamous attraction that hung over it. Jacob would have heart failure if word got back to Galveston of such a daring escapade.

"Well?" Ward whispered. "What do you think of it?"

"It's very nice—warm, cozy, clean," she answered, knowing full well that wasn't what he'd meant.

"Not the place. *You know!*" He motioned with one hunched shoulder toward the bar and the gaudily magnificent frame hanging over it.

Pandora reddened slightly and put one gloved hand up to shield her eyes. Slowly, she turned her head toward the bar. She squinted and peered through a crack between her fingers, seeing at first only a blur of pastels inside the gilt frame. She moved her hand and opened her eyes a little wider.

"My God, Ward!" she gasped, swinging quickly away from the tavern's main attraction—Bouguereau's painting of a naked nymph frolicking with a group of amorous satyrs.

Pandora covered her mouth with her hand to stifle a giggle of embarrassment. What had come over her? She had not only seen nude portraits before, she had painted them herself. Some of her best works were her plump, naked cherubs. Even now, they hung in the rooms of the Sherwood mansion in Galveston. Of course, they were discreetly covered with lace curtains whenever guests came to call. No such curtains protected the modesty of Bouguereau's frolicsome nymph.

Her reaction was more that of a naughty child than a mortified Victorian lady. Pandora could feel no real embarrassment while Ward Gabriel sat across the table from her, stifling a laugh.

A giggle escaped. In trying to suppress it, she choked. Ward started to pound her back, then thought better of it.

"Here, drink this!" He handed her a glass of mulled wine.

She took a sip, then coughed more.

"Don't drown in it! Drink it!"

Pandora downed the rest of hers and then drank Ward's. Her head felt light. She was suddenly warm all over.

"You know," she said thickly, "I've always thought that the life of an artist who paints scandalous pictures like that one must be exciting."

Ward could hardly keep a straight face. "For whom? The artist or the model?"

She shook her head and gazed up at him, trying to make her eyes focus properly. Strong wine! she thought. Then she grinned and said, "I don't know. Maybe one of these days I'll try it." She leaned close and whispered, "I'll let you know afterward whom it excited!"

Ward said nothing. He was too amazed to come up with a quick reply.

Pandora, staring at the painting, went on in an oddly husky voice. "I've always thought it might be fun to run away to Paris and become an artist. I'd have wonderful adventures and many, many lovers."

"Of course," Ward replied, still fighting to keep a straight face.

Pandora went on to tell Ward of her art studies and her plans to continue her painting while in Paris. Her enthusiasm cooled as she said, "Of course, once I'm married, I'll have to confine my subject matter to bowls of fruit and the like."

Ward grinned at her. "Maybe not. You could get your husband to model for you." He nodded toward Bouguereau's shocking masterpiece. "Like that."

Pandora shot him a startled look. "Not Jacob!"

Suddenly, Pandora put her empty goblet to her eye and turned her head toward the painting, squinting through the distortion of the glass, cocking her head this way and that.

"What are you doing?" Ward asked.

"Getting a better perspective," she replied. "The droplets of wine add a new dimension, and the glass makes the whole painting look softer."

Ward picked up his glass and followed Pandora's example. Before long, everyone was staring at them. Moments later, the other customers were holding their glasses to their eyes.

Pandora—slightly tipsy—waved an arm to encompass the entire room and said in a disgusted tone, "Look at them,

Ward! Just look at them! A bunch of sheep following the bellwether. Why are people that way? It's depressing!''

"Can't answer that one, Pan. But if you're getting depressed, let's get out of here. Fast!"

"Good idea! Where to next?"

"I chose the Hoffman House. You choose this time," he said, hurrying her out of the barroom as the other customers all turned to stare.

They were outside now and the stinging cold of the wind felt good in Pandora's face.

"I have an idea," she said. "Let's make this a real adventure. We'll go places one or the other of us has never been. We'll explore the whole city."

"Marvelous," he agreed. "Now it's your turn to take me somewhere new. Where shall it be?"

For the rest of the afternoon, they traded off. She took him to St. Patrick's Cathedral; he took her for a ride across the Brooklyn Bridge. She chose to show him the Dakota Apartments, so named, she informed him, because when the structure was built in 1881, overlooking Central Park, its location was considered to be as far from the center of New York as the Dakota Territory was from civilized parts of the rest of the country. Ward, in turn, insisted they drive down Fifth Avenue and hang around outside the Vanderbilt compound to see if they got invited in for tea.

After they'd been told by a uniformed security guard for the second time to move along, Pandora pleaded, "I'm cold and hungry, Ward. And, as unique an experience as it would be, I really don't relish the thought of spending a night in jail for loitering when I have a lovely, soft bed awaiting me at the hotel."

"Dinner at Delmonico's?" Ward asked brightly.

Pandora shook her head and crinkled her nose in an impish frown. "I've been to Delmonico's. I've even seen them serve a whole roasted bear." She brightened and looked up at him. "Why not something different?"

"You name it!"

Her smile was absolutely devilish. Ward wondered what she had up her fancy beaded sleeve now?

"I've never entertained a gentleman in my hotel suite.

Why don't you join me for dinner? We'll have it brought up from the dining room.''

Ward was too surprised to reply at first. This was not what he had expected at all—what he'd hoped for, perhaps—but *definitely* not what he'd expected! As for entertaining a *gentleman* . . . well, he hoped he wouldn't disappoint her.

"I'm both flattered and delighted, Pandora. It's the best offer I've had since I arrived in New York.''

"Then, shall we?'' she said, hailing a passing hansom without his assistance.

Ward was not nearly as surprised by Pandora's suggestion as she was herself. Inviting a man to her room was something no proper young lady would do. She shuddered to think what Jacob would say if he knew. Cassie and the waiter would be there. She and Ward wouldn't actually be alone. It would be a different matter if she had schemed to get Ward, but she hadn't planned this. After their special day together, it simply seemed right. Ward seemed right, she mused. During the past hours, something had happened between them. They had become close friends. It was almost as if they had known each other for years—for *lifetimes*. Pandora felt so comfortable with him. She would start a sentence, only to have him finish it for her. Their thoughts were in tune. They understood each other. And very few people, she reminded herself, had ever understood Pandora Sherwood.

The beef was rare, the asparagus tender, the Baked Alaska done to perfection, and the champagne was from a vintage year. The only thing that surpassed the excellence of the meal, Pandora thought, was the company. Ward was at his most charming.

Now, as they sat before the fire, relaxing after dinner with brandy and coffee, alone together for the first time all evening, Pandora sighed contentedly.

"That sounds nice," Ward commented.

"It's been a nice evening," she said.

"We could make it even nicer." Ward made no move, but sat very still, waiting to hear her response.

She tensed beside him. "I think I'll ignore that," she answered at length. "Ward, you know I'm engaged. Please don't spoil a perfect day."

"It has been wonderful, hasn't it?" he said, staring into her eyes.

Pandora knew he wanted to kiss her. And—dammit to hell!—she wanted him to. She turned away from his gaze, trying to calm her raging emotions. She belonged to Jacob. She was going to marry Jacob. That was *real!* Whatever she was feeling for Ward Gabriel at the moment had nothing to do with reality.

Sensing her mood, he said, "Perhaps I'd better go. It's getting late."

They rose from the sofa and Pandora saw him to the door.

"Remember," he said, smiling easily again, "tomorrow I have a surprise for you. I'll call for you at eleven. We need to get an early start." He paused, then added, "We've only two more days."

"Time goes so quickly," she said wistfully. Then she smiled up at Ward. "I'm looking forward to tomorrow. I'll be ready."

When he leaned down to kiss her, it seemed the most natural thing in the world that she should let him. A simple thank-you kiss, that's all it was, just as she had given him that night at his cottage.

His lips were warm and soft and brandy-flavored. As the blood in her veins began to stir, he drew away.

"Goodnight, Pandora. Sweet dreams."

Pandora's dreams that night were anything but sweet. Confused images of herself and Ward, herself and Jacob, overlaid other visions of the ebony-haired woman and the green-eyed man.

She watched the phantom pair in her dreams as they lay together in a huge red hammock. Her handsome phantom slipped his arm beneath his lover's shoulders and drew her to his bare chest—warm and bronzed by the sun. When his lips captured hers, Pandora could feel his caressing tongue

98

sliding into her own mouth. A hint of Spanish wine was in his kiss and salt from the sea air, mingled with the sharp, sweet taste of her lover's urgent longing.

One of his hands tangled in her long hair, drawing her head back while his mouth traced a flaming trail down her throat. With his other hand, he untied the string that held her loose peasant blouse on her shoulders. He slipped the silky fabric down over her breasts. They were lying in the open with the noon sun flickering over them through the branches of a tree.

"Darling, no! What about the men?" she protested, trying to pull away.

"Let them find their own women!" he answered against her bare breast.

A moment later, her protests turned to sighs as her blood warmed to his touch and desire flooded through her, making Pandora toss and moan in her sleep.

"Boss! Boss, come quick!" came a male voice from somewhere nearby.

The man in the hammock cursed and quickly pulled the blouse up to hide her modesty. He left her to answer the summons and he left Pandora's dreams.

The vision faded into a blur of hot colors.

"Don't go!" Pandora's own words woke her. She tried to go back to sleep, but tossed and turned instead, aching with need, sobbing into her pillow. Was she going mad?

Who were these strangers who had invaded her life? Why did they haunt her and torment her so?

"What do you want with me?" she moaned, drifting in and out of slumber.

Several times during the night Cassie woke to her mistress's cries. To her total shock and amazement, it was not Jacob Saenger Pandora called for but Ward Gabriel.

Dawn crept over the city before Cassie rested peacefully. Pandora knew only troubled sleep that night as her body and heart ached for something—*someone*—beyond her reach.

Chapter Six

When Pandora awoke at last, it was near ten, long past time for her to be up and dressed.

"Cassie," she called. "Why didn't you wake me? My breakfast, my bath! I have to hurry! I'll never be ready in time!"

After splashing through a quick bath, Pandora charged about the suite like a whirlwind, gulping down scalding, black coffee as she dressed and nibbling at toast smeared with raspberry jam as Cassie did her hair.

When Ward arrived, she was ready, dressed in a fetching Paris walking costume of taffeta, the color of a pigeon's breast. The perfection of her appearance bore no hint of haste.

"Obviously, you are ready to go," he said.

She smiled and nodded. "Whenever you say, Ward."

They hurried out like two over-anxious children seeking a great adventure. Pandora couldn't remember when she'd felt this excited over a morning outing.

The approaching winter weather had forgotten New York for the moment. The harsh winds and chill rain of the day before were replaced by balmy breezes and bright sunshine. The change in weather chased the night's unsettling dreams from Pandora's mind. She clung to Ward's arm, feeling ready to take on the world.

"A perfect day!" Pandora told Ward brightly as they walked out onto the bustling street. "Now, what is this great surprise you plan to spring on me this morning? A circus? An art show? I know—a ride in a hot air balloon!"

"Wrong! Wrong! Wrong!" Ward answered, laughing. "I'm taking you to a museum."

Pandora's enthusiasm cooled slightly. "Oh, Ward, there isn't a museum in the whole city that I haven't visited a dozen times."

"Would you care to lay a small bet on that?" He fished into his pocket and brought out a shiny silver dollar.

Pandora matched his with one from her beaded bag. "All right. Tell me! What museum?"

"Only a few steps away, at the corner of Fifth Avenue and West Twenty-third, the Eden Musée." He turned to her, making a hideous face. "Have you ever experienced its waxwork chamber of horrors?"

With a slight shudder of mixed dread and delight, Pandora pressed her coin into his outstretched hand. "Never!" she said. "I've never even heard of the place."

"Well, dear lady, you're in for a grisly treat, I promise you. We'll see tableaux of the world's most notorious crimes, some of them unsolved to this very day."

"Sounds utterly, gruesomely delightful!" she responded with a shiver.

"If you'd rather not . . ."

"Nonsense, Mr. Gabriel. Lead me to your horror show!"

The Eden Musée was housed in a rickety wooden structure that seemed to hold itself up by leaning into the more solid building next door. The facade was painted to resemble a marble temple, complete with plaster columns and a horrible copy of the Venus de Milo done in some crumbling, chalky substance.

"Why on earth would they put *her* outside a chamber of

horrors?'' Pandora asked, trying to hide her slight nervousness.

"Quite simple, actually," Ward quipped. "Her arms. No one has ever solved that crime. Who chopped them off?"

Pandora gave an exaggerated groan.

"Two, please." Ward paid for the pair of twenty-five cent tickets and they entered the strange little building, following a narrow, dungeon-like corridor that led to a flight of stairs.

Pandora held Ward's arm tightly. Flickering candles spaced along the walls lighted their way, and the floor was rough and uneven. The stairs, leading down into the basement chamber, ended at a tattered curtain. The gloom of the place was exceeded only by its deathly silence. Pandora began to feel uneasy. She tightened her grip on Ward's arm.

"Last chance!" he warned her with an evil-sounding chuckle. "You must turn back now or endure what lies ahead."

"Stop teasing me, Ward! Of course I won't turn back. But I warn you, if I suffer heart failure, my death is on *your* head."

At this early hour, they were the only two visitors to the museum. Pandora felt the hair on her neck rise as their footsteps echoed in the empty, unlighted chamber.

"How are we supposed to see *anything?*" she complained to Ward. "Why, I can't see the nose on my face it's so dark."

Suddenly, as if by magic, dim lights came on before them. Pandora gasped, and sank her nails into Ward's arm, feeling her heart pound at the unexpected scene of gore before them. Julius Caesar, his toga slashed and dripping blood, and the wild-eyed Brutus poised to strike the killing blow, were close enough that Pandora might have reached out and touched the lifelike figures had she dared.

"How ghastly!" she breathed. "Oh, Ward!" She turned her face into his shoulder. "I may be sick."

Ward put his arms around her and drew her close, whispering, "There, there! It's only make-believe."

She pulled away, angry at her own reaction. "I know that. It was just that the lights came on so suddenly and I wasn't expecting to see *that* right before my eyes. Let's move on."

They walked around a bend in the corridor to come face to face with President Abraham Lincoln, his eyes wide and staring blankly as he slumped in his rocking chair. Behind him in the replica of the Presidential Box at Ford's Theater stood John Wilkes Booth, his deadly pistol still in his hand.

Pandora was over her initial shock. Her heart didn't flutter quite as furiously as she viewed the presidential assassination or Jack the Ripper slashing a young maid from stem to stern or Captain William Kidd, hanging by the neck until dead, even though the infamous pirate's eyes bulged and his wax tongue lolled out of his mouth at a grotesque angle.

Ward moved slightly ahead of Pandora and called to her excitedly. "Come look at this! They've added a new attraction since I was here last."

"What on earth?" Pandora gasped, her hand flying to her dry throat. "Oh, that's horrible!"

"It was a horrible crime," Ward assured her. "Haven't you followed the case of the Borden murders in the papers?"

Pandora was barely listening, her attention focused on the grisly tableau—a wild-eyed woman with a bloody axe raised over two hacked-up bodies at her feet. She glanced at the tablet on the wall that identified the crime: "Lizzie Borden executes her father and stepmother with an axe. August 4, 1892, Fall River, Massachusetts."

"Only in New York!" Ward mused aloud. "Why, poor Lizzie hasn't even gone to trial yet, and the Eden Musée has convicted her already!"

"Ward, please," Pandora whispered. "Let's go! I think I've seen enough."

He took her arm, frowning into her pale face with genuine concern. "I'm sorry, Pan. I had no idea the place would scare you so. We have to go all the way through to get out. Close your eyes, if you like. I'll lead you and you won't have to look at the rest."

She did just that. She had no desire to see any further gore. They hurried along, Ward keeping a firm grip on Pandora's waist so she wouldn't stumble. She kept her eyes tightly shut, one hand over them just in case. When Ward stopped suddenly, and she felt him go rigid beside her, without even thinking, she looked.

Pandora's scream reverberated down the winding corridor. The museum attendant, hearing the awful sound and wondering if one of his wax murderers had suddenly sprung to life, ran to locate his two customers.

He found the red-haired woman stretched out on the floor with her gentleman friend kneeling over her, chafing her wrists and pleading with her to wake up.

Ward was feeling none too steady himself as he assured the ticket seller that the lady had only fainted. "Get me a glass of water. That should revive her."

Still bending over the unconscious Pandora, Ward glanced up at the scene that had caused such a violent reaction in him and had promptly sent her into a swoon. The tablet beside the scene read: "Pirate Jean Laffite's wife dies in his arms, murdered by some unseen hand. Galveston Island, 1821."

Pandora was unaware of Ward Gabriel's presence. She never knew that the museum attendant was there, that she had fainted, or that Ward carried her in his arms all the way back to the hotel and up to her bed. All she saw was a deserted beach and her green-eyed stranger, Jean Laffite, his face a mask of agony as the ebony-haired woman in his arms closed her eyes in death, a red stain drenching the breast of her peasant blouse.

The report of a pistol still echoed in Pandora's ears; she still felt the sharp, hot pain of the bullet tearing into her own flesh. She could hear Laffite's anguished words: "No! My God, no! You can't leave me. I love you, darling, too much . . . too much to let you go."

Dense gray fog shrouded the scene suddenly. When Pandora could see again, she spied Laffite's dead wife, lying stiff and cold in her plain coffin. The man—red-eyed from weeping, his face drawn and pale—reached out and removed the two Spanish silver coins from her closed eyes to look on her face one last time.

"Our love is not dead, my darling," he said in a husky whisper. "We'll be together again. I promise you."

He placed the coins in a small wooden box and closed the lid gently. Pandora watched, feeling her own heart break for him, as he closed the coffin lid as well. Pandora's vision followed him to a grove near the sandy beach where she saw him bury both boxes.

Pandora gasped for breath as she slept. She felt like she was inside that coffin. She experienced a terrible burning pain in her breast. There was also a sense of deep relief, brought by the man's parting words.

"Nothing is forever, except our love," she had heard him whisper as he lowered the coffin into its sandy grave.

Suddenly, the scene vanished in a sea of swirling colors. The grove disappeared. The burning pain in her chest and heart was gone, replaced by another sort of agony. Her belly cramped, forcing a scream from her lips.

"Breathe deeply, darling," a man's familiar voice told her. "You can do it. Try to relax."

A cool hand caressed her sweating brow. Warm lips pressed hers. She opened her eyes to find herself staring into his. They were dark green, the color of deep sea water. She tried to smile for him, but she was too weary and the pain was too great. His nearness and his voice gave her strength.

He took her small hand in his and held it. "When the pain comes again, darling, hang on to me. We'll do this together, you and I. We made this child with our love, we'll see it into the world the very same way."

His courage and compassion bolstered her through the next hours of labor. The sea tossed fitfully beneath their ship as if it too were experiencing her pains. At last, the moment came. Jean Laffite knelt to help his child into the world.

"It's a girl!" There was wonder in his voice as he said the words.

"We'll name her Jeannette for her father," the mother said weakly. He was a good, brave man not to show his disappointment. She knew he had hoped for a son. There would be other children, many sons in the years ahead, she hoped.

As the sun sank into the sea, the young mother lay on her pallet with her baby at her breast. Laffite, looking tired, but smiling with love and wonder, watched as the child suckled hungrily.

"You are a marvel, my darling. How can any woman endure such pain?" He shook his head and ran his fingers through his tousled, sun-bleached brown hair.

"We do it for love," she answered tenderly.

He came to her and kissed her gently. "Then you have plenty of reason, my darling. I've never loved you more than I do at this moment—not the first time we met at your father's house in New Orleans, or that tragic evening when I saw you off to Paris, or even the night we jumped the broomstick on the beach at Barataria. The depth of love I have for you now is as newly-born as our little daughter, and yet I feel as if I've loved you since the beginning of time. I know I'll love you until its end."

Suddenly, unbidden tears sprang to her eyes and a pain tugged at her heart as she looked into his dear face. Something was wrong! Not with the baby or with her or with him. Something was wrong with *time!*

"Let's make a pact, Jean," she whispered. "Should anything happen to separate us, let's vow to find each other again, no matter what it takes."

He frowned at her, then laughed softly, winding one long ebony curl around his suntanned finger. "What could separate us, darling? You're only suffering a case of nerves after what you've been through today."

"Promise me, Jean!" she begged urgently.

He leaned down and kissed her damp forehead. "I promise, my darling. Whatever happens, we'll find a way to be together always."

Little Jeannette had fallen asleep at her mother's breast. Soon both of Laffite's ladies gave in to their weariness. The sun sank out of sight. Stars twinkled overhead. The moon rose, silvering the Gulf of Mexico. A kind wind sped the good ship *Pride*, with her captain, his family, and crew, ever closer to their new home.

* * *

"I think we should send for a doctor, Cass." Ward's voice was edged with panic. "It's been almost an hour. She should have come around by now."

Cassie's dark face was filled with concern. "It's one of her spells, Mr. Gabriel. She has them from time to time, but the last one I saw this bad was right after her mama and papa was killed. What you reckon brought it on?"

Ward shook his head and sighed. "It's all my fault. As a lark, I took her to a chamber of horrors. She grew quite nervous. We were on our way out when we came to a frightening depiction of the death of Jean Laffite's wife. I have to admit, it jolted my senses." He shuddered slightly, remembering the lifelike tableau. "I don't know what it was about that particular scene. The figures looked so real. The woman was so fragile and lovely. The pain in Laffite's face . . . it was simply indescribable! I know it sounds crazy, but for an instant I actually felt his anguish."

Pandora began thrashing about in bed, moaning and crying. Ward sat down beside her quickly and gripped her arms to keep her from hurting herself. Suddenly she stopped fighting and smiled. She relaxed visibly.

"Yes, this will be perfect, darling," she murmured.

"Pandora? Pandora, can you hear me?" Ward begged.

She could not. She heard the gentle lap of the waves, the cry of the gulls overhead, the squeak of the warm sand beneath her bare feet, and the contented gurgle of the baby in her arms.

"We'll build our house on the bay side of the island," the tall man beside her said. "That way we'll be sheltered from the worst of the blow when storms roll in."

"A lovely, big house, with lots of room for our family to grow." She smiled up at him, a clear invitation in her blue-black eyes.

Laffite gave a shrill whistle. A young black boy came running.

"Yessir, Boss! What you want me for?"

"Here, 'Gator-Bait, hold the baby a minute."

"Yes*sir!*" The boy's eyes danced with delight as he struggled to manage the tiny, squirming bundle.

"Now," Laffite said, turning to the woman, "what was that about a big house . . . a growing family?"

She smiled shyly and dug her toes into the sand. "Well, not yet!" she answered. "But soon, I hope."

Then she saw why Laffite had summoned 'Gator-Bait to hold the baby. He hadn't wanted to crush their daughter when he took her into his arms.

She could feel the sweat from his bare chest soaking her blouse as he held her. Her hands slid around his lean waist, feeling the rough scars on his sides and back—a saber wound, the deep dimple left by a bullet, and whip lashes from a shipboard flogging years ago. Every inch of his magnificent, scarred body was dear to her. If they lived together for a hundred years, she would never get enough of seeing him, touching him, giving herself to him.

His deep kiss went on and on until her knees grew weak and a wonderful ache seared through her. They had yet to make love since Jeannette's birth over a month before. And they had gone many weeks without each other before that, when she became too large with child. She knew that their time would come soon.

"Tonight, my darling?" He breathed the question into her ear as he drew away.

She glanced up at the noon-high sun. "Suddenly, that seems too long to wait," she whispered.

His eyes glittered with deep green desire. He leaned down toward her once more. Firmly, she placed her hand against his damp chest and smiled. He clasped her fingers and brought her palm to his lips, drawing damp circles there with the tip of his tongue. She trembled and sighed. Another moment, another caress, and she would give in to him— right here, right now!

But a wail from Jeannette, followed by a howl from 'Gator-Bait saved her from her own longing.

"Madame Boss!" the black boy shrieked. "This baby, she all wet and me, too!"

Laffite and his lady laughed as she took Jeannette in her arms. Like it or not, they would have to wait.

* * *

Ward sat very still, watching Pandora intently. One moment she was smiling. The next moment, she would frown or sigh. What could she be dreaming? Why didn't she come out of it?

"The doctor, he's here, Mr. Gabriel," Cassie said from the bedroom doorway.

"Tell him to come right in." Ward rose to greet the physician the hotel manager had summoned. Quickly, he explained what had happened.

The frail, white-haired man proceeded with a cursory examination that took only minutes. Then he turned back to Ward. "You say, you tried smelling salts?"

"Of course! Doctor, she's been unconscious for nearly two hours. What's wrong with her?"

The old man glanced back at Pandora, who was smiling again now. He frowned and shook his head. "I haven't the foggiest. Never saw a case like it before. But I don't think you need to worry, young man. Her heart is strong, her pulse rate regular. She doesn't seem to be unconscious at all. She's simply sleeping deeply. Leave her be. Let her sleep it out."

Ward dismissed the man immediately. After Cassie showed him out, Ward growled, "Quacks! That's all any of them are!"

"Not Mr. Jacob!" Cassie corrected quickly. "Nor his daddy neither. They're both good doctors."

"You're right, Cass, and I apologize for my outburst. I wish to God we had one or both of them here now!"

He sat back down beside Pandora's bed and took her hand in his.

A warm breeze scented with salt and sea blew over the island, wrapping it in a luxurious evening mist. Stars twinkled overhead and a sliver of a moon shone down. The white sand turned to silver at this hour, lending a special enchantment to their new home.

Pandora experienced the dark-haired woman's anticipation as if it were her own. Laffite's lady—dressed in a long, white gown—waited for him in the captain's cabin aboard the *Pride*. Jeannette was sleeping soundly in the sea chest that served as her cradle.

Soon he would come. Soon she would know his love again. How could it be that every time with him was like the first time . . . yet every time was better than the time before? She crossed her arms over her breasts, rubbing the goose bumps that rose as she thought of him.

She glanced at the wide bunk. How dear that bed had become to her! How many long nights they had lain there in each other's arms, their hearts beating as one, while he loved her slowly, tenderly, thoroughly as the sea rocked them gently in its watery embrace.

"Oh, Jean, my love!" she sighed. Why did this feeling of dread linger? If only she knew what it meant.

The next moment, she heard the thud of his boots on the deck. All anxious thoughts fled. Her whole body came alive, knowing that he was on his way to her. Already she was aroused almost beyond bearing. Just thinking of him did that to her.

The door to the cabin opened. He had to stoop to enter. As he did, a slow, caressing smile warmed his handsome face. Quietly, he closed the door, shutting out the rest of the world. His gaze never left her. Without a word, he came to her, kissing her all over with his eyes before he touched her. She was trembling, though he had yet to lay a finger on her. She felt as nervous and fluttery as an untried virgin.

"Come here!" he demanded in a husky whisper.

She hesitated only a moment before going to him. She stood so close, she could feel the heat radiating from his body, yet still, he did not take her into his arms.

She watched, trembling with anticipation, as his hand rose toward her face. His fingers, too, trembled slightly. She caught her breath when he caressed her cheek lightly, trailing his fingertips down the side of her throat, to her bare shoulder. For several heart-stopping moments, he hesitated, stroking the slender strap of the white gown as if he meant to ease it off her shoulder. Instead, he let his fingers slide down the narrow silken thread. He stroked her full breast. Every nerve in her body felt that light touch. Closing her eyes, she sighed his name.

The next moment, he gripped her slender waist in both his hands and drew her hard against him. She could feel the throbbing heat from his loins through the thin fabric of her gown. She wanted to beg him to take her now, here, this minute! But that was not his way. He would torture her first with his gentle caresses and deep, hot kisses. She wanted it that way!

His face hovered over hers. She stared straight up into his eyes—gone deep, smoky green with the intensity of his desire.

"Do you know how much I love you, darling?" he asked in a husky whisper.

She nodded, not trusting her voice. "No more than I love you," she finally managed. "Oh, Jean, whatever would I do without you?"

"You'll never have to find out," he assured her. "We'll always be together, my darling."

She wanted to believe him, but she knew that his promise was as elusive as the moonbeams shimmering on the calm water outside the cabin's porthole. In the years since she first met the great Jean Laffite, their separations had come all too often. With each parting came the painful thought— the awful possibility—that there might never be another joyful reunion. She still ached inside when she remembered the terrible, pain-filled hours and days that she had waited, wondering if Jean was alive or dead, while he and his men helped General Jackson defend New Orleans against the British. That was neither the first nor the last time she had had to bid him *adieu* and pray for his safe return. No, they would not *always* be together!

Ward sat beside the bed all through the night, watching over Pandora. Her condition confounded him. He was unable to rouse her. Her eyelids fluttered and she smiled or frowned from time to time. Once tears ran down to dampen her pillow. She murmured softly or uttered a deep sigh. It was almost as if she had passed over into another level, living a spirited existence beyond sleep.

"Or maybe she's just dreaming," he said to himself.

At the sound of his voice, she half rose in the bed. Her

eyes remained closed, yet she seemed to be looking about, searching for him. He took her hand.

"I'm here," he said quietly.

"You won't leave me?"

"No, I won't leave."

She lay back then, looking relieved, but still clinging to his hand. Ward sat tense, waiting for her next move, her next words. Was she coming out of it?

His hand lay clutched in hers upon her breast. She stroked the dark hair on the back of his fingers, sighing from time to time. Ward began to feel uncomfortable. He shifted in his chair. Her gentle fondling was arousing him, more than he liked to admit. He dared not draw his hand away for fear of upsetting her.

The more she touched him, the warmer the room became. He loosened his collar with his free hand. What if some-one—even Cassie—saw them like this? It was bad enough that he was in her bedroom in the middle of the night. Cassie had dressed Pandora in a thick linen gown with a high collar and long sleeves. But still, Pandora was *undressed, in bed,* and *unconscious!* Far less serious circumstances would be viewed as *compromising* in this day and age.

Suddenly, Ward froze.

He tried to pull his hand away, but Pandora held it tightly. While he'd been lost in thought, she had shifted her position, turning on her side toward him. Now his palm was flattened against her breast. He could feel the pressure of her dis-tended nipple. She held it there as if inviting him to fondle her. To make matters worse, she was now breathing in shallow pants. Ward had bedded enough women to recog-nize what was happening. His touch was arousing her as deeply as her stroking had affected him.

"Yes, my darling! Yes!" she moaned.

Ward pulled his hand from hers and shook her gently. "Pandora, wake up! Can you hear me? You've got to come out of this. I want you to come back to me now."

"Yes . . . always come back to you," she murmured. Then capturing his hand again, she pressed it firmly to her breast, and expelled a deep sigh of longing.

* * *

Jean's strong hand was on her breast—pressing down hard, making her ache. She moaned aloud from the sheer pleasure of his touch.

They were still standing in the middle of the cabin, fully clothed. But now he became more forceful. Almost roughly, he kneaded her breasts through the thin fabric of her gown. A moment later, his hands were at the straps, stripping them from her shoulders. The gown rippled down over her body, leaving her naked—burning for him—before his smoldering green eyes.

He reached overhead and turned up the wick of the oil lamp. It shed a golden glow over her creamy skin.

"I can never get enough of seeing you, my darling," he rasped. "You are the loveliest creature in all creation."

She stood before him, unashamed, her proud breasts full and high, her waist slender, her hips rounded, her shapely legs long and tapered to near perfection. She watched him through half-closed eyes, wondering how much longer her legs would hold her, if he kept looking at her that way.

He came to her again, embracing her, letting his big hands slide down her back and over her buttocks. He bent to capture one taut nipple in his mouth, sighing with pleasure as he tasted her.

The next moment, he lifted her gently in his arms and laid her on the smooth coverlet on the bed. She closed her eyes—waiting, knowing that now, at last, he would take her.

It *was* like the first time! Only it was better, for now he knew what pleased her, and in pleasing her, he satisfied himself. They clung to each other, matching deep, even strokes until she felt the warm tingling in her legs begin to rise. Up and up the delicious heat traveled until her whole body was possessed and burning with a wonderful fire. Then with an explosion of sensations, they reached the heights together. Never had anything been so wonderful, so beautiful, so holy! She slipped her arms about his neck, drawing his mouth down over hers in a long, intimate kiss . . .

Pandora awoke with a start to find herself in her night-gown, in bed, being kissed deeply, thoroughly, and apparently *not* against her will. She pulled away quickly.

"Ward! What are you doing?" She sat up, clutching the covers to her chest. "Why are you in my *bedroom?*"

"Pandora!" he cried. "Thank God! You have no idea . . ."

Suddenly, Pandora became aware of that same sweet weariness she'd felt the night at Ward's cottage. The dull ache was there, the slight soreness, just as before. Panic seized her.

"Ward, please, I don't know what's happened, but I think you'd better go."

"I will! Just stay calm, stay awake. You've been so long coming out of it. I was worried sick, Pandora."

Pandora's kiss had caught Ward off guard. And what a kiss! Surely she hadn't learned that from Jacob Saenger.

"Ward, answer me," she demanded. "Coming out of *what?*"

He stared at her, uncomprehending.

"Ward? Tell me what's happened here. I have a right to know!"

He reached out to touch her arm, meaning to soothe her. She jerked away from him with a cry.

"Don't touch me!"

"All right, Pandora," he said quietly. He didn't want to alarm her. She might slip away again. "Are you telling me that you don't remember what happened?"

She closed her eyes for a moment, trying to bring some order to the clutter of her mind. The last clear memory she had was of getting dressed, waiting for Ward to come and tell her the surprise he had in store for their morning's outing.

"When did you arrive?" she asked suddenly, her eyes wide open. "How long have you been here? Why, it's dark outside!"

The truth was beginning to sink in and Ward was horrified by it. "You don't remember going with me to the Eden Musée?"

She stared blankly at him. "I've never heard of the place."

"Pandora," Ward said gently, "I want you to listen carefully to me. Please, try not to get upset. Cassie tells me you've had these spells before."

The color drained from Pandora's face and she whispered, "No."

"I'm afraid that's what happened. We were in the museum—the chamber of horrors—when you fainted. I couldn't revive you, so I brought you back to the hotel. You've been sleeping for over twelve hours. Now, do you remember?"

Pandora leaned her head down on her knees as he spoke. She raised it up and looked at Ward with dull, anxious eyes. "No, I don't remember any of it."

She remembered his kiss well enough. Her whole body was still tingling. But she refused to admit that to him or the shocking memories of some of her dreams. She clearly recalled the soul-shattering pain of childbirth. She still harbored the dull ache of fear that refused to leave. She could still see her vision of a red hammock, a sandy beach, and a man making love to her on a wide bunk in the cabin of a ship called *Pride*. She still felt warm with the glow of spent passion.

Pandora stared hard at Ward. "Have you been here with me for the past twelve hours?"

He nodded. "Almost every minute."

"Then it was *you*," she said in a flat, dull tone.

"I don't understand."

"Neither do I!" she snapped. "I thought I could trust you, Ward Gabriel."

"Trust me? What are you talking about?" Even though he thought he knew, Ward demanded, "What are you accusing me of, Pandora?"

Tears rushed down her cheeks suddenly and she screamed at him, "Get out! Just get out! I'm still going to marry Jacob, no matter what you've done to me. I'll confess everything to him and he'll still marry me!"

"Pandora, have you gone mad? I never . . ."

In a fury now, she threw a pillow at his head. "Go! I don't want to hear any more. Haven't you done enough? I'm *ruined!*"

In a state of shock, Ward Gabriel departed immediately. Not until he left the hotel did the full weight of Pandora's accusations sink in. Some shrinking-violet of a female might consider herself *ruined* if she woke to find a man sitting beside her bed, sharing a kiss in the middle of the night. But not Pandora Sherwood! Only one thing could ruin her for the man she intended to marry. She had accused him of taking full advantage of her. Pandora believed Ward had stolen her precious virginity.

"Of all the pompous, unmitigated gall! The conceit of the woman!" he muttered, striding angrily down the dark street.

Then, suddenly, he stopped, remembering the way he'd felt after she left his cottage, how he'd given up his plans to visit Abbie Allen's. He had that same feeling now—as if he had just made wonderfully satisfying love.

"Maybe she is crazy," he told himself. "But, if so, I'm as mad as she."

Ward called Pandora's suite the next day, but she refused to speak with him.

"I'm sorry, Mr. Gabriel," Cassie told him. "She's not taking any calls."

"How is she?"

"As good as I ever saw, sir. It's like nothing ever happened."

"Well, thank God for that. I think she really ought to cancel her trip—go back to Galveston. Old Dr. Saenger should see her."

"Lord, Mr. Gabriel, you shoulda heard her blow up when I suggested that very thing. She say we going to Paris and that's that. There's ain't no reasoning with her when she sets her mind to something."

Ward expelled a long sigh. "I know, Cassie. I know."

The following afternoon, Ward was on the dock when Pandora and Cassie boarded the *SS France*. She looked wonderful. He was relieved. Here ended his responsibility toward her. He'd thought a few days with her in New York would get her out of his system. It hadn't happened. He wasn't sure what actually had happened, but now he was certain she never wanted to see him again.

"Just as well," he told himself, trying to deny what he

knew to be the truth. No matter how Pandora felt about him, he *had* to see her again. He *would* see her again.

He could not pull himself away from the dock until her ship had sailed out of sight. Once it was gone, a deep, empty feeling settled in the pit of his stomach. Nothing seemed important now that Pandora was gone. The depth of his emotion confounded him. She belonged to another man. He knew that, he accepted it. So why was he feeling like a deserted lover?

He walked back from the East River docks, not to his own hotel on Broadway, but to the Fifth Avenue Hotel where Pandora had stayed. It was raining, but he never noticed that he was getting soaked to the skin. Only when the bartender said, after Ward's third brandy, "Mr. Gabriel, you're going to catch your death," did he realize he was wet, cold, and shivering.

He shrugged and said, "What does it matter? Give me another, Mike."

Pandora felt dreadfully alone as the ship steamed out of the harbor. She kept thinking about Ward and what fun they'd had together before their dreadful parting. She even allowed herself to dwell on his kiss—the hot, passionate pressure of his mouth and the cool, silky caress of his tongue stroking hers.

She shivered and closed her eyes. "I dreamt it," she told herself. "Ward never . . ." But she knew better.

She had purchased a special gown to wear to the first night gala aboard the *SS France*. But she had decided to have a light supper in her cabin instead. She was in no mood for gaiety.

"Oh, Miss Pan, you'll miss all the fun!" Cassie complained. "Come on now, let me fix your hair and get you ready."

Pandora waved her away angrily. "Please go out on deck for a while. I want to be alone!"

Poor Cass was almost in tears as she hurried out of the cabin.

Pandora sat alone in her stateroom, hoping to regain some of the peace and contentment that seemed to have deserted her forever. The ship rocked gently on the waves, reminding her of her dreams. This vessel wasn't the *Pride;* no lover was on his way to sweep her off her feet and on to ecstasy.

She sighed and poured another glass of Ward's champagne. In spite of the awful row and the vicious things she'd accused him of, he had sent wine and flowers to the ship. She stared at the yellow roses and tears rushed to her eyes. Suddenly, she felt alone—and afraid.

Pandora wanted more than anything to follow Cassie's advice and go rushing back to Galveston, back to Jacob where she belonged. The whole business in New York had been most upsetting. But now more than ever she needed to go to Paris. Twelve whole hours were missing from her life. Twelve hours of *what?* She would never know exactly what had gone on in her bedroom unless she saw Dr. Pinel and let him probe the shadowy depths of her mind.

She laughed humorlessly and toasted her image in the mirror. "Once the truth is out, who's to say that Jacob will even want me back in Galveston?"

A short time later, Pandora crawled into bed. She closed her eyes and held her breath—waiting, listening, hoping, against all reason. No thud of boots sounded outside her cabin door. No warm, caressing hand reached out of the darkness to clasp hers. No kiss touched her waiting lips.

Finally, she cried herself to sleep, praying that her phantom lover would find her in her dreams.

The dark hours passed, the ship rolled on, but no one came to ease Pandora's aching heart.

Chapter Seven

"Interesting case!" Dr. Phillipe Pinel spoke the words in French to his assistant, Madame Celeste. Then, nodding, he placed the long, detailed letter from Dr. Jacob Saenger on his desk and lit his pipe. "What time did you say the young lady will be here?"

"She is due at one o'clock this afternoon, Doctor." The prim, gray-haired woman in her fifties, a stickler for punctuality and accuracy, checked her appointment book to make certain. "Yes. She should arrive within the next few minutes."

"Good, good. Show her in immediately."

By way of dismissing his assistant, Pinel turned in his chair to stare out the window, losing himself in deep thought. The Seine flowed like a lazy silver thread far below his office window in the building adjacent to the hospital. All of Paris seemed shrouded in a cold, gray mist this November afternoon. Winter had arrived ahead of schedule—dreary, wet, and depressing.

The doctor shivered slightly, rose, and poked at the small fire in the grate. He must be getting old, he thought. He could never keep warm these days. Staring down into the orange flames, he thought about Dr. Saenger's letter and the complexities of Mademoiselle Sherwood's case. This "second sight," as his young colleague termed the woman's condition, could be a form of autohypnosis. The trauma of her parents' deaths when she was so young might have caused her subconscious to seek this means of escape from a painful reality. If that was the case, his best course would be to use Dr. Franz Mesmer's techniques to arrive at the root of her problems and thereby affect a cure.

"Yes," he said quietly. "Yes, it should work."

He sucked at his pipe stem, feeling a kernel of excitement bursting to life inside him. It had been many years since a case as complex and fascinating as this had come his way. He would try mesmerism or hypnosis as the technique was called these days. Some still believed that Dr. Mesmer had been a charlatan and his findings worthless. Pinel had used Mesmer's hypnosis to great theraputic benefit in the past. Now, it might be the *only* way to help Mademoiselle Pandora Sherwood.

As he paced his office, planning his strategy, he forgot about the gray autumn rain pouring down on Paris. He forgot that he was cold. He forgot his own advancing age, feeling once again like a young physician in his prime. The Sherwood case would be a challenge for him like none he had dealt with in many a year.

When she wasn't in art classes, Pandora spent her first week in Paris shopping for her trousseau. She did everything in her power to avoid thinking about her appointment with Dr. Pinel. Jacob had assured her the man could help, but she was not so certain. Her lapse of memory in New York frightened her terribly. She dreaded the thought that the French physician might shake his head sadly and tell her there was no hope.

The appointed day had arrived all too quickly. The coach that she had leased in Le Havre to bring them to Paris was dashing through the rain-drenched streets of the old city, carrying her ever closer to her dreaded first meeting with Dr. Phillipe Pinel.

Cassie wanted to accompany her mistress to the doctor's office, but Pandora had convinced her to remain at the hotel. Now she wished that her friend was there. The drive seemed endless, and Pandora was growing more nervous by the mile.

"How much farther?" she wondered aloud.

Just as she spoke, her driver halted the coach. Pandora lifted the window curtain and peered out at a large building, stained dull-gray with age. The place looked like a medieval castle—*complete with torture chambers*—she thought with a shudder.

"Here we are, mademoiselle," the driver announced as he opened the door.

She must find the doctor's office as quickly as possible. She wanted this visit behind her. She glanced about, but saw no signs to direct her. Before she could ask, the driver pointed the way.

Moments later, Pandora stood at the door that bore the doctor's name in gold lettering. When she went in, she was met by a stern-looking gray-haired woman dressed in a stiff woolen uniform of the very same dull shade.

"Mademoiselle Sherwood?"

Pandora nodded.

"I am Madame Celeste, Dr. Pinel's assistant. Please follow me." When Pandora hesitated, the woman added with a flash of annoyance in her watery-blue eyes, "You are already six minutes late. We do not keep the doctor waiting!"

Pandora cringed like a scolded child at the woman's tone. Already she regretted coming. Now she realized that she was truly terrified. How would she ever survive the afternoon?

"Do come along, mademoiselle!" Madame Celeste commanded.

Pandora entered the doctor's office expecting to meet a stern-faced man in a sterile box of a room. She could barely move one foot ahead of the other. The moment she saw the kindly face of Dr. Pinel and looked into his warm brown eyes, some of her panic eased. His office might have been the library of an elegant private home. A fire glowed invitingly, casting its flickering light over the worn leather volumes lining the walls. The office was furnished with a huge, scarred desk, an overstuffed chair, a tea table, and a soft leather couch. Pandora noted everything. Jacob would want to know every detail, down to the paintings on the walls, the worn spots in the carpet underfoot, and the rainbow-colored glass shade on the doctor's desk lamp.

"My dear Miss Sherwood!" Dr. Pinel came toward her with an outstretched hand, speaking to her in perfect English. "I am so happy to meet you at last. Your fiancé has written me in such detail that I feel you and I are great friends already. I hope in our time together that will truly come to pass."

Pandora smiled at the rotund little man in his rumpled black suit as she gripped his hand. "Thank you, Dr. Pinel. I hope so, too. I could use a friend right now."

"Oh, my dear, you sound so distressed. Do have a seat and let me pour you a cup of tea. We'll talk. You'll relax."

Pandora sat carefully on the edge of the leather couch. She still felt nervous, but her terror had eased. Dr. Pinel was not the ogre she had imagined. There was kindness and genuine sympathy in his lined, leathery face.

As he handed her a cup of tea, he smiled and patted her hand. "There, my dear. Drink that. You'll feel much better. It's always difficult for a sensitive young woman when she consults with a new physician. Jacob wrote me that you were against this visit when he first suggested it. He told me something happened that made you willing—indeed, anxious—to pay me a call. Would you like to tell me about it?"

The good doctor's tea, or perhaps it was his open smile and friendly tone, worked magic on Pandora. Soon she was pouring out her whole story to him—the birthday party, her inability to employ her second sight to see herself as Jacob's wife. She even admitted to him what had happened after she'd fled the party—the vision or dream or whatever that she had experienced while kissing Ward Gabriel.

"The kiss was all perfectly innocent," she explained quickly. "He'd given me a birthday gift, you see, and I merely wanted to thank him. But the things I saw and felt and actually *experienced* in those few minutes . . . Oh, Doctor.'' She looked down into her empty cup, unable to face him suddenly.

''Pandora,'' he said gently, ''you don't have to feel embarrassed with me. If I'm to help you, you must trust me completely. Nothing you say to me will go beyond this room. As for your vision of the other man—his making love to you . . .''

''Not to *me*,'' she corrected in a tone edged with new panic. ''It was the dark-haired woman, the one I keep seeing in my dreams.''

''Yes, yes, of course. You told me that.'' He was propped against his desk, standing in front of her. Now he smiled down into her eyes. ''But, my dear, you *felt* what happened to her. That's all I meant. You did, didn't you?''

A warm blush suffused Pandora's cheeks. Tears of embarrassment swam in her eyes. She started to speak, but her voice broke and she fell silent.

''I know this is difficult for you. Take your time, Pandora,'' he cautioned gently. ''And don't be afraid to let me see your tears.'' He handed her a large, clean hankerchief from his desk drawer. ''I know how upsetting this must be.''

Pandora wiped her eyes and blew her nose as quietly as she could.

''There, that's better, my dear. Now, can you tell me what has been troubling you so about that night?''

While the doctor waited for her to speak, his mind was busy, sorting through the facts of her case. Nowhere in his letter had Jacob Saenger mentioned anything about this man named Ward Gabriel. Perhaps Pandora had not told Jacob about that night. She probably feared that her fiancé would be jealous over even an *innocent* kiss, as she had termed it. He smiled. Jacob Saenger's jealousy would be well-placed, he assured himself. Pandora Sherwood was indeed a beautiful woman. She was also secretive by nature. He sensed that already. In order for him to help her, he must gain her confidence and break through the thick wall of emotion she built around herself. If he could not, then hypnosis was out of the question. He would be unable to mesmerize her without her consent and her total cooperation.

Pandora sat before Dr. Pinel wrestling with her own troubled thoughts. She had to know what had actually happened that night at Ward's cottage and what, if anything, had transpired between them the night in New York. She has sworn to herself that she would seek Dr. Pinel's help. Now here he was, offering it willingly, and she could not bring herself to accept. It was so silly. After all, he was a doctor and he would certainly not be shocked by anything she told him. Still, the words simply refused to come.

"If you'd rather go on to something else, Pandora, we can leave that night for the time being. I can see that you are struggling. I don't want to press you."

"No, Doctor! That night is the reason I'm here," she said firmly. Willing herself the courage to speak, she sat up very straight and looked directly into his eyes. "I believe that something terrible happened to me at Ward Gabriel's cottage. I think—no, I'm sure!—that someone made love to me."

Dr. Pinel could hardly have been more shocked—not shocked in the moral sense of the word, but shocked that Pandora could be less than certain if such a thing had happened.

"This is most uncommon," he said quietly. "Do you mean that you believe your *dream* of the green-eyed man and the dark-haired woman was no vision at all, but reality?"

"I know you must think I'm mad." She dropped her gaze, suddenly feeling foolish.

"Not at all, Pandora," he answered quietly. Then, posing his question carefully, he asked, "Or are you telling me that you think this Ward Gabriel took advantage of you?"

Still looking down at her hands, she nodded her head. "That's what I thought at first. But you see, there was the clock. Only a few moments lapsed as we kissed. There was not time enough for . . ."

Dr. Pinel shook his head. Pandora was still holding back. "My dear, you must be *totally* open and honest with me if I'm to help you."

"I know," she whispered. "I'm trying."

"Very well, Pandora. Take your time. I'm a very patient man."

"It was the blood!" she burst out. "When I got home and undressed, my . . . my limbs were smeared with blood. Oh, Doctor," she cried, "I'm afraid I lost my virginity that night. How can I marry Jacob not knowing what he'll discover on our wedding night?"

She was sobbing now. Dr. Pinel came to her and placed a consoling hand on her shoulder.

"Pandora, listen to me, with a simple examination, the question can be settled. Are you willing?"

She looked up at him through her tears. She was trembling with fear, but she managed a weak smile. "Anything would be better than not knowing."

"Very well, Pandora. I'll tell Madame Celeste to prepare you."

Pandora's face flushed scarlet when she reentered Dr. Pinel's office to hear the results of his examination. He smiled at her in a fatherly way and motioned her to take a seat again. She wanted desperately to ask him what he'd discovered, but she could not bring herself to say the words.

"You can relax, Pandora. Your wedding night as Jacob Saenger's virgin bride is assured."

His words took a moment to sink in. When Pandora finally realized what he was telling her, she laughed and cried at the same time. "Oh, Doctor, how can I ever thank you?"

"By being totally truthful with me. By trusting me, Pandora. I want to help you. I *can* help you, if you'll let me."

"I need your help," she said in a sober tone. "I know now that I *must* have it."

He nodded. "That's the first step, my dear, and a very large one."

Suddenly, Pandora felt perfectly at ease with her new doctor. After what she had just been through in his examining room, it seemed she could experience no further, deeper embarrassment. Without hesitation, she asked, "But what about the blood?"

He cocked an eyebrow thoughtfully. "That's easily explained. You'd had an emotionally upsetting evening. It is not uncommon for the emotions to affect the physical functions of the body. Perhaps your monthly cycle was thrown out of phase." He tilted his head and puffed his pipe for a moment. "There's another possibility, but I'm not sure we should go into that just yet. It seems a bit farfetched in your case."

"Oh, please, Doctor. Tell me what you're thinking. I need to know everything."

He nodded. "Yes, I think you do. All right, Pandora, but bear in mind that I am not an ordinary physician. I deal mainly in matters of the mind, and this theory has to do with our peculiar mental processes. It is possible that your body reacted to the scene you imagined between the man and the woman to such a degree that you actually suffered some of the symptoms that she would have experienced on her wedding night. It's known as a physiological reaction. In other words, you believed so strongly that what you witnessed had actually happened to you, that your mind made your body react accordingly. Hence, the bleeding. Do you follow me?"

Pandora was frowning, trying to sort it all out. "I'm not quite sure."

"Well, let me explain it another way. I've seen a number of cases where a woman who was not with child believed herself to be pregnant. Quite often this happens when a woman desperately wants a child but has been unable to conceive. If such a woman can convince herself that she is with child, her body will then do the bidding of her subconscious. Her monthly flow will cease. She will start to gain weight. In extreme cases, her breasts may even begin producing milk. What you experienced seems quite similar to me. In either case, you have nothing to worry about, Pandora."

"I can't begin to tell you how relieved I am, Doctor. I've been worried sick for the past weeks. I'd even come to dread the thought of my wedding." She smiled at him and wiped away a tear. "Now, thanks to you, I can look forward to marrying Jacob."

He chuckled. "No more, I'm sure, than he is looking forward to taking you as his lovely bride. I'm glad I've eased your mind, though I know it was a difficult ordeal for you. Perhaps you would like to end our session for today?"

"No, no." Pandora assured him. Now that she was here, she wanted to get on with her treatment. "I mean, if you have no other patients waiting, Doctor."

"None at all, my dear." He looked pleased. She was a woman of strong will and fine stamina. A good subject, he was sure. "I've reserved the entire afternoon for you. So, if you are willing, I'd like to try an experiment now."

"What kind of experiment?" she wanted to know.

"Are you familiar with mesmerism or hypnosis, my dear?"

Pandora nodded, but frowned at him. "Yes. I saw it performed on stage once in New York. The man who allowed himself to be mesmerized flapped about the stage, clucking like a chicken. It was meant to be amusing, but it made me quite uncomfortable."

Dr. Pinel scowled at her description. "Making you flap about is not exactly what I had in mind. The man you saw was a charlatan. His kind should be arrested for improper use of hypnosis. Hypnosis should not be used as a theatrical trick, but as a tool to help us unlock the mysteries of the human mind. Have you ever been hypnotized, Pandora?"

"Heavens, no!" she gasped.

Dr. Pinel shook his head and sighed. "Are you worried because you believe—as so many still do—that hypnosis robs the subject of his will? If I were able to hypnotize you, Pandora, would you be terrified that I might force myself upon you, seduce you right here on my office rug?"

Pandora didn't know whether to laugh or be shocked. The idea of the kindly, old doctor taking advantage of her or any other woman was the farthest thing from her mind.

"Certainly not." she said with some force.

A twinkle came to Pinel's eyes and he sighed. "Ah well, I suppose my time of seeming a threat to lovely young women is long past." He chuckled then, putting Pandora back at ease.

"What exactly do you have in mind, Doctor?"

"Under hypnosis, a subject will often reveal things that may not be a part of the conscious mind. I believe that your visions or your second sight are a form of autohypnosis that you have been practicing on yourself for a number of years, Pandora."

She was astounded at such a thought. "But why?"

"You had a great tragedy in your early years. Quite often a person who has been deeply hurt will seek some means of escape from the pain. It seems likely that this has been your way. If I could take you back to that time, perhaps we could ease some of the leftover tension from that period in your life."

Pandora looked stricken. "You mean I'd have to relieve that horrible night? See my parents die a second time?" She shook her head furiously. "No! I'm sorry, I couldn't bear it."

"What if I could take you back, but leave no conscious memory of the regression afterward? I am convinced you need to do this, Pandora. I suspect that for all these years you have been experiencing a deep sense of guilt because your parents died, but you lived."

"Could that really be the whole problem?" she asked doubtfully.

"I believe so. Often when a person survives a great tragedy, that individual experiences a senseless guilt for having lived while others perished. Such a deep-seated feeling of shame could play all manner of tricks on your mind and your body. By taking you back, I think I could relieve the problem."

"But your theory still doesn't explain the recurring dreams I've had all my life, even before my parents died, Doctor."

He nodded, hoping to reassure her. "The trauma of your premature birth and your highly developed sensitivity can explain the dreams. The hypnosis should provide a solution to that problem, as well. We will search your mind, find the key, and unlock all your dark, mysterious chambers, young lady."

She looked up at him, still wary of his plan. ""Would I actually have to relive everything?"

"Under hypnosis, you would. Once I bring you out of it, you will have no conscious memory of what you experienced during the trance—only, I hope, a very positive, conscious reaction afterward. Of course, Madame Celeste will be here with us the whole time." The twinkle came back into his deep brown eyes. "She's quite a prude as you may have guessed. So there's no chance that I might take advantage of you. Are you willing?"

Pandora sat very still for several moments thinking the matter through. The whole idea of hypnosis frightened her. So did the thought of continuing to live with her strange dreams and second sight. Now that she knew she was free to marry Jacob with a clear conscience, she wanted their life together to be as normal and happy as possible. If Dr. Pinel's unorthodox technique could accomplish that for her, then she saw no reason to hesitate a moment longer.

"What would you like me to do?" she asked.

He came to her and touched her shoulder, beaming down at her. "Then you agree. I don't think you'll be sorry, Pandora. If you will lie down on the couch, I will call Madame Celeste."

A moment later, the prune-faced assistant took her place in a chair across the room, her notepad on her lap and pen at the ready.

"Madame Celeste will make notes on my questions and your answers, if that's agreeable with you, Pandora," the doctor told her.

She nodded her assent.

"Fine. Then we shall begin."

Dr. Pinel's voice was low and quiet—very soothing. He told her to focus on the lamp on his desk, the one with the rainbow-colored shade. He reminded her that she was to retain no conscious memory of anything that transpired during the session.

"Your eyes are growing very heavy, Pandora. You will want to close them soon. You will want to close out the whole world—the noise from the street, the ticking of the clock, everything except the sound of my voice. Slowly, now. Slowly, let your eyes close. That's very good, my dear."

Pandora tried at first to fight him, to keep her eyes open. Dr. Pinel's voice wrapped her in its warmth and security, and soon her heavy lids closed, leaving only the swirling colors of the lamp's bright shade.

"Now, Pandora, I want you to let your mind travel back in time. The days and months and years will fly backward, like the flipping of pages in a picture book. When you reach the year of the great storm, you will stop."

She lay very still on the couch, letting her mind drift back. Her body felt very heavy at first, then she experienced a lightness. It seemed as if she had left her being entirely to float through space and time.

"You remember the hurricane, don't you?"

"Yes, I remember." Her voice sounded far away to her own ears.

"Tell me about it, Pandora."

"There's a strange cast to the sky. Brickdust! A bloody tint as if bricks had been powdered and blown all about. The wind is rising. I can hear the waves pounding on the beach. It's going to be a terrible blow!"

"And how do you feel?"

"I'm afraid! I want to leave, but I refuse to go alone and the others insist they'll ride it out."

Dr. Pinel glanced at Jacob Saenger's letter. Yes, this all fit. Jacob had written that Pandora tried to warn her parents of a nightmare she'd had a few nights before the storm struck. They regarded her forebodings as childish prattle. They stayed and they died.

"So you will have to remain at Indianola."

Pandora's eyes flew open suddenly. She stared blankly into the doctor's face, seeming to focus on some point beyond the man, beyond the room.

"Indianola?" she said in a strangely accented voice. "I know of no such place."

Dr. Pinel shifted in his seat. This was outrageous. Had Saenger sent him the wrong information?

"Where are you, then?" he asked quietly. "Tell me the name of the place."

"We thought it was Campeachy when we came."

"Mexico?" he asked.

"Yes. But we were wrong. This island was not on the charts. The Indians call it *Isla Serpiente.*" She smiled, then chuckled softly. "My husband, of course, still calls it Campeachy. He is a stubborn man. He insists that all the other charts are wrong and only he is correct. He will go to his grave insisting that we reached his planned destination, although he knows we did not."

"Your husband?" Dr. Pinel's voice boomed in the room. He paused for a moment, collecting himself. Somehow, something had gone wrong. Pandora Sherwood was only ten years old when her parents died. She had no husband. Where was she now?

"Do you know what year it is, Pandora?"

She made no reply.

"Pandora, can you hear me?"

"Are you speaking to me, sir?"

"Yes, of course I am."

"Then use my name, please."

The doctor was leaning forward, watching her intently. "What is your name?"

She laughed. "You had better call me Madame Boss as the other men do. My husband is a jealous man. He would fight you if you dared address me by my Christian name, Nicolette."

"Very well, Madame Boss, can you tell me the year?"

She laughed. "Why, where have you been that you don't know the date? It's been three years since the end of the great battle at New Orleans. It's fall now, the fall of 1818."

"Doctor!" Madame Celeste gasped. "What have you done?"

He motioned the woman to silence. He had to get his thoughts together before he could go on. Finally, he framed his next question.

"The storm. You were going to tell me about the storm."

Pandora twisted uneasily on the soft leather couch and her face lost its calm expression. She cradled her arms to her breasts and her head tossed from side to side.

"Oh, please, let's leave before it's too late!" she begged. "We can still make it to the mainland. But I'll go only if you come with me. The baby and I will not be separated from you, darling!''

"What baby?" Dr. Pinel demanded. "Who is your husband? Tell me your child's name. Madame Boss, can you hear me?"

The woman on the sofa heard none of Dr. Pinel's frantic questions. She was far away in another time and place, with the rain and wind slashing the island, the water rising steadily, and the ship that might have saved her from the storm now foundering at its anchorage.

Stubbornly, she remained, determined, even if it meant her death, to stay by the side of the man she loved.

Chapter Eight

A sound like cannonfire thundered in the distance out over the Gulf. Disturbed by the noise and by the tension she could feel in her mother's body, the baby left off suckling and began to cry.

"Oh, sh-h-h, Jeannette," the ebony-haired woman crooned. "It will be all right. Papa will keep us safe."

The words trembled on Nicolette's lips. How she wished she could believe those assurances! Perhaps she had made a mistake in refusing to leave the island. The storm was of uncommon savagery—no coastal gale, but a full-blown West Indian cyclone.

She glanced out the window of the bedroom. Through the blowing sand and hard-driving rain, she could just make out the faint outline of the collection of huts where her husband's men and their families lived. Shaking her head sadly, she thought how he had warned them to build better, stronger homes like his own—houses that would survive the stormy months of fall. But the band of nearly a thousand displaced men who now called Campeachy home had more adventurous things on their minds. There were Spanish ships to be taken, treasure chests to be plundered, women to be brought home and ravaged as part of the spoils of war.

Nicolette tried not to think of that sordid side of the island's life. She could do nothing about it, so she tried to put it out of her mind. Here in her own fine home, she was insulated from the ugliness of the village. When she went out, her husband saw to it that she was never alone. If he was unable to accompany her, he sent one of his trusted men to guard her from the others. She had had one narrow escape at the grove, when two men accosted her. If they had not been drunk and argued over which of them would have her first, and if 'Gator-Bait had not run for help, she shuddered to think what might have happened. Her husband had arrived in the nick of time, putting a bullet between the eyes of Thomas Corkland even as he held her to the ground, preparing to violate her. Frenchie McCabe, the other brigand, had dangled from the yardarm of the *Pride* for nearly a week—until the gulls and terns had done with him—a warning to any others who might take it into their heads to lay a hand on the Boss's woman.

For a time after that, she had been confined to *Maison Rouge,* the great scarlet-painted mansion that was her home. Only when she finally agreed to an armed escort, was she once again accorded the freedom of the island.

She loved this bare sand spit in spite of its reprobate crew, its snakes, its mosquitoes, its multitude of dangers. She loved it, quite simply, because she was here with *him!*

Now, as the howling wind beat relentlessly at her windows and the water rose at the stone steps of the mansion, she wondered why she—the gently-bred daughter of a fine Creole family—had ever left New Orleans to come to this godforsaken speck of sand. She knew the answer without ever having to think about it. She was here because she loved Jean Laffite with every shred of her being. She had loved him, not from the first moment she saw him, but from the very beginning of creation. She would continue to love him to eternity's end.

"Darling?" His voice brought her out of her reverie.

"Oh, Jean, you're back!" She placed the sleeping baby in her crib and ran into his open arms.

He was soaked to the skin, his hair and shirt were plastered with wet sand, and his mouth tasted of salt, but none of that mattered. The feel of his body pressed to hers and the sweetness of his kiss filled her senses.

When he drew away at last, she saw that his green eyes were deeply troubled.

"It's bad, isn't it?" she whispered.

He shook his head. "The worst I've ever seen. The whole island's flooding. We've lost two ships. A dozen men have drowned already. How high the water will rise is anyone's guess." Suddenly, he clutched her to him in an embrace of sheer desperation. "Why, in God's name, didn't I send you to safety while there was still time?"

She looked up into his eyes, her own wide with fear. But her words were calm and determined. "You could not have made me leave you, darling. You would have had to drag me on board that ship in chains and lock me away like a prisoner."

"Then, by damn, that's exactly what I should have done! If anything happens to you and Jeannette . . ."

"If anything happens, my darling, it will happen to all of us together. Do you think I'd want to live if you were gone?" She was trembling with fear. "What can we do to make sure nothing does happen, Jean?"

"I want you to carry Jeanette up to the attic. The water will flood the first floor any minute now."

She glanced about at their snug, dry bedroom—the room she loved most in the house. The Turkish rug glowed like a warm jewel beneath her bare feet. A driftwood fire crackled soothingly on the hearth. The bed, with its gilt cornice and crimson drapes looked its most inviting. If they pulled the heavy drapes at the windows, she would hardly know that a storm was in progress. They could make love until it passed.

"But, Jean, we should be perfectly safe upstairs here in the bedroom. I don't want to leave."

He shook his head furiously. "There's no time to argue, darling. When the storm surge comes, the water will rush in so quickly and with such force that this floor could be flooded before you have time to run to the attic stairs. I want you up there *now!*''

"I'll do as you say," she answered submissively. "But it's so dark and close up there, with only that one tiny window."

"Another point in our favor. The shacks in the village are beginning to blow apart. Soon the wind will be carrying loose boards like deadly missiles through the air. You could be killed if one smashed through the bedroom window. In the attic you'll be safe. Hurry now! I want you settled before I leave."

Icy fingers closed around her heart. "You aren't going back out there?" she cried. "Jean, that's madness!"

"I have to, darling. The men and their families need help. I'll bring as many as I can back here to the house. They can't stay out in the open. Take the sick and injured and the children up to the attic with you. The rest will have to fend for themselves down here."

For the next hour, Jean and Nicolette hauled supplies up the attic stairs—food, clothing, blankets, jugs of water and wine. Then they set about carrying furniture from the first floor up to the bedrooms. When they could not jam another chair or table or piece of china into the second story, Laffite ordered his wife to the attic.

"Where's 'Gator-Bait?" Nicolette asked suddenly.

Laffite glanced about as if he expected to find his wife's lazy little servant loitering about as usual. "Isn't he with you?"

"No," she answered. "He went out shortly before you arrived. He said he'd left Jeannette's toy chest in the garden and he didn't want her doll to drown."

"Goddammit!" Laffite exploded. "That little bastard causes me more trouble than he's worth. I should have let those Kaintucks feed him to that 'gator and good riddance!"

"Jean, please! He's only a child."

He gave an angry snort, then smiled at her in apology. "I'll see if I can find him for you, darling. You stay in this attic. And, remember, only women and children are allowed in." He shoved a loaded pistol into her hands. "Use this if you have to. Some of the men aren't above taking advantage of the worst situation.''

"Oh, Jean, surely they wouldn't!"

"Well, you know what to do if you have to, darling. Don't hesitate. *Shoot to kill!*''

He gave her a quick farewell kiss. His boots, thudding down the stairs, seemed to echo with a hollow sound in her heart. She felt utterly, completely alone—cut off not only from her husband, but from the rest of the human race. She would even have welcomed a fretful cry from Jeannette. Her daughter, once settled in the old sea chest in the attic, was now sleeping soundly. Only the constant howl of the wind and the drumming of rain on the roof broke the lonely silence.

When she heard pounding on the front door, she hurried to the attic stairs, bent on welcoming whoever had come. Perhaps 'Gator-Bait had finally returned. Or it might be the first refugees arriving from the village.

"Come in out of the storm!" she called from the head of the attic stairs. She heard the door slam shut, but no one answered her.

"Gator-Bait! Is that you?"

Still no answer.

She hesitated for a moment, then started more cautiously down the stairs to the first floor. She could hear footsteps, someone sloshing about the flooded living room below. Already the ground floor stood in almost a foot of saltwater.

Edging slowly down the stairs, her heart pounding frantically, she called out, "Who's there?"

She heard a cabinet slam shut in the pantry, then the watery sound of someone walking back toward the front of the house. Instinctively, her hand slid into the deep pocket of her shirt, closing on the pistol her husband had left her. Her finger gripped the trigger as she saw a man's boots at the foot of the stairs.

Quickly, she pulled the gun out and aimed. He was coming up. She could see his boot tops and the wet, sandy knees of his canvas britches. She held the pistol with both hands, trembling all over, but ready to squeeze the trigger, if she had to.

137

"Don't come another step!" she ordered.

"Ma'am?" said a familiar voice. "Is that you, Madame Boss? It's me, Frisco. Your husband said I should come keep an eye on things."

Nicolette went weak all over with relief. Slowly, she lowered the pistol, then slipped it back into her pocket. *Frisco*. She should have guessed. He was the young man her husband usually assigned as her bodyguard—in his early twenties, red-haired, blue-eyed, and born, he claimed, to the madam of the finest sporting house in all of California. Frisco looked like a mere boy, but according to Laffite, the lad was "mean enough to rip out a man's gizzard with his bare fingernails."

"Frisco, you scared the life out of me!" she said. "I'm glad you're here. I was getting so nervous I was about ready to jump out of my skin."

He grinned up at her, parting a million freckles with his smile. "Hell, ma'am, you couldn't be no gladder than I am. I sailed three times 'round the Horn and back, and I ain't never seen nothin' like that storm out yonder. I's tickled plumb pink when the Boss told me to get on up here to the house to see was you and the baby all right."

"We're fine, Frisco. But I'm worried sick about 'Gator-Bait. You haven't seen him, have you?"

"No, ma'am. You want I should go out and have a look around?"

She hesitated. She hated to send Frisco or anyone out in this weather. "It's just . . . He can't swim!" she cried. "You know I got him from those awful men who were using him as bait to hunt alligators—tying a rope around him and throwing him into the bayou. He's been terrified of water ever since. Frisco, he'll drown out there!"

"I'm gone, ma'am! Now don't you worry none. I'll find the little bugger and bring home safe and sound."

Frisco had no more than shut the front door when it flew open again, crashing against the wall. Three half-drowned women came tumbling in, blown by a fierce gust of wind. Nicolette bit her lip as she realized who they were. They were not sailors' wives, but inmates of the only other structure on the island called a "house." The women there came from all over, lured by the smell of adventure and gold. Some had followed the *Pride* from New Orleans, but the vast majority hailed from much more exotic ports—Havana, Lisbon, Naples, Santo Domingo.

"Welcome," she said solemnly. Her delicate nostrils twitched as she became aware of the odors they brought with them—unwashed flesh, French perfume, and the strong, rancid smell of shark oil, used to repel the island's dense winged population.

The trio eyed her curiously. They had seen her before, but only from a distance. They seldom strayed far from the house and Madame Boss never ventured near it.

A heavy-bosomed woman with copper-colored skin spoke for them all. "Your man told us we should come here. We ain't just bargin' in."

Nicolette nodded. "I said welcome and you are. This may be the only safe place on the island soon."

The thin girl with long, blonde hair began to sob. She turned to the woman who had spoken. "Lord, I'm so scared, Tildy! We're all gonna' die and go straight to hell!"

Without changing expression, Tildy slapped the girl's face. "Shut yer yap, Sal!"

Nicolette stiffened, but Tildy's cruel methods worked. Sal's hysterics ceased immediately.

The third woman—a tall, elegant beauty with the look of a Spanish aristocrat stood away from the others, ignoring the scene. She obviously felt that she was above the other two in station. A curious attitude, Nicolette thought, for one of the island whores.

"What's your name?" Nicolette asked her.

The woman cut dark, suspicious eyes toward their hostess, but retained her disdainful silence.

"That one there, she's the Queen of Spain!" Tildy answered with a loud guffaw. "Ain't you, Señorita Honey-Drawers?"

The Spanish woman's face went crimson with rage. "Close your filthy mouth!" she snapped at Tildy. "They do not touch me, those awful men of yours! Not one of them, ever. I am as pure as the day they stole me from my father's ship."

"In a pig's eye," Tildy taunted.

"Ladies, ladies. Please," Nicolette soothed. "We're all in this together. Let's not make it worse by fighting among ourselves." She turned to the young Spanish woman, whose eyes were still blazing pure hatred at Tildy. "I asked your name."

The black-eyed beauty held her head up proudly as she answered, "I am Señorita Isabel Maria Estella Consuela Estaban y Alejandro, madame. My father's ship was attacked by these pirates three weeks ago. They stole the cargo, killed my father, and burned the ship. I alone survived, but I would have preferred death. I will take my own life if ever one of those filthy pigs so much as touches me. I swear it!"

Nicolette felt a sudden kinship with the poor Spanish girl. She, too, had once been on a ship that was attacked by pirates. Her father's merchantman, the *Fleur de Lis*. She had been returning from a year in Paris with her aunt, returning to marry a man she had never met. Jean Laffite had saved her—from the pirates and from the dreadful marriage.

"It's all right, Isabel," Nicolette soothed. "Don't upset yourself needlessly."

"That's right," little Sal added, mistaking Nicolette's meaning. "It ain't so bad, really once you get used to it. I hadn't never known no men neither before I run away from home and come here with my big sister, and I was mighty scared of what they'd do to me. Shoot, I like it fine now."

Tildy cackled with delight. "You tell her, Sally-girl! She'll get the itch one of these days, you mark my words. There won't be nothing to cure it but some big, husky sailor-man with a bulge in his britches fit to kill and enough rum in his gut to fool with a goddamn puny virgin in the first place."

Isabel, her dark eyes flashing, uttered what sounded like a Spanish curse.

"Come upstairs with me, all of you," Nicolette ordered. "I'll find you some dry things."

Sal and Tildy followed immediately, but Isabel lagged behind, defiant to the end. When they reached the attic stairs, Nicolette said, "You'll find dry clothes and blankets up there. Try not to wake the baby. I'll go down and persuade Isabel to join us."

"Good luck," Tildy said with a sneer. "We had to drag her here. I think she *wants* to get herself drowned."

As she turned, Nicolette heard the front door open again. Sure that Isabel had fled back out into the storm, she hurried down the stairs. What she saw when she reached the first floor froze her blood. Isabel had not left. A man had entered—a man Nicolette knew well by his horribly scarred face and his equally repulsive reputation. Emilio La Paz was feared by every man on the island except Jean Laffite. He took orders from no man and claimed no country, but every woman, as his own.

"No! Let me go!" Isabel screamed, clawing at her attacker's eyes.

Nicolette could see that La Paz had one thick arm about the girl's slender waist in a crushing grip. With his other hand, he was ripping away the bodice of her gown. One firm, white breast sprang free. He clamped his big hand down hard and Isabel cried out in pain.

"Release her!" Nicolette screamed. "Do you hear me, La Paz? Let her go!"

The huge man swung around with a roar of rage. For a moment, he stood motionless, staring at Nicolette. Then an ugly grin twisted his hideous face.

"Ah, it's Madame Boss." The words oozed sickeningly out of his mouth. With one quick jerk of his arm, he tossed Isabel across the room. Then he started for Nicolette.

"This seems to be my lucky day," he growled. "I came looking for rum, but just see what I've found instead. *Two* pretty women panting for me!"

He lunged for Nicolette, but she ducked under his thick, hairy arms. He howled with delight. "A playful minx. No wonder Laffite keeps you all to himself." He inched toward her, grinning. "Come to Emilio," he coaxed. "Come let him show you what it's like with a *real* man."

Nicolette's heart was in her throat, pounding so that she ached all over. Her head was spinning. Any moment now he would make another lunge for her and this time she might

141

not be so lucky. The floor was slick with slimy silt washed in by the water. If she lost her footing . . .

La Paz was inching ever nearer, unlacing his britches as he came. "Come closer, my pretties," he said with an ugly laugh. "I'll give you a peek at what you've been missing. You take a real good look, then you two whores will be tearing each other's hair out, fighting to see who can climb on first."

When he yanked the great, throbbing thing from his britches, Isabel screamed. La Paz's revolting actions had the reverse effect on Nicolette. Her head cleared suddenly. The gun. She reached into her pocket and brought the small pistol out, taking careful aim.

"Get out of my house," she said in a voice that was deadly calm.

The pirate's bearded face registered surprise the moment he spied the pistol. He broke into a huge roar of laughter and moved toward her once more.

"You think you can ruin my fun with that little toy of a weapon? Such a tiny bullet would not even pierce my thick hide. So, you will hand it over to me and then we will get on with this."

"I'm warning you!" Nicolette said in a shaky voice.

"And *I'm* warning *you!*" the man bellowed in reply, his face twisting into a hideous mask of rage as he rushed her.

It all happened so quickly. She saw him coming for her. She felt her finger squeezing the trigger. She heard her husband's words in her head: "Shoot to kill!"

When the shot rang out, Emilio La Paz did not fall. He stood inches away—so close that Nicolette could smell his foul breath in her face. She watched his black eyes go glassy with pain. His huge mouth lolled open for an instant before he roared out his agony. Then she watched him turn, clutching his genitals as blood streamed through his thick fingers. Bellowing like a wounded bull, he stumbled out of the house and disappeared in the storm.

Quickly, Nicolette gathered her wits about her. "Isabel, we will not mention this to the others. If Tildy and Sal ask about the shot, I'll tell them a snake swam into the house."

The girl mustered a shaky laugh. "Not far from the truth

is that lie. You are right, madame, there is no need to alarm the others." Then she tossed her head, her spirit returning. "Besides, knowing those two, they would probably rush out into the storm to bring him back for their own amusement. But that one will not be of much use to a woman ever again."

Nicolette allowed Isabel to think what she would about her reasons for keeping La Paz's visit a secret. In truth, she was ashamed. Not because she had shot the evil pirate, but because her husband had told her to shoot to kill. She had missed her aim. Jean must never know that after all the lessons he had so patiently given her, she could still miss such a large and threatening target.

The storm raged on outside, and *Maison Rouge* filled with women and children. The water crept higher and higher in the house. Night was coming on. There was no word from Jean. 'Gator-Bait was still missing and Frisco had not come back. The full weight of managing the crowd in the house and trying to soothe their terror fell to Nicolette. She felt weak, exhausted, and as frightened as she had ever been in her life.

"Try to sleep for a time. I'll take over your duties," Isabel offered. "I'll wake you if Jeannette needs feeding."

Nicolette, who was stretched out on the floor beside her sleeping baby, smiled weakly up at the girl. She was sweet and kind, and she seemed to have gained new confidence from their episode with Emilio La Paz. It was clear that she counted Nicolette as her friend now.

"I don't think I can sleep, Isabel. I'm so worried about my husband and 'Gator-Bait."

"They are probably together and safe, madame. All will be well, you'll see."

"I wish I could be so sure," Nicolette answered, trying to return the girl's confident smile.

Just then, the house shuddered. Women screamed and children began to sob.

"What was that?" Isabel cried, her calm slipping suddenly.

"The storm surge," Nicolette said quietly. "The whole

island must be under water now. The worst is yet to come. Pray that my husband built this house well. It *must* hold up against the force of the tides!''

The surge came as Laffite had predicted—suddenly and with awesome force. The women and children clung to each other, hearing the great wave crash into the Gulf side of the house, feeling the floor move under them, seeing the dirty, angry water race up the stairs to flood the second floor. Those in the bedrooms climbed on top of furniture to keep their heads above water. Only inches of breathing space remained.

The roof shifted over their heads and rain poured down over Nicolette and the baby. ''Oh, God, please!'' Nicolette prayed softly. ''Don't let me go without telling him good-bye!''

The night seemed endless, but somehow *Maison Rouge* held its own against the fierce hurricane. When the first hint of dawn began to color the sky, Nicolette knew that the worst was over. Those in the house had survived. As for the others, until the water receded she could do nothing to find out how bad the news was. The long hours of that second day dragged by.

Finally, near sunset, she heard a shout from below. ''Hallo! Is anyone there? Madame Boss?''

Handing Jeannette to Isabel, Nicolette hurried down the stairs. The water was still knee-deep on the first floor, but she paid no attention.

''Frisco!'' she cried with relief, wanting desperately to hug the weather-beaten young man. ''You're safe!''

''This 'un here made it, too, ma'am!'' Frisco yanked at the rope in his hands and Nicolette saw wide round eyes staring at her from a very black, very frightened face.

'''Gator-Bait!'' she cried, lifting the terrified lad out of Jeannette's toy chest that had served as his lifeboat to ride out the storm.

The little boy clung to his mistress, whimpering incoherently.

''What about my husband?'' She was almost afraid to ask.

Frisco avoided her gaze and brushed nervously at a lock

of hair that had fallen over his eyes. "Sorry, ma'am. I ain't seen the Boss since yesterday. By the time I found ole 'Gator-Bait here, the water was mighty high. Me and him just had to hang on and ride her out. We been drifting with the tide all night." He paused, considering his next words. "We seen some bodies."

Nicolette gasped.

"But wasn't none of them his," Frisco added quickly. "I'll go see can I find him right now, ma'am."

Nicolette nodded, her throat too constricted with tears to answer. Why did Jean have to go back out in the storm? Why couldn't he have stayed with her where it was safe?

"No need to bother yourself, Frisco."

Jean's familiar, well-loved voice sent a sudden thrill through his wife. She looked up through her tears.

"My darling," she whispered.

The next moment, she was in his arms, holding on as if she'd never let go.

Slowly, the waters sank back into the Gulf. The rain stopped. The last exhausted gasp of wind died away. The sun shone once more on the tiny speck of sand between the Gulf and the bay.

That night, Nicolette and her husband shared a dinner of soggy crackers and Spanish wine in their attic—the only dry spot in the house. She could not take her eyes off him. It seemed to her that if she looked away for the barest instant, he might vanish again.

"The clean-up will be a major task," he told her. "I've lost four ships with all hands. The village is gone, except for the house and three or four shacks on the bay side. Dozens are dead. It's the worst I've ever seen."

Suddenly, he gripped her hand and brought it to his lips. His eyes took on new light. "But, you and I, we still have each other, darling. You can't imagine what I went through last night—not knowing if you were safe."

"Believe me, Jean, I *can* imagine."

He rose and gently led her from the table, drawing her down with him to the blanket beside their daughter's cradle. Then blowing out the candle, he showed his wife, sweetly and tenderly, how much he had missed her, how much he had worried about her, how much he loved her.

Pandora's eyelids fluttered slightly and she stirred on the couch.

"She's coming out of it," Dr. Pinel said to Madame Celeste. "The storm outside and the storm of her emotions have both ceased."

"Jean has made me understand tonight how very deep our love for each other truly is. We are no longer two separate people, but two halves of a single soul. We cannot be parted!"

"Pandora, can you hear me?" Dr. Pinel's raspy voice cut through the tense silence in his office. "Pandora, I want you to come back now. I will count slowly. When I snap my fingers, you will wake feeling rested and refreshed. You will remember nothing that has transpired here. Now, Pandora, one . . . two . . . three!" He clicked his thumb and forefinger together.

Pandora felt as if she had been sucked under by a whirl-pool and was not drifting peacefully to the surface once more. She gave up her struggle, letting the warm tide carry her safely back to the light.

Slowly, slowly, she returned to the present.

Chapter Nine

Pandora blinked once and then again. She shook her head, trying to clear it. She felt wonderfully relaxed, but for a few seconds she had no idea where she was. Then things began to fall into place and she smiled up into Dr. Pinel's kindly, but concerned face.

"Goodness!" she said. "I must have fallen asleep."

Dr. Pinel and Madame Celeste exchanged glances.

"We have finished for the day." The curt tone of Dr. Pinel's voice startled Pandora.

She sat up, a look of disappointment on her face. "But I thought you were going to hypnotize me."

"I did."

"You couldn't have!" she argued stubbornly.

"Look at the clock, Pandora."

She glanced toward the mantel. The brass hands were almost straight up and down.

"Six o'clock?" she asked, unbelieving. "In the *evening?*"

"Exactly." The doctor watched her closely as he answered, trying to gauge her reaction. "You've been in trance for nearly four hours."

"Did I tell you what you wanted to know, Doctor?"

"Not exactly," he evaded.

"You were unable to take me back?"

"Oh, you went back, most certainly! But somehow, Pandora, you managed to disregard my instructions totally."

"I *must* know what happened, Doctor! My whole future depends upon my recalling what I saw in the past, doesn't it? If I can't remember it, you have to tell me, Dr. Pinel."

He put a calming hand on Pandora's shoulder. "There's no need for alarm. The things you told me could not possibly be true. I suspect your fear of hypnosis and your active imagination simply took things out of my hands."

"I don't understand, Doctor."

"I think I do," he answered. "You believe in reincarnation, don't you, Pandora?"

She stared at him as if he'd lost his mind. "Of course not. That's sheer foolishness. I've always believed that we get one chance on earth so we have to make the most of it. I've lived my life thus far by that golden rule."

He expelled a long breath. "I'm surprised to hear that you and I agree. If you are telling me the truth, young lady, then this whole session has been a waste of time. You were never in trance at all, were you? You made up the whole story."

Pandora stared at him, horrified. "I don't even know what story you're talking about, Dr. Pinel. Please, I came to you for help."

He shook his head, but avoided looking at her directly as he answered, "I'm afraid I can't help you."

A chill passed through her. Maybe he was making a joke, hoping to lighten the mood.

"Are you going to tell me what I said?" Her voice was shaky now. In fact, she was trembling all over.

Dr. Pinel almost whispered his next words to her. "I can tell you some of it, Pandora. The rest you can read for yourself in Madame Celeste's notes, if you like. You never mentioned your parents or the storm that took their lives. You said your name was Nicolette, a married woman with a child." He went on to list other details while Pandora sat listening, trying to take it all in, trying to understand.

It was as if he were talking about someone else—telling her a fairytale of long ago. She had to make his words connect with reality somehow.

"Where did this Nicolette live, and when, Doctor?"

"You said she was raised in New Orleans. The exact location later was unclear."

"*I said,*" Pandora whispered, trying to make herself believe.

He nodded. "While you were supposedly under hypnosis, you told me all about this woman. The year was 1818. When you went into trance and I commanded you to go back to the storm, you followed my instructions, but not to the letter. I told you a specific storm. However, you chose another and made up quite a tale about it. The hurricane you chose to revisit was another that struck somewhere along the Gulf of Mexico many years before you were born. You couldn't possibly have been there."

Pandora paled suddenly and began trembling violently. Dr. Pinel ordered, "Quickly, Madame Celeste, a glass of brandy!"

The fiery liquid burned her mouth and throat, but stilled Pandora's shaking enough so that she could speak. "How could that happen, Doctor? How could I go back so far, against your specific instructions?"

Dr. Pinel shook his gray head. "I don't know. I simply have no answers for you. In all my years as a physician, nothing like this has ever happened before. Apparently, you have been practicing autohypnosis as I suspected. Once I put you under, you took over the reins, telling me whatever you wished, making it up as you went along."

"It all sounds outlandish!" Pandora was still reeling from the shock. She looked up at the doctor, pleading with her eyes. "Can't you give me more detail?"

Dr. Pinel suddenly withdrew from her. The afternoon had tired him.

"Please, Doctor," Pandora begged gently. Obviously, he

did not believe a word of what she'd said. The name, Nicolette, gave Pandora an odd, uneasy feeling. She suspected there was more to this memory of hers than simple fantasy. "You can't imagine how strange all this makes me feel. Tell me as much as you can, won't you? It's frightening!"

He nodded, but his frown remained. With a weary sigh, he said, "You told me you were better known as Madame Boss among your husband's friends and followers." Her face remained blank and impassive; the name meant nothing. "You said you were *Madame Jean Laffite.*"

Pandora, who had braced herself for any kind of shock, found that she was unprepared for this. The name seemed to echo through her head, through the stillness in the room. Waves of dizziness passed over her. Bits of visions flitted through her brain—a red hammock, a great golden bed, a man with a scarred body that could arouse her own flesh like no other on earth.

"Jean," she murmured softly, unconscious of having spoken.

Dr. Pinel adjusted his spectacles, then squinted hard at her. "Yes, Jean Laffite was the man in your dream." His tone held a hint of derision.

"You don't understand," she said quietly. "It was never a dream at all. You see, I've always had a passion for stories about Laffite. Now I think I understand why. I suppose I spoke of *Maison Rouge?*"

Dr. Pinel nodded. "You did. You said it was your home."

"It was *Jean Laffite's home.* The ruins of the house are still on Galveston Island. It was one of my favorite hiding places when I was a child. I still find myself drawn there often. I still feel like I belong there."

Dr. Pinel stood up abruptly as if to signal an end to their session. "The whole story can be attributed to your vivid imagination. Madame Jean Laffite, indeed!"

"Please, Doctor," Pandora begged, "don't be upset with me. I came here for your help. Don't send me away. I have nowhere else to turn."

He waited so long to reply that she was afraid he would tell her never to darken his door again. Instead, he said,

"Well, perhaps we'll have more luck next time. That is, if you're willing to try again in a few days."

She smiled and gripped his hand. "Of course I'm willing. I'm surprised you want me to come back after I wasted your entire afternoon."

"Nothing that happens in this office is ever a total waste, Pandora. Come back on Monday afternoon at one."

"Yes, Doctor, and thank you for everything!"

On the long ride back to her hotel, Pandora mulled over everything that had happened that afternoon. Her ramblings about Laffite and his wife meant nothing to Dr. Pinel. She realized now that Jean and Nicolette were the couple who had haunted her dreams these past months. Now she understood why she seemed obsessed with the pair. At last she knew who the green-eyed man and his ebony-haired lover were. Perhaps now that she had that information, she would see them no more. She smiled at her own reaction to that thought: She would miss their tender moments together and the warm feeling they left with her.

Soon she and Jacob would share their own tender moments. She would not have to rely on a pair of phantoms to make her feel that special tingling. What a relief it was to know that now she could go to Jacob with no apprehension. If nothing else, the certain knowledge that her virginity was still intact made her afternoon with Dr. Pinel a success. How she had worried over that! But now she could go to her wedding bed free of guilt.

Cassie was waiting anxiously when she returned. She hurried to take Pandora's coat. "Where in the world have you been? I was worried sick that something had happened to you in this wicked city. Why, it's dark already!"

"It was a long session, Cass. But it went fairly well. I like Dr. Pinel. His assistant is something out of a waxwork chamber of horrors . . ."

The moment Pandora spoke those words, a strange dizziness came over her. It passed in an instant, but left her feeling weak and shaken.

"Are you all right, Miss Pan?" Cassie quickly felt her forehead.

"I'm fine. Just tired and hungry. I think I'll have a long, hot soak in the tub and then we can go down to dinner."

"Mercy, I almost forgot!" Cass cried excitedly. "You got mail today from Galveston, and there's something from New York, too, from Mr. Gabriel."

Pandora took the letters and settled quickly on the sofa, ripping first into the envelope with Jacob's neat handwriting on the front.

> October 10, 1893
> Galveston Island

My Dearest Pandora,

You've been gone less than a month, but already it feels like a lifetime. You will never know, my dear, how often I think of you. But I know that this separation is in your best interest. Dr. Pinel will help you. And after we are married, we will both rejoice that you took this time to visit him in Paris.

You are much missed by the socialites of the city, who seem involved at the moment in a never-ending round of teas, balls, dinners, and theater parties. Even this poor doctor has been pressed into escort duty.

Pandora bristled at those words, but relaxed when she read on.

It seems since you are away that your little cousin is much in demand at all social functions. Your aunt and uncle, although hesitant to give her free rein at such a tender age, see me as a trustworthy squire for Angelica. Mark my words, in a year or so she will have many a young man panting on the doorstep. She certainly keeps this old fellow on his toes!

My practice is growing daily. The most marvelous thing happened yesterday. I delivered a baby! Although I have assisted at many births in the past, this was my first time to go it alone. I'm proud to announce that young Mrs. Kempner was delivered of a beautiful little girl, her first child. What a miracle!

Someday, my dear, you and I will share this same miracle. What a wonder that will be! You know I want many children. How I have longed for the day when I will take on the responsibilities and the delights of fatherhood. And I could never have found a more suitable mother for them.

I ran into Ward Gabriel on the Strand today. He's just back from New York. He told me the two of you spent a day together in the city. There was no time to press him for details. I was happy to hear that you were well and accounted for. I must admit, however, to a slight twinge of jealousy. How I would have enjoyed being with you that day!

Pandora clutched the letter to her breast and breathed a long sigh of relief. Thank God, Ward hadn't told Jacob that he'd spent a *night* with her as well. In her bedroom!

Well, my dear, it's quite late and I have a busy schedule ahead of me tomorrow so I must close now and get some sleep.

Yours most sincerely,
Jacob Saenger

Pandora sat for a long time staring at Ward's envelope before she opened it. His handwriting, unlike Jacob's neat script, was a bold, dark scrawl. The two men, she mused, were as different as their styles of penmanship. Jacob's life, like the letters of his words, was predictable, well-ordered, and controlled. Ward, on the other hand, led a bizarre life— all twisted and turned and confused like his letters—never knowing from one day to the next where he would be or what exactly he might be doing. Granted, he had a successful career. He was a businessman of the first order. There, too, he and Jacob differed.

Slowly, she opened Ward's letter, with trembling fingers. She realized she was tingling all over with excitement. Whereas Jacob's letter had contained the expected, any communication from Ward promised the unexpected. His message was scrawled hastily on a sheet of stationery from the Fifth Avenue Hotel. There was no date, no greeting.

I was down on the dock when your ship left an hour ago, Pandora. I wanted to board and say good-bye. But I had a feeling I wouldn't be welcome. So, here I am, back at your hotel, getting royally drunk for no reason that I can understand. And if I hadn't had several brandies, I wouldn't be writing this to you in the first place.

I don't know what happened to you at the wax museum. All I know is I've never been so afraid in my life! If I angered you by staying until you came out of it, I'm truly sorry. Wild horses couldn't have dragged me out of there before you came around. I just wanted to make sure that you understand that you neither said nor did anything to be ashamed of while I was there. As for me, tempted as I might have been, I am not in the habit of taking advantage of unconscious women. So you can rest easy on that score. As for the kiss, consider it a fond *adieu* between friends.

I'm not sure why I wound up here at your hotel. The place feels empty and cold now that you're gone.

It's back to Galveston for a few days, then I'll be heading to California, South America, and Cuba for several months. I suppose the next time we meet, you'll be Mrs. Jacob Saenger.

A few words were scribbled after that, then scratched out. Pandora squinted her eyes, trying to read what Ward had written before he changed his mind. Finally, she made it out: *That lucky bastard!* She smiled in spite of herself.

I'll probably miss the wedding of the decade. Just as well, I guess. But you have my best wishes, Pandora, I hope you know that. I wish you only happiness . . . *always!* And if anything should ever happen—I don't know what, just *anything*—you can always count on me. I hope you know that, too.

Say hello to Paris for me. If I were there, I'd take you to see the can-can dancers. Any woman with nerve enough to go to the Hoffman House must certainly drop in at the *Moulin Rouge*. More likely you'll visit the Louvre, to see the *real* Venus de Milo, after having been forced to endure that hideous fake we saw the other day.

Pandora frowned at Ward's letter. When had they seen this fake Venus de Milo?

I won't say good-bye, Pandora. We'll meet again. Until then, I remain—

Your slightly drunken servant,
Ward Gabriel

"Well, he was right about *that!*" Pandora said aloud. His handwriting toward the end of the page was barely decipherable. He must have written to her from a table in the tavern while he was drinking. She sniffed the paper. The brown stain at one corner reeked of brandy. How dare he write to her from a bar!

She found, to her surprise, that she wasn't really angry with him. She was touched. There was something so lost and alone in his words to her.

The weekend weather was miserable. Sheets of cold rain lashed the streets of Paris, making the whole world seem dull and gray. Pandora decided to stay in until the deluge ended. No need risking pneumonia! She had enough problems for Dr. Pinel to deal with as it was.

Pandora had Cassie set up her easel near the window. All she could see was rain, but she could paint sunshine. She closed her eyes, imagining the chestnut trees in full flower lining the Champs-Elysees and the shops along the great boulevard brightly dressed in red and white striped awnings. Yes, springtime in Paris. That was what she would paint.

When she put her brush to the waiting canvas, an entirely different scene emerged. The chestnut blossoms she'd meant to paint became exotic lotus flowers of rose, aqua, scarlet, and gold on a flowing field of heliotrope. Their stems and leaves twisted and twined, forming an endless design that seemed to bloom on forever. Out of the hectic pattern, the full scene sprang to life—a wild, desolate beach with turquoise water beyond the sandy stretch. Three lone trees stood sentinel on the shore and beneath them a man and a woman, she wearing a lotus-flowered skirt and a thin peasant blouse, clung to each other, embracing as if in farewell.

Even though her hand held the brush, Pandora seemed to have no part in painting the picture. Somehow the scene emerged of its own accord, as if it had been there on the blank canvas all along—as if her brush had merely swept away the covering that had hidden it from her eyes. When it was done, she stood back staring at the woman's flowing skirt. The pattern seemed symbolic to her—love blooming with all the vibrant colors of deep emotion, going on endlessly, uninterrupted.

"Forever," she whispered, then a chill ran through her.

"Oh, Miss Pan! That's beautiful!" Cassie enthused. "Why, that's Laffite's Grove back home! I never saw it look all lonesome like that."

"I have," Pandora answered quietly. And suddenly she realized that she had indeed!

She knew the exact year, the exact moment of the scene. She knew not only the woman's name, but her pain at having to say good-bye to the man she loved. She closed her eyes, willing the ache in her heart away, but it only intensified as the moment came alive for her.

"I won't be gone long, darling."

They had come to the grove to be alone, to make love one last time before he sailed. But their final precious moments together were at an end. Even now, the *Pride* awaited her captain's boarding before she set sail.

"Jean, a day, an hour, a minute without you is too long."

Still holding her in his arms, he bent down and pressed her lips, slowly parting them for one final taste of his love.

"I promise you, darling, I'll come back safe and sound. Why do you worry so? I've lived through battles, duels, every fever known to man, and three other marriages.

Nothing's going to take me away from you for good. Now that I've finally found you, you'll never be rid of me. You have my word on that.''

Somewhere deep down in her heart, she knew that he would come back to her. But during the long, empty days while he was away she would be as good as dead without him.

"Jean, you will be careful?" she demanded for the dozenth time.

He smiled down at her, his green eyes dancing with his urgent longing for adventure. Sometimes she thought it would be easier if he took a mistress. Another woman, she could fight, but his love of the sea and the life with his men on the *Pride* stirred up deep fires of jealousy in her heart. How could a mere woman fight the passion her man felt for the adventure of the high seas?

"A fast run to the Yucatan, darling," he told her. "Two weeks, a month at the most. I'll bring you back a golden trinket."

The woman gripped his waist, burying her face against the warmth of his bare chest. "Just bring me back my man, Jean Laffite! That's all I ask!"

"Done, madame!" he said. "You'll have your man back before you have time to start missing him."

She looked up into his dear face—boyish with excitement over this new adventure—and tears streaked her cheeks. "I miss him already," she whispered.

Suddenly, the scene dissolved from Pandora's mind. She found herself standing before the painting, sobbing her heart out for Jean Laffite.

Chapter Ten

Ward Gabriel stood frowning as he looked out over the glittering crowd. His gaze focused on one particular couple on the dance floor. He wished he had not come. He'd had the perfect excuse. Tomorrow he would leave Galveston by rail for California. Who could be scintillating at a party when his trunks were still to be packed?

His empty suitcases weren't the cause of his distress at the moment. What he was feeling came astonishingly close to jealousy. An odd reaction, he mused. He had no interest in Angelica Sherwood, and what Jacob Saenger did was certainly none of his concern. But it seemed to him that for an engaged man Jacob was holding the lovely young lady entirely too close and that Angelica's chime-like laughter was too gay, too flirtatious.

His scowl deepened. He had half a mind to write to Pandora and warn her to come home immediately. But, no. It was not his place to interfere. Besides, spreading tales was not his style. Still, he wished that one of the over-bustled, diamond-bedecked wags at the party would take it upon herself to drop Miss Sherwood a line. Surely, they had all noticed what was going on.

Tonight was only the start of Galveston's holiday festivities—the pre-Thanksgiving Ball. Ward was glad he was leaving town. He didn't relish the thought of a whole string of these fancy soirees. And seeing Jacob Saenger enjoying himself so thoroughly with his fiancée's luscious young relation was definitely not to his liking. Pandora deserved better.

A slow, calculating smile spread over his face. His dark eyes narrowed. Perhaps he would have a bit of sport with the pair. After all, Jacob Saenger wasn't the only man Angelica had flirted with at the party. She had given Ward himself a generous fluttering of eyelashes when they'd said good evening earlier.

With Pandora still in his thoughts, Ward put on his most alluring smile and strode toward the dance floor.

He tapped Jacob's shoulder. "Mind if I cut in, old chap?"

Angelica gripped her partner even tighter, ready to refuse until she glanced up into Ward's handsome, smiling face.

She released the dumbfounded Jacob and went immediately into Ward's waiting arms. Jacob scowled at the pair as he stalked off the dance floor.

"That's a lovely gown you're wearing, Miss Sherwood."

He pulled her closer, feeling her breasts snuggle against his chest. She uttered a deep sigh of pleasure.

"Please call me Angelica, Ward. Or, even better, simply Angel."

"Angel!" He whispered the name close to her ear. "That fits you—all white and silver like your hair and your gown. My guess is that you have a bit of the devil in your heart."

"Ward Gabriel!" She tried to sound shocked. Ward knew by the sparkle in her ice-blue eyes and the faint blush on her cheeks that he had pleased her no end.

"You've certainly been bedeviling Dr. Saenger. For an engaged man, he seems uncommonly infatuated with his fiancée's little sister."

"Pandora's not my sister!" Angelica snapped. "She's only my cousin. Why, my parents never cared enough for her to adopt her legally. As for her claim on Jacob, she must take that rather lightly.''

''Oh? Why do you say that?''

''She ran off to Paris and left him here all alone, didn't she? The poor man is just dying of loneliness. Why, if he didn't have me to keep him company, I don't think he'd survive.''

Ward felt ice down his spine. Hearing Angelica state her case was like listening to a spider, defending her reasons for inviting a fly in to tea.

He wondered if Pandora knew what a threat her cousin truly was. Angelica was no longer the pretty little girl she had been such a short while before. In the two months since Pandora's departure, Angelica had blossomed. Her strait-laced mother had finally allowed her to cast off child-hood and become a woman. Her clothes were different—scandalously-cut designer gowns from Paris. She wore her hair up and twined with jewels. She seemed to have matured physically as well. She was now thinking a woman's thoughts, scheming a woman's schemes.

''You must be very fond of Jacob to put forth such an effort to amuse him,'' Ward commented.

She laughed softly and her voice dropped. ''*Fond* is hardly the word I'd use. Jacob is good and kind and sweet and gentle.''

Ward's dark brow rose as he wondered, *Gentle at what?* He started to ask her, but decided he really didn't want to hear about it.

''Pandora was just plain foolish to leave him here all alone,'' Angelica continued. ''It would serve her right if she lost him. Why, if I were engaged to such an attractive man, I'd marry him this minute. It never pays to wait too long, you know.''

Ward laughed. ''No, Angel, I don't know. Fortunately, I've yet to meet the woman who makes me think of wedding bells and orange blossoms.''

She cocked her head at a saucy angle and smiled up into his eyes. ''Well, Ward Gabriel, maybe you've met her at last!''

Ward managed to hold back his laughter. The girl certainly had nerve, he'd give her that. The fact that he was old enough to be her father didn't stop her from her mating dance.

"Are you—how shall I put this delicately?—throwing your lovely body on my matrimonial altar, so to speak?"

Angelica gasped, truly shocked, but delighted by his boldness. *"Mr. Gabriel!* Why, I never! You are far too old for me. Papa wouldn't allow it."

He grinned at her. "But *you* would?"

Her eyelashes fluttered like butterflies in flight. "Perhaps," she purred.

Never taking his eyes off Angelica and Ward, Jacob refilled his punch cup from the great silver bowl.

He experienced the oddest sensations as he watched the pair. He felt betrayed and alone and downright jealous. That was ridiculous, of course. Angel meant nothing to him. She was a lovely, warm, exciting young woman to spend an evening with now and again. But that was all. He had Pandora, and soon they would be married just as he had always planned. So why did the sight of Ward Gabriel holding Angelica close, whispering to her quietly, enjoying himself so thoroughly bring such a twisting pain to his gut?

He ladled another cup and drank it down, still watching them.

"What kind of woman are you looking for, Ward?" Angelica asked innocently.

"What kind of woman or what kind of wife?" Ward purposely leered at her as he asked the question. He was determined to frighten her into acting her tender age.

Angelica cuddled closer and whispered, "Dear me, you say the most shocking things. What kind of wife, of course."

Ward cocked his head and looked thoughtful for a time. "Well, she must be cultured, a gifted hostess, of good family, preferably wealthy, and quite beautiful."

"But what about love, Ward?"

He gave her a bleak smile. "What about it, Angel? Do you still believe in fairytales?"

"Well, no," she stammered. "But I always figured that

there's a man somewhere meant just for me and that I'd find him and fall in love one day."

"I hate to burst your pretty bubble, but love is an illusion. If you believe that there is only one person in the whole world who's meant for you, then you are out of luck if that lover happens to live in China or even in Houston, aren't you?"

Angelica pouted, looking truly perplexed. She didn't like having to think about such things. If she wanted to fall in love, she would. She didn't care what Ward Gabriel said.

Ward's voice and the tightening of his embrace drew her attention once more. "Perhaps you don't mean love, Angelica. Perhaps what you're longing for is *passion*. That *is* very real and it can be found quite easily."

"You shouldn't say such things to a lady!" Angelica gasped.

"Why not? Are you telling me you've never known passion? Not even for Jacob Saenger?"

"I don't know what you're talking about, Mr. Gabriel."

He had her flustered now—on the run. Good. She deserved it.

"When Jacob kisses you, do you feel weak and hot all over?"

"I never said . . . I never let him kiss me! Not *that* way!"

"Perhaps you're feeling passion right this moment, Angel." He whispered the words beside her ear. "You are very warm, perspiring in fact. Most unladylike. I can even feel your breasts trembling against my chest."

"Oh!" she cried. Pushing out of his arms, she ran for the nearest door and out into the night.

Ward cursed softly, feeling his face flame. People were staring. He'd gone too far with his little game. Horace Sherwood would be outraged when he found out his daughter had been embarrassed in public, and by one of his own employees. Ward would likely lose his position and all for the pleasure of making little Miss Angelica squirm a bit for Pandora's sake.

Shouldering his way through the crowd, Ward headed for the door to find Angelica. He would have to apologize. Too bad he wasn't drunk. He could have used that as his excuse.

Jacob saw Angelica tear away from Ward and run out the door. She looked upset. He should go see about her. He was her escort and she was his responsibility for the evening, he reminded himself. But the butler had just refilled the punch bowl. And besides, Ward was going out to check on her. She'd be all right. After all, Ward had taken good care of Pandora, hadn't he? He could do as well with Angelica.

He'd just pour himself a fresh cup, sip it along, and *then* he'd go find Angel.

Angelica knew Ward would come after her. She only hoped that Jacob wouldn't follow. She'd dashed out so quickly—perhaps her escort had taken no notice. He was getting quite drunk, not an uncommon occurrence lately. Her little fun in the garden would serve him right.

She hid behind a large oleander bush until she saw Ward coming down the steps.

"Angelica, where are you?" he called softly. "I know you're out here. Answer me. I only want to apologize. I was out of line."

Angelica worked herself into a suitable state of hysterics. Ward heard her sobs and followed the sound. He found her collapsed like a crumpled white flower on one of the garden seats. He felt utterly ashamed of himself, especially since he knew that his disgraceful performance with Angelica had something—no, *everything*—to do with the way he felt about Pandora. Since that night in her hotel room, he hadn't been able to get her out of his system.

He went to the weeping girl and touched her shoulder. "Angelica, please stop crying and listen to me. I'm sorry. I acted like a perfect cad. A gentleman has no right to say such things to a lady. Since you are definitely a lady, I suppose that makes me no gentleman at all."

Suddenly, Angelica gripped his hand tightly and brought it to her cheek. Soon she was showering his fingers with kisses.

"Oh, Ward, you don't need to apologize. Don't you

understand? Those things you said to me in there—they were all true. When you held me in your arms, I grew weak and warm all over. My breasts did tremble, they're trembling now." Still clutching his hand, she pressed his palm to her chest—to the warm, damp flesh just above the low-cut neckline.

"Angelica, no!" he growled, jerking his hand away. "You don't know what you're saying. Just tell me that you accept my apology and I'll go."

He was backing away slowly, waiting for her answer. Suddenly, she rushed at him, throwing her arms around his neck and smothering his mouth with hot, wet kisses.

"Ward, oh, Ward." she breathed through her attack. "You make me feel like a *real* woman! Kiss me. Oh, please kiss me."

He was trying to get away from her, trying to unclasp her arms from around her neck, but she had locked him in her embrace. Her mouth was open on his and her tongue smoothing over his lips.

"Angelica? Are you out here?"

Ward put extra effort into his escape when he heard Jacob Saenger's voice behind him. He broke free at last, but not in time.

"What the hell do you think you're doing, Gabriel?" Jacob was unsteady on his feet and he slurred his words drunkenly.

"Simply apologizing, Jacob, and saying good night." He backed away toward the garden gate, but Saenger stumbled after him.

"What exactly were you apologizing for?" he demanded.

"I said something to upset Miss Sherwood, that's all. Now if you'll both excuse me . . ."

Ward turned to unlatch the gate. Jacob threw an uncertain punch.

"Nobody fools with Angel, but me!" Jacob roared.

Avoiding a glancing blow to the side of the head, Ward hurried through the gate. Slamming it behind him, he saw Angelica rush to Jacob.

"Oh, darling!" she cried. "Oh, Jacob dearest, are you hurt?"

Angelica quickly found Jacob's mouth and gave him the kiss she had meant for Ward.

"Damn good thing I'm leaving Galveston in the morning," Ward muttered as he headed at a quick stride for his house on the beach.

Pandora had slept miserably on Sunday night and had awakened with the dawn the morning of her second visit with Dr. Pinel. The rain had stopped, leaving Paris spanking clean and the skies brilliant with the luminous colors of sunrise.

Without waking Cassie, Pandora had dressed, written a hasty note to her companion, and headed on foot to the Louvre. She knew she would have a long morning, waiting for her appointment, if she did not find something to occupy her mind.

Now, as she strolled the vast halls of the silent museum, she felt totally immersed in Rubens, Rembrandt, Titian, and Caravaggio. Here and there, students sat silently before their easels copying the great masters of old. Pandora felt that she had the fabulous collection of art all to herself. For a time, she was able to forget her visions, her problems, her very existence. She lived and breathed *Tournament Near A Castle*, *Christ Crowned With Thorns*, and *Women of Algiers*.

She became totally entranced by the world of art about her. She never wanted to leave the Louvre. A glance at the fragile, gold watch fastened to her lapel, told her she hadn't much time left. It was nearing eleven. Another half hour and she would have to leave for Dr. Pinel's office. She sighed with regret and walked a bit faster, wanting to see everything in the short time that remained.

Her inner peace remained undisturbed until she turned suddenly and spied a gleaming marble on the stairway—the Venus de Milo. In an instant, the Grande Galerie and everything in it vanished in a swirl of confused, glowing colors. Once more, she stood outside the Eden Musée in New York on Ward Gabriel's arm, staring at the terrible fake perpetrated on the armless Goddess of Love.

"Two please," she heard Ward say as he purchased their tickets for the chamber of horrors.

Then, the time that had been lost to her until now, unfurled before her eyes. She saw again Nicolette Laffite's tableau of death and again felt the bullet pierce her own breast. She remembered the night, the visions. Everything that she had experienced under hypnosis returned to her mind. She knew the terror of the hurricane and her fear that her husband was lost. Before the colors swirled again to dissolve the scenes, she knew it all. With this new clarity of vision, Pandora saw into her past life. The woman named Nicolette was a part of her even now.

In the next moment, a troubling thought struck her. What of Jean Laffite? With his passionate love for his wife and his shock and grief at her sudden death, he must surely have come back to find her. Where was he now? *Who* was he?

"Jacob?" Pandora whispered softly. A frown stole over her face and she shook her head as a bleak chill closed around her heart.

When her head cleared, Pandora touched her lapel watch with trembling fingers. Only a few moments had passed. She hurried out of the museum and hailed a carriage, giving the driver directions to Dr. Pinel's office.

"You are early!" Madame Celeste accused when Pandora entered.

Before Pandora could respond, Dr. Pinel stepped out of his office. He noticed her agitation at once and, without a word, motioned her to come with him.

"What's happened?" he demanded.

Pandora sank to the familiar couch and poured out her tale to the doctor. She told him everything she had seen while she stood before the statue of Venus in the Louvre. Pandora looked up at the doctor with pleading in her eyes, willing him to reaffirm her belief in her own reincarnation. "It's true, Doctor, I'm sure of it. What I've just told you is the same as you heard from me while I was in trance, isn't it?"

The doctor nodded. "Exactly Pandora, but it proves nothing except that you can spin a fine tale."

"I *know* I was Nicolette!" she insisted.

Pinel shrugged. "Believe what you wish, but what is the point?"

She glared at him, her eyes blazing. "The point is that now I know my purpose in life. I must find Jean Laffite!"

"You can't be serious!"

Pandora stared down at her hands. She had worried her thin handkerchief to shreds as she talked. "What am I going to do, Doctor? Am I truly going mad? How do I know these things, if I haven't lived them before? Where do they come from?"

Dr. Pinel sat down beside her and covered her hands with his, knowing that he had been too sharp with her. "I'm sorry, Pandora, I have no answers for you."

Her eyes searched his face. "You don't actually believe that all these things really happened—that I lived before?"

He shook his head. "I don't think you really believe it either."

Pandora gave up arguing with the man. "So, where do we go from here, Doctor?" she asked in a disheartened voice.

Pinel had already given this question much thought. Pandora could not keep the thread of this fantastic narrative going forever. For some reason unknown to him, she wished to believe in this dream of hers. By delving deeply, he might be able to prove the unreality of her beliefs. He would demand more details today.

"Will you consent to being hypnotized again, Pandora? It could be that we can find the source of this problem locked away in your subconscious."

She considered his proposal for only a few moments before she agreed. "But only if I am allowed to remember everything this time."

"As you wish."

Pandora lay back on the couch, ready to begin. As soon as Madame Celeste entered with her pad and pen, Dr. Pinel's calm voice filled the quiet room. He had hardly finished his first sentence before Pandora slipped into a deep hypnotic trance. This time he told her that she would remember everything when she awoke.

"Nicolette? Are you there?" Dr. Pinel asked.

"I am," answered the woman on the couch. "What do you want with me?"

"I have only a few questions. Can you tell me your father's name?"

She laughed. "Who in New Orleans does not know my father? His name is Claude Vernet and he deals in import goods."

Dr. Pinel glanced at Madame Celeste, frowning. He had not expected such a quick and thorough answer. "You mentioned an aunt who lives in Paris? What is her name?"

"She is my mother's sister, but she doesn't live in Paris now. She left there after her husband died and came back to New Orleans with me. She was against the marriage my father had arranged. She did not believe in the old Creole ways. She said love was the only reason to marry. She approved of Jean. I should have listened to her."

"Her name?" Dr. Pinel insisted.

"Madame Gabrielle Vernet."

"Vernet?" the doctor questioned. "You said she was your mother's sister, yet she bears your father's name?"

"She married a Frenchman named DelaCroix first. For many years after his death, she remained a widow. After my mother died, Aunt Gabi married my father. They had been in love when they were young. Vernet, of course, became her name then."

Dr. Pinel was not smiling. Pandora's answers were all too detailed to please him. Try as he might, he could not trip her up. He decided to put an end to the session.

"That's exactly what I wanted to know. Nicolette, I must say farewell for a time. Pandora, when I count to three and snap my fingers, you will awake, feeling rested and refreshed."

A moment later, Pandora sat up and looked directly at him. "Well?" she demanded. "Are you convinced now? How could I have known the right answers, if Nicolette and I are not one and the same?"

"You gave me answers, but how do I know they are facts?" He shook his head. "No, Pandora, I am still not convinced. I only hope you are not playing some game with me. I am a busy man with patients who need and are willing to accept my help.''

"This is no game," Pandora assured him. "Doctor, I need your help," she begged. "I must know what's happening to me."

Placing the file back on his desk, he sat down and studied Pandora for some moments. He chewed at his pipe stem, trying to make up his mind. Finally, he said, "Pandora, you know I don't believe in reincarnation. You admitted to me at first that you were also a skeptic. I can't understand what has changed your mind."

"My visions . . . my experiences, Doctor," she insisted. "If only you knew how real they are. It's as if I'm leading two separate lives, not knowing which one I truly fit into or if I belong in either. I love one man in my dreams, but I am going to marry another in real life. What if I'm making a mistake? What if the man who is Jean Laffite is out there somewhere, searching for his Nicolette at this very moment? What if I marry Jacob and *then* he finds me? I don't believe in divorce, Doctor. When I marry it will be forever. I *must* know the truth before I return to become Jacob's wife."

Pandora slumped back, breathless after her long speech. Until this moment, she had not realized how uncertain she felt about her relationship with Jacob Saenger. She had never been given a chance to question their engagement. It had always been an accepted fact to her because her parents had wanted it that way.

"Is there nothing you can do for me, Dr. Pinel?"

He shrugged, "I can lead you through more of these sessions. I can help you find out all you want to know about Nicolette Laffite. But I can't interpret the meaning of the knowledge we gain. I have no experience in this field. Still, if you are so curious about all this, I suppose we can pursue it a bit further."

Pandora stood up and walked to the window. She looked out over the Seine, glittering in the bright sunlight as if its surface were strewn with diamonds. When she turned back to Dr. Pinel her face wore a calm, determined expression.

"*Curious,* Doctor, does not begin to describe the way I

feel. I'm *frantic* to know what's going on. If you are willing to continue, then I feel I must.''

"There is one matter I think we should discuss before we begin again, Pandora. In Dr. Saenger's letter to me, he mentioned that your visions include glimpses into the future. He further stated that on one occasion you sought to summon the vision of your life after your marriage to him, but you failed.''

"That's correct,'' Pandora admitted softly.

"I think I can help you in this area. It seems to me that you are having grave doubts at present. Perhaps you are not destined to marry Jacob Saenger?''

"My parents wanted this match,'' she explained. "I have a duty to them, especially now that they're gone.''

"You have a duty to yourself—to your own happiness and peace of mind, Pandora. I'm not trying to dissuade you from marrying Dr. Saenger, I merely want you to search your mind and heart. Often, patients with problems similar to yours are only reacting to unhappiness of the present. If you can understand what is troubling you in your present life, these past and future life visions will, in all likelihood, go away of their own accord.''

Pandora shook her head, thoroughly confused. "I'm willing to do whatever you say, Dr. Pinel. But I still don't understand.''

"Your willingness is all that is required,'' he assured her. "The understanding will come.''

"What must I do?'' Pandora asked.

"You must tell me everything you have ever imagined about Nicolette Laffite,'' Dr. Pinel said. "Little children often make up imaginary playmates.'' His words brought to mind the visions of Jeannette. "When an adult does such a thing, it is far more serious. We must understand why you identify so strongly with her personality, what you want of her and from her. Her reasons, in your mind, for living, and for dying.''

The wax tableau flashed into Pandora's mind. "She was murdered!'' she murmured, still finding the fact difficult to believe.

Pinel nodded. "We know that. But why and by whom?''

"I don't know," Pandora answered.

"Then shall we find out?" Dr. Pinel said gently.

Pandora nodded.

Pinel came to her, motioning for her to lie down. He felt confident that if he could rid Pandora of all thoughts of Jean Laffite and his wife then her problems once she awoke would be solved.

"I am going to put you into trance again. I want you to try to concentrate on the time after the great storm. The time between then and Nicolette's death in 1821."

"I'll try," she said. Already, focusing her eyes on the many-hued lamp, she felt herself slipping away. As she traveled back, she tossed fretfully on the couch.

All was not well at *Maison Rouge!*

Chapter Eleven

•

"Jean has sailed to Mexico," Pandora began, speaking in Nicolette's Creole-accented voice. "Perhaps while he is away, I will be able to sort things out in my own mind and heart. It was dreadful when we said good-bye in the grove today. We both tried so hard to pretend everything is as it used to be between us. We do love each other. Perhaps *too* much. Surely, such a love as ours is not meant to die so suddenly . . . so needlessly!"

"What year is this, Nicolette?" Dr. Pinel asked.

"1820. We have been on the island for over two years. Jeannette is a beautiful child now, running everywhere, talking like a pretty little magpie. Life would be so perfect, but for . . ."

"What?" Dr. Pinel insisted when she paused.

"But for *her!*" Nicolette's voice turned bitter and hopeless.

"You don't mean Jeannette?"

"Of course not!" Nicolette laughed humorlessly. "Without my daughter, my life would be a constant misery now. I speak of the other female under my roof. How foolish I was to bring her here. She seemed little more than a child herself, and so helpless and alone. It was *my* idea to rescue her from her terrible fate. How I have come to rue that day two years ago. The day Isabel came to live at *Maison Rouge*.''

"Tell us about that day," Dr. Pinel instructed.

Pandora related the scene in the bedroom of the Laffites' home in 1818, only a few days after the great hurricane that wrecked the island. Dr. Pinel, still skeptical, leaned forward, held in thrall, as the hypnotized woman told her tale.

They lay together, still locked in an embrace—their early-morning passions spent. Ever since the storm, Nicolette had tried to bring up the subject of Isabel's coming to live with them. Now seemed the perfect moment to try once more to convince him.

"Darling," Nicolette whispered, stroking his bare chest with her fingertips, "I've been worrying about the Spanish girl. Isn't there something we can do?"

He heaved a weary sigh, indicating that this was not a subject he cared to discuss. "I'm sorry, Nicolette. No, there isn't! I thought we'd finished with that topic."

She begged him then, "Jean, please, I know it goes against the laws of the island. She was taken by Captain D'Angelo's crew and by rights she is part of their spoils from the Spanish ship. But she's so young, and still a virgin. Would you have her passed around among those terrible men to use her as they will? There's only one place on this island where she'll be safe. Here with us."

Laffite rose from the bed, running his fingers angrily through his rumpled hair. He stood naked, staring out the window. Then he pulled on his robe and turned back to face his wife. "Nicolette, why must we discuss this now?" he began. "The whole island is a shambles after the storm. We still have to recover bodies, prepare for a mass burial at sea, then rebuild and reorganize. She'll still be safe for a time. The men will be far too busy to think about deflowering virgins."

Nicolette rose and went to him, laying her head against

his chest, trying to make him understand. "You're wrong, my darling. If something isn't done now, it *will* be too late." She stared up into his face, letting her eyes help her plead. "Already La Paz has made the attempt. The others will not hold off much longer. I don't know how she has managed to protect herself for the time she's been here. Please, Jean, only *you* can save her!"

A smile curved his lips when Nicolette mentioned Emilio La Paz. She guessed its source. Although she had not told him of the incident during the storm, Isabel had spread the tale far and wide, calling Madame Boss a heroine of the first order. Everyone on the island laughed about the wounding of La Paz, making cruel sport of that terrible scene. Nicolette could find nothing amusing about it.

Laffite's half-smile turned to a grimace, again Nicolette guessed what he was thinking. Emilio La Paz was another of his problems. The man—maimed for life by her faulty aim—had left the island for the mainland. Before departing, he had vowed revenge. Jean was worried that he must keep an even sharper eye on his wife now. La Paz was a villain to be reckoned with, who had sworn to do unutterable horrors to Nicolette upon his return.

"Jean, are you listening to me?"

He answered in a pleading voice, "Nicolette, how can you even ask this of me? If I bend one rule here and another there, I will lose control of this place. The men will not stand for it. When it comes to a woman—especially a woman taken in fair capture . . ."

"Fair capture?" she railed at him. "You call it fair that her father was murdered before her eyes, that the ship was burned, that she was taken prisoner by that band of thugs? Jean, you are thinking like one of them."

He turned and searched her face. His own was hard with sudden hurt and anger. "If you believe that, then there is little I can say or do that will make you happy. Perhaps I had better send you back to your father in New Orleans."

Jean's words turned Nicolette's blood to ice. She knew then that she had gone too far. No threat could have been more painful to her. She ran to Jean, embracing him frantically. "My darling! I didn't mean that. I'll never leave you.

174

It's just that I know how terrified Isabel is. I remember so well the way I felt when Browne and his men took my own father's ship. Why, if it hadn't been for you, I'd be dead or worse!''

Laffite's grim expression told Nicolette that he, too, remembered that day and the sight of her, tied to the mast of the *Fleur de Lis*, while Silas Browne taunted her mercilessly. Had Jean not arrived when he did, she would have fallen victim to gang rape by those pirates.

"All right, Nicolette. I'll do as you ask. But I must remind you, this girl is Spanish. I don't trust anyone with that nation's blood in their veins. I'll bring her here, on a trial basis, to work as your maid. At the slightest sign of trouble, back to the house she goes.''

Nicolette embraced him then and kissed him, tears of relief flooding her eyes. "Oh, Jean darling, there won't be any trouble. I promise you. Isabel will be eternally grateful, even as I am this minute.''

"How well I remember that day.'' The woman on Dr. Pinel's couch spoke those words in a voice filled with hopelessness. "The memory has pained me these two years past. I can still see Isabel's tearful gratitude over having been rescued. The girl swore that she would do everything in her power to repay my husband for his kindness. And she did try. She waited on him hand and foot, while he raged at her for the slightest infraction; it seemed she could do nothing to please him.''

Pandora paused, her eyelids fluttering, taking in a thousand scenes in a glance.

"Life under the roof of *Maison Rouge* grew worse by the day,'' she continued. "Little Jeannette cried more often and took to sucking her thumb again. With Isabel always there, the privacy Jean and I had cherished vanished. Our lovemaking, which had always been spontaneous and passionate, changed most of all. No more could my dear Jean, when the sudden urge struck him, close the living room drapes and cajole me into abandoned embraces on the bright-colored carpet. Nor could he pull me down into the big red hammock in the yard without her seeing. With Isabel always about, we had to lock ourselves away in the bedroom, after dark, confined behind closed doors.

"With the casual flame of our love so abruptly squelched, Jean became irritable. He made love to me less often because as he said, 'I like variety, excitement, something different every time.'

"I did my best to keep him happy. But it was clear that he would not be satisfied as long as Isabel remained under our roof, invading our sacred privacy. My husband's grim moods kept me always on edge, ever wary of a temperamental explosion. As my nerves frayed, my imagination began to get the better of me. Or was it my imagination? I could never be sure."

She paused in her painful monologue and uttered a long, weary sigh. A single tear and then another slipped from the corners of her close eyes.

"More than once I came into a room to find Isabel hovering too near my husband. Time and again I noticed the young woman's hand brush Jean's as she handed him a sniffer of brandy. Isabel was no longer a child. In the months since her arrival on the island, she had blossomed into full and radiant womanhood. Jean could hardly be oblivious to her new-found maturity and sensuality. As hard as I tried to guard against it, I became jealous.

"To make matters worse, Jean seemed suddenly to temper his reactions to the girl. This was exactly what I had prayed for. But in unguarded moments when my imagination would run wild, I allowed myself to believe that the reason for my husband's softened temperament was the dawning of his awareness of Isabel as a passionate and available female.

"Isabel exuded her need for a man, *like a cat in heat.*"

Restless on the doctor's couch and quite obviously experiencing extreme mental anguish, she went on slowly, explaining her fears and doubts. "Two years after her arrival, Isabel was truly a woman to be reckoned with. Her figure had gone from lovely to luscious—her high, proud breasts accentuating her slender waist and gently curving hips. She had affected the island costume—a long full skirt and loose-fitting peasant blouse. I could swear that when Isabel served

Jean at the table, she bent low enough to give him a glimpse of her magnificent bosoms.''

Again, Pandora tossed on the couch and threw an arm over her eyes as if to hide her tears.

"Go on, please," Dr. Pinel prompted gently. "You must tell us everything. Purge your mind of all these disturbing thoughts.''

Pandora sighed wearily before she continued. "I could no longer swallow my food at meals. Looking at her took my appetite away," she confided unhappily. "Consequently, I began to lose weight at an alarming rate. My face grew thin, making me look much older than my twenty-five years. While Isabel's breasts strained temptingly at the fabric of her blouse, my own poor bosoms dwindled to small mounds of soft flesh as I grew thinner and thinner.''

Suddenly, Pandora's eyes opened. She raised her hands before her face, staring at them in sad wonder. "My poor hands, see how spindly they've become. You can see the veins through my flesh. They look like the hands of an old woman. I am no match for Isabel's voluptuousness. I can see that plainly. Surely, Jean must have noticed as well.''

"You say Jean went to Mexico?" Dr. Pinel asked gently, trying to distract Pandora's attention.

She closed her eyes and nodded. "On the night before Jean was to sail, I vowed to send him away with pleasant memories. I suggested the 'something different' that my husband always seemed to be longing for in those days.''

Once more, the listeners found themselves drawn into her tale.

They were alone for a time that final afternoon. Isabel disappeared from *Maison Rouge* on an errand. Tension stretched between the two of them as Jean packed his bag to leave the next morning.

Nicolette was half-afraid to mention her idea, terrified that Jean might refuse. Finally, she found the courage. "Why don't we take a blanket to the grove, darling?" she asked with as much cheer as she could muster. "I'll pack our supper and your favorite wine. We'll share an intimate maroon before you have to go.''

Jean looked at her and that wonderful green fire she remembered so well flared to life in his eyes. "The grove, you say, and wine to tempt me?"

His words cut her to the quick. "You never needed wine for that before!" she snapped at him, wishing even as she said it that she had bitten off her tongue before allowing such harsh words to escape.

But he wasn't angry. Instead of flaring back at her, he pulled her close, kissing her deeply until she grew weak all over. Neither of them realized that Isabel stood in the doorway spying on the tender moment.

"I don't need wine to fire my passions for you, my love." Jean leaned against Nicolette, letting her feel the hot, throbbing stirrings that her plan aroused in him. "Ah, my darling," he whispered into her ear, "it's been too long."

"It had indeed been too long—almost a month since he'd held me and loved me. My whole body ached with wanting him and with fearing that he was finding his release with *her*." Pandora's voice became bitter.

Their night together in the grove, she went on to explain, had been almost enough to reassure her. Laffite came to her as in the old days—his patience infinite, his passion endless, his love a real and tangible force. For hours, they had lain together beneath the trees with only the faint light of the moon clothing their sweating bodies. Had it not been for the nagging in the back of her brain, this night, she confided, would have been as magnificent as their first time together.

Tears gushed from Pandora's eyes as she told the doctor of her doubts. "In the afternoon, shortly after Jean agreed to our rendezvous at the grove, both he and Isabel disappeared for over an hour. Although they departed separately, they returned to *Maison Rouge* together. I could not help but note the warm flush of Isabel's cheeks and the glitter in her dark eyes. She had the look of a woman well and quite recently loved. Jean seemed nervous, too jovial, too anxious to please me. Try as I might, I could not lay to rest the thought that my husband had said *two* fond farewells."

Madame Celeste's eyes never left her pad, and her pen never faltered in its hurried jottings, but her face flamed scarlet as Pandora elaborated on the intimate details of the couple's last night together there in the grove on Galveston Island.

"Jean knelt over me, stroking deeply with wonderfully powerful thrusts, sighing my name, lifting me up and up until the very peaks of ecstasy were within my grasp. I finally released my hold on all uncertainties to embrace my lover with all the depth and strength of my passion. Whatever might have happened in the past, whatever might come in the future, at that moment we were totally, undeniably one."

Nicolette's voice, coming from Pandora's mouth ceased then. Dr. Pinel's office grew deathly silent for a few moments. Only the scritch-scritch of Madame Celeste's pen defiled the quiet void. The doctor sat motionless, on the edge of his seat, leaning anxiously forward as he waited for Pandora to continue.

Finally, the voice from long ago resumed. "My euphoria passed as quickly as our time together. Soon the sun came up and we could see the *Pride* riding at anchor, waiting off shore for her master. I had often wondered how I might handle the situation if Jean ever desired another woman, but I knew I could never tempt my husband away from his first love—the sea.

"I joked with him in parting. He snipped a lock of his dark hair, telling me I should sleep with the curl beneath my pillow to have a part of him near me always. I managed to hold back the flood of tears until I was alone. *He'll be back soon*, I reminded myself. But that thought held little consolation. When he returned, would I have him all to myself?

"Yes, I determined. *Yes, I would!"*

Pandora went on to tell of the terrible row she'd had with Isabel when she returned to *Maison Rouge* and found that she was not the only one crying over the departure of Jean Laffite. When Nicolette saw Isabel's eyes all damp and red-rimmed, she confessed to feeling no sympathy for the other woman.

"Isabel," Nicolette said, "I've come to a decision. My husband's brother Pierre is sailing to New Orleans in a day or two. It is high time you went to my family as I've suggested in the past. My father and stepmother will welcome you and will introduce you to society. You are a lovely young woman; you will be beseiged with offers of marriage."

Isabel shied away from Nicolette's direct gaze. "I have no desire to marry, madame," she answered defiantly. "I wish to stay here. I am happy here."

"I think you will be happier in New Orleans. Go upstairs now and start packing your things," Nicolette ordered. "I'll tell Pierre that you plan to go with him. He will see you to my father's house once you arrive in the city."

Turning quickly, Nicolette left Isabel standing in the middle of the living room of *Maison Rouge*, a rebellious expression on her beautiful face.

"Isabel offered no further argument," Pandora continued. "But she gave me a look of such sheer hatred that I felt as if I had been mortally threatened. However, my problems seemed solved by this move. Once Isabel left for New Orleans, my life with Jean would naturally fall into its old, happy pattern."

Pandora shifted uneasily on the couch, muttering angrily under her breath.

"What is happening?" Dr. Pinel whispered.

When Pandora failed to respond, he tried to prod her into further revelations, but, for the moment, she was oblivious to his anxious questions.

"The plot thickens," he said quietly to Madame Celeste. "It seems we have two possible murderers. The man La Paz and now Isabel, unless she went to New Orleans."

"She did not go," said Nicolette in a bitter voice. "When Pierre sailed two days later, Isabel was nowhere to be found."

"What happened to her?" Dr. Pinel asked.

"At the far west end of the island lived a band of three hundred Indians—the Karankawas. They were terrible savages who ate human flesh. They never came near our village. I suppose they feared and respected the sound of the cannon. Determined not to leave the island, but terrified of going back to the house of women, Isabel struck out on her own, planning to hide out until Jean returned. But the Karankawas found her. What she endured at their hands is too terrible to tell. She returned to us a strange and vacant-eyed woman. I always blamed myself for what happened to her. I drove her away with my jealousy.''

"When did she return?" Dr. Pinel asked.

"By the time Jean came back from Mexico the following month, we knew where Isabel was. There was a plot afoot among the men to fight the savages for her return but nothing came of it until Jean arrived home. He was wild—murderous—when he heard the news. I'd never seen him that way. He took two hundred men and two cannons down the island and laid seige to the Indian camp. The battle raged for three days. Then the Karankawas fled in their boats and never returned. Isabel was found in one of their abandoned huts. Jean brought her back to *Maison Rouge,* where she lived until we were ordered off the island the following year.''

"I suppose I must bring her out of trance now," Dr. Pinel said. "She is nearing the end of Nicolette's life. I cannot allow her to relive the moment of her dying, it might be dangerous. Besides, it would serve no purpose since Nicolette probably never saw the person who killed her.''

Dr. Pinel went through the usual soft-spoken routine to bring Pandora out of her hypnotic trance. When she sat up, staring at him oddly, he said, "Are you all right?"

"Why did you bring me back so soon? There was more I had to tell.''

"It could have been life-threatening to allow you to continue," Dr. Pinel informed her. "You were drawing near the point of Nicolette's death.''

"Oh," Pandora's eyes grew wide. She remembered suddenly the burning pain in her breast when she'd seen the tableau at the Eden Musée. "Do you mean that I might actually die from the very bullet that killed her?''

Dr. Pinel, unsmiling, nodded in the affirmative. "It is possible, since you seem to believe all that you have told me. We must move with extreme care from this point.''

Pandora rose slowly and went to the tea tray, pouring herself a restorative cup. "I feel very odd at the moment, almost as if I came back too quickly. I seem like two people instead of one. Nicolette was so desperate to save her marriage, to keep her husband's love." Pandora paused for a moment and seemed to be searching the distance for something or someone. "No, that's not quite right," she corrected. "It was not Jean's love she feared she might lose. She knew she had that. But she was afraid that Isabel might lure Jean away with her body. The thought of him with another woman—even a woman he didn't love—was more than Nicolette could bear."

Dr. Pinel leaned forward in his chair, studying Pandora as she spoke. She was right; it was almost as if she were two entities at the moment—Pandora Sherwood *and,* deep down inside, this woman from her visions, Nicolette Laffite.

"Pandora, how can you be so sure of Jean and Nicolette's abiding love for each other? More times than we like to think, another man or another woman comes between two lovers, disrupting the pattern of their lives for all time."

Pandora shook her head emphatically. "No. Not between Jean and Nicolette. There is no love as great as theirs!"

"*Is?* You speak of it in the present, as if they still lived and still loved," Dr. Pinel pointed out, his skepticism painfully apparent to Pandora.

She looked confused for a moment. "Yes, I did say that, didn't I?" She closed her eyes as if she were very tired. When she opened them again, a new light blazed deep within, like a dancing green flame. "That is exactly what I meant to say, Doctor! You insist reincarnation cannot be a fact. Well, the love of Jean Laffite and Nicolette is a fact at this very moment even as it was three quarters of a century ago. Their love lives on through me and through . . ."

"Ah, that is the underlying question at the very heart of all this, isn't it?" Dr. Pinel said excitedly. "Your problems are not of the mind, young woman, but of the heart. We come right back to Jacob Saenger and your proposed marriage once again. A mere doctor can hardly measure up to your fantasies of such a bold pirate lover as Jean Laffite, can he, Pandora?"

"I never said I was comparing the two." Pandora resented the doctor's accusation and let him know it.

She was near tears. "You're twisting everything! You sound as if you haven't believed a word I've told you about anything."

"I never promised to believe, Pandora, only to listen. You alone must decide what is truth and what is fiction."

For several moments, silence reigned in the room as Pandora fought to maintain control of her frayed emotions. Only the soft crackling of the fire and the ticking of the clock shattered the tense stillness.

"You think I'm mad, don't you?" Pandora's heart pounded frantically as she awaited his verdict.

The old French doctor sighed and shook his head. "I never said that. I never meant to imply it. I think that you are a very confused young woman who does not know her own mind or heart. I believe you are deluding yourself with romantic notions as a means of escape from a reality not of our choosing. And I don't think that you are ready for marriage, Pandora, not to Dr. Saenger or any other man."

His words infuriated Pandora. She jumped up from the couch. "I've heard all I care to hear. I *will* marry Jacob! And sooner than I had planned," she informed him. "Now that I know you can be of no help, Doctor, I'm going back to Galveston. Jacob and I will marry immediately."

All manner of disturbing thoughts swirled about in Pandora's brain. Were her visions real or imagined? Could she really have been another woman in another time? If so, could she find the man who had been her lover as Jean Laffite? And was it fair to marry Jacob when she was so uncertain of all these things?

Regardless of what Dr. Pinel said, she knew what she wanted to believe. Nicolette, Laffite, and their love *were* real! Jacob and his feelings for her were real, too. And right now she needed him more than she ever had in her life.

There was so much to be taken care of—boat tickets,

shopping, packing, and she must write to Jacob immediately. No, she decided suddenly, she would surprise him! She would simply turn up in Galveston. He would be deliriously happy at her unexpected return. She could explain all this to him in person; it would be so much easier talking to him than trying to tell him everything in a letter.

Her mind made up, Pandora calmed herself enough to clasp Dr. Pinel's hand. "Thank you for trying to help," she said.

"I hope you and your husband will have a very happy life together," he told her.

"And happiness in *all* our lives to come," she answered, defying him to the last.

Pandora rushed into her hotel suite as if she were blown by the high winds of a West Indian cyclone.

"We're going home, Cassie!" she sang out with feigned gaiety. "Start packing the trunks."

Cassie was used to her mistress's whims but this revelation took her completely by surprise.

"Home, Miss Pandora? Back to Galveston? So soon?"

"It can't be soon enough!" Pandora assured her.

"But what about the doctor? What about your art lessons? What about your trousseau?"

Pandora was moving quickly about the room, sorting her belongings already. "The doctor has released me. My art lessons can wait. And most of my trousseau will be ready by the end of the week. The rest can be shipped to Galveston. Tomorrow, first thing, I'll arrange passage on the next ship to New York. We'll be home shortly after the first of the year." She paused and gazed out the window. "I would have liked a Christmas wedding, but I don't suppose even the fastest ship could get us there in time."

"A Christmas wedding?" Cassie cried. "But you got your plans with Mr. Jacob all made for next June."

"Not any longer, Cass," Pandora told her. "We'll be married the minute I get home."

Cassie shook her head in confusion. "Lord, Lord, Miss Pan, you moves too quick for me!"

While Cassie went into the bedroom to begin packing trunks, Pandora gathered up her paints and brushes, carefully packing them away in their straw basket. The painting of the grove and Galveston beach still sat on the easel beside the window. She gazed at it with new feeling after having lived through that very moment earlier in the day.

As she continued staring at the picture, a feeling of utter desolation swept over her. She felt totally alone and unloved. How she wished she were in Galveston this very minute. How she would love to see Jacob, to feel his arms around her, his lips on hers.

Closing her eyes, she tried to summon his image. She let her mind stray, trying to guess what he would say, how he would look at her, what she would feel when next they met.

A scant week later, Pandora and Cassie sailed out of Le Havre, bound not for New York, but for New Orleans.

"I still can't imagine our good luck," Pandora said to her companion as they entered their stateroom. "Once we arrive in New Orleans, we'll have only a few hours' sail to reach home."

"New Orleans!" Cassie sighed wistfully. "I always wanted to see that place. Maybe we'll stay overnight, Miss Pan?"

Pandora thought for a moment. The idea was tempting. She would love to search through the city's record books to see if she could find any mention of Nicolette and her family. Surely, the house where the Vernet family lived must still be standing in the old French Quarter. But all that would have to wait for another time. More pressing business was at hand.

"No, Cassie. We'll leave for home as soon as we arrive. There's a ship running daily from New Orleans to Galveston. I plan to go home by the fastest route possible. I intend to become Mrs. Jacob Saenger *immediately*. That's all I've ever wanted, all I've ever dreamed of. I don't need fancy

French doctors to tell me who to marry. I only need Jacob to love me and care for me.''

Cassie frowned. It had been impossible to mistake the edge of hysteria in Pandora's voice as she made her empassioned declaration. Cassie couldn't guess what it might be, but something was very wrong.

Chapter Twelve

Jacob Saenger stayed up most of Christmas night laboring over his letter to Pandora. He was not much of a correspondent by nature, and his heavy work schedule provided him with a good excuse on most occasions, but this letter had to be written. He had put off composing it for too long already.

He glanced at the stack of perfumed envelopes lying on his night stand. All from Pandora, all written to him while she was away. What a good and faithful woman she was. He didn't deserve such a prize, he told himself.

It had become his habit over the last months to reread her letters before drifting off to sleep at night. He still did that, but now with a feeling of distance that seemed to grow ever wider with each passing day. It was all his fault. He was the one who had insisted they wait to marry; he had sent Pandora off to see Dr. Pinel in Paris.

He leaned low over the piece of stationery before him—blank except for the date and his salutation, simply "Dear Pandora." With a heavy sigh, he ran taut fingers through his hair. How to begin? What to say? It hardly seemed to matter somehow, by the time she received it, the deed would be done. There would be no turning back, no second chance.

He crumpled the paper and tossed it across the room. Taking another sheet, he penned the date, then "Dearest Pandora." Yes, that was what he'd wanted to write from the start. Damn convention! That expressed what he felt for her far better than his first bland salutation. How he wished he could pour out his honest feelings to her. If he dared, his first sentences would read: "I know now that I truly love you. I will never let anyone come between us!"

But it was too late for such declarations. Clenching his teeth, he wrote instead:

> This letter will come as a cruel shock, I know. But there is no painless way—at least for me—to write this news to you. I must break my solemn promise to the one woman in the world who means more to me than I can tell.
>
> Pandora, by the time you read these lines, I will be married to another. I cannot bring myself to ask your forgiveness. What I have done and am about to do is unforgiveable. You and I have shared so many plans and dreams over the years. Through no fault of yours, those dreams have now vanished into thin air.
>
> If you hate me, I will understand. In my own mind, I am beneath your contempt. I almost hope that once you read this you will decide never to return to Galveston. This, too, is pure selfishness on my part, for how I will ever face you again, I do not know.
>
> Forgive me, forgive me, sweet Pandora! On my knees, I beg you!

Jacob reread the letter. It sounded pitifully wanting—cruel, in fact—but then how else could it sound? He could not bring himself to tell her who he was marrying or why. Hurriedly, he scrawled a farewell and sealed it in an envelope before he lost his nerve.

Exhausted, he crawled into his rumpled bed, but slept not a wink that night.

* * *

Pandora's ship left New Orleans in the early afternoon on January 6, 1894. The day was crisp and bright—the breeze cool and the sun shining warmly, turning the Gulf of Mexico into a gleaming jewel that glowed all the colors of the tourmaline. At the railing of the small steamer, Pandora looked like a bright flower, dressed in a traveling ensemble of ashes of roses silk, her smiling face shaded by a broad brimmed hat on which bloomed a veritable garden of silk poisies.

Cassie hurried up on deck, a scowl of disapproval marring her face. "Miss Pan, you gonna look like a octoroon once you get to Galveston if you don't come in out of the sun."

Pandora waved her objections away and continued staring out over the broad expanse of water before them. "I'm not leaving this spot." she declared. "I want to see the island the moment it comes into view. I feel as if I've been away for years; it will be wonderful to get home."

"Well, at least use your parasol!" Cassie opened the elegant sunshade of gray lace trimmed with rose-colored fringe and forced it upon her mistress. "There, that's better!" Seeing that Pandora was deep in thought, Cassie went back below deck.

Pandora's mind was indeed busy, deciding her first move when she reached Galveston. It would be late afternoon by then. She thought about going first to Jacob's office where she would surprise him with her early return and the news that she wanted to get married immediately.

"No," she murmured. "That won't do." All his patients would be witnesses to their reunion. She had a better idea, one that would ensure the intimacy of her welcome home. He had written her that he'd rented a small but comfortable apartment where he was living now and which the two of them would share after their marriage. "But only until I've saved enough for our new house," he had assured her. She smiled, thinking how Jacob, with his stern German upbringing, insisted they live on his earnings, not her vast fortune once they were married. Yes, she would go to the apartment and wait for him. Their reunion would be private and, oh, so sweet!

She closed her eyes for a moment, imagining how she would feel when she first saw him, when he first touched her, kissed her, held her in his arms. Putting aside all the disturbing uncertainties of Paris, she told herself she was about to fulfill her destiny. She was more than ready to continue loving Jacob where Nicolette's love for Laffite had left off.

In her mind's eye, Jacob's image became confused with that of Jean Laffite. Both were tall and lean, but there the resemblance ceased. Jacob's hair was lighter, his eyes warm-brown instead of green, his features smooth instead of rugged. Yet Pandora imagined that she could see some of Laffite in Jacob Saenger. She wanted to so desperately.

A moment later, the boat's whistle blew, interrupting her thoughts. She opened her eyes and there it was—Galveston Island. The sandy spit seemed to float just above the water, all shimmering white with touches of green here and there. The tin roofs blazed in the afternoon sun as they drew nearer. She imagined that she could smell the sweet perfume of the oleanders although she knew they never bloomed until the hot weather came. Her heart quickened and her cheeks grew warm. Tears suddenly flooded her eyes.

As they steamed past the east end of the island, with Bolivar Point to starboard, Cassie rejoined Pandora on deck.

"Won't be no one to meet us, Miss Pan. How we gonna get home?"

Pandora never took her eyes off the busy docks as she answered, "You go straight to the Emporium, Cassie. Uncle Horace will have one of the boys pick up my trunks and drive you home. I have an errand to take care of. I'll hire a buggy."

"But, Miss Pandora, what am I supposed to tell Miz Tabitha when I come in without you? She's going to be powerful upset."

"Tell my aunt that I had some important business. Tell her she can expect me for dinner. There won't be a problem, Cassie."

Knowing that there was no use arguing with her mistress, Cassie sighed resignedly. Soon the two women were in the crush of passengers crowding down the gangway. Pandora hailed a cabbie. He eased his one-horse buggy through the throng of disembarking passengers, porters, and waiting vehicles.

"Where to, ma'am?" the young driver asked as he helped Pandora mount the step.

She gave him Jacob's address on Mechanic Street, between Sealy Hospital and St. Mary's Infirmary. The driver clicked his tongue at the old black horse, who broke into a smart trot once they cleared the dockside traffic.

As they moved down Water Street, Pandora's gaze locked on the tumbled ruins of *Maison Rouge*. She saw more than the broken stone steps and the weeds overgrowing the foundation; she saw a great, scarlet-painted mansion with a tall, green-eyed man and a ebony-haired woman standing arm in arm on the broad veranda. She blinked and the vision vanished, but the warm glow of their obvious love for each other remained in her heart.

Soon, she heard the driver call, "Whoa there, Lightnin'!" as he pulled back on the reins.

Quickly, Pandora paid the man and walked up the narrow stairs of the wooden house built on stilts to guard against Galveston's seasonal "overflows." When she knocked at the door, a stocky, gray-haired woman answered.

"Yes, miss, can I help you?" She gazed curiously at Pandora through the thick lenses of her spectacles.

Pandora didn't quite know what to say. She wanted to wait in Jacob's apartment, but she wasn't at all sure his landlady would allow that. She looked the prim and proper sort.

"I have an appointment with Dr. Saenger. Of a delicate nature," she confided in a whisper. "He asked that I meet him here at his apartment after regular office hours."

Exactly what the woman thought of her tale, Pandora didn't know. Her gray eyebrows lifted for a moment, then her harsh expression gentled to a conspiratoral smile. She put her hand out to touch Pandora's arm, drawing her quickly into the hallway.

"I understand, dear. Dr. Saenger usually gets home about this time. Come with me. I'll let you in."

Pandora felt slightly uneasy until the woman left her.

Obviously, Mrs. Gray—fitting name, she mused—believed that she was unmarried and with child and that Dr. Saenger had agreed to help her. Oh, well. Pandora dismissed her worries. The landlady would know the truth of the matter soon enough. At least she was here, and in a short time Jacob would arrive home to a great and happy surprise.

Pandora moved about the tiny apartment shaking her head. "Poor dear," she murmured. He was no housekeeper at all. His clothes were tossed this way and that. His bed was unmade—a messy tangle of sheets and spread. Dirty dishes were stacked to towering heights on the kitchen table. While she waited, she began tidying up, feeling comfortably domestic already.

When she heard his footsteps in the hallway and his key in the lock, Pandora stood back in the shadows. She hoped that Mrs. Gray had not told him someone was waiting. She wanted to surprise him.

Pandora watched in silence as Jacob entered, closed the door, and switched on a small lamp on the table. Her heart went out to him. He looked tired and drawn. His hair and suit were rumpled. Taking his coat off and slinging it casually in the general direction of the sofa, he went immediately to the spirits' chest and poured himself a straight whiskey. Pandora frowned. Jacob was drinking heavily again—his one and only fault in her eyes. He had promised her time and again that he would stop. He had given up everything but wine shortly before her departure. She watched as he belted down one straight shot, then reached for the bottle a second time.

Pandora stepped into the light. "Jacob," she whispered.

He nearly jumped out of his skin. "What the hell?" He swung toward her, crouched as if to defend himself against an intruder. When he saw her standing there, he straightened up. He looked confused and unbelieving. *"Pandora?"*

She came toward him, her arms outstretched. "Yes, Jacob! I'm home."

"Pandora, didn't you get my letter? The one I wrote you Christmas night?"

"Why, no, Jacob, I left Paris before Christmas. I must have passed your letter in the crossing. What does it matter?

192

We don't have to write letters any longer. I'm home. I came straight here from the boat. And I'm with you to stay. I want to get married immediately.''

Jacob Saenger was fighting a thousand devils. *Pandora did not know!* How could she? She hadn't received his letter and she'd spoken to no one in her family yet, he was sure. He'd have to tell her everything, face to face, this minute.

"Oh, God, how I've missed you, Pandora!" His words came out in a harsh, breathy sigh. "Come here!"

He led her toward the sofa and pressed her down gently against the cushions. For a long time, he leaned over her, staring down into her wide, green eyes. His own, she noted, looked troubled. He seemed on the verge of saying something to her, but no words came. She thought for a moment he meant to argue with her over the wedding date. When he leaned down and captured her lips, she knew that that was the farthest thing from his mind.

"Pandora, oh, Pandora," he breathed against her hair. "I want you right now more than I've ever wanted you before in my life."

He was sitting next to her, leaning over her. Suddenly, he clasped her in his arms, gripping her so tightly that pain shot through her back and shoulders.

"Jacob, please! You're hurting me," she cried.

He swore under his breath. "I know I am, my dear. I know . . . I know!"

Pandora stayed with Jacob only a little longer. He kissed her again, but with a restraining hold on his passion. She began to feel a creeping dread. Something had happened to Jacob while she was away. He was still the same man she cared for so deeply, but some great burden was weighing heavily on him now. If only he would talk to her about it, but he remained as silent as a statue.

"Pandora," he told her firmly, "I think you'd better leave now. It's getting dark. Your family will be worried."

Rebuked in such a fashion, she had no option but to go. For whatever reason, her fiancé did not want her just now. Obviously, he had had a bad day. His disheveled look when he arrived, the drink he so quickly tossed down, the strange expression on his face when he first spied her. Perhaps her surprise visit had not been a good idea after all. Yes, she would go. But tomorrow, she vowed, they would set the date.

Jacob collasped, face down on the sofa, the moment Pandora left. He couldn't tell which ached most—his heart, his conscience, or his groin. Sitting up, he slumped forward, burying his face in his hands. What a *bastard* he was! Why had he held her and kissed her when he knew he had no right any longer? Why hadn't he confessed the whole bloody truth to her the minute she told him she hadn't received the letter? He'd meant to, but . . .

Now he had sentenced her to a more heartbreaking shock than he had experienced the moment he spied her in his room. Who would tell her? Her uncle? Her aunt? Some stranger on the street as she hurried home? Or—oh, God, please no—*not Angelica!*

Jacob rose slowly from the sofa. He felt like a corpse. No, dead men had no feelings. For a moment he wished he could claim that blessed, final oblivion. Instead, he went to the bottle he'd left sitting on the table. Not bothering with a glass, he grasped its neck in a stranglehold and tipped it up to his lips.

By the time the bottle was empty, an alcoholic haze dulled the pain, but the ache in his groin intensified. He could have had her; she'd wanted him. And he'd certainly wanted her. He blew out a long breath and tried to focus on his slightly blurred image in the mirror.

"Well, it seems even the worst bastard in the world has a grain of nobility lurking deep inside."

Shedding his clothes as he went, Jacob stumbled into the bedroom, falling upon his neatly made bed. He took no note of Pandora's handiwork, but the lingering scent of her perfume was there where she had smoothed the spread. He breathed in deeply, seeing her smiling face before his closed eyes.

"Pandora," he whispered with pain in his voice and guilt in his heart. "My darling Pandora!"

Then the blessed oblivion he had sought from his bottle closed over him.

Pandora decided to walk the few blocks home. She needed to think, to clear her head. And she needed to make plans. Aunt Tabitha, she knew, would want a big wedding. But Pandora could not wait that long. She needed the comfort and reassurance of becoming Jacob's wife as soon as possible. She would simply insist that they have a small, private ceremony. If her aunt and uncle put up a fuss, she would threaten to be married in a civil service at City Hall. Yes, that would do the trick! That would silence all objections.

The sky lost its scarlet and golden sunset tints. Purple shadows deepened as she walked down 8th Street toward Broadway. A pair of hardy cyclists passed her. As evening settled, most of Galveston's citizens had gone inside to sit by their fires and await the call to dinner. When a buggy pulled up beside her, she barely noticed until she heard someone call her name.

"Pandora, is that you?" the man's voice repeated.

She stopped, gazing through the darkness, trying to make out who it was. A moment later, the tall figure came striding toward her. She was as surprised as he was.

"Ward Gabriel?" She offered her hand and he gripped it warmly. "I thought you were off in California or South America."

The husky rasp of his laughter sounded good to her—intimate and caressing. "A bit of luck came my way unexpectedly and I had to rush back to Galveston to confer with my attorneys. And you, young lady, are supposed to be in Paris having a high old time of it. Did you see the can-can girls?"

She shook her head. "No, I hadn't time for that, I decided to come home ahead of schedule."

"I wondered if you would." Suddenly, his voice lost its jovial tone. He sounded like someone consoling the bereaved.

"Why would you think I'd return early?" she wanted to know.

"Oh, no reason." He answered too quickly, arousing her suspicions. "Why *are* you home so soon?"

Ward thought back to the night of the dinner dance before Thanksgiving. Had Pandora had some advance warning of trouble ahead? Had one of the society ladies written to her then, hinting that all was not well? Somehow that didn't seem likely from her bright spirits. Either she knew nothing of her former fiancé's upcoming nuptials or she was playing it cool, trying to avoid the subject in order to hide the pain of rejection. She was probably still in shock.

"To be honest, Ward, I came home because Dr. Pinel, the specialist Jacob arranged for me to see, was no help at all. Instead of solving my problems, he only confused me more. I'm not even sure of who I am any longer. I didn't just come home, I escaped Paris, running back here in desperation. Jacob is the only one who can help me now. I need him. I mean to marry him right away." She paused, embarrassed by her own confession. Then she smiled up at Ward and touched his arm in a friendly gesture. "I'm glad you'll be here for the ceremony, Ward. Truly glad."

He was glad that the street was dark so she couldn't see his shock. She didn't know! How could that be when all of Galveston was buzzing with the news?

"When did you arrive?" Ward asked.

"Late this afternoon. I went directly from the boat to see Jacob. I've just left him."

"Your arrival must have come as quite a surprise to him."

"Oh, indeed!" Now it was Pandora's turn to bless the darkness. She could feel the frown on her face as she thought back to Jacob's odd reaction. "Ward, has something happened while I was away . . . something Jacob didn't want me to know? He seemed troubled."

Ward waited so long to frame an answer that Pandora thought he must not have heard her. "Ward?" she prompted.

"Let me give you a lift home. We can talk on the way."

Once Pandora was seated beside Ward, he seemed disinclined to speak. She prodded him with further questions, but he refused to respond.

Ward was undecided. Certainly, it was not his place to

break such shattering news to her. He couldn't imagine Jacob holding his silence on the subject. But then he couldn't imagine what Saenger could be thinking, breaking off his engagement to Pandora and planning this other unexpected and hasty marriage. Why, he'd move heaven and earth not to disappoint Pandora Sherwood.

"Ward, please," Pandora implored. "I'm beginning to feel like I'm being left out of some deep, dark conspiracy. There's something you're all keeping from me. What is it?"

Ward slowed the horse and turned toward Pandora. Her face looked pale and drawn in the darkness. She seemed only a ghost of herself.

"Pandora, did you receive the letter I wrote you from New York?"

She nodded, embarrassed suddenly that she'd failed to answer it. There would have been no harm in a brief, formal note of acknowledgment. "Yes, Ward, I received it. I'm sorry I never . . ."

He waved his hand in an impatient gesture, brushing aside her apology. "Do you remember what I told you in that note—that if anything ever happened, you could count on me?"

"Yes, I remember, Ward. That was very sweet of you, but I don't understand what that has to do with anything . . ."

"It has *everything* to do with the situation right now. I meant what I wrote to you, Pandora. I still mean it. I didn't realize until that night in New York—the night you were so ill—how I truly felt about you. You're no longer a dirty-faced little girl climbing trees in the grove. No, Pandora." He paused and brushed her cheek with his fingertips. "You are a very lovely, very *special* woman."

"Ward, please, you're out of line."

"No," he whispered, "I don't think I am, Pandora. You asked what everyone is keeping from you. I'm about to tell you, but I had to say all that first."

"Well?" she demanded, her heart in her throat.

"Jacob is going to be married the day after tomorrow." He stated the fact bluntly because there was no gentle way to tell her.

Pandora heard Ward's words clearly, but she managed to fit them into her own mold, reshaping them to suit herself. Somewhere in the night, a bird called out a few musical notes. Pandora matched it with her own trill of laughter. "Well, I can't say for sure that it will be the day after tomorrow, Ward. But I'm certainly willing, if we can arrange it that soon."

Ward reined the buggy to a full stop and turned to stare into Pandora's face. "You are not listening to me, or rather, you refuse to hear what I'm saying. Jacob Saenger is marrying someone else, Pandora."

Dead silence descended between them. Only the sleepy bird in the distance could be heard. Then suddenly, Pandora's self-imposed barrier to understanding shattered and she cried, *"No!* He can't! Why would you tell me such lies, Ward Gabriel?" She slid away from him, ready to escape the buggy, to run back to Jacob, but Ward caught her arm.

"Pandora, listen to me!" he implored. "It isn't the end of the world. Painful as they are, these things happen. We survive. Life goes on, I promise you."

"Spare me your clichés, Mr. Gabriel!"

Pandora was fighting for her life now. She could not, *would* not believe what he'd told her. The tears she'd been battling back suddenly rushed to the surface. Ward was telling her the truth. Why would he lie about such a thing? He had nothing to gain by hurting her so; he was not a malicious man. He spoke the honest truth. And this terrible truth meant that her entire, well-ordered destiny lay about her now in crumbled ruins, like the tumbled walls of *Maison Rouge*.

As her choked weeping turned into pathetic sobs, Ward put his arms around her and drew her close, trying awkwardly to comfort her. "Please, Pandora, don't." He could think of nothing else to say. They sat there for a long time until finally Pandora had cried herself out.

With great dignity, she withdrew from Ward's embrace, sat up straight, and smoothed the skirt of her gown.

"You haven't told me the woman's name," she said, her voice steely quiet. "Do I know her?"

This was the moment Ward had dreaded most of all. But

he couldn't ignore her question, not even to spare her more pain. "Jacob is marrying Angelica."

Sitting as straight and rigid as one of the palm trees that lined Broadway, she inclined her head slightly, unable to speak a word. Angelica! How like her cousin this was. Angelica, who had all the beauty, all the attention, all the love she could ever want, was never satisfied with what she had. She was never satisfied until she had what was Pandora's, whether it was a party dress, a piece of jewelry, her parents' attention, or a man to marry.

"I should have guessed," Pandora said softly.

"What will you do now?"

They had drawn up in front of the Sherwood mansion on Broadway, but Ward still held the reins poised in his hands as if he was ready to speed away should Pandora request such an escape.

"Now?" she said wistfully. "Now is not the problem; I shall do what I must do. It's the future that stretches ahead like a great, arid desert." She put her hand on his and looked directly at him. "Thank you, Ward."

"For *what?*" he asked, astounded.

"For everything!"

He watched, feeling Pandora's hurt in every muscle and sinew of his own body, as she climbed out of the buggy. Her back straight, her regal head held high, she moved along the walk with great dignity.

"Pandora?" he called after her.

She turned slightly to glance back at him.

"If you need me . . ."

She nodded, then approached the steps.

Pandora's walk from Ward's buggy to the front door seemed to her like a condemned felon's last mile. She still felt in shock as her mind gnawed at the problem facing her. She had no idea how this had happened. Jacob had squired her cousin about while she was away—with her full approval—but she'd been gone only three months. How could Angelica have stolen Jacob so quickly?

More importantly, how should she react? What should she do? Her first impulse, of course, had been to tear into the house, find Angelica and "snatch her baldheaded," as Cassie would have said. But what good would that do?

Her aunt and uncle could not be counted on to intercede in her behalf. After all, Angelica was their only child—pampered, petted, granted her every wish and whim. She was sure that the Sherwoods must have tried to head off the romance somewhere along the line. But, with the wedding scheduled for the day after tomorrow, their attempts had obviously failed. Now they would be on Angelica's side, not wanting Pandora to stir up needless gossip by disrupting the happy couple's announced plans.

As her hand touched the cool brass of the doorknob, Pandora suddenly knew what she must do. There was nothing left for her in Galveston. She would get through the next few days and then she would simply vanish. The old Pandora was dead. Now she must set out in search of some new identity.

Perhaps she might even find the man who was Jean Laffite. But first, she must find herself.

Chapter Thirteen

The first person Pandora saw when she opened the door was Aunt Tabitha. The woman's face went ashen when she spied her niece.

"Oh, my dear, we hadn't expected . . . I mean, of course, we knew you were back since Cassie . . . but I thought you'd come later, when dinner was . . ."

Pandora moved forward smoothly, forcing a smile, kissing the flustered woman on her pudgy cheek. "Aunt Tabitha, you must have known I'd want to be here for the wedding. After all, Angelica has been like a sister to me these past years. And Jacob is my *dearest* friend in the world."

"How could you have known? We all agreed it would be best to keep it a secret." Her aunt, in her nervousness, realized that she had let the cat of conspiracy out of the bag and quickly covered her little bow mouth with her hands.

"I have my sources," Pandora whispered. "Now that I'm here, you must tell me everything. When did they decide? How did they break the news? And, for goodness sakes, why the rush? All of Galveston will be thinking the most improper thoughts.''

Pandora's hint that the island's citizens might suspect Angelica of having dallied before her time caused the color to drain from Tabitha Sherwood's face. Noting her aunt's reaction, Pandora raised an eyebrow. Could she have hit upon the truth of the matter?

Just then, Angelica appeared at the head of the stairs, a smug smile on her lovely face. Pandora took several deep, even breaths to maintain her control as she seethed inwardly. The pleasant expression remained, through no small effort on her part.

"Angelica!" The name oozed like warm honey from Pandora's lips. "My, you are full of surprises! I left thinking you a child and return to find you a bride. What a difference a few short weeks can make!"

Angelica started slowly down the stairs with a regal toss of her silvery hair. "All the difference in the world, Pandora. Why did you cut your trip short? Jacob and I had no idea you'd be back before June at the earliest."

"Why, Angelica," Pandora said sweetly, "I wouldn't have missed this wedding for the world! Everyone in Galveston will be here to wish you well. Such a handsome couple. I'm sure that you and Jacob will be deliriously happy together. He's a fine, hard-working man."

Angelica's smile of bravado wavered. She looked hard at her cousin, suspecting some trick. Surely, Pandora couldn't have taken the news so calmly. Could it be that something had happened while she was in Paris . . . that she'd met someone else . . . that she was actually happy to find that she was no longer obligated to Jacob? Pandora was acting as if she didn't care for Jacob Saenger; how could that be?

"Pandora, I hope you understand," Angelica purred. "Neither Jacob nor I wanted to hurt you, but you know how love is . . ."

Pandora fought her urge to smack Angelica's cool, smiling face. Yes, she knew all about love! But had her cousin ever understood the meaning of the word? Pandora doubted it!

Before Pandora could frame a suitable reply, Angelica

went on in her patronizing tone. "I'm sure you'll find someone to marry sooner or later."

Angelica's blatant attempt to wound her fired Pandora's determination to keep her true feelings to herself. She vowed she would get through these next two days and then she would go far, far away.

Pandora motioned her cousin to a couch in the Gold Room. "You must tell me all your plans. Jacob wrote to me that he has rented a lovely, little apartment near the hospital. So that will be the Saengers' love nest after the honeymoon, I assume?"

Angelica's ice-blue eyes narrowed and her delicate nostrils twitched. "There won't be a honeymoon right away." From her outraged tone, Pandora guessed that the two of them had argued heatedly over this point. "With Jacob's practice, there's the financial side of things to be considered. Father wanted to give us a large sum as a wedding gift, but Jacob is too proud to take it. Sometime later we'll go to Europe for a few months, maybe a year. He promised. I've suggested that he raise his fees so that we'll be able to afford the trip as soon as possible."

Pandora nodded, her face solemn. "Sensible of you to wait. Doctors don't make that much actually. The apartment will save you money as well."

"Humph!" Angelica tossed her head again and looked both angry and pained. "That grubby little flat, I'll *never* live there," she hissed. "We will move in with Jacob's father while our own home is being built."

Pandora clucked her tongue in feigned sympathy. "Oh, what a pity! I can't imagine you living in that old house on Avenue O after being raised in this beautiful mansion on Broadway, Angelica." Then she smiled brightly, enjoying her cousin's anguished expression. Angelica remembered her own words and did not enjoy having them thrown back in her face. Pandora waited expectantly for Angelica to remind her that it mattered little where one lived as long as she was with the man she loved. But instead, Angelica answered her with grim silence.

Pandora had suspected that there was no love on Angelica's part. She couldn't quite figure where Jacob stood in all this. Certainly, after his initial shock at seeing her, he had seemed wonderfully happy having Pandora in his arms again. She frowned, not listening as Angelica talked on about guest lists, reception plans, and Jacob's stubbornness where money was concerned. Her own mind was traveling other channels. Could it be that something *had* happened between Angelica and Jacob? She stared at her cousin—her beautiful pale blonde hair, her long-lashed blue eyes, her porcelain complexion, her tempting figure. Could Jacob have lost control one evening, perhaps after a few too many drinks? Might Angelica be carrying his child? The thought was staggering.

"Angelica," she interrupted her cousin's mindless chatter, "do you have anything you'd like to tell me? Anything *really* important about you and Jacob?"

Angelica's icy gaze sidestepped Pandora's probing stare. "I can't imagine what you're talking about."

"All this haste, it's rather unusual. Normally an engagement is much longer, unless there's some reason to hurry the vows."

Pandora watched a bright flush creep into Angelica's cheeks.

"You're just imagining things—trying to find some reason why Jacob stopped caring for you. Well, I refuse to sit here and listen to your veiled accusations."

Angelica ran from the room. Pandora rose with a sigh and headed upstairs. She found Cassie there unpacking her things, looking grim-faced and sour, muttering angrily to herself. She froze when Pandora walked in, scanning her face with wide eyes, wondering what her reaction to the news had been.

Pandora went to her and touched her hand, trying to sound less than grim for the woman's sake. "It's all right, Cass. I know all about the wedding. I've just had a talk with Angelica. Maybe it's all for the best."

But Pandora's feelings belied her words. She sank down on the bed, hiding her tears in the fur of her much-missed kittens as they climbed into her arms to welcome her home.

Her thoughts strayed to Ward, soothing some of the ache from her heart. He had been so kind to her tonight, so understanding. He would help her through this dreadful wedding. He was the only one who could.

Pandora had read Angelica like a book. The very moment that she pretended approval of the match and a lack of interest in her former fiancé, Angelica's passion had begun to wilt as quickly as a moonflower fades when the dawn approaches.

On leaving Pandora's side, Angelica had grabbed her cloak and headed straight for the carriage house. Moments later, she was on her way to Jacob's apartment. She would confess her deception to him and call off their plans. Nothing had happened that night in the garden after Ward Gabriel left them. But Jacob, convenient to her scheme, had been too drunk to remember anything the next morning past their kiss in the garden following his final stop at the punch bowl. When she'd confronted him a few weeks later—tearful, injured, terrified—with her invented story that their encounter that evening had left her carrying his child, he agreed to the wedding immediately. What else could he do?

She could still remember how triumphant she had felt when she'd left him that day. Jacob had looked terrible, old beyond his years. His shock at her accusation had left him pale and shaken. He begged her to tell him that it was a mistake. He pleaded, saying that he and Pandora were meant for each other; to break off their engagement was unthinkable. He had gone on to tell Angelica that he did not love her and he was sure they would both be miserable if they wed.

She had answered his arguments defiantly. "There is no *if* about this, Jacob; you *will* marry me. The sooner the better. I do not relish the thought of looking like a cow in my wedding gown."

He had agreed—hesitantly, angrily, miserably. Now she was on her way to release him from his promise and his torment. Let him marry Pandora, if she would still have him. Angelica had more exciting things on her mind than giving herself to a man who could not even afford a honeymoon or a proper home. That fascinating Ward Gabriel was back in town. She'd been thinking about him ever since the night of the party back in November. Rumor had it that a fortune had just come his way. He had resigned from her father's business to see to his own ventures. Angelica knew what Ward wanted in a wife because he had explained it all to her as they danced. She would try to make him love her. If that failed, she would approach him as if their marriage were yet another promising business venture. She cared little on what terms she got him so long as she did.

Old Mrs. Gray sniffed with disapproval when the second young woman that evening came pounding on her door, demanding to see Dr. Saenger. It seemed that he was in a highly improper line of medicine. She would have to speak to him immediately about finding other lodgings.

Jacob roused slowly when he heard the pounding on the door. The whiskey made his head buzz and his eyes refused to focus properly. He rolled off the side of the bed and, after some effort, gained his feet, if not his balance.

"Coming," he called as he stumbled toward the door.

Angelica waited in the drafty hall, tapping her foot impatiently. The longer she stood, the more she wondered how she could ever have considered marrying a man who expected her to come as a bride to such a shabby place. She even began to wonder what Pandora saw in him. Well, she had certainly learned her lesson. Never again would she be contented with what Pandora wanted. Obviously, her cousin had very poor taste. If Jacob ever got around to answering the door, she planned to make short work of this. She would confess her little white lie, call off their wedding, and say good-bye to Dr. Jacob Saenger *forever!*

Jacob was still blinking, trying to focus as he opened the door. The last person he expected to find there was Angelica Sherwood. The sight of her sobered him slightly.

"Angelica, what on earth are you doing here?" he managed to say as she swept past him into the room.

She stopped directly under the overhead light, looking for all the world like a heavenly vision with her long, glowing hair and tight-fitting gown of white lawn. Her bosom rose and fell temptingly as she took deep, excited breaths. As he stared at her—slightly in awe of her beauty—the desire

Pandora had aroused in him earlier came back to plague him.

"Jacob, we have to talk," Angelica announced.

He moved toward her, smiling, wanting to touch her skin to make sure it was real and not made of china or glowing wax. When his fingers brushed her bare shoulder, Angelica shrugged away.

"What's wrong, Angel? You seem upset." He slipped an arm about her waist and drew her to him, meaning to give her a comforting kiss. She was, after all, about to be his bride. He had certain duties and certain rights.

"Stop it, Jacob . . ." She struggled against his grip. "Jacob, you've been drinking again!"

His answer to her accusation was to silence her lips with his. He drew her very close, letting his hands caress her back, her waist, and finally her trim little buttocks. She gave up her struggle quickly, enjoying the unexpected intimacy. She had to admit that he could fire something in her when he was forceful this way.

Jacob, still holding her, kissing her, moved slowly toward the bedroom. The die had been cast the night of the party. What was done was done. There was no longer any need for him to suffer so. Angelica would be his wife in only hours. She might as well begin her duties this minute. He was in painful need, and she possessed the cure for what was ailing him; the doctor prescribed his own treatment.

Angelica felt strange. Whatever had come over Jacob? Never, in all the times they'd been together had he ever shown such masculine command. It was quite thrilling. The way he was holding her, kissing her, touching her! It set her senses all adrift. She had never felt this way before. Up till now, she had always been the one to set the rules between them, the aggressor of the pair.

She opened her eyes for a moment. They were in his bedroom, where he had skillfully maneuvered her even while kissing her expertly.

"Jacob." She tried to open their discussion again, but he had other things on his mind. "Jacob, what are you doing?"

"This," he murmured as he pressed her down to the bed. "And *this,*" he said, drawing up her skirt and petticoats,

letting his hand slide above her stockings to the tender bare flesh between her thighs.

He was holding her down, kissing her again—deeply, wetly, taking away her will and her reason.

"Jacob, no!" she managed. "No, I've come to tell you I don't want . . ."

But suddenly it was too late. She felt the tearing pain as he plunged through her maiden's barrier. Her eyes were wide, staring into his face. Jacob too looked startled, then angry.

"You lied," he ground out the words between clenched teeth. "You told me . . . but you were still a virgin! Damn you, Angelica! Damn you! Damn you! *Damn you!*"

Each time he cursed her, he rammed deeper, making her cry out in pain and fear. Had he withdrawn, they might have settled things short of matrimony, but a fever was in Jacob's blood now. He wanted to punish Angelica for her deceit. In punishing her, he also sentenced himself to the altar. When he finally climaxed and rolled away from her, Angelica lay there sobbing in her fury.

"No, Jacob Saenger," she said with deadly quiet, *"damn you!* I came here to tell you the truth, to call off the wedding. You could have had your precious Pandora and good riddance to the both of you. Now you've done it; I may *truly* be with child! Now you *will* marry me!"

Angelica rose from the bed with as much dignity as she could muster. Jacob still stood there, his britches open. He stared at her with an idiot's expression on his face. His head ached, but he was cold sober now.

She was gone within minutes, leaving a trail of lusty curses in her wake. Jacob, sick at heart, still reeling from what had happened and what she had told him, stood in the middle of the room unable to make himself move.

"Yes, now you have done it." He parroted Angelica's accusing words, feeling his blood turn to ice water in his veins. "You have no choice now but to marry her. What she lied about before, you made fact."

He hated the whole idea of taking Angelica as his wife. Suddenly, he told himself he did not have to marry Angelica. With calm deliberation, he strode to his desk and drew out the pistol he kept against intruders. He cradled the gun in his hands as if it were a newborn infant.

"I have another choice," he said aloud.

Slowly, determinedly he put the muzzle to his head and closed his eyes. He had no idea how long he stood there. He imagined every second was his last. It would be so simple and painless—a bullet to the brain and then oblivion. After a long time, his finger still frozen on the trigger, he lowered the gun.

"Coward," he accused bitterly though in the deepest part of his heart, Jacob Saenger knew that living would take far more courage than death.

Pandora felt like a corpse with a frozen smile on its face. Yet she knew by her pain that she still lived.

She gazed about, seeing the flowers everywhere, the guests, the gifts, the minister, the couple standing before him, speaking their vows even now. It all seemed like one of her visions—a terrible nightmare that would go away as soon as she awoke from her trance. But it was all too real. This was the here and the now and the forevermore. The wedding gown she should be wearing was worn by another woman and the man she should have married was slipping a heavy gold band on another bride's finger.

Angelica was *Mrs. Jacob Saenger!*

Pandora couldn't bring herself to believe that this moment had actually arrived. Since her return home, she had forced herself to imagine that Jacob would call it off.

To the very last moment, Pandora had expected Angelica to back out, if Jacob didn't. Yes, that would be like Angelica, she had told herself, to wait to the final possible instant. She would enjoy the show, the excitement, the wearing of the fabulous gown, all antique satin covered with pearls. Her greatest thrill would come as the minister asked her to repeat her vows; she would shock all of Galveston as she shamed Jacob, refusing him publicly, humiliating him before friends and family at the instant they would have been wed.

But it hadn't happened. Pandora stood stiffly, feeling cold seep into her heart as she watched Jacob kiss his new wife.

Nothing was left for her except to return to Paris, where

she would search her soul, trying to discover who she was and where she should go from here. She would live her own life, uncluttered by husband and children.

I am an artist, she reminded herself, silently, desperately.

This was why she'd been unable to see her future with Jacob. They had no future! She thought for a moment of Jean Laffite and Nicolette. Perhaps a soul was allowed only one such love to last through all eternity. If that was so, then she must find her Jean or live alone for the rest of this life.

At that very moment, Ward Gabriel, who was standing close at her side, took her hand and squeezed it gently. "Pandora, are you all right?"

She looked up into his handsome, anxious face. His dark eyes caressed her, sending a shiver along her spine. The lines about his mouth showed his genuine concern.

"Of course not," she admitted, trying to smile at him. "But I shall survive."

"I'd say you've held up magnificently. Were I in your place, I'd be screaming and throwing things. Or I would have escaped last night under cover of darkness. Why did you stay, Pandora? Why did you put yourself through this?"

She smiled weakly at him. "The truth is I never believed for a moment that she would actually go through with it. Even this morning . . ." Tears choked off her words. She looked down and shook her head.

Ward heaved a great sigh. "I should have told you everything, even the gossip, but I was hoping to spare you some pain," he said.

"Gossip?"

He leaned down close so that no one else would hear, although the whole island was buzzing about it already. "Rumor has it that Angelica is *enceinte.*"

Pandora had guessed as much, but the trembling that suddenly seized her made her realize that for the first time she truly believed it.

"Ward, may I ask you a great favor?" Pandora whispered.

He glanced down at her hands, gripping his arm. Her eyes, he noticed, glittered with unshed tears.

"Anything," he told her gently.

"Tonight, if you have no plans, will you take me to dinner? It's terribly important to me that there be no rumors that I still care for Jacob. I won't be laughed at or pitied. That I could not bear!"

Ward covered her hands with his. "Dear Pandora, if I had any plans I would certainly cancel them to be with you. As it happens, you beat me to the punch. I had planned to invite you out tonight. I had thought of the same reasons as you. I had another purpose as well."

"Which was?"

He laughed—a good warm laugh—then shrugged. "I wanted to be with you. It's as simple as that."

The lavish reception would have been a torture had it not been for Ward. He stayed at Pandora's side, acting the jealous protector all the while. When Jacob—stiff-faced and nervous—pleaded with Pandora for a moment alone, Ward's ominous demeanor quickly sent the groom back to his bride.

"He looks terrible," Pandora remarked sympathetically.

"I'm sure any man would view Angelica with a touch of fear. She even tried her wiles on me one evening. She is a formidible schemer, that one. Perhaps motherhood will settle her down."

Finally, the bride and groom left amidst a showering of rose petals and good wishes. They would spend two nights at the Tremont Hotel before moving in with old Dr. Saenger. The good German physician, a widower for many years, had made no bones about his plans for his new daughter-in-law's future. Beaming at the horrified Angelica, he had said to her earlier during the reception, "Ah, it's good Jacob and I will have a woman about to cook for us again. You know how to make sausage and sauerkraut, my dear?"

When Angelica refused his suggestion with a violent shake of her head, the old man beamed at his son. "Then Jacob will teach you, Angelica. A German wife must always be a good cook."

As the guests were departing, Aunt Tabitha slumped, exhausted, into an overstuffed chair. Uncle Horace, spying

Pandora and Ward, came to them, beaming with the pleasure only a father can feel on having successfully married off a daughter.

"Ah, Ward my boy! I haven't had a moment to speak with you. I don't know how I'll manage without you. Buyers of your excellent taste and superior bargaining power are hard to find." Horace grinned and slapped Ward on the back. "Remember the time I over-bought on those copper bathtubs—could have cost me a mint. You said not to worry, you'd unload them. Sold the whole lot to that tribe of cannibals in South America. Told them they were fancy cookpots. And you let them pay in trinkets. *Solid gold trinkets!* Made a damn fortune on the deal. Ah, Ward, those were the days. I wish you luck. You say the silver strike was a big one?"

Pandora hadn't any idea what her uncle meant. "Silver strike?" she said.

Ward nodded and his smile became as self-conscious as a boy's. "Yes. A well-kept secret from my frivolous youth. I foolishly sank most of my inheritance into a silver mine in Mexico years ago. For the longest time, it seemed I'd been set upon by a shifty trader. The fellow had salted the mine. When I found that out, I figured I'd bought a dud. Since all my money was in it, there was nothing to do but keep digging. While you were away, we struck a rich vein."

"The damn mother lode is what he struck, so I've heard, my dear," Horace Sherwood put in. "Rich as a lord, he is. Probably be moving to Mexico now, eh, Ward?"

"No, Horace. I plan to stay right here in Galveston. Of course, I'll make frequent trips to the mine. I'm going to build here, put my money in the place I think of as home."

"Good for you, Ward! Good for our local economy, too."

Horace wandered off, puffing his cigar, making Pandora choke as the smoke drifted her way.

"A silver mine!" she gasped when she could speak again. "That sounds very romantic."

Ward laughed. "It's a lot of dirty hard work. Very little romance, I'm afraid. But it's paying off, Pandora. I stuck to my dream, and finally after all these years . . ."

"Yes, it does pay to stick to one's dreams, or so I've heard," she said wistfully.

Pandora wanted to go to the Tremont Hotel for dinner that night, but Ward thought that would be going a bit too far to prove her point. Granted, Dr. and Mrs. Saenger were hardly likely to put in an appearance in the dining room, but Ward worried that Pandora would be unable to eat, thinking of the couple upstairs somewhere, doing what brides and grooms do.

"I suggest the Beach Hotel instead," Ward offered. "Even though it's off season, there's a big private party there this evening. Mrs. Landes and her Concert Society patrons. If you want to be seen tonight, that's definitely the place to go."

Pandora finally agreed. After all, the whole purpose of their being out together was to let all of Galveston know that she was not home crying into her pillow on her former fiancé's wedding night. If they went to the Tremont, it might seem as though she was trying to spy on Jacob and Angelica.

Ward looked especially dashing tonight, Pandora mused, as she entered the hotel dining room on his arm. It almost seemed as if he had gone to special effort to make a good showing for her benefit. She certainly had taken extra pains. She'd spent the whole afternoon in her bedroom, trying to decide what she should wear. Finally, she settled upon one of her "trousseau" gowns. The dress of patterned maroon on a light ground was made of *velours frappe* or stamped velvet and fit her slender figure with sheath-like closeness. The simple design of the long-sleeved gown was set off by a high collar and deep cuffs of lace, and a sweeping caftan of beige velvet trailed gracefully behind her like the foam of a wave. Her only jewelry was the single gold and opal earring from the box Ward had given her on her birthday.

As the head waiter led them to their table, Ward whispered, "Don't look now, Pandora, but everyone's staring at you. Probably because you're wearing only one earring." He squeezed her arm and chuckled. "Or it could be they're staring at me because I'm with the most gorgeous woman in the room."

With that remark, Ward set the tone for the evening—light bantering, nothing too serious. Pandora was glad. Ward, as she had learned in New York, was better for her than celery tonic. He was so easy to be with, so interesting to talk to, and such a good listener. She hadn't the least doubt that most of the heads that turned, did so to stare at Ward Gabriel—not only because he was so handsome, but because he was now a celebrity in Galveston, with his newly-struck vein of Mexican silver. It gave Pandora a delicious feeling inside to realize that she was the envy of every woman in the room. She hardly spared a thought all evening for the newlyweds.

Not until after dinner, when they were seated side by side in Ward's surrey headed back toward Broadway, did the old familiar ache come over her again.

"Ward, I don't want to go home yet," she said.

"Where would you like to go? Name the place and my chariot shall speed you there, fair lady!"

"Could we go to your cottage?" she asked hesitantly.

Ward frowned. That was the one place he'd hoped she wouldn't suggest. He didn't want to be alone with Pandora. Or, to be perfectly honest, he wanted that far too much.

"Pandora, are you sure that would be wise?" he asked gently. "You know how people talk."

"I don't care! Let them say whatever they like. I won't be here to listen to their gossip much longer."

When he still hesitated, Pandora said, "I need to talk to you, Ward, where it's quiet and I don't have to be afraid of others overhearing."

Ward had wanted this chance with Pandora for so long. He'd be a fool to turn it down. Maybe he could make her understand tonight how much he truly cared for her. He might even be able to convince her to stay in Galveston. He agreed, then turned the horse toward home.

Ward's cottage was just as Pandora remembered it—the shells, the shark, the lovely paintings, and the view of the beach. It was such a cozy place that she immediately felt relaxed and comfortable. When Ward closed the door behind them it was as if he had closed out the rest of the world and all its troubles and worries.

Ward laid a fire from the basket of driftwood on the hearth and soon had a blaze roaring brightly.

"Would you like a brandy, Pandora?"

"Please." She was moving slowly about the room, her fingertips trailing over the backs of chairs, across tabletops. Finally she stopped to finger the objects on the mantelpiece.

"You told Uncle Horace you plan to build, Ward. What will you do with this place when your new house is ready?"

"Oh, sell it, I suppose. I hadn't really thought that far ahead."

"Would you sell it to me?" she asked.

"To you? I thought you meant to leave Galveston. Pandora, I'll give you this place, if it will keep you here. You know I don't want you to go."

Their eyes met as he handed her the brandy sniffer. In that instant, Pandora didn't want to go. If only she could stay here forever, locked away from the rest of the world—with Ward—safe and secure in his cozy cottage. But, of course, that was impossible.

Ward sat down on the couch in front of the fire, patting the place next to him for her to come sit. She did, settling very close to him, desperately in need of his warmth and understanding.

"I feel so strange tonight, Ward," she said solemnly. "As if I've been set adrift. I don't really know where I'll go or what I'll do. Only one thing is clear: I must leave Galveston."

Then the whole tale of Dr. Pinel and the treatment she'd undergone came tumbling out. She confessed her belief in reincarnation and her former existence as Nicolette.

Ward sat, silent and staring at her, wondering if she'd drunk too much champagne at dinner. Mesmerism! Reincarnation! It was all a bunch of drivel! He listened patiently to Pandora's narrative, all the while marveling at the firelight dancing mysteriously in her wide green eyes. The light in her eyes matched the intensity of the blazing fire inside the single opal earring she wore.

"So, you see, Ward, if Jean Laffite is alive now in another incarnation, then I must find him." She gazed into the fire, a faraway look on her face. "But the chances of such a discovery are slim. I have to admit that to myself."

She stared up at him, waiting for some response. She had just poured out her whole heart to this man. She had a special reason for doing so, but somehow everything depended upon his reaction to her story.

"Poppycock!" he burst out. "Pandora, you can't be serious! All this talk of reincarnation, I don't believe a bit of it." He smiled and leaned toward her, letting his fingertips stroke her cheek. "If you're convinced you must find your passionate pirate lover, I suggest you begin your search right here and now. Maybe I'm your lost love. Wouldn't that be convenient for both of us?"

Ward gave her no chance to answer. He closed his arms around her and covered her tempting mouth with his. He'd been waiting a long time for this. Now that she was a free woman, he meant to have his chance. Pandora did not resist.

She was shaken by Ward's unexpected kiss. This was not at all like the other times, yet it almost seemed to have happened just this way before. What else had they done before? She had to find out.

"I've known friendships to turn into love, Pandora," he said as he drew away. "If you stayed here and I wooed you properly, we just might fall in love. Are you telling me that if that happened you would absolutely refuse to marry me, only because my soul is the wrong one?"

"Absolutely," she replied, still slightly dazed. "I would never marry you." She offered him a flirtatious smile and whispered huskily, "I would become your lover instead."

Ward felt the hair on the back of his neck rise in warning—for Pandora as well as for himself. She was treading dangerous waters. If she was about to propose that they become lovers starting this very night, she would get little argument from him. In the past few months, the idea had crossed his mind more often than he liked to admit.

"Well, I'm relieved to hear that you don't plan to die a virgin." He laughed and stroked her cheek. "What a waste that would be."

Pandora hoped that Ward would take the excited blush of her cheeks for heat from the fire. He had given her the very opening she sought. Now it was time to make her move. She stood and glanced toward the bedroom and the water closet beyond.

"Excuse me for a moment," she whispered.

"You know where it is—far side of the bedroom," he told her.

As Pandora eased between the curtains, Ward sat back, staring into the fire. What a pleasant evening it had been. Maybe he would do as he had suggested, pay Pandora court just to see what would happen. He'd known from that first night here in the cottage that he wanted her. Yes, he could finally admit it to himself—he *loved* her! But maybe Pandora was right. They might discover that marriage wasn't for either of them. In time he and Pandora would become lovers, growing old together, but never allowing the dull routine of married life to blunt the sharp edge of their passion. He closed his eyes and sighed. They would travel the world together, making love in Paris, Rome, London, Moscow, and in his little shack outside the silver mine in Mexico—even right here in Laffite's Grove.

Some sound caught his ear. His eyes flew open. Pandora stood before him, dressed only in his burgundy velvet robe.

"I want you to make love to me, Ward," she said matter-of-factly. One hand fluttered up to her hair, held in place by dozens of garnet-studded golden hairpins. "I left it up," she said hesitantly. "I've been told a man enjoys taking it down himself—slowly, letting each pin fall to the floor."

When he recovered enough to speak, all Ward could say was "My God, Pandora!"

"I've thought it all out, Ward. It's what I want."

"You can't just come into a man's home, shed your clothes, and say, 'Take me!' That's not the way it's done, Pandora!"

Although this was exactly what Ward had dreamed of for so long, he was taken aback by her forwardness. *He* had meant to initiate their lovemaking. It was his responsibility, his *right* as the man. When he saw her lips begin to tremble and a tear dribble down her cheek, he was on his feet immediately, sorry for his outburst. He drew her into his arms and said, "Don't cry about it."

"You don't want me," she whimpered.

"I never said that. Yes, Pandora, I want you. God, how I want you! I've wanted you for as long as I can remember." He fumbled at the belt of the robe and opened it, slipping his hands inside to touch her breasts. She sighed and leaned her head on his shoulder.

"Oh, yes, Ward," she sighed as his touch turned her weak. "Make love to me!"

He kissed her softly and fleeting glimpses of Laffite and Nicolette together in their great gilded bed passed through Pandora's mind. Laffite's hands were stroking Nicolette's breasts, just as Ward was fondling hers. Suddenly, Ward released her, closed the robe, and moved away.

"Are you sure, Pan? You won't wind up hating me?" he asked quietly.

"No, never!" There was pleading in her tone.

"You're very young, Pandora. You've had a great shock. It's natural for you to think now that you will never marry. But in years to come, you'll change your mind. How will it make you feel, going to your husband knowing that I stole his treasure long ago?"

Damn his conscience! Why was he trying to talk her out of it? He was a man of appetites and Pandora Sherwood was high on his list of desirable delicacies.

Pandora felt doubly rejected—first by Jacob and now by Ward. It was almost more than she could bear. She had her life mapped out in her mind. She would soon return to Paris but tonight she longed to feel desired, cherished. Now she realized there was something more to her need. She had thought about the possibility before and found it to her liking. Tonight when Ward had first kissed her, mere possibility had grown to probability. What if Ward Gabriel was indeed her Jean Laffite?

"Please, Ward," she whispered urgently, "love me . . ."

Slowly, Pandora sank to the sofa beside him. She leaned over, pressing her lips to his, her mouth open, inviting. He drew her into his arms, once more slipping his hands inside the robe even as his tongue slipped into her waiting mouth. Her whole body burned and tingled at his touch. Their kisses grew more passionate. Her breathing came in short, shallow bursts.

Silence reinged except for the soft crackling of the fire and the dull metallic sound of gold striking wood as Ward slowly, carefully drew the hairpins from Pandora's thick red-gold tresses, never taking his eyes from hers. She sighed with pleasure as he ran his fingers through her hair. This was so good . . . so right.

Then, griping the silken skein, he forced her head back. "Oh, God, Pandora! You can't imagine how long I've wanted to hold you like this!" His eager mouth burned a fiery trail of kisses down her throat.

Suddenly, the room vanished. She was once again in *Maison Rouge*—before Isabel's coming. She lay wrapped in her husband's strong arms, feeling his hardness pressed to her naked belly while his hands moved over her back, stroking, fondling, sending waves of desire searing through her. She could stand no more. She must have him!

"Oh, Jean darling," Pandora cried, digging her nails into Ward's muscled arms. "Now, please, take me now!"

Part
II

Chapter Fourteen

The view from the window was breathtaking. Naples lan-
guished about the gently undulating hills like the many-
colored petticoats of some voluptuous peasant maiden as
she lay in the arms of her lover. Beyond the staggered
houses that dotted the lush green Posilipo area, wavelets
danced on the bay like floating diamonds. A plume as white
as snow stretched to heaven from the cone of Vesuvius. In
the distance, Capri rose from the water, its limestone cliffs
a purple shadow, beckoning the rich and the decadent to
come and play.

Bright Mediterranean sunshine spilled in through the open
window, pouring over Pandora's shoulders to shower golden
highlights on Franco's naked body. Staring at him, she had
to admit that she had never seen such a flawless male form—
broad shoulders, tapered waist, trim hips, and the long,
muscled legs of an athlete. In every way, Franco was as
sleek and powerful as a stallion. His perfection allowed
Pandora to reach new heights that until now had seemed

223

unattainable. Her excitement grew as her hands moved boldly, caressing his strong, earthy maleness with sure strokes. Ah, how good it felt, how magnificent the end result would be!

Her nose itched, but she dared not pause to scratch it. Franco would rage if they weren't finished in the allotted time.

"How much longer?" he demanded, reminding her what an impatient man he was. "I ache all over. Can't you hurry?"

Pandora quickened her strokes, dashing sunlight-colored oils across the smooth belly of the figure on her canvas. "It shouldn't take much longer, Franco."

He sighed deeply, tragically, but held his pose.

Pandora went on with her masterpiece, adding the finishing touches as her mind strayed to other times and other places. Each painting she had done in the past three years seemed a small lifetime in itself. Her existence with Franco had begun a mere five weeks ago. Now once again, she was about to end her work. What would come next? Would she stay on in Naples or move on? She wasn't sure.

At least the weather was warmer now. She and Franco had both shivered in her cold studio during the first weeks' sessions while the late winter rains poured outside and the cold mistral blew down from the snow-covered mountains to the north lashing the coast with a vengeance. A sudden gust of warm wind filled the room with the familiar perfume of oleanders, conjuring up visions of Galveston and the pink, yellow, and white flowers that bloomed so profusely there. A little stab of pain shot through Pandora's heart. How long had it been since she last saw her home?

Paris, London, Vienna, Rome, and now Naples. For the past three years—since she fled to France the day after Jacob and Angelica's wedding, the morning after that dreadful scene with Ward—she had stared at disrobed models in dirty, drafty studios all over Europe. Her bold nudes now hung in galleries, in restaurants, in private villas all over the Continent, and were peddled from stalls on the banks of the Seine.

The paintings, which she signed "Nicolette," were now

more famous than Bouguereau's naked nymph at the Hoffman House in New York. The thought of New York brought a fleeting mental glimpse of Ward Gabriel's handsome, smiling face. She wondered briefly where he was, what he was doing, if he had married. The ghost of her memory sent shivers of longing coursing through her. How she wished she could reshape their final hour together!

But the past could not be altered. Her only reality existed in the here and now. She had left Galveston with a mission: she had wanted to be known. Now she was famous all right. At least the recluse named Nicolette was known round the world. Pandora had not been bold enough to put her own name on her paintings. The art world rumors concerning Nicolette were rampant. Many artists and patrons spread tales about her that grew with each telling. It was said that she had an insatiable sexual appetite, that she paid her male models with favors, not cash.

How ironic that half the men in Europe bragged of having slept with Nicolette, but not a single man had yet made love to Pandora Sherwood. No doubt Ward Gabriel, if he knew, would find that fact amusing.

Ward Gabriel! How often she thought of him. How long it seemed since she'd seen him last.

"Carissima," Franco crooned softly, casting a leering grin her way. "What can you be thinking of? Your nipples have puckered. No gutter thoughts, *per favore*. Keep your mind on your work or we'll never be done."

Ignoring Franco's annoying interruption, Pandora went right on thinking what she pleased but a flush of embarrassment warmed her face. Without moving, she glanced down at her thin smock. Her thoughts of Ward had indeed aroused her.

The last time she'd seen him . . . it seemed long, long ago. Her final night in Galveston—the night of the wedding—the night Ward had rejected her desperate plea that he make her a woman. After that disgraceful scene at his cottage, she'd had no choice but to run away. She could not have faced him again.

She still smarted with shame whenever she thought about that night. She still blamed herself for his turning back at the last moment. It embarrassed her now to remember how innocent she'd been at the time. What an enormous amount of naive courage it had taken to throw herself at him that way.

She could still imagine his kisses and the way she'd felt as his hands played over her breasts. Heat rose in her body at the very thought. Oh, how she had wanted Ward to make love to her that night; he had wanted her, too. She was as sure of it this minute as she had been then. On the very brink of taking her, her vision had begun. She'd sighed Jean Laffite's name and Ward had quickly drawn away, raging at her about her fantasies. She must have been out of her head that night. Why had she tried to make Ward fit her image of Jean Laffite? Even if she still thought he might be the one, Ward believed none of her talk of reincarnation.

To this day she could still see the scowl of anger on his face. "You don't want *me* to love you!" he'd accused. "You want your precious pirate ghost! Well, I won't play your games, Pandora. If ever you decide that I'm the man you desire, I'm more than willing. Just let me know!" He'd flung the robe at her then. "Get dressed. It's time I took you home."

She'd been stunned, shamed, furious at the time. Their ride back to Broadway had been in strained silence. He'd seen her to the door, wished her a cool good-night, and driven away. No kiss, no touch, no word of comfort.

She'd spent the rest of that night sobbing and packing. The next morning, she'd caught the first boat leaving Galveston, headed for New Orleans. She had literally run away from home, leaving only a note behind, addressed to her aunt and uncle.

Her week's stay in the Crescent City while she waited for a ship to take her to France had been most enlightening. She'd spent her time searching through old record books, gleaning facts about the Vernet family. Nicolette's birth was recorded in the church archives, the same day as the great fire that leveled most of the city in 1794. Ironic, she thought that she and Nicolette had both come into life during times of great danger—birthed in fire and flood.

She also located Nicolette's marriage certificate—but not

to Jean Laffite—to a man named Diego Bermudez. Oddly enough, however, there was no record of his death in the book. Could that mean that Nicolette and Jean Laffite were never legally married, but lived together as lovers?

She'd even found the old Vernet home in Toulouse Street. She thought it resembled a beautiful Creole woman who had fallen on hard times. Its cream-colored sand brick facade had gone dingy with age and want of paint. The delicate wrought iron balconies, used now by some poor family to hang out their wash, were rusting badly.

She'd knocked at the front entrance, curious to see if the interior would spark any memories. A fat Irish woman with a squalling infant in her arms answered the door. Pandora had a difficult time explaining why she wanted to come in and look around. Finally, she'd lied, telling the befuddled tenant that she was considering buying the property, but needed to see it first.

Moving from one cluttered, dirty room to the next, she'd tried to imagine its former grandeur. In one of the bedrooms upstairs, she'd experienced a warmth that was certainly lacking in the rest of the unheated house. "Nicolette's room," she'd said to herself. She'd closed her eyes and concentrated, finally conjuring up a vision of a great tester bed with filmy mosquito netting and heavy brocade curtains, a rosewood dresser on which lay a silver toilette set, and for a fleeting instant she'd seen a young, ebony-haired beauty, standing by the window, weeping.

Pandora had caught her breath and reached out, whispering Nicolette's name. Her hand had passed through the fading image, and when she looked about again, she saw only a pile of papers, peeling plaster walls, a sagging cot, and a mouse scurrying through a hole in the baseboard.

She learned a great deal about the Vernet family in New Orleans. Nicolette's mother had died in a madhouse. Soon after his wife's death, Claude Vernet married his sister-in-law, Gabrielle, just as she had told Dr. Pinel. As for Jean Laffite, he had sailed away from New Orleans shortly after the great battle against the British, never to return again. Everyone she spoke with agreed that he had headed for Mexico, but had landed on Galveston Island by mistake.

Some said he died in the Yucatan of a fever in 1826. No one seemed certain. One elderly woman told her that Laffite had been seen in Alton, Illinois, as late as 1854.

Gooseflesh prickled her arms when she met an old man who said he'd actually known Jean Laffite.

"Knew his brothers Dominique and Pierre, too, and their uncle Rene Beluche," he told her.

The thought that this man's life had overlapped both of hers was somehow staggering. She'd stared into his weathered face, wanting to ask a million questions, but not knowing where to begin.

"You really knew him?"

His egg-bald, sun-bronzed head tilted to a jaunty angle. "Not so's I could call him friend. Me and him we fit the British Dragon together. I was just a lad, a beardless drummer boy. One day I stood so close to him I coulda reached out and touched that scarlet sash that held his sword." The old man's voice took on a wistful tone then as he gazed off into the distance, remembering. "Tall he was and straight as a swamp cypress. With green eyes that could pierce you through. There was pure devilment in his smile. He could even laugh while them Brits was trying to make us all into buzzard bait. I tell you, lady, now there was a man! The women loved him; the men feared him. His band of bloody roughnecks would've stormed the gates of hell if Laffite told them he wanted old Lucifer taken captive."

"What about his wife?"

"Wife?" The old man squinted up at her with eyes as sharp as a hawk's and a face to match. "Don't know that he had no wife. I heared tell he had himself a right pretty woman, though."

"They weren't married?" Pandora had trouble containing her shock.

"Hell, no! If we're talking about the same woman—the one that run off to Galveston with him. She still had her a husband. Spanish Creole the man was, and something of a bounder as I recollect."

"Was his name Bermudez?"

"Yeah." He stabbed at her with his pipe and nodded. "Yeah, that was it. That was one big scandal in this town, I can tell you. Jean Laffite won that woman in a poker game from her husband. Imagine, a man putting his own wife in the pot." He chuckled then and winked at Pandora. "Hell, I reckon it ain't such a crazy thought after all. Many's the time I'd of liked to got rid of my Mabel that easy, rest her soul."

"What happened to Bermudez?"

The old man stared down at his gnarled hands, sorting out the past in his mind. "Don't rightly recall, ma'am. He was a no-good, though. Only married that pretty little gal for her papa's money. Treated her real mean, he did. Even tried to kill her once, so they say. As I recollect, Bermudez just up and disappeared." Suddenly, his eyes lit up. "No, wait, a old whore name of Josepha told me he died of the yellow fever on her flatboat. She claimed Laffite hisself deep-sixed the body. Since there wasn't no corpse or no death certificate, the church never recognized him as dead. To their way of thinking, his wife was married to him to the day she died. Poor woman, reckon she had good cause to run off with Laffite."

Pandora now realized that the broomstick marriage was all, except their love, that had united Jean Laffite and Nicolette. She could not have been his legal wife, could never have hoped to be. All the more reason, she thought, for their souls to seek each other in a new existence, since, by church law, Nicolette had never been allowed to marry the man she truly loved. If Pandora had ever doubted before that Nicolette had come back through her, all misgivings vanished during her stay in New Orleans.

From there, she had traveled on to Paris, arriving in rainy, dreary March. Dr. Pinel had agreed to resume their sessions, even though he still scoffed at her belief in reincarnation. With his help, she'd relived much more of Nicolette's life, especially her younger years, including her brief but dreadful marriage to Diego Bermudez—gambler, womanizer, liar, cheat, and sadist. That Nicolette survived the man's cruelties was a miracle.

Dr. Pinel had listened patiently as she told of losing Jacob and of her feelings for Ward Gabriel.

"Whether you discover the man you were meant to marry

seems to me to lie entirely in the hands of fate. Pandora, you must simply live your life as best you can and never give up hope,'' Pinel encouraged.

At that point, Pandora ended her sessions with the doctor to begin living her life. She had no choice. Although she was a wealthy young woman, her vast fortune was in trust and would remain there until she married or turned twenty-five, whichever came first. She was still one husband or three years short of that. Her uncle had been most generous with her while she remained under his roof. But now she must make her own way. After only a short time in Paris, her funds were all but exhausted. She had to find some way to support herself.

She had told Ward once that she would be an artist and now was the time to try.

As for the rest of what she had told Ward—that she would take many lovers—that now seemed laughable! Having known the Francos, the Vincents, the Edouards of the art world, she had serious doubts that Laffite would have come back as an artist's model. Never—not if she lived a thousand years—would she ever forget her first experience with one of the mad models of Paris. Edouard was tall, painfully thin, elegantly beautiful, with intense violet eyes and a voice as rich and smooth as aged brandy. She could see their meeting now as if it were happening for the first time.

He walked toward her as she stood at her easel, painting the Seine and the boats. She had not yet worked up the courage to ask a man to pose for her. She glanced up to see the tall man drawing near, but had no idea he was headed directly to her.

He stopped before her, blocking her view, and in a voice that was as rich and sweet as warm honey, he whispered ''Let me model for you. I ask no pay. It would be my honor, beautiful lady.''

Shocked speechless, Pandora found she could only stare at him. Her first impulse was to run away, but she couldn't make her legs move.

''Please, mademoiselle, I am not mad.'' He shrugged in that eloquent Gallic manner. ''Well, perhaps, just a bit. But then are not all artistic people better if they are slightly insane? You must let me pose for you. I see in your eyes that we share a great, secret passion." His gaze then traveled the length of her, coming to rest at her bosom and making her tingle inside. "I beg of you, mademoiselle! May I you come to your studio . . . pose for you?"

Pandora finally agreed. She was nervous beyond all reason, having never painted a male model from life. When she arrived at her studio—a cold, wretched garret in Montmartre, but the best she could afford—she changed her mind again. "No, no, Edouard!" she told him. "I'm sorry. Please go." The slightly mad man would have none of it. He began disrobing before her shocked eyes.

Beautifully naked and weeping real tears, he begged on his knee, "My very life depends on you, mademoiselle. If you make me go now, I will have no choice but to kill myself."

When he lunged toward the table, taking an evil-looking bread knife, threatening to plunge it deep into his thin, but beautiful breast, Pandora finally relented.

She could still remember her uneasiness as she'd glanced about her, uncertain how to go about posing the man.

When she remained frozen to the spot, Edouard came to her, an imploring smile on his full, beautiful lips. Before she could move away, he took her in his arms, whispering reassurances, telling her that he was sure they would be magnificent together once the painting was done. And then, Edouard kissed her . . . and kissed her . . . and kissed her. Deep, wine-flavored kisses that melted her will and set her trembling inside and out. By the time he finished with her, she found herself totally, overwhelmingly infatuated with him, as mesmerized as if Dr. Pinel had spoken his magic words over her.

Edouard is Laffite!

It had to be, she told herself as she arranged his wondrous body with trembling, loving hands, then set to work creating her first masterpiece.

To her vast disappointment, Edouard, pleading fatigue, did not make love to her when they finished their first session. Nor did he on any other occasion. She remained, their whole month together, trembling on the very brink of ecstasy. Before each sitting, Edouard kissed her, stroked her, fondled her almost to the point of release. But never further. He told her she kindled his fires of passion and that they made her canvas glow with a special light to inflame the viewer. He promised her their time would come. She accepted that, dreaming all the while of the day she would finally finish her work and of the marvelous, passionate love they would share in celebration.

While Pandora had a room elsewhere, she allowed Edouard to live in the studio. On the day she was to finish the canvas and be fulfilled at last, she arrived early, glowing with expectancy.

Today was the day! she told herself. Edouard would make her his woman at last!

She arrived *too* early! She burst in to find her beautiful Edouard in the arms of his lover—a husky, hairy brute named Gaspar. She would never forget that sight. The two men lay naked and entwined on the very couch where she and Edouard had lain together, kissing and fondling and waiting—waiting for what could never be.

With a cry of sheer anguish, she had ordered her would-be lover out of the studio, warning him never to return again.

Edouard's portrait sold almost immediately. The buyer's agent contacted her and offered an enormous sum. She did not know the new owner's name, nor did she care. She only wanted all memories of Edouard wiped from her mind. Rave reviews of her work were published in the Paris papers. The painting was the hit of the season in Paris when it was shown at the "luxurious studio of the renowned art connoisseur, Monsieur Gaspar Lemercier." The whole city was guessing who this female genius was who had painted such a masterpiece. Names were suggested in gossip columns and whispered at coffee houses. Many claimed a man had actually done the work. Edouard and his lover kept silent and no one else knew for sure.

Pandora was careful to keep her two lives separate. Her friends had no idea that she was the much whispered about artist, Nicolette. They would never have suspected that a gently raised American lady could paint such scandalously realistic portraits of male nudes. She told her models no details of her personal life—not even her real name. She spoke French, Italian, and German fluently. The men who posed for her knew nothing of her American background. Only two people might guess her true identity by the way she signed her works, Dr. Pinel and Ward Gabriel. The doctor would keep her secret in professional confidence. As for Ward, she only wished he would make the connection and come back into her life.

Putting the final touches on Franco's portrait, Pandora thought ahead to her plans for the evening. Tonight she would see an old friend from home. Magnolia Hempstead, who had married an Italian count, was giving a masked ball at her villa on Capri. The occasion for the party, other than the usual frantic round of post-Easter festivities, was Count Bellini's recent acquisition of one of her early French portraits.

Pandora, hearing about the purchase, had considered declining the invitation. But the party promised much amusement and very little danger of discovery. Besides, she missed her old friends and longed for news from home.

She sighed suddenly, thinking that if she did not finish with Franco soon, she would not be dressed in time to catch the boat that the Bellinis were sending over to transport their guests from Naples.

"Not much longer," she told her model.

"Un momento, cara?"

Franco was teasing her again. A moment to her, he had told her, could mean an hour or a day. He often accused her of painting out more than she painted in during most sessions.

Her hand and shoulders ached. Pandora closed her eyes for a moment, but her mind refused to be still. For some reason her thoughts kept flying in all directions. She felt as if something were about to happen to her yet she had no idea what it might be. Perhaps she was only excited about the gala tonight, about seeing someone from Galveston after so long. Magnolia would have all the latest news from home.

When she had run away three years ago, she had cut all ties. She had written her aunt once, to tell her that she was in Paris, but did not intend to remain there much longer.

She had given her family no address. They could not write to her and she did not write to them. Sometimes she felt sorry for that. There were things she would like to know. By now, Jacob and Angelica's child must be a toddler. Perhaps their second or even their third was on the way.

"Finito!" Franco's cry of exultation made her jump. While her mind wandered, he had left his spot to come look at the canvas. She stared at him, then at her work. He was right. It was finished.

The naked model grabbed her and hugged her enthusiastically. Pandora could not share his excitement, feeling only relief. She stretched her arms over her head, experiencing a prickling sensation like tiny needles stabbing her flesh. Then reaching to a nearby chair, she grasped a green velvet drape and tossed it to Franco.

"Get dressed!" she ordered good-naturedly. "You're embarrassing me."

Franco gave her a sound kiss on her cheek. "Ah, *signorina,* I would like to do more than that to you. You are *molta artista . . . molta femina!"*

She laughed at the sexy come-on. "You're not so bad yourself, Franco. Would you settle for some wine?"

He still stood there, gazing at the painting with sheer delight in his dark eyes. *"Magnifico!"* he whispered.

Pandora turned and took a blood orange from a bowl by the window. She sank her teeth into the tough skin, taking a deep bite of the red and orange flesh. Juice dribbled down her chin, but she didn't care. She was famished.

Franco opened a bottle of chianti and brought two glasses. They toasted the masterpiece, she paid him handsomely, then he dressed, and left.

A short while later, Pandora left the apartment. Outside the late afternoon sunshine was warm. It felt good on her face. She decided to walk the few blocks to catch the boat to Capri. She felt wonderful. Perhaps it was because the portrait was finally finished or more likely, she mused, it had to do with seeing someone from Galveston again. She sighed, wishing she could go back. Surely by now she had matured enough to return and accept all that had happened to her there.

Countess Bellini, a tall slender woman three years Pandora's senior, rushed to greet her childhood friend. Pandora stared, wondering at the vast change in her, until she realized that Magnolia had hennaed her blond hair for the occasion. The fiery tresses transformed her entire appearance. Her hazel eyes were hidden behind a jeweled mask.

Magnolia was costumed as Queen Zenobia of Palmyra, complete with the heavy golden chains about her wrists and ankles that the Emperor Aurelian was said to have used on his lovely prisoner. Magnolia's costume was not quite authentic, for according to the histories Pandora had read, Zenobia wore nothing but those gold chains as she was paraded through the streets of Rome so long ago.

"Pandora dearest," the countess cooed, kissing her old friend on both cheeks. "I am furious with you. Why didn't you let us know sooner that you were in Naples? You could have stayed with us. I won't scold you; you're here now." She held her friend at arm's length. "Let me look at you. Oh, you are *gorgeous*. I know now who will win the prize for the best costume of the evening."

A dozen guests were assembled already in the spacious, airy ballroom of the Bellini villa. The moment Pandora entered, the buzz of conversation ceased as all eyes drank her in. She became self-conscious under such close scrutiny. She hadn't planned to draw undue attention to herself this evening. Perhaps she'd gone too far with her costume. She was dressed as the huntress goddess Diana, her form caressed by a gauze-like, clinging silver drape. Ropes of silver formed a girdle at her waist. She wore silver sandals. Her hair, piled high in flaming waves held in place by golden hairpins, was crowned by a crescent moon that glittered with brilliant stones. Her golden mask, too, was encrusted with the sparkling glass gems.

"Come, Pandora," Magnolia insisted, tugging her from the staring crowd. "Let's have a glass of wine and talk. There's so much I want to know about home. I love Italy, but sometimes I think I could die for the tiniest glimpse of Galveston."

Pandora was relieved to be alone with her friend in a quiet sitting room, but she admitted that any news she had to share was at least three years old.

After her first disappointment, the countess's face brightened. "Then I'll simply have to tell you *everything*. Mother and my sisters write every week. I know of course about your broken engagement." Magnolia studied Pandora's face to see if the subject offended. When her friend only nodded and smiled, she realized she was on safe ground.

"Was it a boy or a girl?" Pandora asked. The other woman looked puzzled by her question. "Jacob and Angelica's child."

Magnolia slapped her fingers to her lips and drew in her breath, delighted to be the first to tell Pandora this choice bit of gossip. "My goodness, you have been out of touch," she whispered. "There was no child. Angelica lied to Jacob to get him to marry her. Why, it was the scandal of the whole island. Can you believe it?"

Somehow Pandora could not share her friend's shock. How like Angelica. How very like her. Poor, dear Jacob. He had counted so on having a son to carry on the family name and medical practice.

"They've had no children?"

"None, rumor has it that Jacob left her bed after he found out that she had deceived him."

During the next few minutes, Magnolia told her about everyone she knew in Galveston, everyone she cared about—everyone except Ward Gabriel. Pandora was dying to ask about him. Was he still there? Had he built his fine house? Had he married? But she couldn't bring herself to mention his name. Everytime she thought of him, she felt guilty and ashamed.

"Ah, ladies, here you are." It was Count Salvatore Bellini, Magnolia's darkly handsome husband—older than she, but obviously wild about his American beauty. "You must join us now. It is time to unveil my new masterpiece. Come, come." He offered an arm to each of them and smiled down into Pandora's eyes. "We are honored to have you here, *signorina*. And later, we have a special surprise for you."

Again, Pandora felt her heart give an extra beat. She convinced herself that he referred only to the contest; there was no way that they could have found out she was the artist, Nicolette.

The painting of Vincent was unveiled by the count amidst much sighing and exclaiming from the guests. Pandora stared at it, remembering those strange days in her cold, drab studio in a back alley of Paris. How she had shivered as the winter rains pelted the city. And Vincent, ah, Vincent—with his wild hair and one cocked eye, but the most magnificent body.

When she had complimented him on his physique, he had been quick to warn her off. "Be careful, mademoiselle. I know of your reputation. I will allow you to paint me, but I will not make love to you." She could still hear his pompous voice in her head. She had not asked him to. "You see," he'd continued, "I no longer allow myself the luxury of taking a lover while I'm posing. To make love is to sap the spirit of its strength. The model must be as great a genius as the artist. The creative juices can flow in only one direction. The wise genius allows them to flow from his fingers and his spirit. The stupid one spews them out through his penis. You will remain celibate also while I am posing for you. Am I understood?"

He had refused all but meager payment, thinking her deprived because he would not bed her. Pandora smiled at the memory and at the painting. Vincent had insisted on creating his own pose. He stood naked with his hands caressing the marble breasts of a statue of Cleopatra. Despite her best efforts to the contrary, Pandora had been unable to give the painting anything other than erotic overtones. Vincent looked as if he were either about to make love to the cold marble or plead with the exotic queen to come back to life to soothe his passionate longings. It was almost comic art, albeit masterfully done. She had the urge to giggle, but everyone around her was rapt with awe.

"Magnificent!" she heard a woman behind her say in a

voice choked with emotion. "What I would not give for one night with such a man."

"You *have* such a man, madame," Pandora heard the woman's husband remark in a gruff whisper. "That pretty fellow who tends the horses at our country place. I know all about him."

After the initial excitement over the painting, the party went into full swing. Musicians began to play and Pandora found herself whirled about on the smooth marble floor for hours. As midnight and the unmasking neared, she felt ready to drop. Perhaps she would excuse herself and hide away in Magnolia's bedchamber, escaping the final waltz and the inevitable soggy kiss of some stranger at the moment of the unmasking.

As she started to slip away, someone caught her hand.

"Signorina, per favore?"

Trapped! She was in the masked man's arms before she could say a word. One of the count's Italian friends she could tell. They were all dark and earthy-looking, although this one was taller than the others. He spoke to her only in Italian, but with an odd accent she couldn't quite place. Every province had its own peculiar accent; Pandora found it impossible to keep them all straight.

"Your costume, *signor?*" she asked. He was dressed in high boots, tight pants, a wide sash, and a full-sleeved shirt, all in brilliant colors. She noted the golden ring in his ear and the bandana covering his head. "You are a gypsy prince?"

He laughed and the sound of it struck a chord deep in her heart. "No, I was never any good at disguises, signorina. I am supposed to be a pirate—that French scoundrel, Jean Laffite."

Pandora missed a step and then another. Some latent fury from long ago boiled up in her. "He was neither a pirate nor a scoundrel, *signor!*"

He bowed in apology, still smiling, and swept her back into the waltz. "I will not argue that point with you since I know little of the man. If one so gentle and lovely as you defends him, then I am sure he was a gentleman of the first order. But I am disappointed. I chose this disguise hoping o emulate the man's personality as well. I hear he had quite a way with the ladies.''

Pandora was angry. Was the man purposely trying to goad her? Then she realized how silly she was being. This stranger could know nothing about her and certainly he had no inkling of her past with Jean Laffite. His choice of costume and his words were mere coincidence. She willed herself to relax in his arms.

"That's better." He breathed the words close to her ear in perfect English and drew her hard against his chest.

She stared up at him, at the almost black eyes glittering at her through the slits in his satin mask. Something stirred inside her. Then suddenly the villa was thrown into darkness. The moment of unmasking. The moment of the kiss.

He held her face between his warm palms. Pandora tried to reach up and give him the required brief kiss to be done with it but her partner had other ideas. His lips moved across her brow, down to kiss her eyelids, her nose, her cheeks. She felt the light touches deep down inside, stirring up a maelstrom of old memories and desires. Then his hands moved from her face to slip around her waist. He drew her close. When his lips captured hers and he teased gently, urging her to open for him, she went weak all over. For a brief moment, their tongues caressed. Even before the lights came on, she knew . . .

"Ward," she whispered, staring up at him as the room flooded with lamplight. "What on earth are you doing here?"

He only smiled at her, tracing one finger over her moist, puffy lips, making her tremble all over.

Chapter Fifteen

Pandora could not quite remember the sequence of events at the Bellinis' party after the unmasking and Ward's kiss. She knew she had stayed at the party for a time and that she had left with Ward. The rest remained a warm, hazy cloud of light and color and sound in her memory—like one of her visions.

As she sat on the terrace of Ward's nearby villa, still clutching her prize in her hands, it came back to her that her filmy Diana disguise had been chosen the party's best costume. Everyone had cheered and toasted her. All the while, Ward Gabriel had clung to her as if he meant never to let her out of his sight again.

Ward handed her a brandy and nudged the long, slender package she was holding. "Why don't you open your prize, Pan?"

She smiled at him, still not quite able to believe they were really together again. "I forgot all about it," she said, stripping off the bright wrappings. By the wavering light of the flambeau on a nearby wall, she could see the gleam of silver inside the velvet box when she lifted the lid. She gasped in surprise.

"That's no trinket. It's the real thing," Ward told her, unable to mask the pride in his voice. "Mexican silver, handworked by Italian artisans. What do you think?"

"Why, it's beautiful! But I'm amazed. I thought the Bellinis' silly contest warranted only a silly prize."

"Here, let me fasten it for you."

Ward took the delicate necklace from her. She trembled as his cool fingers brushed her bare shoulders.

"Lovely," he murmured. "Perfect for you. I knew it would be."

She stared at him quizzically. "What do you mean?"

Quickly, he explained the whole plot, or at least a version of the truth fit for Pandora's ears. "I told Magnolia that I'd provide the prize, but only if it went to you."

Pandora touched the cool silver at her throat and feigned a disapproving look with the lift of an eyebrow. "A rigged contest? Ward, for shame!"

He laughed and went on to explain. "Magnolia thought it was a fine idea. In fact, our hostess was my co-conspirator for the whole evening. Over the past couple of years, she has come to look on me as one of her special charities. She's taken me under her lovely wing like a mother hen protecting a prize chick. This villa was her idea. I'd planned to stay in a hotel while I was in Naples on business, but she insisted that I lease this place instead." He glanced at the pastel stucco walls, pale in the moonlight. "I haven't been sorry. I may even buy it. At any rate, Magnolia knew that you and I were old acquaintances. She loves bringing people together and she loves surprises. She's always had a flair for the dramatic. When she found out you were in Naples, she told me she was working on a plan to get us together. Then her husband bought that painting by *Nicolette* and Magnolia had the perfect vehicle for a party that she could turn into a surprise reunion. It was her idea to spring me on you unexpectedly. She said you deserved no less for having been in Italy weeks before you let her know. She planned tonight's festivities with all the care and attention that she

241

might have lavished on her own daughter's wedding. I'm sure she's hoping that she's just engineered the match of the season."

Ignoring his last statement, Pandora said, "So you knew that I was there all evening. Why didn't you show yourself sooner, Ward?"

He laughed. "*You* were there all evening but I have been down in Sorrento for several days. I decided to take my boat from there to Capri, but I misjudged the time and distance. I very nearly missed the whole damn party. Magnolia would never have forgiven me."

"So that's why I didn't see you before." Her hand went again to her throat, to the necklace of delicate silver filigree set with tiny cameo roses of pink and white. "You certainly came as a shock, but a pleasant one, Ward. I love my prize. Thank you!"

He came toward her and sat beside her on the low wall overlooking the bay. "Somehow I knew it would look perfect on Nicolette," he whispered.

"You know about me?" Suddenly, Pandora felt ill at ease.

He raised her hand to his lips and held it there. "I guessed the first time I saw one of the paintings. Who else would choose that name? Besides, you told me you were going to Paris to paint. I never doubted for a moment that you'd become famous."

She looked away from him. "Oh, Ward, I didn't want anyone to know."

"It's our secret," he murmured, slipping his arm around her and drawing her close. "You are quite the loveliest artist I've ever seen, Pandora. You should be on canvas yourself."

"You're making me blush," she whispered.

He laughed. "All over, I hope. You told me something else that you planned to do in Paris, Pandora. Do you remember?"

"I do," she answered, knowing full well what he meant. Suddenly, it seemed desperately important that she tell Ward she had not taken any lovers after all, but she was too embarrassed to confess to him that she was still the chaste maiden he had rejected three years before.

Silence stretched between them. Ward was still holding her hand, still gazing at her. A gentle breeze, scented with lime blossoms, danced over the terrace, riffling through Ward's thick, dark hair. A lock fell over his forehead. Without realizing what she was doing, Pandora reached up and gently brushed it back in place. Ward felt a shock surge through him.

It was hard to believe that she was really here, that she was so close he could feel her warmth and smell her expensive French perfume. How often he had dreamed of this moment! How often he had rehearsed what he would say, what he would do. Instead of confiding in her, confessing that he had searched the Continent for her for the past three, long years . . . instead of telling her his plans, his dreams, his hopes, he sat like a statue, unable to do anything but stare at her, drinking in the passionate woman that the precocious child had become.

Her voice jolted him. "What are you doing here, Ward? In Italy?"

"Consulting with Italian craftsmen." He answered her, but his mind was not really on her question. "My silver mine has put me into another sideline—jewelry. This necklace is only one of the designs I've commissioned. Soon every woman in America will feel naked unless she's wearing a piece of my silver. It's all the rage in Galveston. Your uncle carries a whole line of my baubles at the Emporium. What about you, Pandora? What are you doing in Italy?"

She shrugged and offered him a girlishly guilty smile. "Still painting, of course. To be more honest, still searching for something or someone."

"Oh." Ward could not hide the disappointed tone in his voice. If another portrait was in progress, then her handsome model was probably her present lover as well. The gossip in art circles said she flitted from lover to lover. No model had ever posed for more than one canvas. Her latest affair would end the moment the painting was finished.

No, by God, it will end now! he vowed silently. He didn't care how many lovers she had had, he still wanted her. They would both wipe their past slates clean and begin again together. He was about to tell her all this when she cut him off.

As if reading his mind, Pandora said softly, "Franco and I, we are through. I'll miss him. I admired him greatly. He never looked down on me because I was a woman. He was extremely sensitive—wonderfully warm." She looked up at Ward from under her long lashes and grinned almost impishly. "He was able to bring out the very best in me. We were good together."

Unable to contain his shock and dismay, Ward rose and strode across the terrace, pouring himself another brandy. How could she speak so openly to him of her lover's talents in bed? Had she no consideration for his feelings? Surely, she must realize how he felt about her, even if he hadn't spoken of love yet. But that wasn't his fault; when had she ever given him the chance?

"You were good together, eh?" He fired the words at her.

The deep growl in his voice confounded Pandora. Why was he suddenly so out of sorts, when a moment before he had been mellow with good cheer?

"Yes, I consider Franco the finest, the most sensitive model I've ever known. He demanded perfection of me. At times it could prove tiring, but never disappointing."

Ward, raging inside at her words, gave her a long, cool look. "No doubt his perfection comes through long, careful practice."

"I suppose," she answered. "He was most complimentary of my skills. None of the others ever told me what they thought of my talents."

"My God, Pandora!" Ward was staring at her, unable to believe his ears. Surely, after three years in Europe and God alone knew how many lovers she could not still be so naive, needing praise from the men who bedded her. "I can't take any more of this. Forget your painting and your models and everything else in the world. We've waited too long to let anything spoil this night."

"You're right, Ward," she said softly. "You and I have a lot to discuss. That last night, I wasn't myself. I don't think you were either."

He'd dreaded her bringing up this subject. He didn't want her ever to know the hell she'd put him through that night. He'd damned himself a thousand times over for being so quick to dismiss her. If he had another chance—and he certainly intended to—she could call him anything she liked, so long as she came to him with love on her mind.

"If you want an apology, you have it," he said quickly.

"I'm the one who should apologize. You were right. I shouldn't have asked you to make love to me," she admitted. "You must have thought me an absolute wanton."

He laughed. He couldn't help himself. This was so outrageous. She'd just been explaining to him about her last in a long string of affairs, now she was apologizing for begging him to be her first three long years ago. He was the fool; he was the scoundrel.

Ward had been as nervous as a boy about their meeting tonight. He'd spent three years going over in his mind and heart their last time together—the night of Jacob and Angelica's wedding, the night Pandora had offered herself and he had refused. All because of his foolish hurt pride. In a fit of passion, she had called him by Jean Laffite's name, bruising his delicate ego. Bah! Laffite was long dead. What kind of man was he if he allowed himself to envy a ghost?

On that night—before she'd asked him to make love to her, before he had rejected her—his own mind had been set. He had planned to begin his earnest pursuit of Pandora Sherwood. He had thought it all through carefully. She was the only woman he wanted. Granted, she was outrageous and cared nothing about what anyone thought of her. She was given to eccentricities that often proved shocking, but wasn't he as well? That night he knew he loved her.

He had told her about the silver mine and that he planned to build a fine home in Galveston. He had not told her that he had already purchased four of the best lots on Broadway, that he had engaged architect Nicholas Clayton's services, and that he was planning his magnificent mansion with *her* in mind. He had never had a chance to tell her any of this. He had never had a chance to tell her how much she meant to him because he had not realized until after she was gone.

Again, he hesitated. If he could not deal with his jealousy at the simple, whispered name of a dead man, how could he live with ghosts of her many living lovers? He set his jaw in a grim, firm line.

"Ward, something's wrong. Tell me what it is." Pandora's voice shocked him out of his contemplative silence.

"It's seeing you again, Pandora. You've changed so."

"Have I?" There was pain in her question. She had changed and she knew it. She had hoped that Ward would not notice.

He came to her and took her hands in his, drawing her up to stand before him. Searching her face, his own unsmiling, he said quietly, "Yes, Pandora. The last time we were together, you felt a woman's need, but you were still a little girl. A precious child, tottering on the brink of life. Uncertain. Untried. Now you are a lovely, exotic, passionate woman. You've come into full bloom. You know who you are and what you want. There's a depth and a meaning to you that were never there before. I'm not even sure any longer that I'm man enough to deal with you." He drew her close, brushing her cheek with his lips—seeking, testing. "But I'm damn well going to try!"

Oh, Ward, you are man enough! Only Pandora's heart spoke the words as she leaned against his hard body, offering her parted lips to him, offering him *everything*— everything she had to give. Suddenly, three years of her life vanished in the blink of an eye. She was totally innocent again, wanting him, aching for him. They were not in Italy, but back in Galveston. She was pleading once more that he make her a woman, that he love her as she had never been loved before.

His hand brushed the side of her breast. She tensed. He hesitated but only for a moment. She moaned softly as his fingers closed around her, teasing the nipple through the thin fabric of her gown.

"Oh, Ward, please," she whispered between their feverish kisses.

In answer, he swept her up into his arms, carrying her inside to his bed.

He stared down into her face. Her green eyes gazed steadily, boldly up into his. He saw a lazy sensuality there that he had never seen before. She could speak silent volumes with those eyes. They were dark now, like the mysterious ancient hue of the soft moss that grew on the ruined walls of Pompeii. Her eyes were suffused with a softly glowing light, as if her very soul shone through. These were the eyes that had haunted his dreams since that last night in Galveston.

Pandora was the only woman he really wanted. And now, she was about to be his. But she was no tender virgin as she had been three years ago. She was an experienced woman, wise in the ways of love and passion. His skills would be tested to their very limits, but he vowed to please her, to erase all the others from her mind and from her heart. He leaned down to capture her lips.

Pandora's heart was beating wildly. She felt as if the whole world were moving in slow motion; her body felt heavy, her mind drugged. How many times had she thought of this moment, prayed for Ward to come to her? She had dreamed at night of their last time together. Only while she lay sleeping they had continued the scene beyond that evening's true ending. There was no rejection, only the warm melding of two bodies—aching for each other, dying to be one. Her dream was about to begin all over. Only this time her fantasy was real.

"Ward." His name whispered over her softly pouting lips.

He was beside her. She closed her eyes, trembling with pleasure, feeling his hands on her body. He kissed her deeply, drawing his breath through her open mouth until they breathed as one and it seemed as if their life forces mingled. His strong hands tangled in her hair, forcing her to lie as she was so that he might take his pleasure. Slowly, lightly then, he kissed her forehead, her eyelids, her nose. He nibbled at her lips, at the tip of her tongue. She squirmed with pleasure, with growing need.

His hands slid from her hair, gliding down her face and

throat, coming to rest on her breasts. Through the thin, silvery fabric, he kneaded and caressed. Her nipples rose to him in sweetly painful desire. He leaned down to suckle them. The smooth silk of her gown and the wetness of his mouth created a searing, engulfing heat.

With gentle expertise, Ward unwound the silver cord from her waist. The touch of his hands made her quiver as he loosened her gown. He was impatient. So was she.

He unfastened her silver sandals, fondling her tender soles until she writhed with pleasure. The heat of his caresses flowed up her legs, centering between them, throbbing like a fresh-burned brand. She needed him *now!*

But instead of taking her immediately, Ward rose from the bed. He poured a glass of wine, took a sip, then handed it to her.

"Drink," he ordered.

Pandora raised up on one elbow. Her gown slipped from one shoulder, exposing her right breast. He stared, a hungry look in his dark eyes, and smiled.

"And the other!" he commanded.

The silvery cobweb of fabric slipped to her waist. For a long time he stood some distance away, gazing at her until her nipples grew hard under his hungry stare.

He came back to stand beside the bed, still looking at her, but now his eyes held hers. As their gazes remained locked, he reached down with both hands, fondling her lovingly.

Pandora began to tremble. His hands, teasing her breasts, seemed to be reaching inside her to tug at new cords of desire. He sat beside her then, and eased the gown down over her hips, letting one of his large, smooth hands slide over her quivering belly.

"I was a fool to send you away. I wanted you that night," he said, still staring into her eyes, still letting his hands play over her body. "I think I've always wanted you, Pandora. I know I always will."

She shook her head. Why did his words sound so familiar? Right now she couldn't think, she could only feel. At the moment, his hand was touching the tight red curls between her thighs. Her eyes flickered closed for a moment, avoiding his gaze, and the tip of her tongue smoothed wetly over her lips. He saw the movement and quickly pressed his mouth to hers for an instant, touching tongue to tongue.

"Tonight," he began. He drew away slightly, only his lips still teasing her mouth as he spoke. "Tonight, right now, I'm about to make love to you. The way I've wanted to for so long. There will be no holding back, no turning away. I'm going to kiss you . . ." He did. "And touch you . . . and make you want me like you've never wanted any other man in your life."

"Oh, Ward, I *do* want you!"

He smiled and drew an invisible line with one finger between her breasts. "And after we're done," he continued, "I'm going to sleep inside you so that when we awake we can begin all over again."

Something between a soft moan and a gasp escaped Pandora's lips. Ward's eyes blazed at her, daring her to refuse him as he had refused her on that night so long ago.

"And, Pandora," he added, matter-of-factly, "I am going to marry you!"

Before his words even had time to sink in, he stripped her gown from her, then shed his own clothes. His bold gaze never left her face as one by one his garments were cast in a heap on the floor—shirt, boots, stockings, britches. She felt heat flush her face. The lamp overhead blazed brightly, casting a golden glow on his naked body. Muscles corded his shoulders, arms, and thighs. His waist was narrow, his stomach flat, his legs long and furred with dark hair as was his chest, his belly. And that secret part of him, the part she had dared not visualize even in her dreams, rose toward her stiff with desire. She had seen many a naked man in her studio. But never had the sight made her ache with the exquisite need she felt as she gazed at Ward.

Hands on hips, he turned, showing her his taut buttocks and the thick muscles of his back. "Take a good look," he said. "Along with a silver mine and a thriving jewelry business and a pink marble palace on Broadway, Pandora, this is what you get in the bargain."

She tried to speak, but her vocal cords seemed paralyzed. All she could do was stare at the naked, godlike body before her and feel the heat and desperation of her need. She lay back on the bed, limp and waiting. She had never been so afraid in her life. Nor had she ever felt such excitement.

When he came to her, she wrapped her arms around him, devouring his lips, urging him on with whimpers and sighs.

Ward had to hold himself in check. Pandora was like a tigress. She clawed his shoulders and back, bit his neck, kissed him with long wet strokes of her tongue. But he knew better than to act too soon. He let his hands trail lightly down her sides as she lay pinned beneath him. He felt a shudder run through the length of her body. A low moan escaped her. She whispered his name over and over again. *His* name this time! He slid down over her, holding her tightly about the waist. With the tip of his tongue, he made tight wet circles around her nipples, her navel, then trailed farther down to leave a damp design on her quivering white belly.

"Ward darling!" she gasped. "Oh, please . . . please!"

But he was determined not to be rushed, not to let her convince him that the time had come.

"Please *what?*" he whispered into the thatch of flame between her thighs. "Tell me, Pandora."

Her fingers, tangled in his hair, gripped convulsively. She moaned again. Another shudder racked her body.

"What, Pandora? What do you want?" he demanded again.

Her hips arched suddenly upward.

"You," she cried. "I want you, Ward! All of you!"

Her whole body was aflame by the time his first thrust found its slick, hot mark. Pandora barely felt the pain, the release was so great . . . and the wonderful feeling of being filled. She relaxed for an instant and sighed with pleasure, but then her hips began to move rhythmically.

Ward, too, paused a moment after he entered her and met the unexpected barrier. "My God!" he cried aloud. Could it be? But there was little time to think of anything but his own aching need and the insistent motion of Pandora's hips.

They loved each other frantically, savagely, as if they had been waiting lifetimes for this one moment. They could not get enough of each other—mouths, tongues, hands, bodies. Everything kissed and touched and stroked and coupled.

Pandora gripped Ward's waist with her legs, drawing him deeper, deeper, deeper. All that she had felt before—the need, the burning, the aching, the pleasure—combined into one explosive moment of such intense sensation that she thought she might die in that instant. The purest kind of ecstasy washed over her time and again like great crashing waves in a storm.

Scenes unfolded in her mind—Laffite and Nicolette in the hammock, on the beach, at the grove, in their gilded bed— always together, always making love. All the while, she was totally aware that the man filling her, surrounding her, stroking her on toward this whirlpool of bliss was Ward Gabriel.

Afterward, Ward stayed as he had said he would—inside her. They lay face to face, exhausted, overwhelmed, but unable to draw apart, still as one in each other's arms, still joined intimately.

"Pandora," Ward whispered against her hair, "you should have told me."

"Told you what?" she asked dreamily.

"I thought you'd had lovers. Many lovers. After all this time, I never dreamed . . ."

"Sh-h-h!" she whispered. "It doesn't matter."

"Like hell!" he cursed. "It matters to me! I was too rough with you. You should have told me."

She laughed softly. "Well, next time we won't have to worry about that, will we?"

Next time, she knew, would come very soon. Already, as she lay with him, kissing him deeply and stroking his thighs, she could feel Ward growing again inside her—filling her once more. The sensation aroused new need within her. Soon his hips began a slow undulating motion. She followed his lead. All the suspense and wonder and pleasure began building again.

By the time they finally slept, gold and coral streaks of the new spring dawn were slipping in through the open window, creeping across the cream-colored marble floor where their clothes lay intimately tangled, even as their bodies were on the bed.

They sat across from each other at a round table on the terrace. Pandora traced the blue and yellow pattern in the Spanish tile of the tabletop with one finger. Ward carefully peeled a blood orange with a silver knife.

Pandora sipped her strong Italian coffee, wondering what to say, wishing Ward would begin the conversation. He seemed totally absorbed in his sticky task. What was he thinking? It was all well and good in the dead of night to defy morality in order to satisfy desires. But the hot light of day was another matter, bringing a burning feeling of guilt blazing down on her head.

Finally, with a sigh of resignation, Pandora began, "Ward, what you said last night . . . did you really mean it?"

He grinned at her—a mischievous, boyish grin. "I said a lot of things, Pan. Which thing?"

"About marrying me?" she said hesitantly.

Still concentrating on his orange, he nodded. "Yep!"

"Then last night made you realize the truth." She sighed with relief, hardly able to believe this wonderful turn of events.

"What truth?" he asked. "That we love each other? I've known that for a long time, darling."

"No, that's not what I mean, Ward. You know now that you were truly Jean Laffite. That's such a relief . . ."

"Damn the man!" He stared at her, his knife still poised. "Are you trying to tell me that *he* loved you last night, that I had no part in what went on? Pandora, I'm the one who loves you! I'm the one who's going to marry you! Now, forget your silly dreams."

Pandora felt a sudden pain shoot through her heart. "Ward, I can't marry you," she said quietly. "Not if you won't admit the truth about our love." She expected another outburst from him and braced herself for the explosion.

Instead, he grinned again and handed her a slice of

orange. "I figured you'd say that. But it's no use arguing with me. You're as good as Mrs. Ward Gabriel already. If Jean Laffite wants you, tell him to come get you himself. But you'd better warn that damned pirate that I just might challenge him to a duel." Ward brandished his small, silver blade and laughed. "Fruit knives at ten paces! I'm the one who's going to marry you, Pandora, like it or not."

His flippant attitude enraged her. She shot him a mutinous look with her green eyes. "I'd say that's my decision to make."

He nodded. "You're right."

"And I say *no!*"

Suddenly, she felt his hand on her bare knee. She was dressed in another of his robes, better she'd thought than her skimpy costume for this time of day. Flipping the soft fabric aside, Ward slid his hand up between her thighs. She felt herself begin to tremble and protested softly. Her leg muscles responded to his touch, hugging his hand, urging it upward until he easily reached his goal.

"See?" he said, withdrawing his exploring fingers. "There's nothing more to discuss. We'll do whatever you like—marry here, on the ship home, or we can wait and have a huge affair back in Galveston."

Pandora put the heel of her palm to her forehead. Her head ached as if she had been pounding it against a brick wall. There was no reasoning with him. How could she marry him when he considered their past lives together one enormous joke? "Ward, you aren't listening to me?"

"Words don't matter. Actions do!" He stood up and stretched, then came to stand over her, staring down into her eyes. They had a slight tilt to them when she was being stubborn. It was there now. He leaned down and kissed her—deeply, expertly.

"I'm telling you, Pandora," he whispered, smiling down into her eyes, "last night was the ruination of us both. You don't have any basis for comparison, but I do. There is no doubt in my mind that you and I were made for each other. As a businessman I know a good deal when I find one and the two of us, my love, are the best deal I've ever come across. You'd be a fool not to marry me. Besides, I've already written to your uncle and we have his permission. I took care of that matter months ago, as soon as I realized that I was hot on your trail. Everyone in Galveston knows that we're engaged. There'll be a real scandal if you refuse me.''

Pandora jerked away from him, but realized immediately that this was just the sort of thing Laffite would have done. ''Of all the pompous . . .''

Ward nodded. ''You have me pegged exactly! That's another thing—we understand each other. Now, to the details. How many children would you like? I'd thought two a nice number, but if you really want a large family . . .''

Pandora jumped up and stamped her bare foot on the terrace, looking perfectly adorable in her rage, Ward thought. *''Children?''* she shrieked at him.

He shrugged.

''Ward Gabriel, you are the most horrible, insufferable, stupid, unfeeling, despicable . . .''

''Don't forget *devious,*'' he added with a husky laugh.

''Oh!'' Pandora whirled away from him to storm into the villa, meaning to get her clothes and leave. But she never escaped the terrace. Ward caught her hand and twirled her around into his arms.

''I love you, too,'' he whispered. Then he captured her angrily pouting lips, silencing her, while his hands inside the robe took away her fight and turned it into a different kind of fire.

Two weeks later, the *Corsica* sailed out of Naples on a fine, clear day. Puffs of pure white clouds floated like angels' wings high above in the cerulean-blue sky. As the escort boat towed the great ship out of Naples Bay, Captain Marco, in full dress uniform, stood in the ballroom against a bank of white lilies. Many of the passengers gathered to see the ceremony. They all agreed a wedding was a lovely way to begin a voyage.

''I now pronounce you man and wife!'' the captain boomed in his best shipboard voice.

Pandora stared up at Ward, so tall and handsome beside her, and wondered vaguely how this had happened. After the morning at his villa, he had dogged her every step. He showered her with lavish gifts, flowers, candy, banquets delivered to her rooms. He had insisted they take a carriage to Pompeii's ancient ruins. He had told the guide there that they were on their honeymoon and she had blushed all day at the stares they received. They had climbed Vesuvious and tossed pumice stones into the glowing crater. They went to the opera, to the ballet, and to another party at Magnolia's Capri villa. -

The countess, glowing with pleasure, announced their engagement in front of a huge crowd that night and Ward had slipped an enormous diamond on Pandora's finger. She had been told only that it would be an "intimate supper" with the Bellinis. She had been furious, amazed, and finally delighted in spite of herself.

That evening, after the party, they had gone back to his villa—"to talk," she'd insisted. Pandora determined to make Ward see the light or take back his ring. But whenever she brought up Nicolette and Laffite, Ward only scoffed. There had been little time for conversation in Ward's bed. They made love all night—beautiful, wonderful, heart-stopping love. The next morning, she still wore his diamond.

And now, here she stood, gowned in bridal lace and satin, staring up into the warmest, most dazzling gray eyes she had ever seen—eyes that were making glorious love to her at this very moment. Making her weak in the knees. Making her ache in that special place. Making her want nothing in the world but to be with this man, to hold him, to love him, to bear his children.

Ward smiled down at her, pleasure and triumph clear in his expression. "Happy, Mrs. Gabriel?" he whispered.

"How should I know?" she answered curtly. "You haven't given me a moment to breathe, much less to think."

He leaned down and gave her a light kiss. "Well, when you have time to think, my darling, think about this: I love you! I always have and I always will!"

It was hopeless. She could no more fight her feelings for him than she could swim back to Galveston. What did it matter if Ward believed or not? She remembered and she knew. "I love you, too, Ward. I *really* do!"

They leaned into each other, their lips meeting in a deep and lingering kiss that sent tongues of fire racing through Pandora's blood. The captain and the passengers applauded, but Pandora heard nothing but the sound of her own heart beating against Ward's.

Chapter Sixteen

The last patient of the day had left the office over an hour ago. But still Jacob sat at his desk—creating paperwork, cleaning out a drawer, finally sitting and simply gazing out the window at the glorious Galveston sunset. The red-gold riot in the sky reminded him of the fiery shade of Pandora's hair.

"Pandora," he sighed aloud. "Ah, Pandora, what a mess I made of things."

Never a day went by that he didn't think of her, wondering how she was, where she was. It would seem reasonable to expect that after three long years his memory of her would have faded. But now—*especially* now, the day she was due to return to Galveston—her image was sharper in his mind than it had ever been.

Tonight he would see her again. The ship bringing her back was scheduled to dock within the hour. Ward Gabriel had sent word from Italy that he was bringing Pandora home with him, that they were to be married. Of course, Tabitha

Sherwood had wasted no time in arranging an elaborate engagement party for the night of their arrival. In a few hours, Jacob would be forced to go with Angelica to the Sherwood mansion on Broadway to celebrate the betrothal of the woman he should have married.

"How different my life would have been, if only . . ." He stared down at his hands and sighed.

Everyone in town would be there tonight. All talk would center around the coming "joyous event," as Angelica insisted upon calling it. She mentioned the wedding a dozen times a day, purposely rubbing salt into his wounds. He knew well enough the mistakes he'd made. No one needed to remind him, least of all his wife.

Jacob shook his head sadly. "Yes, what a mess!" he muttered.

Three years since he'd seen her. These last three years had been hard, the most difficult of his life. Not only had he been faced with the demanding work and long hours of setting up his practice in Galveston and making his reputation, but there had been his wife to deal with as well. And the gossip, always the gossip. Wherever Angelica went, whatever Angelica did there was gossip. The worst had come a few months after their marriage, when her still-slender waist made it obvious to everyone in Galveston that Angelica Saenger was not with child. They all whispered that she had tricked Jacob into marrying her.

He laughed humorlessly at the thought. "Wouldn't their tongues wag if they knew the *whole* truth?"

He didn't care. He could close his mind and his ears to their idle chatter. Angelica was different. Even while she seemed determined to stir up talk—as if she was trying to top her cousin's former notoriety—each new rumor, each whispered remark set Angelica off in a rage. Her anger was the easy part; Jacob had learned to deal with that. It was the depression that came afterward that confounded him. Lately it had seemed that she might be losing touch with reality altogether.

Each month Angelica imagined herself pregnant; each month she visited his father for an examination. And each month she came home screaming and sobbing and threatening him with divorce when his father gave her a negative report.

"You don't want me to have a child!" she would shriek. "I know you, you're doing something to prevent it. I won't have it, Jacob. Do you hear me? Damn you to hell, I married you, you *owe* me a child!"

She was obsessed with becoming a mother. As if motherhood could instantly make their shambles of a marriage perfect and silence the wagging tongues. Jacob sighed. Angelica wanted a child for all the wrong reasons. Perhaps that was the very reason she was unable to conceive.

Last week, she had come to him, her pale blue eyes redrimmed from her most recent fit of crying. But her tears had dried abruptly, leaving her eyes glittering with excitement. "We can have a child. I know a way, my darling." He'd winced. She never called him that unless she had reached the point of extreme hysteria—so extreme that she actually became deceptively calm.

She'd gone on to confide her plan to him. She would quietly whisper to the right women in town that she was expecting. Then she would go away for a few months, to visit a cousin of her mother's in Mobile. At the right time— say, five months later—Jacob was bound to deliver the right baby for them. A boy she thought would be nice, but that really didn't matter as long as the child was healthy and perfect.

"What of my patient, the baby's mother?" he'd asked, horrified, but trying to maintain a calm facade. "What do I tell her?"

Angelica had flipped her lace fan in annoyance. "That the baby died, of course. Don't act dull-witted, Jacob."

Jacob had explained as patiently as he could all the reasons that such a plan was impossible, the most obvious one being that if he gave Angelica the infant, there would be no body to present to the sad parents when he announced the death of their child.

Her lovely face had twisted into a grotesque mask as she'd thought this problem over. From her expression, Jacob had dreaded to hear her solution. No doubt her next step would involve robbing graves.

"Angelica, you can't be serious about this."

"I am, Jacob!" Her voice had been as cold as death. "If you don't agree to help, then I'll simply divorce you."

She knew that was her one effective weapon. Jacob worshipped his father and the old man believed that marriages were binding and made in heaven. Even though Jacob realized that no kind and understanding God would have had any hand in joining him to Angelica for eternity, old Dr. Saenger believed it totally. A divorce might truly mean the end to him. His heart was bad; he couldn't stand the shock. So Jacob kept his peace and let Angelica think that he was considering her insane proposal.

He ran a shaky hand through his rumpled hair and shook his head. A glance at the clock told him that he could hide in his office no longer. It was time to leave, time to go home and prepare himself as best he could to see Pandora again.

Angelica heard her father-in-law call her once, twice, a third time from the downstairs hall. He had misplaced his heart pills and was calling for her to find them.

She ignored him. "Tiresome old fool!" she muttered, making a face at her reflection in her mirror. She had better things to do than act as his nursemaid. She had to look perfect tonight. Pandora was coming home.

She smiled at her mirror image and let her tongue glide sensually over her lips. Pandora was coming home, but that wasn't the important part. Ward Gabriel was returning, too. Angelica had been waiting a long time for this. Ward had made it very clear that night as he'd held her close that he found her quite attractive. If Jacob—in his drunken haze—hadn't stumbled out into the garden that night, Ward and his silver mine and the fabulous pink palace he'd built would all be hers now.

"But never mind," she told her image. "I still have a chance."

After all, Ward and Pandora were *only* engaged. "There's many a slip 'tween the cup and the lip," she sang softly.

She stood and gazed at her full reflection in the looking glass. She smoothed her hands down over her slim waist. For once, she was glad that she wasn't carrying Jacob's

child. She was deliriously happy that she hadn't conceived.
That would have complicated things.

As she appraised her figure with half-closed eyes, she had
to smile. Her black silk gown fit her full bosom and narrow
waist like a second skin before belling out over her hips into
an extravagantly full skirt. A curved line of cherry silk roses
swept from one shoulder down to the waist, and the petticoats that peeked out when she walked were cherry and
white striped. The gown was cut so low in front that she had
to breathe carefully or her nipples rose startlingly above the
black silk. She would be careful, she vowed, until she got
Ward alone. Then she planned to use every womanly wile
she knew.

No one understood better than Angelica herself what a
mistake she had made in marrying Jacob Saenger. She still
blamed her cousin. Pandora had known all the while that
Angelica would want the man she chose. Angelica was
firmly convinced that Pandora had become betrothed to
Jacob first, realizing that Angelica could and would take
him. With her cousin safely married and out of the way,
Pandora could now go after the real man of her dreams—
Ward Gabriel.

"You were a little fool to fall for her ploy!" Angelica
snapped at her reflection. She'd been only a child when she
married Jacob; now she was as much a woman as Pandora,
with a woman's understanding of things. If her cousin
thought she had the last laugh, she was sadly mistaken.

The smile that curved Angelica's lips had a feral look
about it. "Yes, they are only engaged," she reminded
herself again. "After tonight, who can tell?"

Galveston reminded Pandora of Poseidon's temple on
Atlantis as described by Plato, all overlaid with gold and
coppery orichalcum, as the setting sun blazed over her
island home.

"I'd forgotten how beautiful this place is and how much I
love it," she whispered, squeezing Ward's hand.

"You're catching it in its best light, darling. It's not so
magical when the tropical cyclones threaten to wash it
away."

261

She gazed up at him and he saw tears in her large emerald eyes. "Any time, any weather, it's the best place on earth as long as you're here with me. I don't ever want to leave again, Ward."

He put his arm around her and hugged her close. "Then you don't have to, my love. We'll stay right here on our little speck of heaven and raise our children and watch them raise our grandchildren. We'll become pillars of the community and when I've grown a long white beard and you have turned into a charmingly plump dumpling of a woman, we'll hold court at our castle and still be just as much in love as we are this very moment." He brushed her temple with his lips.

"We *are* in love, aren't we?" After their honeymoon voyage home, she wondered that there could be any doubt left in her mind. But Ward still bristled when she made the slightest reference to Laffite or her other life as Nicolette. Why couldn't he simply accept the truth as she did?

On the journey home, Ward had taken every opportunity to show her how much he loved her by taking her to their bed whenever the spirit moved him.

"We'll christen Pandora's Palace the moment we arrive, darling," he whispered. "Then you'll know how much you're loved. As for whether you love me . . . well, I'm willing to settle for what I have. If you loved me any more, I'm afraid I might die from it. I'm only mortal after all. There are limits to my endurance."

Pandora flushed scarlet and avoided his eyes. She could hardly believe that statement after the prowess he'd shown in bed last night. She was still tired and guessed that she would be slightly sore for days to come. Her new husband continued to amaze and delight her.

"Just wait until we get to your palace, my darling." He whispered the words against her ear, sending a shiver of anticipation through her.

"You *are* joking about this palace, aren't you?" She tried to lead him away from his passionate thoughts. The other passengers were staring at them and whispering.

"Joking?" He threw back his head and laughed. "Wait till you see it, darling! Nicholas Clayton outdid himself this time. It's been three years in the building. The materials and furnishings came from all over—Italian marbles, Spanish tiles, French antiques, South American mahogany. And our bed!" he whispered. "No, I'm not going to ruin the surprise."

Pandora was about to press him for more details, especially about the marvelous bed, but the gangway was in place and it was time to disembark.

She sighed wearily as they set foot on the dock. "I'm so tired, darling. I can hardly wait to get home."

Ward squeezed her arm. "I can hardly wait either," he said, but obviously being tired had little to do with his thoughts.

"Miss Pandora!" someone called.

She glanced about and saw Cassie coming toward them from the Sherwoods' buggy. The woman was crying and laughing all at the same time. She rushed to her mistress and they embraced, both sobbing happily.

"Lordy, you look so fine!" Cassie said at last. "You, too, Mr. Ward. We got to hurry now."

"Hurry?" Pandora asked. "Why? What's wrong?"

"Nothing's wrong, Miss Pan. But Miz Tabitha's got the whole town coming to your engagement party tonight. You'll just have time to change."

"Engagement party?" Pandora cried. "But Cassie . . ."

Ward squeezed her arm to silence her. "I think I can explain, darling," he said. "I sent a message to your aunt and uncle a few days before we left Naples. At that time, you still hadn't decided when you wanted to get married. So, they don't know."

"Don't know what?" Cassie asked, her big dark eyes suspicious suddenly.

"That we're already married, Cass!" Pandora hugged the surprised woman as she cried out her news.

"Lordy, Miz Tabitha'll be fit to be tied!" Cassie said, rolling her eyes.

Pandora looked worried. She knew her aunt would be disappointed that they had spoiled her grand evening.

"There's really no problem, ladies," Ward told them. "You go back and tell them, Cass, that we'll be there shortly. Don't break our news to anyone. We'll go home and change, then arrive a bit late for the party. We'll tell everyone the truth as soon as we get there. Won't they be surprised!"

Pandora laughed. "I like it, Ward. Your plan has just the sort of flair I enjoy most."

He hugged her right there on the dock with passengers, coachmen, and stevedores looking on and grinning. "I thought you'd agree. I know the woman I love."

Pandora's Palace, as Ward insisted on calling his mansion, was everything and more that he promised. The new Mrs. Gabriel could hardly believe her eyes as she drove up in front. The four lots on which it stood had been a wilderness three years ago. Now "Gabriel's folly," as many Galvestonians were calling her new home, rose to a height of three stories with circular towers, wide verandas, balconies at the upper floors, and a profusion of stained glass, wrought iron, and exquisite statuary.

"Ward, I don't believe it!" she kept murmuring as he led her from room to room, delighting in her praise.

"Library, front and back parlors, music room, conservatory, formal and informal dining rooms, a study for me, an artist's studio for you, eight bedrooms . . ."

"Oh, Ward, stop it!" she cried. "You're making me dizzy!"

He swept her up in his arms then and kissed her deeply. "And *the* bed!" he whispered.

Ward carried her up the wide, mahogany staircase with its curving banister and intricate carvings. In moments, they were in the master suite—bedroom, sitting room, dressing rooms, and bath—all done in scarlet damask and gold.

"Your bed, madame!" Ward announced.

Pandora, who had been laughing and snuggling in his arms, suddenly fell silent. Dizziness blurred her vision for an instant. She blinked her eyes rapidly and looked again. It couldn't be, but it was!

"Ward, where did you get that bed?" she demanded.

His face fell. "You don't like it?"

"It's not that. It's just . . ." Her words broke off. How

264

could she tell him? How could she explain to him that she knew this bed, that she had slept in it before, that it was the same bed in which Jean Laffite had made love so often to his Nicolette. There was not the slightest doubt. The design was exactly the same. It had the same ornate crest on the headboard. She could still hear Laffite laughing, telling Nicolette, the first time she slept in it, that he had "borrowed" it from a Spanish king just for her.

"Ward, tell me where you found it," she pleaded.

He shrugged. "In Paris. A dealer there heard that I was buying only the finest antiques for a home I was building. He contacted me. I went to see the bed and I knew it was perfect for this room . . . for *you,* Pandora."

"Did he tell you any of its history?"

He nodded and walked over to touch the design on the headboard. "That's the emblem of King Carlos of Spain. The bed was made for him and he took it with him from place to place. The dealer told me that a gang of cutthroats stole it from his ship and it eventually wound up in America. Some pirate, he said, was supposed to have owned it for a time. How it got to France from the States is a mystery. Now it's right where it belongs."

Pandora nodded. "Yes, exactly where it belongs," she said wistfully, remembering how it had looked in the bedroom at *Maison Rouge.*

Ward let out a whistling breath of relief. "You do like it then? I was afraid you were going to tell me you didn't."

She put her arms around him and hugged him soundly. "Yes, darling, I love it." She almost added, "I always have," but she caught herself in time.

Everyone who was anyone in Galveston was waiting expectantly at the Sherwood home for the couple of honor to arrive. Although word of Pandora's success as an artist had not leaked back to Galveston to set tongues wagging, the gossips still relished the scandal of her broken engagement and her unexplained disappearance immediately following Jacob and Angelica's wedding. Now she was returning home, triumphant, to a vertible palace built in her honor.

The best silver, china, and crystal had been brought out

for the occasion. The second best set had been used when Pandora's engagement to Jacob had been announced. But Ward Gabriel was different, Tabitha Sherwood had told her husband; he was special, the catch of the decade.

Jacob and Angelica were the first to arrive. Angelica insisted they be early in spite of the fact that Jacob was late getting home from his office. Just like him, she thought, to work past the usual hour when he knows we have important plans for the evening.

Jacob had been pleasantly surprised when he'd arrived home. He'd expected his wife to throw one of her tantrums. Instead, she had simply ignored him, refusing to say a word after she ordered him to hurry and dress. Fine, he'd thought. They really had nothing to say to each other anyway.

Now, Jacob stood in a far corner of the Gold Room, watching his extravagantly gowned wife flit about like an excited monarch butterfly in her black and scarlet costume. He wanted to point out to her that black was inappropriate for the occasion, but he decided to let it go. Her mother had taken care of the admonishment the moment they'd arrived.

Horror stricken, Tabitha Sherwood had clutched her throat and shrieked, "Angelica, how could you? A *black* gown! One never wears black to any sort of nuptial occasion and you know it."

"One wears what one chooses to wear, Mother, and I choose black. I want to stand out in the crowd."

Well, she certainly did that! Jacob mused. She had every man in the room at her beck and call—bringing her cups of punch, tiny cakes, or just standing over her leering at her dangerously low cleavage, praying for her to take a deep breath. Jacob had to agree with his mother-in-law on this one occasion. Angelica's costume and behavior were scandalous. She looked more suitable for an assignation on Postoffice Street than for an engagement soiree on Broadway.

Angelica knew Jacob was staring at her, but what did it matter? She'd had all the lectures she could stomach on the proper behavior of a doctor's wife. She'd also had quite enough of her husband, his father, the old house on

Avenue O—enough of everything, she told herself, except Ward Gabriel.

She stood surrounded by men of all ages, each one elbowing the other to get a bit closer to her. Just now her father's short, balding lawyer, Mr. Weatherbee, had the choice position directly before her. The poor man was not quite tall enough to get a proper view down the front of her dress. Feeling suddenly indulgent and giggling girlishly, Angelica bent forward, allowing the short fellow a bird's eye view of her pale bosom. Old Mr. Weatherbee blushed to the very top of his bald head and wiped a sweating palm over his eyes.

She touched his ruddy cheek. "Poor dear, you must be coming down with a fever," she crooned. All the others in the circle howled with delight as Weatherbee scurried away.

At the sound of a carriage out front, all the guests pressed toward the door, each one wanting to be the first to catch sight of the guests of honor. Jacob frowned, noting that Angelica hung back. That surprised him. He'd thought she would have shoved past the others in order to be the first to greet Pandora and Ward. She was up to something. He didn't like it.

Jacob was right. Angelica had her campaign map carefully drawn. She wanted to surprise Ward, to catch him alone when he least expected to see her. While all the others gathered around, she had a chance to gauge her opposition. Pandora, she admitted grudgingly, looked marvelous. She was gowned in seafoam satin, embroidered with pink pearls in a shell pattern that covered her bodice and half the full skirt. Petticoats of silver tissue gleamed beneath the deep ruffle at the hem, and a fabulous necklace of silver set with pink and white cameos covered her throat and seemed to point like an arrow to the full swell of her breasts.

As all the guests pressed in around Pandora, Ward stepped back to avoid the crush. He stood by smiling, feeling understandably proud as he watched the ladies gush over his beautiful bride while the men looked on with envy. He still had to pinch himself now and again to believe that she was actually his. He wondered why he had waited so long to pursue her. He had realized years ago that she was the only woman he could ever love. He grimaced slightly, remembering how close he had come to losing her. If it hadn't been for her scheming little cousin . . .

A hand touched his. "Ward, how wonderful to see you again."

"Why, Angelica." He smiled down into her glowing face, his eyes going, in spite of himself, to the deep valley between her breasts. "I was just thinking about you."

She laughed softly. "I'm glad to hear that. I've been thinking about you more often than I like to admit." She went up on tiptoe and brushed his cheek with her lips. "I'm glad you're back, Ward. Welcome home."

Pandora turned just in time to see her cousin kiss her husband. It all seemed very innocent. But something about the look on Angelica's face, the gleam of her pale eyes struck a warning chord in Pandora's heart. She moved as swiftly as she could toward the two of them.

Angelica saw her coming and quickly whispered to Ward, "I'm leaving Jacob so you don't have to marry Pandora after all. I remember everything you told me that you wanted in a wife. I'm the one you need, Ward, not her. Go ahead and announce your engagement. We'll work out our plans later. Of course, you'll want to let my cousin down gently. I understand that. You needn't worry. Jacob will welcome her back." Then, quickly, Angelica moved away through the crowd.

Ward stood stunned, staring after her. He tried to think back to what he might have said to her on that night so long ago. The whole evening was a blur.

Pandora interrupted her husband's frenzied thoughts. "Darling, I think it's time now," she whispered.

Ward stared down at Pandora lovingly. He decided not to tell her about her cousin's crazy declaration. What did it matter? In a few moments, Angelica and all of Galveston would know the truth.

"Yes," Ward agreed. "We shouldn't wait any longer."

Before they could make their announcement, Horace Sherwood took the floor, calling out for attention. "My dear friends, we all know that we are here tonight to welcome

Pandora and Ward back to Galveston and to wish them well on their coming marriage. I think a toast is in order.''

A murmur of excitement swept the room. The guests applauded and cast congratulatory smiles toward the couple.

Taking Pandora's hand, Ward led her toward Mr. Sherwood. "Horace, we'd like to say a few words, if we may.''

"Of course, Ward. Come right up here.''

Ward kept an arm protectively about Pandora's slim waist as they turned toward the crowd. Oddly enough, it was Angelica's face that stood out when he looked about the room. She was smiling, a secretive, mysterious smile meant only for him.

"When I wrote to Horace, asking his permission to marry his lovely niece, I assumed that we'd come back home for the biggest, finest wedding Galveston ever saw.'' He paused and looked down at Pandora, gazing into her eyes adoringly. "Well, I hate to disappoint all of you, but . . .''

An anxious murmur rustled through the room. Only Angelica seemed pleased by what Ward had said so far.

Ward raised his hand for silence. He laughed and said, "Don't get me wrong, folks! Pandora and I aren't breaking our engagement. It's just that we couldn't wait. We were married on the ship coming home.''

Once again, Ward's gaze fell on Angelica. Her smile froze for an instant, then her expression turned into something as near hatred as he had ever seen. A moment later, she fled the room. No one else noticed. The guests were too busy oohing and ahing and offering congratulations to the happy couple.

It was long after dinner before Jacob Saenger approached Pandora and asked her to dance.

"I've been trying to get a moment to speak with you all night, Pandora, but you've been surrounded.''

Pandora had noticed when she first set eyes on Jacob earlier that he had changed. Now the full impact of the difference hit her. When last she'd seen him, Jacob had looked years younger. Tonight, he wore the expression of an aging man trying desperately to hold on to his youth.

Lines of fatigue creased the corners of his eyes. A worried frown seemed permanently imprinted on his face. His gaze was dull and troubled. His shoulders sagged as if he carried some great weight.

"I've been wanting to talk to you, too, Jacob," she said quietly. "Come. Let's go out to the veranda."

The warm night breeze outside was scented with salt and the sweet perfume of oleanders. For a moment, Pandora closed her eyes and the years blew away, taking her back . . . back to her lonely childhood, when she'd never felt that she truly belonged. How different her life was now.

"Where's Angelica?" Pandora asked. It suddenly dawned on her that, though she had seen her cousin earlier, they had not even said hello all evening.

Jacob shrugged. "I suppose she went home."

"Without even telling you?"

"She seldom tells me anything these days. She probably had one of her headaches."

"I'm sorry, Jacob." Pandora wasn't sure what she was sorry about, but it seemed the proper thing to say at the moment.

Jacob reached out and touched Pandora's hand, not looking into her face. "No, Pandora. I'm the one who's sorry. I made a terrible mistake by not marrying you."

Gently, Pandora drew her hand away. "Jacob, we're *both* married now. I don't think we should talk about that. I'm happy. I'd hoped you were happy, too."

Gripping her shoulders, he turned her to face him. His eyes blazed with emotion. "How could I be happy with anyone but you, Pandora? Our parents understood what I was too foolish to see—that you and I belong together."

"No, Jacob!" Pandora shrugged away from his touch and his gaze. "You mustn't say such things. You have a wife and I have a husband. I'll always feel something special for you, but *I love Ward!*"

"Then I suppose there's nothing more you have to say to me."

Pandora stared at Jacob. How could he do this to her? After all that he had put her through! She wanted to rage at him, to remind him that he had broken their engagement

. . . that he was the one who had sent her fleeing to Europe in despair. But his voice was so filled with pain that she could not lash out at him. Instead, she gripped his hand and said softly, "Jacob, you know I'll always be your friend. If you ever need me, I'll be there."

"Thank you, Pandora. As it happens, I need a friend just now. *Desperately!*"

Jacob went on to tell Pandora everything—far more than she wanted to hear about his life with Angelica. She ached for him, but what could she do? When she asked as much, Jacob replied with a weak smile, "You've done more than your share already, Pandora, just listening to me whine about my misery."

Then he turned and walked back inside, leaving Pandora alone in the starry, perfumed night. As she gazed up at the sky, trying to dispel the gloom of Jacob's tale, another hand touched hers.

"Darling, it's getting late. Are you ready to go home?"

Pandora turned and clung to Ward. How strong and good and loving he was. Suddenly, she wanted nothing more than to be with him, to show him how much his love meant to her.

"I'm such a lucky woman," she whispered, staring up at him through tear-misted eyes. "Yes, take me home, my darling. Please, take me home."

The great golden bed cradled Pandora as if it had been awaiting her return, lo, these many years. Late in the night, as she and Ward held each other—touching, kissing, making glorious love—visions of the past mingled with the present in a strange, exotic mirage. One moment, Ward was staring down into her face with his stormy-gray eyes, watching for the instant when total ecstasy would claim her. As the height of pleasure arrived, she saw his eyes turn green and cunning, and her hands on his naked body felt the old, dear scars.

The shade of Jean Laffite haunted the bed, stealing into Ward's body to love her from the grave. Pandora found his ghostly visitation doubly satisfying. She knew for certain that the long-sought spirit of her soul-mate resided in her new husband's body. A body that even now was a part of hers.

Ward knelt over her, stroking slowly, whispering his litany of love words, caressing her breasts, and smiling into her wide green eyes.

"I love to watch the expression on your face, darling. You seem always surprised when the moment comes. Your eyes grow wide and gleam. Your lips part and the tip of your tongue glides out." He quickened the pace just a bit. "Now!" he cried. "Now it's beginning!"

Ward guessed correctly. Even as he spoke the words, Pandora felt the hot flash of sensation flowing up her legs, spreading through her belly, and flooding her breasts. Even as the moment of total ecstasy came, Pandora stared up into Ward's face, seeing his eyes change from gray to green. One moment he was her husband, the next, her long lost lover. She could feel both of them, moving as one, inside her, bringing such exquisite pleasure that it was almost painful.

Finally, she could bear it no longer. Closing her eyes, she moaned as the storm tide of passion ebbed.

When he had seen it all, Ward lowered himself to her and kissed her deeply. For a long time, they lay coupled, letting the pleasure slip away slowly.

In the warm, love-scented darkness after Ward turned out the lights, it seemed to Pandora that both men held her and stirred within her and kissed her lips and breasts. There could be no doubt that Ward and Laffite were one.

The thought was not shocking, but rather a soothing, fulfilling truth. Pandora kissed her husband and sighed contentedly. She felt totally, beautifully, wonderfully loved.

Chapter Seventeen

Pandora and Ward spent the rest of the summer and early fall settling into their cozy castle. Marriage had performed the most extraordinary miracle for them. Single, they had both been considered eccentric and even a bit bizarre. By simply speaking a few vows and exchanging rings, they became honored members of Galveston society. All of Galveston looked on the couple as trendsetters. Wherever the Gabriels went, so went the rest of the island. When Ward had a new silver brooch designed especially for his wife—a crescent moon set with diamonds and attached to a constellation of tiny stars by the thinnest of silver chains— every woman in town wanted one like it. When Ward and Pandora announced, after a trip to his silver mine, that Mexico was definitely the place to vacation, European travelers from Galveston changed their plans. When Ward presented Pandora with a pair of blue-eyed, white angora kittens to replace the ones which drowned mysteriously in the fountain in her uncle's garden while she was away, angoras became the favored pets all up and down Broadway. When Pandora discovered a new and daring designer in Paris, the House of Worth found itself deserted by the ladies of Galveston society.

Mr. and Mrs. Ward Gabriel—handsome, social, charming, rich, and obviously in love—could do no wrong as far as their neighbors were concerned. They were the perfect couple. No one suspected that tension still smoldered and sometimes flared to full life when Pandora mentioned Jean Laffite to her husband.

Only Dr. and Mrs. Jacob Saenger looked on the couple with anything short of total approval. To Jacob's credit, he kept any further declarations of his feelings to himself—suffering long, but silently. Angelica, however, was less discreet in her continuing flirtation with Ward. With each passing day, it seemed that she inched ever closer to the dangerous edge of sanity. Jacob tried to control her, but there was nothing he could do. Things became so bad in his father's house, that Jacob was forced to use the last cent of his savings to buy Angelica her own home—a handsome frame house with gingerbread trim just off of Broadway.

"You call this a proper house?" she shrieked as he proudly took her on a tour of their fine new home. "Why, this isn't even as grand as Pandora's servants' quarters!"

Jacob curbed his temper, answering as evenly as he could manage, "And I am not Ward Gabriel, Angel."

"Don't call me that!" she snapped. "Don't you dare ever call me that again."

"I'm only trying to make you understand that I'm not a rich man. I don't own a silver mine or a fleet of ships or even a mercantile store. I will never be wealthy, Angelica. You knew that when you married me."

"No!" she shrieked. "You tricked me! You promised me a honeymoon in Europe, a fine mansion, a life of luxury, everything that Pandora has."

Jacob shook his head wearily. How many times had he heard all this before? There was no use arguing with her. Angelica would never be happy. Not even if she had everything her cousin possessed, not even if she had Ward Gabriel.

Gently, Jacob suggested for the thousandth time, "Perhaps if we had a child, Angelica? That's what you've always wanted. Why did you give up hope? A baby might change everything for us."

Her ice-blue eyes narrowed and she moved away from him. "Oh, no. You think I'll let you back into my bed if you promise me a child. *You* are the reason I haven't conceived. *You*, Jacob Saenger! You're not man enough to father children. I won't put up with your fumbling and groping ever again. I've told you what to do. Get me a baby! I've waited long enough. My patience is wearing thin."

Jacob felt his gut twist. He had hoped that Angelica would forget all about her wild scheme. She hadn't mentioned it in a long time.

As for trying to worm his way back into his wife's bed, that was sheer nonsense. He wasn't sure he could ever bring himself to make love to Angelica again. He had lost his desire for her many months before she began refusing him. An occasional visit to Postoffice Street kept him satisfied these days.

"Well, Angelica, what do you want me to do?" he asked finally, a tone of weary resignation in his voice. "I've put all our money into this place. I can probably sell it, but we can't buy anything else until after the sale. That would mean staying on with my father. I leave it up to you."

Again she turned on him. "You'd like that, wouldn't you? It makes you happy to see me waiting on that dreadful old man as if I were a servant. Well, no more, Jacob! I'd live in Crazy Nettie's shack just to get away from him."

So it was settled. Dr. and Mrs. Saenger moved into their pleasant, new residence on 13th Street. Jacob felt even the street number bode ill for their disintegrating marriage.

At first, Pandora and Ward invited the Saengers to their new home frequently. As time went on and Angelica became more blatant in her pursuit of Ward, Pandora left their names off her guest lists more often than she included them.

"I hate excluding them, Ward, but what else can I do? Jacob understands. He even spoke to me about it. He said he feels uncomfortable going anywhere with her these days.

He's especially embarrassed by the way she throws herself at you. The whole island is talking and he knows it.''

Ward leaned back in his easy chair in the library and puffed his pipe, trying to read his wife's thoughts. "I hope you don't think I've encouraged your cousin, darling."

Pandora laughed. "Angelica needs no encouragement, Ward. I know her all too well. If you had given her the slightest sign that you were interested, she would have left Jacob by now." Pandora shook her head as she stared down at the guest list for their upcoming dinner party. "Sometimes I feel so sorry for both of them. How horrible it must be for a husband and wife not to love each other . . . not to trust each other totally."

Ward frowned. Was Pandora making a veiled accusation that he was leading Angelica on? He brushed the troubling thought aside and went to her, wrapping his arms about her. "We'll never know about that, will we, darling?"

He kissed her deeply, letting one hand stray inside her dressing gown to explore and arouse.

"Ready for bed, dear?" Pandora whispered.

Ward grinned and nuzzled her ear. "I thought you'd never ask."

Once they were undressed and in their bed, Pandora gently fended off her husband's eager advances. "I have something to tell you first, Ward," she said.

He continued holding her, petting her as he answered. "Then you'd better tell me quickly."

"Remember last week I mentioned to you that I'd seen Nettie?"

"Yes, I remember." He tried to disguise his annoyance. After seeing Crazy Nettie, Pandora invariably experienced one of her disturbing visions of Jean Laffite. He'd begged his wife to stay away from that old woman.

"Well, she said the oddest things to me. She'd sent me an urgent note, asking me to meet her at the grove. When I arrived, she acted very strangely."

Ward laughed humorlessly. "There's certainly nothing unusual about that, Pan. Nettie's a strange old woman."

"No, I mean strange in a different sort of way. She frightened me, Ward."

He sat up, all attention now as Pandora told him of the incident.

"I drove alone to the grove that afternoon as Nettie instructed. The place looked deserted when I arrived, but I had this peculiar feeling that someone was watching me as I approached. I climbed down and hitched the horses to a post near the three trees, then wandered into the deep shade, calling Nettie's name softly.

"Suddenly, Nettie appeared from out of the shadows. I can't imagine why I felt so nervous, but I actually cried out in alarm, she startled me so. I know the grove is supposedly haunted, but I've never felt afraid there before."

Pandora paused for a moment to collect her thoughts. Ward, anxious for his wife's emotional well-being, said, "You've seemed especially edgy these past few days, Pan. Maybe you should see old Doc Saenger. But go on, tell me what she had to say."

"She apologized for frightening me, saying she was concerned that I might have been followed."

"By whom?" Ward asked.

Pandora looked at her husband sheepishly as she answered. "Her exact words were: 'You know . . . that woman, the one with the dark hair and eyes. She ain't to be trusted, that one.' "

"Who on earth was she talking about?" Ward demanded.

Pandora shook her head. "I don't know. I tried to think who she might mean. I had no idea at the time. Later that night, in a vision, the answer came to me."

Ward felt his anger rising. As always, this meeting with Nettie upset Pandora, giving her bad dreams.

Pandora sensed Ward's change of mood and reached out to touch his hand. "Nettie mentioned that she hadn't seen much of me since our marriage. That made me feel guilty. I have been neglecting her. I asked how Daniel was." Pandora laughed. "You should have heard her, Ward." Pandora mimicked Nettie's speech as best she could remember. " 'Damned old fool's the same as always—ornery, lazy, just plain cussed. It's just as well, though, that he don't know nothing about any of this. He's not real sharp anymore—sort of out to pasture, if you know what I mean.

He'll find out when the time's right. But there's no need him worrying about things now.' "

Ward truly lost his temper now. "What the hell was she babbling about?"

Pandora frowned. "That's just what I asked her, only in a kinder tone. I told her I didn't understand. Nettie just shook her head and told me I'd know soon enough. She said there's trouble brewing, more than I could guess. 'Fire and flood and fornication,' she said. She warned me that this dark-eyed woman would be the cause of it all."

"That old woman's as crazy as hell, Pandora," Ward insisted hotly. "You know better than to listen to her wild tales."

"I tried to tell myself that her words meant nothing, Ward. I turned to leave, to get away from her, but she caught my arm. 'I ain't quite finished,' she told me. 'The news ain't all bad. I saved the good for last.' Then she advised me to make an appointment to see Dr. Saenger."

Now Ward's concern intensified. "Did you see the doctor, darling?"

"I hadn't planned on it," Pandora admitted. "But I have had a few spells of light-headedness lately. So, I went while you were at the office this morning."

Ward was sitting up in bed, staring at Pandora, worry lines etching deep patterns in his face. "What's wrong, Pandora?"

Noting her husband's expression, Pandora kissed him quickly and held his face lovingly between her soft palms. "Nothing, darling. Nothing at all. Everything's perfect now." She took a deep breath, beaming into his eyes as her own glittered with happy tears. "You're going to be a father."

Ward continued staring at his wife, but now the fierce light in his dark eyes softened. Slowly, a smile spread over his face. He reached out his hand and touched her breast. "A baby," he whispered. "We're going to have a baby!"

Pandora nodded and hugged him. "Oh, Ward, isn't it wonderful?"

"A miracle!" he agreed. Then taking her into his arms, he loved his wife tenderly, carefully for a long, long time.

After Ward fell asleep—the smile still on his face—Pandora lay, wide-eyed, in the dark. She hadn't had the nerve to tell him the rest—the part about the dark-eyed woman. How could she? He would never understand. She didn't understand herself. Ward had no patience with her visions from the past. Sometimes she thought he was actually jealous of her memories of Laffite.

She lay in the great golden bed, next to her sleeping husband, and let her mind relive what she'd seen the night of her visit with Nettie. The memory still sent chills through her.

She'd awakened with a start sometime later that night, so she knew what she saw was not a dream, but a vision from her far past. It all began innocently enough. Nicolette was in the kitchen of *Maison Rouge*, little Jeannette playing at her feet as she prepared one of Jean's favorite dishes to surprise him—wild strawberry pie.

The day was warm and fine. Summer had settled over the island, but the scorching days of July had yet to inflict Campeachy's inhabitants with its mid-season torpor. No fierce West Indian storms threatened to sweep over the island before the hot months melted into fall.

The pie looked crisp and brown with sugary perfection. Nicolette lifted it from the oven with a thick cloth to keep from burning herself. Carefully, she set it on the table.

"There," she said to Jeannette. "Won't your papa be pleased?"

Little Jeannette, sucking her thumb, tugged at her mother's skirts, wanting to be picked up. Nicolette scooped her daughter into her arms and kissed her. "I have an idea. Let's go pick a few more berries. I'll mix them with the cream to go on top."

With the baby in one hand and a pail in the other, Nicolette left the house in search of more strawberries. The best patch, she knew, grew near the grove. She headed for the beach with Jeannette.

By the time Nicolette reached the grove, her face and arms felt hot and tingly from the bright sun. Her bare feet were crusted with warm sand. She felt invigorated from the exercise and fresh air. It was good to be out alone, with only Jeannette for company. For once she had evaded her armed escort.

As they neared the grove, Jeannette's pretty face broke into a happy grin. "Papa, Papa, Papa!" she called.

"Silly baby," Nicolette chided, "Papa's on his ship. He won't be back till suppertime."

Only then did Nicolette notice the *Pride* riding at anchor in the Gulf. She frowned. Jean always brought his ship into the bay on the far side of the island. The only time he'd ever anchored in the Gulf was the night the two of them had spent together in the grove before his departure for Mexico some months ago.

"Papa! Papa!" Jeannette kept up her singsong chorus.

"Sh-h-h!" Nicolette cautioned, edging carefully toward the three spreading oaks.

Suddenly, she froze as she heard a woman's laughter and then her sigh of pleasure. Hiding behind a high stand of sawgrass, she peered through its sharp blades. She saw two figures in the grove, lying on a blanket in the shade. She stifled a cry, feeling suddenly as if a bullet had pierced her heart. There, beside the dark-haired woman Isabel, lay her own husband, his hands playing over the woman's bare breasts, his lips searching her willing mouth.

Nicolette closed her eyes against the painful scene. Pandora watched, sharing Nicolette's pain. As she stared toward the pair, colors swirled, then reshaped themselves. When the images cleared, Pandora saw not Jean Laffite, but her own husband, Ward, there in the grove. And in his arms lay, not Isabel, but Angelica!

"Fire and flood and fornication!" Nettie had said. Before the vision faded, Pandora had seen them all. Through hot, dancing colors that seemed to throb with a life all their own, she witnessed flames eating the very beach. A moment later, a huge wave crashed over the island, carrying all in its wake. She felt herself swept along on the storm tide. Through it all, she kept reaching out, crying Ward's name, begging him to save her . . . to save their love.

Finally, the mad fury of her vision faded to shades of gray, black, and silver. The gray of an angry dawn. The black of skeletal hands reaching out to her. The silver of a pulsing cord that seemed to pull her ever closer to the groping, bony fingers.

The old nightmare was now even more horrible. No matter how hard she fought against it, she could not repress the suspicion that her husband secretly enjoyed Angelica's flirtation. Her cousin was a beautiful, desirable woman. Ward, after all, was only human—with a man's weaknesses, a man's vanities.

As desperately as Pandora tried to deny her fears, it seemed that history was about to repeat itself. She knew for a fact that Jean Laffite had betrayed his wife with Isabel. Could it be that she was destined to suffer Nicolette's pain once more when Ward succumbed to Angelica's charms? It was more than she could bear.

Pandora tried to go to sleep, but it was no use. She knew she had to tell Ward what was happening to her. She reached out, placing her hand on his arm, hoping the comfort of feeling his warm flesh would be enough to reassure her. She had thought all this was behind her. She had had no troubling visions for some time after their marriage. But now it began again. Somehow, she must share all this with Ward. Trying to cope alone would drive her mad.

"Ward, are you awake?"

Still half asleep, he reached out, drawing her near. "What's wrong, darling? You're trembling."

"The visions, Ward. I'm having them again. The other night, after my talk with Nettie, I saw the most horrible thing. I've tried to tell myself it's all in my mind. Darling, I'm so afraid."

"Pandora, what is it?" Ward was fully awake now, cradling her close.

"Everything's all mixed up—you and Jean Laffite, Angelica and the woman named Isabel. I'm so confused, Ward. I'm so afraid of losing you."

"Hush now," he soothed, holding her close and kissing her tear-streaked cheeks. "You couldn't lose me if you tried. I love you. I'm here to stay. As for the vision, it's nothing, darling. Women often have bad dreams when they're expecting.''

"No, Ward, this wasn't a dream. I know the difference. This was something that really happened, a long time ago. It happened to me . . . and it happened to you." She stared at him, wondering if she dared tell him the whole truth. "Ward, I know you don't believe any of this, but you *were* Jean Laffite."

Feeling pain and anger twist through his heart, Ward willed himself to remain calm. He forced a soft laugh and cuddled her close. "Yes, so you've told me before. You were my wife then and we loved each other and we still do. Darling, try to love me for myself, not because you have this fixation about Laffite."

"It isn't a fixation, Ward, and neither is this thing with Angelica. She's vicious, Ward! She won't rest until she's taken you from me. If Jean Laffite couldn't resist Isabel, then how can I hope to keep you from Angelica?"

Ward, wounded and angry, drew away from Pandora. "Do you know how it makes me feel when you talk about him?" His tone was sharp with resentment. "I swear, I'm more jealous of that pirate than I could ever be of any real, flesh and blood man. As for this business with Angelica, I'd think you'd have more faith in me. If you're jealous of her, think how jealous you make me, always sighing over your damned dead pirate!"

"Don't say such things," Pandora pleaded, reaching out to stroke his cheek. "Please, Ward! You have no reason to be jealous."

"I can't help it. I want you to love me for who I am *now!*"

"I do!"

"Then show me how much."

He silenced his wife with a deep, searching kiss. Some of the tension eased from her body. When Ward made love to her, she could think of nothing else. She wanted nothing else.

As he entered her this time—slowly, careful not to disturb their unborn child—the room filled suddenly with the ringing of bells, the colors swirled, and Pandora knew that she was no longer in her husband's embrace, but in the arms of Jean

Laffite. She stiffened, seeing him again as he held Isabel— or was it Angelica?—there in the grove.

"I'm sorry," Jean whispered. "What must I do to gain your forgiveness? I don't love her. I love *you! Only you!* It just happened—I can't explain how or why. I promise you, darling, when we leave Campeachy in a few days, she will remain here. We'll go to Mexico without her. She'll never have a chance to threaten our love again. Things will be as they were before."

"It's too late!" the woman in Laffite's arms answered tonelessly.

"It's never too late, not if we love each other," he insisted. "You still care for me, don't you?"

"You know I love you, Jean. More than life itself. But . . ."

"No buts," he commanded.

His strong hand trailed down her naked body then, and his lips touched her breast. A moment later, as he moved inside her, the hot colors swam in her mind and consumed her whole being.

Even at that most precious moment, when the heavens parted and she knew the best there was to know, the words still rang in her ears: "Too late! Too late! Too late!"

A moment later, the vision dissolved. Pandora clung to Ward. *He* was her husband, her lover, her best friend. And he was right about Jean Laffite. She had to stop thinking about him and about the past. The here and now—her husband and their unborn child—were the things that counted. The past—whatever it had been—was dead and gone and buried. As for Angelica, Pandora would simply have to trust her husband to do the right thing.

Angelica sat in Jacob's father's office, waiting to be called in for her monthly visit. As her father-in-law, she despised the man. As her physician, she had grown accustomed to him over the years. She would not have considered going to any other doctor. This month, she would not have dreamed of canceling her usual appointment.

Jacob laughed cruelly when she'd announced at breakfast where she would spend her morning.

"Still thinking you might be pregnant, are you? Well, it will be a miracle child, if you are. It's been my experience as a physician that immaculate conceptions seldom occur."

She had scowled at him, but kept silent. Inwardly, she had been half-relieved, half-disappointed that he didn't know. Waiting to be called into the examing room, Angelica smiled to herself. What a surprise it would be for Jacob. He'd built a lovely, little potting shed out back, hoping to interest her in gardening. The garden held no fascination for her, but the young gardener from the west end of the island captured her imagination. He could make *anything* grow— or so Angelica hoped.

Moments later, Dr. Saenger's nurse called Angelica in. The examination was blessedly brief, but painfully disappointing.

Her father-in-law avoided looking her straight in the eye as he broke the news. "I am sorry, Angelica. Not this time. My son is a strong young man. You have nothing to worry about. You must be patient."

Angelica bit her lip to keep from laughing out loud. *His son,* indeed!

Angelica left then. She was disappointed not to be carrying her lover's child, but there was still a better way to become a mother. She had no desire to go through the misery of pregnancy and the pain of childbirth. If her plan worked she would not have to.

It was such a lovely fall day that Angelica decided to drop in at the Gabriels'. Ward seemed to have been avoiding her lately. If she was in luck, he might be at home. If not, she could have a nice heart-to-heart with Pandora—who better to tell that she was about to become a mother. The seed for her gossip needed to be planted very soon since she planned to demand this very evening that Jacob get her a child.

Pandora spotted Angelica coming up the walk and felt a cold shudder inside. "Why *this* morning?" she begged of heaven. Her dinner party was set for eight o'clock that evening, and she had left the Saengers off her guest list. Angelica was sure to notice the preparations in progress.

Motioning to Cassie, Pandora stripped off her apron and

said, "Let Miss Angelica in and show her to the front parlor. Tell her I'll be there in a moment."

Pandora ran up the back servants' stairs to warn Ward that they had a visitor. He was working in his upstairs study, totally engrossed in the latest sketches of jewelry designs that had just arrived from Italy.

"Darling," she said quietly, "Angelica's here."

Ward ran his fingers through his hair and groaned. "I don't want to see her."

"I know but she's sure to ask for you. What shall I tell her?"

He looked at Pandora, his dark eyes blazing. "That I'm damn sick and tired of her silly little games. That I'm a married man who's perfectly happy with my wife and that she's making an absolute fool of herself!"

Pandora went to him and gave his slumped shoulders a quick hug. "I'd love to, darling but perhaps it would be better if I simply told her that we're about to add to our family."

Ward reached up, his face shining now, and pulled her down to receive his kiss. "You're a wonder, you know that, darling? That could be the perfect solution."

Pandora shrugged. "It's worth a try. Besides, she's bound to find out soon and it would be better coming from me."

Moments later, Pandora entered the parlor, still glowing from her husband's sweet kiss and the reassuring fact that he did not want to see their guest.

"Angelica, this is a surprise."

Angelica had sized up the flurry of activity at the house already. Putting two and two together, she'd guessed that Pandora and Ward were having a party and that she was not invited. "Oh, I'll just bet it is. Obviously, you hadn't planned to see me today?"

Thinking quickly, Pandora replied with a straight face, "Well, not until the dinner party tonight. You and Jacob are coming, aren't you? You never replied to the invitation I sent."

"Invitation?" Angelica looked blank. She often misplaced mail these days—especially bills and requests for

285

contributions. "Why, I never received it, Pandora. It must have gone astray. Of course, Jacob and I will come."

Caught! It was just as well. Pandora had been feeling guilty ever since she'd decided to leave the Saengers off the guest list. So now she was being punished. It served her right, she told herself. She dreaded telling Ward.

Cassie came in with a tray of tea and honeyed almond cakes. Pandora poured and settled back, wondering at the reason behind Angelica's visit.

"Isn't Ward home?"

Pandora smiled.

"He's working today."

"Oh!" Angelica made no attempt to disguise her disappointment. Then she brightened. "He'll be here tonight, of course?"

Pandora nodded. "Of course!"

"Well, then you and I can just have a nice chat over our tea. How have you been, Pandora? It seems ages since I've seen you, although I run into Ward quite often."

"Yes," Pandora answered coolly, "I know all about your frequent meetings. You see, Angelica, my husband tells me *everything*. We keep no secrets from each other as some married couples do."

Angelica let Pandora's pointed remark slide over her as easily as a raindrop off an oleander leaf. She laughed, then whispered, "You're a brave one, Pan. Jacob would have me tarred and feathered if I ever dared tell him *everything*. Sometimes I think the secrets Jacob and I keep from each other are the only things we have in common any longer. Not that there was ever any real bond between us. I should have let you marry him, Pandora. I've been meaning to tell you for some time now how sorry I am that I came between you."

Pandora looked up, amazed to hear such an apology coming from Angelica. The minute she stared into her cousin's ice-blue eyes, she realized that this was no apology at all. Angelica wasn't sorry for Pandora's or Jacob's sake that she had come between them. She was simply sorry that she had married Jacob Saenger.

"Let's not talk abut the past, Angelica. What's done is

done. Besides, the future is much more exciting." She set her cup down and leaned close. "I have a secret to tell you. After Ward, you are the very first to know."

Angelica, always anxious for a juicy bit of gossip to spread, stared at Pandora, her face alive. "Then don't keep me waiting. Do tell!"

"I'm pregnant! Isn't that wonderful?"

Angelica's bright expression faded. "You're sure?"

"Positive!" Pandora nodded. "I saw Dr. Saenger just last week."

To Pandora's utter amazement, Angelica laughed. "Well, isn't this a coincidence! I've just seen him myself, this very morning. It seems we'll both be mothers soon."

Pandora stared at her cousin, stunned by the news. Only last week, Jacob had stopped by. He often came to see her when life began to wear him down. They would sit on the veranda—sometimes with Ward, sometimes without him— and simply talk. Usually, Jacob did most of the talking and most of it had to do with Angelica. On his last visit, he had been in a particularly somber mood. He had poured out his heart to her that day and told her that Angelica was no longer a wife to him.

"Jacob doesn't even know yet," Angelica continued. "I'm sure he'll be delirious with excitement. You know how he's always wanted a big family."

Pandora nodded, frowning. "Yes, I remember. He'll be a fine father, I'm sure."

Angelica's laugh tinkled in the sunny parlor. "Much better at it than Ward, I imagine. Somehow I can't picture your big, strapping husband burping and diapering babies."

Pandora's head jerked up. *"Babies?"* How could Angelica know? Had Dr. Saenger said something to her? She hadn't even told Ward that they might be having twins. The doctor had said he couldn't be sure yet. Then she realized she was only imagining things. Still, she didn't want anyone else to know before she'd told her husband.

"Let's take this one baby at a time, shall we, Angelica?" Pandora laughed to cover her own tension. "Motherhood has me a bit nervous as it is. I don't want to think beyond the first one."

"When's your baby due, Pandora?" Angelica asked innocently, her mind working in crazy, frantic patterns.

"In the spring—April, Dr. Saenger said."

Angelica widened her eyes in feigned surprise. "Well, my, my! Isn't that a coincidence? Mine too!"

Pandora didn't know why, but she suddenly had a strange feeling in the pit of her stomach. It had something to do with Angelica's announcement that she was also pregnant and the fact that she knew Jacob could not possibly be the father. Something about the situation seemed to threaten her and her family and their well-being.

Pandora managed to mask her uneasiness as she said, "We'll all have to celebrate tonight. I know Jacob will be as surprised and excited as Ward was when I told him my news."

Angelica only nodded and smiled. There was something in those cold, blue eyes that sent a shiver down Pandora's spine.

Chapter Eighteen

By early 1898, the news was out. All of Galveston twittered about the fact that both Pandora Gabriel and Angelica Saenger were expecting babies in the spring. It seemed a miracle that the Saengers were finally to be blessed after all this time. Of course, the Gabriel infant was the more important of the two as far as the island's citizens were concerned.

"That child will surely be born with a sterling silver spoon in its tiny mouth," Mrs. Rosenberg informed the ladies of the Thursday Evening Literary Guild at their March meeting.

They all nodded their agreement, glad to have the opportunity to discuss the matter openly since both women in question were absent from the spring meeting—Pandora being too great with child to attend and Angelica being out of town, visiting her mother's cousin in Mobile.

"The Saenger child won't fare too poorly either," Mrs. Landes pointed out. "After all, Angelica will inherit the mansion on Broadway and the Emporium and her father's other stores some day. Why, even if her husband is only a poor struggling doctor, she'll be rich in her own right in time.''

The others murmured thoughtfully over this, then Mrs. Rosenberg said, ''Those Sherwood girls could own the whole island before it's done. Suppose Pandora has a son and Angelica a daughter or vice versa. If those children married, they'd bring enough wealth together to buy and sell every last one of us.''

''No,'' Mrs. Landes gasped. ''Never! There's too much queerness in that family already what with Pandora's visions and Angelica's emotional instability. If those two little cousins grew up to marry, it would be madness for their offspring for sure.''

The ladies left off their gossip then to return to their discussion of one of Lord Byron's oriental tales, ''The Corsair.''

'' 'He left a Corsair's name to other times, Link'd with one virtue, and a thousand crimes,' '' Mrs. Rosenberg read aloud in her stentorian voice.

''You know,'' interjected Mrs. Landes, ''they say that Lord Byron was inspired to write this piece after reading in the newspapers of Jean Laffite's bravery at the Battle of New Orleans.''

Mrs. Rosenberg sniffed indignantly at the interruption. ''I don't believe that for a moment. Laffite was a scoundrel and a pirate, unworthy of such a lofty poet's notice. Byron obviously wrote this about himself.''

One of the younger members of the group spoke up for the first time, timid, but determined to be heard. ''I think Jean Laffite was a terribly romantic figure, Mrs. Rosenberg. Did you know that after his wife died in his arms right here on Galveston Beach, he swore, as he buried her in the grove, that he would find her again in another life?''

''Poppycock!'' Mrs. Rosenberg huffed. ''That's a tale made up for the sake of tourists and feather-headed young women. Where did you ever hear such nonsense?''

The young woman blushed as everyone stared at her. ''Old Nettie told me.''

Mrs. Rosenberg's brows rose officiously. ''There, you

have just proven my point." Then she went back to her reading.

Pandora's one problem during her pregnancy was that everyone was trying to pamper her to death. Ward cancelled several business trips, unwilling to leave her side. Cassie hovered like a mother hen, refusing to allow her mistress to lift a finger. The other servants were no better.

Finally, one fine morning in mid-March, Pandora declared her independence. "Ward," she commanded, "you are going to your office this morning!"

They were at the breakfast table, Pandora refusing to be served in bed as she had been, at Cassie's insistence, for the past four months.

Ward looked up at his wife as if she had suddenly gone soft in the brain. "I wouldn't think of it, darling. Any work I have to do today, I can do right here in my study."

"No!" she said flatly. "I honestly believe that you intend to smother me before these babies arrive. I want you out of here today. I have things to do and I can't do them with you underfoot."

A short time later, Ward Gabriel, looking bewildered and rejected, put on his coat and left for his office on the Strand. As he walked out the door he was still protesting.

Before he left, Pandora kissed him gently, trying to soothe his injured feelings. "I ask only an hour or two alone, darling. I promise you, I'll be perfectly safe."

"She will be that, Mr. Ward!" Cassie assured him, standing nearby with her arms crossed imperiously over her bosom. "I'm not letting her do a thing you wouldn't allow. No, sir!"

The moment Ward was gone, Pandora turned on her overbearing servant. "I will do what I please this morning. Is that understood, Cass?"

"Not nothing that will hurt them babies."

"Certainly not. Now, I'm going to my studio and I don't want to be disturbed."

Cassie looked horrified. "You ain't planning to paint? No, ma'am! You can't do that."

291

Pandora, already headed up the stairs, turned on the woman. "And why not?"

"Them paints, they smell something awful, Miss Pan. Might harm the babies, all them noxious fumes."

"That's ridiculous. As I said, I'll be upstairs."

"What about your morning nap, Miss Pan?" Cassie's question received no reply.

Pandora entered her studio with the feeling of returning, after a long absence, to an old friend. There, just as she had left them months before, were her easel, her palette and her boxes of paints. Warm yellow sunshine flooded the room, pouring down through the skylight. She closed her eyes for a moment and breathed in the wonderful, familiar smells of turpentine, linseed oil, and paints that Cassie had branded "noxious."

Slipping into a long smock, Pandora set to work. She had two projects in mind. First, she would paint a chubby, pink-cheeked cherub on the headboard of the white double cradle. She also wanted to decorate the lovely, antique box Ward had given her for her eighteenth birthday. Someday, the box would belong to her children. She wanted to add something of herself to it that would last for many years.

She set right to work and two hours later, she was still at it. She had to admit that she was tired—that she could not possibly finish both projects in one morning. The cherub even now was smiling at her from its ground of blue sky and white clouds. The antique box still sat on the table, untouched by her brush.

She picked it up and smoothed her hands over the dark wood. What scene would be appropriate for its lid? She couldn't decide. She opened the box and browsed through the contents. Over the past years, she had made a habit of hiding away all her treasures inside the tiny chest. She hadn't looked through these things in a very long time.

Going to the sofa, she eased herself down and carefully perused the contents—pressed flowers from Ward, their marriage certificate, special invitations, bows from gifts Ward had given her. The shell with the painted rosebud from Nettie. Finally, in the very bottom, she found the single gold and opal earring and the antique coins. Then her heart gave a sudden lurch. Something was missing—the dark curl tied with scarlet ribbon. Frantic, she shuffled back through everything in the box. She thought maybe it had slipped inside one of the envelopes but it was gone, nowhere to be found.

Fighting tears, Pandora replaced the contents, feeling an odd emptiness deep down inside. She chided herself for being such a silly, sentimental woman. It wasn't as if the lock of hair had belonged to some long-lost lover. Still, it had been a part of Ward's gift. Losing it distressed her deeply.

Rising slowly and with some effort, she roamed about the studio, unconscious of the fact that she was still searching. In one corner of the room, she came upon a covered canvas. She lifted the linen cloth covering the picture. She gasped and her heart all but stopped; it was the painting she had done in Paris of the man and woman in the grove. Now, *three* figures stood among the trees. A second woman with long dark hair had intruded—a woman she had not painted herself and never would have. The scene looked out of balance and the lone man seemed torn between the two of women.

With a soft cry, Pandora let her hand drop from the canvas and clutched her belly. Silver dots swam before her eyes. Bells rang inside her head. The whole room seemed to be turning upside down.

Cassie found Pandora a short time later. Anxious that her mistress had been alone so long, she entered the studio and almost fainted herself.

"I found her just lying right there in the middle of the floor," the still-trembling Cassie told Ward when he arrived home a short time later. "I told her them fumes would be bad. Mr. Ward, she wouldn't listen to me."

"Take it easy, Cass," Ward soothed. "Dr. Saenger says she's going to be fine. He thinks she should stay in bed until her time comes. We aren't going to argue with her anymore, we're simply going to tell her."

"That's fine by me," the weeping woman sniffed. "Belonged there all the while is what I say."

Ward returned to the bedroom to find his wife looking pale and shaken. "Darling, how are you feeling?"

"Strange," she answered, not looking at Ward, but staring vacantly out the window.

He sat down beside her on the bed and took her hand. "You should have listened to Cassie, darling. Those paint fumes . . ."

She whipped around to face him, a fierce light in her eyes. "It wasn't the fumes, Ward, it was the painting."

"What painting?" he asked gently. "I don't understand."

Pandora, between sobs, spilled out the tale of the picture she'd done that long ago rainy afternoon in Paris, of how she'd meant to paint the Champs-Elysees, but instead Laffite's Grove had flowed from her brush. "Ward," she stammered at length, "now it's changed! There's someone else in the picture—*Isabel!*"

Ward held her and tried to soothe her with soft words, assuring her that it had been only another of her visions. Pandora refused to be convinced. Finally, he said, "I'll prove it to you. I'll bring the painting in here."

"No!" she gasped. "I can't bear to look at it, Ward."

"Then I'll go look at it myself." He left her then, a worried scowl on his face. What was happening to her? Her imagination was getting out of hand.

Pandora lay trembling in the bed, dreading Ward's return. The change in the painting frightened her more than any other vision she had seen.

A moment later, Ward returned, carrying the canvas. "It's lovely, darling. One of your best, I'd say." He laughed heartily. "Why, the man even has all his clothes on!"

When Ward started to turn the picture toward Pandora, she cried, "No! I don't want to see it!"

"It's all right, darling," he said gently. "See? It's just as you described it to me—a man and a woman embracing in the grove. There's no other figure in the picture. You must have had one of your visions just before you blacked out."

Pandora stared at the canvas, unable to believe her eyes. She *had* seen the other woman! She didn't care what Ward said. Yes, it had been a vision and it had also been a warning. But a warning against what? She still equated Isabel with

Angelica. However, Angelica posed no problem that Pandora could see. She was not even on the island. What could the vision mean?

"Why don't you try to rest now, darling?" Ward suggested. "You look done in."

She reached out for his hand. "Will you stay here with me?"

Leaning down to kiss her forehead, Ward whispered, "Of course I will, as long as you like. Dr. Saenger says you're to remain in bed from now until your time comes. Understood?"

She smiled and nodded, feeling far too weak and frightened to argue.

So for the next weeks, Pandora became a prisoner of her bed, with Ward and Cassie as her loving keepers. She did convince them finally to let her have her paints and the antique box. She promised to work on it only for short stretches at a time. She had decided at last which scene she would paint—the grove, with only two figures there, herself and Ward, embracing and vowing their love for all time.

While the rest of the island's citizens anxiously awaited the two April births—some even laying bets on the sexes and arrival dates of the pair—two Galvestonians could not get caught up in the almost carnival atmosphere surrounding the coming blessed events.

The Drs. Saenger—father and son—knew that Angelica was not now nor had she ever been carrying a child.

"I don't understand, Jacob." The old doctor sat across his son's desk, shaking his shaggy, gray head. "What can she be thinking?"

Jacob sighed and clasped his hands together before him. "I haven't wanted to say anything about this to you before, Father. I was sure Angelica would give up her wild scheme. Unfortunately, that hasn't happened, so I suppose you must know. After all, you're Pandora's doctor, too."

"You mean Angelica is only pretending to be pregnant because her cousin is?"

Jacob shook his head. "If only it were that simple. Angelica demanded some time ago that I *steal* an infant for her. She announced to me that she was pregnant the very day that she found out Pandora was expecting. Then she dashed off to Mobile. I've just received a letter from her. She's in Houston now, awaiting word from me that I have procured a baby for her. When all is ready here, she will slip back into Galveston under cover of darkness, claim the child, and explain to everyone that it was born before her return.''

"Great God in heaven, your wife's gone mad!"

Jacob nodded, a pained expression on his face. "I'm afraid that's exactly what's happened, Father."

"Ah, Jacob my boy, how twisted life seems at times! Here is your wife, longing so to become a mother, yet seemingly unable to conceive, while her cousin carries twins."

Jacob looked up, all attention. "You're sure now about the twins?"

A twinkle glittered in the older man's brown eyes and he nodded with some enthusiasm. "There is no doubt in my mind any longer. For some reason, Pandora wants to keep the news a secret. She is a dramatic woman. I suppose she thinks it will be even more exciting to surprise all of Galveston this way." He laughed softly.

Jacob shoved up from his chair and walked to the window, gazing out toward the Gulf. "Well, thank God Angelica doesn't know! That could push her over the edge. Things are bad enough as they are."

Old Dr. Saenger muttered in German under his breath. He looked at his son with pity in his eyes. "Of course, you have no intentions of going along with this wicked plan."

"Of course not, Father!" Jacob blew up. "Angelica may be totally mad, but I am alarmingly sane in spite of her." Jacob slumped back down in his chair, wondering if he dared mention divorce to the old man—his only way out now. He decided it was too risky. His father had had several mild attacks in the past months. Sighing again, Jacob asked hopelessly, "What am I do to?"

Dr. Saenger gripped his son's arm. "I wish I could tell you, Jacob. If only there were an easy answer to all this. Life is seldom simple, my son."

Jacob uttered a humorless laugh. "How well I know that, Father."

On the first of April, Angelica, tired of waiting in Houston for Jacob's reply, sneaked back to Galveston. She *would* have her way, Jacob be damned!

Disguised in mourning, her face covered by a heavy black veil, Angelica took the early train from Houston, arriving at the Galveston station while thick fog still shrouded the streets. She took a hired cab to the house on 13th Street and slipped in without being noticed.

The bedroom shades were drawn and Jacob was still sleeping when she arrived. She went to him and yanked the covers off.

Jacob woke instantly. Rubbing his eyes, he stared up at the black-clothed figure before him, half-believing that the Angel of Death had come for him.

Without preamble, she launched her attack. "I suppose you have an explanation for me?"

"Angelica?" Jacob would almost have preferred the Dark Angel.

"I've been waiting in Houston for over a week. Why haven't you contacted me? What did you expect me to do?"

Collecting himself and pulling on his robe, Jacob tried to kiss her cheek, hoping to soothe her near-hysteria. She shoved him away.

"I expected you to do exactly what you have done— come home where you belong," Jacob said coolly. "I hope you've finally realized what an insane plan it was."

Angelica whipped off the veil and Jacob saw the mad, eerie light in her cold-blue eyes.

"No, I haven't given up on my plan. I slipped back into town. No one knows I'm here." She gave him a sardonic smile. "No one who counts, that is. I hope you've made proper arrangements by now."

"I have not!" Jacob answered, his voice rising dangerously.

"Well, when will you?" she demanded.

"You're crazy. I haven't given the slightest thought to

your outrageous scheme nor do I intend to. You might as well forget it, Angelica.''

"Forget it?" she screamed, coming at him with fists flying. "I will not! I cannot!"

Jacob caught her wrists and wrestled her down to the bed, pinning her on her back. She writhed and kicked at him.

"Now, you are going to listen to me, *my dear wife!*" Jacob said through clenched teeth. "There will be no stolen babies! Since you've come home and you are obviously not pregnant, we will tell everyone that you lost the child while visiting in Mobile. You stayed away recovering. And if you persist in this baby-snatching madness, I will sign the papers to have put you away."

A long silence followed before Angelica finally conceded. "All right, all right," she said. "Just let me go!" She began sobbing hysterically, the fight gone out of her.

Jacob released her and rose, feeling a sickness in the pit of his stomach. Angelica had given in too easily. He had no idea what she had in mind, but he had not heard the last of this, he was sure.

Ward Gabriel was sick with worry. Why *now* of all times? Here it was the end of the first week in April, with Pandora's babies due any time, and he'd just received word of trouble at the mine in Mexico. A cave-in trapped several miners in one of the tunnels. He was needed immediately to supervise the rescue operations. How could he leave Pandora now?

"I'll be fine," Pandora told him after finally prying the distressing news out of him. "The babies won't come for another two weeks at the earliest. Dr. Saenger said the end of April. That gives you plenty of time to make your trip and get back. I promise I'll behave while you're away, darling."

Ward sat beside her bed, holding her hand, stroking her soft palm with his fingertips. He hadn't had an easy moment since she'd confided in him about the twins. His own mother had died giving birth to Ward and a twin brother, who had lived only a few hours. Now he might have imposed the same fate on Pandora. What would he do if anything happened to her? He couldn't begin to imagine life without her.

Ward stared into her face. She was so beautiful—lovelier than ever before. Perhaps everything would be all right. Motherhood seemed to agree with her. She'd never looked healthier or stronger or more in bloom. An ache shot through his heart and then his groin. How he longed to hold her and love her again. It had been so long.

Reading his thoughts, Pandora leaned forward to kiss his brow. "It won't be much longer now, darling. I miss you so!"

In the end, Pandora finally convinced Ward that he must go see to the business of his mine. He left her grudgingly and only after receiving reassurances from old Dr. Saenger.

Pandora settled into her last days before delivery by letting Cassie pamper her. She finished the painting on the lid of her box. She smiled at the thought of twins. One child seemed a miracle to her, two would certainly be a double blessing.

On the morning of April tenth, Angelica waited until Jacob had left for his office. Donning her widow's weeds, she set out for her father-in-law's house, where he still maintained his office.

The converted back parlor, which was usually filled with patients waiting to see old Dr. Saenger, was conspicuously empty this morning. White-haired Mrs. Kuntz, who kept his records and collected his bills, stopped Angelica from entering his private office.

"The doctor isn't seeing patients this morning. He's not feeling well. One of his heart spells, I'm afraid." She peered over her spectacles, trying to see through Angelica's heavy veil.

"I'm not here for medical advice," Angelica told the woman. "This is a matter of an extremely private nature." She swept past the woman, not even bothering to knock on the doctor's door.

"I must speak with you *now*," she said to the pale, ill-looking man at the desk.

Recognizing his daughter-in-law's voice, Dr. Saenger waved the flustered Mrs. Kuntz away and rose to shut the door.

"Won't you have a seat, Angelica?" he offered in a tired but polite voice. "Actually, I've been expecting to see you. I'm surprised you waited so long."

"Jacob told you I was back? I should have guessed." She sat down across from him and drew up her veil. "If you expected me, then you must know why I'm here."

Dr. Saenger nodded. "Jacob refused you. There's no sense wasting my time or yours because I won't be a party to this either." He frowned at her and leaned forward. "Jacob said that you had agreed to forget this madness. He also told me that he didn't believe you when you gave him your promise."

The pain around Dr. Saenger's heart had increased. His daughter-in-law's visit wasn't helping matters any. He had vowed to maintain control, but suddenly he felt compelled to let her know exactly what he thought of her. "Let me tell you now, young woman, that just because you want a baby doesn't give you the right to demand such a horrible crime from my son. You've treated him miserably from the start— lying, cheating, demanding everything in the world. You're a bad one! I've known it all along. Why my Jacob married you instead of your sweet cousin is something I will never understand. The good are rewarded, Angelica, but the wicked are forced to pay for their sins. Perhaps that's why you remain childless while Pandora awaits the birth of her twins."

"Twins?" Angelica gasped. Her mind flew suddenly in a dozen different directions at once. She thought of the daintily appointed nursery at the house on 13th Street—the dimity curtains, the white wicker furniture, the *empty* crib. Then her thoughts went to Pandora—huge with child, carrying two babies, enough to fill her own empty nest. She glanced up at her father-in-law. He was indeed ill this morning and his fiery lecture had taken its toll. His face was the color of wallpaper paste; his eyes were dull and filled with pain. His breathing seemed labored. Angelica's gaze shifted to the bottle of pills he took for his heart ailment, sitting there within reach on the corner of the desk.

She rose suddenly, as if she meant to leave. Turning abruptly, she let her cape sweep the edge of the desk, knocking the pills to the floor. With the toe of her shoe, she nudged the bottle out of sight under the rug.

She didn't leave. Instead, she turned back to Dr. Saenger. "I haven't come to argue with you or to hear what you think of me. Frankly, I don't care. I've had enough lectures from your son to last me a lifetime. In fact, I've come to tell you that I've had quite a belly-full of your dear Jacob. Our marriage was doomed from the start. I know about his pretty little whore in Postoffice Street. I've decided to divorce him on grounds of adultery."

She watched the old man's face closely, feeling the warmth of triumph in her breast. At first he looked startled, then disbelieving, one hand clutched at his chest as he opened his mouth to speak.

The effort of the words took a great toll on him. "No, Angelica. You wouldn't do that to him. Think of the scandal. You're his wife for better or for worse. You can still have a child. No divorce, please . . ."

Angelica tossed her head defiantly and stared at the old doctor with a look to kill. "I've decided I don't want a child of my own—not if Jacob is the father. I don't love him. How could I possibly love a baby he had fathered? That is, if he is even capable, which I doubt. No, a divorce is what I want and a divorce is what I shall have! Your son can go to hell without me!"

Dr. Saenger's face flushed with rage, then drained of all color. Frantically, he reached out for his pills, but found only empty air as he slumped across the desk.

"Call Mrs. Kuntz," he choked out. "My medicine . . ."

Angelica smiled down at the ailing man. "Aren't you feeling well, Father dear?"

"Please . . ." he gasped.

"I'm leaving. I'll send Mrs. Kuntz in on my way out." She smiled at him and her blue eyes flashed like the Arctic sun striking an iceberg. "Such a sudden attack—I do hope it was nothing I said."

Angelica informed Mrs. Kuntz that the doctor needed her. Without waiting another moment, she swept out of the house and headed home, glowing with triumph under her long, black veil.

Old Dr. Saenger would not be delivering babies anytime soon. Jacob would be forced to take over those duties for him, smoothing the way for Angelica. The strait-laced old man might have presented a problem, but Angelica knew how to manipulate her husband. Jacob *would* do as she commanded!

Long before Angelica had set out for her visit with Dr. Saenger, Pandora realized her time had come. In the hours before dawn, she tried to deny the pains. She had promised Ward that she would wait for his return. Unfortunately, Mother Nature had other ideas.

Cassie came in with her mistress's breakfast tray to find Pandora's face a mask of agony.

"Lord, help us!" she cried, slamming the tray down on the nearest table and running to the bed. "It ain't time yet, Miss Pan!"

Pandora managed a weak laugh. "Oh, yes it is! You'd best call Dr. Saenger right now, Cassie. I'm afraid these babies are rather anxious to get out into the world."

Muttering frantically, Cassie fled to the study to telephone the doctor. When Mrs. Kuntz finally answered the doctor's phone, she sounded as hysterical as Pandora's maid.

"No, the doctor cannot come. He is ill, they're taking him to the hospital now."

"What I'm supposed to do, then?" Cassie wailed into the receiver. "Miss Pandora's fixing to have her babies. I got to have a doctor over here *now!*"

"I'm sorry, but I can't help you. Call someone else. I must go to Dr. Saenger." Then Mrs. Kuntz abruptly hung up on Cassie.

Cassie hurried back to the bedroom to see how Pandora was. She had no training in midwifery and the only other doctor she could think of was Jacob Saenger.

"Is he coming?" Pandora demanded, realizing by the frequency of the pains that there was no time to lose.

Cassie shook her head and rolled her eyes as she explained their predicament. "What can we do?" she moaned.

Pandora clutched her belly and gritted her teeth, trying

desperately not to scream as another contraction gripped her body. "Call Jacob," she managed. "Quickly, Cass!"

"Oh, God, no," Jacob whispered into the telephone.

Less than an hour ago his father had been rushed to the hospital. He'd been unable to leave his office until he'd finished splinting a ten-year-old boy's broken leg. Now this. Cassie, hysterical on the phone, sobbing to him that Miss Pan was having her babies!

Jacob allowed himself only a moment to remember that this was the woman he'd hoped would bear his own children—the woman he wished he had married. He could not afford to ponder such things right now. Pandora was simply a patient—a patient who desperately needed his help.

"I have an emergency," he told the people waiting in his office. "Leave your names with my nurse and come back later. I'm sorry."

Within minutes of Cassie's frantic call, Jacob was pounding the knocker on the massive front door of the Gabriel castle. One of the servants opened it immediately and showed him upstairs. Some of Jacob's panic fled when he saw Pandora, lying propped up on pillows in her huge bed, looking tired and in pain, but smiling bravely.

"Thank God I made it in time," he said, hurrying over to her.

She laughed softly. "I'll second that! How's your father?"

" 'Holding his own,' is all they'll say at the hospital. What about you?" He was busy now, taking her pulse, listening to her heart, tossing instructions over his shoulder to Cassie.

"I'm much better now that you're here, Jacob. I was beginning to get nervous. Things seem to be happening so quickly."

Jacob looked into Pandora's eyes for a moment, allowing her a fleeting glimpse of his own nervousness. "I'm sorry my father couldn't be here," he whispered. "This can't be easy for you."

"Nor you, Jacob," she returned. "But I didn't know who else to call."

"You did the right thing. No one will take better care of

you and these babies than I will. No one else would feel as deeply . . ." He broke off, knowing that he was about to go too far.

Three hours later, Pandora lay in bed, beaming down into the two tiny, red faces of her twin daughters. She kissed each girl on the forehead, then held out her hand to Jacob.

He squeezed her fingers warmly and beamed down at the three of them. "I never saw a lovelier sight, Pandora. I'm so proud of you."

"You should be equally proud of yourself, Jacob," she told him. "It isn't every day that a doctor brings *two* beautiful babies into the world. No one could have managed it better," she assured him. "Thank you, Jacob. With all my heart, I thank you."

"Have you thought of names for your young ladies yet?" Jacob asked, embarrassed by Pandora's gratitude and wanting to get on a safer topic.

She smiled down at her daughters. "Ward and I talked about that before he left. We decided that if they were girls, we would call them Miriam and Meraiah." She glanced up at Jacob with a bewildered expression. "But which is which? They are identical!"

He laughed. "I supposed you'll have to tie a different color ribbon around their wrists or something of that sort until they develop their individual personalities."

Just then a soft knock at the bedroom door made both of them turn. Jacob frowned, but Pandora smiled her welcome.

"Angelica, I didn't know you were back in Galveston. How nice to see you," Pandora said.

Jacob stared at his wife, hardly able to believe his eyes. Gone was her black costume and with it her hateful expression. She was dressed in a becoming spring gown of pale blue to match her eyes. Her face shone with innocent pleasure at the sight of her cousin and the two newborns.

Angelica hurried to the bed and kissed Pandora's cheek. "My, my, but you and my dear husband have done a fine morning's work. Just look at those two beauties. Pandora, I'm so happy for you."

Suddenly, Pandora lost her smile as her eyes took in the

other woman's slender waist. "Angelica, what about your baby?" she asked softly, not certain if the tidings would be happy or sad.

Angelica looked down and she shook her head gently. "I lost it," she whispered. "While I was away."

"Oh, I'm so sorry!" Pandora sympathized. "Jacob didn't tell me."

Angelica forced her sweetest smile. "I asked him not to. I'm terribly superstituous; I was afraid it might bring you bad luck."

"It was kind of you to be concerned," Pandora answered.

Jacob stood back, silent, observing his wife with new respect for her acting abilities. What was she up to now? He couldn't begin to guess.

Angelica turned to Jacob, her arms open to embrace him. She went to him and kissed his cheek affectionately. "I just found out about your father, darling. I do hope it isn't as serious as it sounds. I've been to the hospital, but they wouldn't let me see him."

"We'll go there from here and see what we can find out about his condition, Angelica." He stared down at her, puzzled. "That is, if you have nothing more pressing."

Angelica turned back to Pandora and the twins. "Well, I had planned to visit here for a bit."

Ah, here it comes! Jacob thought. She means to wait for the right moment and then steal away with one of the twins. I should have guessed, he told himself.

"But I'm sure Pandora needs to rest," Angelica continued. "We can go to the hospital and I'll come back at a more convenient time."

Jacob stared at his wife, dumbfounded. Had something happened to snap Angelica out of her madness?

After the Saengers left, Pandora drifted in and out between napping, nursing, and just smiling down into the adorable faces of her two little girls. She couldn't make herself believe that they were real and all hers.

What a joy it would be when Ward returned and she could present his two daughters to him for the first time.

The late afternoon sun warmed the room. The sweet

scents of flowers drifted in through the open window, and the soft drone of bees at work on the jasmine-covered trellis lulled Pandora into a half-sleep.

Suddenly, the room was filled with shadows. Pandora's eyes flew open. A tall man stood at the foot of her bed. She sat up from the pillows. "Ward?" she whispered, but she knew better.

Another man who loved her had come from far, far away in time and space to pay his respects to her and her beautiful daughters. The twins were a part of him even as they were a part of her husband.

She relaxed against the pillows and stared at him—his big, rough form, his wind-blown hair, the shining green of his eyes.

"You've done well, madame," he said at length. "Well, indeed!"

"Thank you." Pandora wasn't sure if she said the words aloud or only thought them.

"Our Jeannette and now Miriam and Meraiah. All lovely little ladies born to the most beautiful woman in the world out of the greatest love any man could ever know." He bowed to her. "I salute you!"

She held her sleeping daughters toward him. "They are as much yours as mine. Your love helped create them."

He nodded and smiled, then walked to the side of the bed. Fishing into the pocket of his canvas britches, he brought out two necklaces of tiny, delicately carved beads. "To tell them apart," he explained. "I think pink coral for Miriam. Yes, she will be as gentle and soft as an angel's wing. And for Meraiah, who bears her mother's spirit and fire, turquoise to match her eyes and to protect her."

Gently, he fastened the necklaces about the sleeping infants' necks. He seemed to know which child was which. He leaned down and kissed the twins on the soft, fiery down of their heads. When he rose, his eyes met Pandora's. She felt his loving gaze warm her through. A moment later, she felt his kiss on her lips, stirring long-slumbering embers to flame.

"I must say good-bye now," he whispered. "But I could not let you be alone when our babies came."

"Wait!" Pandora cried. But he vanished as quickly as he had appeared.

Hours later, she awoke as dawn was coloring the room. She lay very still, staring out the window, thinking of the strange dream. Had it been real or only another vision?

When Cassie brought the twins in for their early morning feeding, Pandora's heart sank. Jean Laffite's gifts had vanished; the necklaces were gone. Did she imagine his visit?

"No," she whispered to herself. "I know he was here. I can still feel him near me."

Pandora smiled; for the first time, Jean Laffite had actually kissed *her* lips, not Nicolette's.

Chapter Nineteen

"No, don't tell me, darling! Let me guess."

Ward Gabriel, still travel-dusty and unshaven, stood with his arm around his wife's slim waist. He was gazing down at his week-old daughters as they slept in their cradle under the merry, watchful eye of the fat-cheeked cherub their mother had painted for them.

"That has to be Meraiah on the right and, of course, Miriam on the left."

Pandora, still not quite able to believe that Ward was really home, looked up at him with a twinkle in her green eyes. "A lucky guess!" she answered with a laugh.

Suddenly, Ward's face clouded. "No!" he said emphatically. "Oddly enough, it was no guess at all. I don't know how, darling, but I knew for certain. I had the oddest dream the night they were born. It seemed as if they came to me and told me their names. The next morning I went out and bought these so other people can tell them apart."

Pandora gasped aloud when he fished the two necklaces out of his pocket.

"Turquoise for Meraiah because she has her mother's spirit and fire," he explained, "and coral as soft as an angel's wing for sweet little Miriam." Ward shook his head in wonder. "I don't understand it. But I knew exactly when they were born and that they were girls. I was here in spirit when you gave birth to them, darling."

So you were, my love! Pandora thought. She dared not mention her odd dream to her husband. He would not be pleased to hear that Laffite had paid a personal call while he was away.

She squeezed his arm affectionately. "I'm so glad you're home, Ward."

Staring down at her, his dark eyes gleaming, he whispered, "I've been gone *too* long. From now on, I'm staying here with you and our girls where I belong."

Then closing his arms around the woman he loved more than life itself, Ward pressed her close and sought her lips for a real welcome. He felt his body harden as he held her, and he was pleased when Pandora clung to him as if she never meant to let him go again. She had missed him, he could tell. Almost as much as he had missed her.

They were together again, and their daughters were with them, and all was safe and secure and right with their world. In a few weeks, they could make love to each other again. Oh, what a glorious time that would be!

Pandora, luxuriating in her husband's embrace, became instantly aware of his arousal. She smiled. How good it felt to be held and kissed and desired again.

Secure in Ward's love, she almost told him of her vision of Jean Laffite. *No, it was no vision,* she corrected in her mind. Phantoms did not kiss that way! Her husband was not likely to take kindly to another man in their bedroom—real or imagined. She decided against telling Ward. Things were good between them now; there was no need to stir up trouble. He would never understand what she had seen; she wasn't sure she understood it herself. Talk of Laffite at such a tender moment would only hurt Ward's feelings and spoil his homecoming. She was determined not to let that happen. There would be plenty of time later to discuss the matter.

When Ward drew away at last, he looked down into his wife's face with concern. "Shouldn't you be in bed? You've had quite an ordeal; giving birth is no easy task."

Pandora laughed. "And how would you know?"

"Well, it just seems that you ought to be resting."

She shook her head and smiled to reassure him. "Jacob says I'm in tip-top shape. He told me that I would know when I needed to rest; he doesn't hold with new mothers being totally confined to their beds and waited on like invalids." She laughed and tossed her long, bright-coppery hair. "Goodness knows, darling, I had enough of that before the twins arrived. Besides, Jacob stops by every day on his way to the office to see that all three of us are behaving ourselves."

Now Ward was truly frowning. His whole face took on a menacing expression.

"What's wrong, darling?" Pandora demanded. "You look like a hurricane about to roar in over the Gulf."

Ward waved her question away. "Nothing, nothing at all, Pan." Then he confessed, "It's just that I wish old Doc Saenger had been here for the delivery."

"Well, of course, we all wished that. Poor man, he's much better now, thank goodness."

Pandora had missed his meaning, but it was just as well, Ward told himself. Better that she not even suspect how the news of Jacob's tending her at the births had affected him. Jealousy was not his most endearing trait, but he could do nothing about the way he felt. After all, Pandora and Jacob Saenger had planned to marry and have a family of their own. The thought of his wife's former fiancé presiding at her delivery seemed almost indecent to him.

"I'm glad to hear the old man's doing well," Ward answered. "When will he be able to leave the hospital?" He left the rest of his question unstated: *And when will he be able to take over your care from his son?*

"Jacob said he'll be released by the end of the week. He's going to stay with Jacob and Angelica for a time. She'll nurse him until he's able to go back to his own home."

Ward bellowed a laugh. *"Angelica?* Nurse her father-in-law? I thought she despised him; I can't imagine her taking decent care of anyone."

Arm-in-arm, they quietly made their way out of the nursery and down the hallway to their bedroom as they talked.

"You are in for another fine surprise, my darling," Pandora said. Her voice promised him exceptionally good news, but even as she spoke, her face betrayed her misgivings. "Angelica, it seems, is a changed woman."

"It seems?" Ward repeated suspiciously.

She waved her hand in the air as if to dismiss her doubts. "I shouldn't have said it that way. She *has* changed, Ward. I think it has something to do with her losing the baby. Perhaps she's mellowed from that tragic experience. At any rate, she has been a perfect dear since our girls arrived. She's over here every chance she gets, helping me and Cassie with the twins. She's really going to make a wonderful mother someday, and already she's like a dear aunt to our babies."

Ward knew his wife too well not to sense her lingering distrust of her cousin. "But all the same, you suspect her of ulterior motives, eh, darling?"

"No, Ward!" she said flatly, trying to make herself mean it. "I will not allow myself to continue doubting Angelica. I think that for whatever reason she has finally decided to grow up. She's even confided in me that she and Jacob are sharing their bed again."

"Sharing a bed, eh? Now there's a thought to savor!" Ward stood in the middle of their bedroom, looking about him, caressing his wife and the room he loved most with warm eyes. "Ah, it's good to be home!" he sighed.

Pandora went to him and slipped her arms about his waist, laying her head on his chest. "I've missed you so!" she whispered. "There is no *home* without you, my love."

She knew the effect she was having on him. Ward could take little more of holding, kissing, touching his wife; he strained to keep himself in check. He needed a bath desperately. He would make it a *cold* one, he decided.

"How's that newfangled bathtub working?" he asked.

Pandora laughed. "How would I know? It's been so long since I used it. I certainly couldn't get down into it before the twins came. I must do with sponge baths for another five weeks, Jacob tells me."

Jacob again! Ward moaned inwardly.

Aloud, he said, "Well, I'm about to find out how it's working, and not a moment too soon. I must smell like a Mexican mule."

Shedding his coat and shirt as he went, Ward headed for the marble and tile bathroom off their dressing room. To both his pleasure and his dismay, Pandora followed, saying, "I'll scrub your back for you, darling."

It seemed to Pandora that she had been waiting months to see *all* of her husband again. Her eyes misted as she caressed his naked torso lovingly with her warm gaze. She felt herself blush when he shucked off his trousers. He turned his back to her, but not before she saw his full, pulsing erection.

"Here, let me turn on the taps for you," she offered.

"Make it cold!" he commanded, setting her cheeks burning again.

They both stood watching the faucet like nervous children. The pipes gurgled and sputtered for a time. Finally, a thin stream of water from the cistern trickled into the claw-footed, porcelain tub. Ward eased himself down, gritting his teeth against the first shock. The tepid water had the desired effect. Ward pretended not to hear Pandora's sigh of regret as he shrank before her eyes.

Cool water could not dampen his desire for long . . . not with Pandora's gentle hands smoothing over his back and shoulders, around his neck, and down his chest. He leaned his head back and let out a long, pleasured sigh.

"There's not another woman on earth with hands like yours, Pandora. Do that again. Yes! Lower . . . lower. Ah-h-h!"

By the time Ward's bath was finished, Pandora's loose gown was drenched. Her hair was damp and her nose tipped with soap. Her whole body tingled for her husband, but she knew she would have to wait. However she had taken care to relieve the need that plagued him. She felt it her duty and her joy to satisfy Ward as best she could—with slick, soapy hands and deep, probing kisses.

Jacob shared Pandora's suspicions concerning the change in Angelica. There was a change, too, in the way she gave herself to him in their bed. Before she had deserted him for the gardener—oh, yes, he knew all about that!—Angelica had been at best a reluctant partner; now she seemed insatiable. Almost every night and morning . . . and when he hesitated, she went out of her way to seduce him into taking her. Jacob couldn't decide if he should be flattered or alarmed. He felt like a greedy child turned loose in a candy store. The variety of sweets she used to tempt him was beyond his wildest imaginings. Where on earth, he wondered, had she learned such erotic tricks?

A month after the twins' arrival, Jacob awoke on a steamy May morning to find Angelica, naked, her body poised over his. Her hair was a wild mass of silver, spilling over his belly and thighs as she took him, deeply, into her mouth. He lay rigid, willing control over his body. Flames seemed to shoot from her tongue, consuming him totally.

"Oh, God, Angelica!" he moaned. "What are you doing to me?"

When he felt himself about to explode, she lifted her face and stared directly into his eyes, her own heavy-lidded, her lips puffy, her delicate nostrils flared. For several moments, she stared at him, a vacant expression in her pale eyes. Then with movements as swift as those of a striking snake, she stradled him and let his hot, moist member glide into her. Hair flying, head thrown back, hands clutching his hips, she rode him frantically to the finish.

Then, to Jacob's total amazement, she rolled off of him, curled in a fetal position at this side, and wept. When he tried to soothe her, to thank her, she became almost hysterical. It was as if she had enjoyed none of the performance, as if he had forced her into her wanton acts for his pleasure alone.

Finally, he gave up trying to talk to her. He rose and dressed silently, feeling guilty as hell. But why? It had been all her idea. Granted, he had enjoyed it, but he would never have suggested any such thing to his wife.

"I have to go to the office now, Angelica," he said at last.

No answer.

"That was nice . . . what you did."

A sob.

Jacob reached out to touch her quaking shoulder, but she shrugged away. He gave up.

"I'll be home around six."

Angelica, to be on the safe side, kept up her sobbing until she heard the front door slam shut. Then she sat up in bed and wiped away her tears, smiling at herself in the mirror across the room. She smoothed her damp palms down over her breasts and felt her nipples tingle.

Jacob must never know that she actually enjoyed their lovemaking. Let him think that she gave in to him only as a humble, repentant wife—a servant to her master.

"Let them *all* think what they will about me and be damned!" she told the smiling image in her mirror. It was enough that *she* knew the truth. Jacob Saenger was only a tool to be used until she had what she wanted.

She half-closed her eyes and continued staring into the mirror as she reached under her pillow and drew out a dark curl tied in faded scarlet ribbon. She kissed the coarse lock, cradling it gently in her palm. This was her talisman, her charm. She had slipped upstairs and taken it from the box in Pandora's studio that night of the dinner party back in the fall. A lock of Ward's hair. For now, it was all that she possessed of him, but soon . . .

She stared at the dark curl, visualizing Ward's strong, determined face, his muscular body. She tried to imagine how she would feel the first time they made love. She flung her head back, closed her eyes, and sighed. Jacob had never satisfied her, but *Ward* would! Ward Gabriel was more than man enough to tame her; very soon now she would give him his chance.

Smiling to herself, Angelica thought through her plans. How clear her thinking had become these past weeks! Her whole childhood had been spent in Pandora's shadow, but no more. Now, she knew what she must do. Ward Gabriel was the key to everything—her happiness, her life, her very existence.

She had watched him closely since his return from Mexico but had done nothing to arouse his suspicions. She would never get him away from Pandora by flaunting herself as she had in the past. She realized that now. Ward was a man of deep loyalties and still deeper emotions. He loved with all his heart and soul. Only one person in this life would ever challenge his love for Pandora—his little daughter Meraiah. Angelica had seen the way he looked at her, the gentle way he held her. He loved Miriam, too, but not with the depth of feeling he had for the bolder of the twins.

"So-o-o," Angelica sighed, lolling back against her pillows, "where Meraiah goes, Ward Gabriel is sure to follow."

She thought back to the morning she had visited old Dr. Saenger—the morning of his attack. How like Pandora to ruin her plans! As soon as she heard about the expected twins, a new scheme had taken shape in her mind. She had meant for Jacob to deliver the babies, she had planned to be there, and to take one for her own. Damn Pandora for coming early! By the time she found out that Pandora was in labor, with Jacob at her bedside, it had been too late. She smiled, thinking of her new and better plan.

Angelica rose and dressed in a demure pink dimity morning gown. She would go to the castle on Broadway to take the twins for their stroll as was her custom of late.

"How nice that they trust me so," she said to her scheming image in the mirror.

The bright spring turned to the brassy heat of summer; the hot Gulf breezes blew the sweet scent of oleander about the island. The tiny spit of sand that was the greatest city in Texas took on the lush green of the tropics. Life slowed to a lazy pace. Offices closed in the heat of the afternoon. Adults and children alike napped after dinner at noon. Then as the sun sank with blazing glory into the Gulf and the sea air cooled in the evening, Galveston came alive. Carriages and bicycles cluttered the streets. Servants pushed their masters and mistresses along the beach in great, wheeled wicker chairs. Laughing children played in gardens. Mr. and Mrs. Ward Gabriel proudly strolled their twin daughters up and down Broadway, greeting friends and neighbors and basking in the compliments paid Meraiah and Miriam.

Pandora felt that this particular July evening was inordinately fine. Her life lately had been so full and so perfect that it almost frightened her. Fate was not usually so kind. She glanced up at Ward. He was tipping his hat to a couple coming toward them.

"Jacob, Angelica, so nice to see you!" he greeted.

Something like a cool, dark shadow suddenly passed over Pandora's soul. The smile on her face mirrored nothing of her inner feelings. Why didn't she trust this change in her cousin? She hated herself for being so suspicious. Angelica had challenged her all her life; could a person change so drastically in such a short span of time?

Angelica hurried to the white wicker pram and bent over the babies. "Oh, my two little darlings!" she crooned. She smiled at Pandora and said, "I declare, it seems that if I miss seeing them for one single day they grow and change so I hardly know them. Just look how plump they're getting, darling." She squeezed her husband's arm.

Jacob glanced down at the babies and nodded. "I have to compliment you, Pan. You're doing one fine job of mothering."

Pandora couldn't be sure, it seemed she glimpsed a flicker of annoyance in Angelica's pale blue eyes.

"I've had a lot of help," Pandora replied. "I don't know what I'd do without Angelica. She's been wonderful with the babies. A great help to me."

"We haven't seen either of you in almost a week," Ward said, secretly grateful for their unusual absence.

"Busy season," Jacob answered. "Seems like the heat brings out every illness known to man and some that aren't. I'm at the office everyday from dawn till after dark. This heat today," he shook his head and wiped his brow, "it's even been too hot for the sick to come out for attention. Thank goodness, it's finally cooling off."

"It's been a scorcher, all right," Ward agreed.

Angelica had been standing by silently. As she gazed at Ward she felt a hunger rise inside her. She decided that the time had come; she could wait no longer.

"Pandora, have you any plans for tomorrow?" she asked. "I thought I might stop by in the morning."

Pandora tried not to let her relief show as she answered, "I'm afraid I do have an appointment in the morning, Angelica. My dressmaker is here from New Orleans. I suggested we meet at the hotel so she wouldn't have to bring all those bolts of fabric to the house." Pandora smoothed her hands down over her slender waist. "Motherhood has taken its toll on my figure. I'm having a whole new summer wardrobe made, with a few inches added. So, I'll be with Madame Leone all morning."

Angelica beamed a glorious smile at her cousin. "Why, that's perfect! I'll come by early, before it gets too hot, and take the girls out, if that's all right with you. That way Cassie will be free to take care of her other chores and the twins will still have their morning outing. Jacob says that babies need lots of fresh air and sunshine, isn't that right, my darling?"

Jacob nodded and mumbled his agreement, noting the slight look of displeasure in Pandora's eyes. He'd known her too many years not to be able to read her expressions. She didn't trust Angelica any more than he did.

"Angelica, perhaps Pandora had other plans for the girls," Jacob suggested.

Pandora shook her head, relenting. "No, that will be fine. It's very generous of you to offer, Angelica."

The Saengers walked on. Pandora was no longer smiling and chatting; the lovely evening had soured.

"Oh, Lord!" Ward said suddenly, in a disgusted tone. "I knew we should have gone back to the house a while ago."

Pandora looked up to see old Nettie bearing determinedly down on them, her flowered hat flapping in the stiff breeze.

"Be nice to her, darling," Pandora pleaded, touching Ward's arm in a placating gesture. "She's harmless enough."

"I don't like her around the girls."

Before either of them could say another word, Nettie was upon them. "You shouldn't let that one near them babies," she scolded.

"Who do you mean?" Pandora asked.

Nettie leaned forward, glanced this way and that, then whispered, "You know who! That bad woman! Ain't you ever gonna learn? Ain't she caused you enough trouble already?"

Realizing immediately that Nettie meant Angelica, Pandora felt her skin prickle. Nettie's words seemed to confirm her own nameless fears, but Pandora refused to admit to herself that Angelica might be a true threat.

"Here, I brung these for the twins." Nettie shoved two bags decorated with feathers and bones toward Pandora. Whatever was inside the little sacks reeked of dead things and strong herbs. "To keep 'em both safe," she explained. "This one's for Meraiah. She'll need a more powerful charm. Even that turquoise necklace her daddy give her won't be strong enough for what's coming."

"I don't think they need . . ." Ward began.

Nettie cut him off. "Time you was coming around to see old Dan'l, Miss Pan. He's got real lucid of late. I reckon his wait's almost over. Now that his old brain's unscramblin', he'll know you soon."

Before either Pandora or Ward could say another word, Nettie shuffled away, her long skirts flapping out behind her like the bright wings of a bird.

"Crazy old coot!" Ward snapped. "I want you to keep her away from the girls, Pan. And I *don't* want you going to that filthy shack to see old Daniel. He might be carrying some disease that you'd bring home to the twins." He looked at Pandora hard suddenly. "What 'bad woman' was she referring to?"

Pandora sighed. "Ward, I think it's time we had a long talk. Let's go home, shall we?"

"You know that I love you, don't you?" Pandora asked, almost dreading his answer. She knew the jealousy that consumed Ward at times, even if he tried to hide it.

The twins were in bed. Pandora and Ward sat together in the garden, cool glasses of wine punch before them on a round, wrought iron table.

"What kind of question is that, darling? Of course you love me and I love you!"

She touched his hand. "Well, I just want you to remember that while you're listening to what I have to say. We've been married for some time and now we have the twins to cement our union further. Angelica tried to come between us, and I know how uneasy you've felt with Jacob taking care of me these past months. But I don't believe that there is anyone or anything that can separate us."

"Certainly not," Ward affirmed, feeling guilty that Pandora had guessed his secret feelings toward Jacob.

Pandora smiled at him a little sadly. "I'm glad you agree, darling, because it's going to take all your love and understanding to help me through what I have to tell you."

Pandora began at the very beginning—going back over all the things she'd learned in Paris in Dr. Pinel's office. She told Ward everything, including her most recent vision of Jean Laffite and the necklaces—the very ones that Ward himself had brought for their daughters. "I don't know what part old Nettie has in all this but she seems convinced that you and I both share ancient souls. In our lives as Nicolette and Laffite, we experienced great tragedies, the final one being Nicolette's murder."

Ward twisted uneasily in his chair, remembering the oddly personal desolation he'd experienced that day at the Eden Museé when he'd come upon Nicolette's death scene. He still saw it in his nightmares.

"Nettie seems to think," Pandora continued, "that the evil from our past lives has somehow followed us into the present. Nettie does not trust Angelica. So there it is, darling. The whole truth! I need to have you share this with me. I'm afraid our relationship will never be complete until you accept all these things. I hope you understand."

Ward Gabriel didn't understand any of it. Nor did he want to. The one emotion raging through him at the moment was anger. He had hoped that Pandora had put aside these wild notions. He felt now exactly as he had that first night that he'd meant to make love to her—the night she had lain in his arms and called him by another man's name. The jealousy tore at his gut and raged in his heart like acid eating away at raw flesh when she spoke of Nicolette's love for Jean Laffite. He feared that what Pandora really described was her love for some other man.

"You must be tired, Pan," he said at length, his voice cool and abrupt. "Why don't you go on up to bed?"

Pandora did as he suggested, but with a heavy heart. Ward was not pleased with what she'd told him. He didn't understand at all. He didn't believe her. How could she ever make him see the truth? How could they ever be totally one, if he refused to accept what was?

All night she tossed and turned, alone in their big bed. Ward never came to her. When she rose in the morning, Ward had already left to go to his office. With a dull ache in her head and her heart, she dressed. She almost cancelled her appointment with the dressmaker. Nothing seemed right this morning. It was more than a simple headache, it was like a premonition. Yet, try as she would, she could see not the slightest shadow when she willed her mind into the future. Finally, she told herself she was only being silly. She would go on with her day as planned.

On the way out, she told Cassie that Angelica would stop by to take the girls out for a stroll. Before she left, Pandora went to the white wicker pram and tucked Nettie's two foul-smelling fetishes under the pillows. She felt an odd sense of relief as she went out the door.

Pandora was hardly down the front stairs before Cassie came to put a clean coverlet in the pram. Plumping the pillows, she came across Nettie's charms.

"Them pesky cats," she complained. "Been in the babies' stroller playing again and hiding their dirty old toys!"

She tossed the two smelly objects in the nearest trash basket.

The Beach Hotel had been closed since the beginning of the season until proper sewer lines could be laid. So far, no work was in progress. Angelica had been careful to scout

out the building's possibilities. She knew that the only living beings in the place were the night watchman and his bull terrier. On the night of July 3, preparing carefully for this day, she had sneaked into the place, lured the dog with a bit of poison meat, and disposed of its body in the Gulf. The barking terrier had been a problem. The watchman was not. She knew from careful observation that the man left his dog on guard alone while he went down the beach every night to drink with his buddies. So far as she knew, the lazy man had not bothered to get another dog.

As she walked along Broadway, pushing Meraiah and Miriam in their stroller the morning of July 22, she went back over her plans carefully in her mind. She left no detail to chance. She had stocked one room in the empty hotel with everything she would need. She had her train tickets. She had reservations at a cheap, out-of-the-way hotel in Houston under the name of Smith. Now all that was left was for the day to pass.

After her outing with the twins, Angelica made a great show of leaving for Cassie's benefit. But the moment the servants were all out of sight, she slipped back into the castle and up the stairs, hiding in Pandora's studio.

The afternoon was long and hot. The paint and turpentine smells made her head swim. She should have gone ahead with her plan earlier. Waiting was making her jumpy. Still, she reminded herself, she needed the cover of darkness.

Slowly, the afternoon faded into evening. The supper hour came and went. She cracked the door open slightly for a breath of fresh air. She could hear voices down the hallway—Pandora and Ward arguing.

"Dammit! I can't help the way I feel! I figured we'd both be better off if I left last night."

"But where were you?" Pandora was crying, Angelica could tell.

"I slept at my office—*alone!*" He was almost yelling. Angelica smiled. "I figured you wouldn't mind."

"But I do mind, Ward! I want you here with me!"

His laugh was cruel and hurtful. "It gets a bit crowded

with *three* of us sharing a bed! You let me know when Laffite leaves and I'll come back."

"Ward, please!" Pandora sobbed.

Angelica heard Ward's heavy footsteps in the hall, then the front door slammed.

"My poor darling," Angelica whispered, closing the studio door carefully and smiling to herself. "Don't worry, things will be all right soon."

A short while later, it was dark out. Time! Angelica knew from listening at the door that Pandora was still in her bedroom. The servants, sensing that all was not well above, had remained on the first floor. It was easier than Angelica could have wished to slip down the hall to the nursery and take the sleeping infant. The back stairs, too, were clear. She hurried down and out the servants' entrance. In less than half an hour, she was hurrying up the side steps of the deserted Beach Hotel.

Her heart pounded with a mixture of fear and excitement.

"We've done it!" she cried aloud to the baby in her arms. "You're mine now. Don't worry, little love, soon your daddy will be with us."

Angelica moved cautiously across the front veranda, listening for the slightest sound. The watchman was off at his usual nightly amusement. She felt in her pocket for the knife she had brought just in case, hoping she wouldn't have to use it.

Going to a door with a broken pane, she reached through and flipped the lock. The place looked eerie and strange at night—all dark shapes and shadows. The wooden structure creaked and groaned and the wind howled at the eaves. She trembled slightly, but forced herself to remain calm.

"We have nothing to fear now, Meraiah. The hard part is over. No one will find us here. Nothing can hurt us."

Suddenly, out of nowhere a black shape charged toward them. The creature's snarls, Angelica's screams, and the baby's wails filled the silent building. It all happened so quickly that Angelica did not have time to realize the true extent of her fear until the new watchdog lay in a bloody heap at her feet, her knife lodged in its ribs.

Trembling badly, Angelica soothed the crying child as she made her way to the room where they would wait until it was time to leave for the train.

She slumped to the floor of the windowless pantry, placing Meraiah on a blanket she had hidden there earlier. Feeling about for her supplies, she located a kerosene lantern and a box of matches. The light helped. Her trembling ceased. Carefully, she took stock of everything—her packed carpetbag, food for herself, a bottle and milk for the baby, and her traveling clothes. Quickly, she changed into the widow's weeds she had worn back to Galveston. She had her story all planned. Mrs. Smith's husband had been lost at sea. She was traveling with her newborn child, back to her family in the East.

"Yes, a new mother in mourning. My privacy will be ensured," she told Meraiah. "Nothing and no one can stop us now!"

Pandora cried for more than an hour after Ward walked out. It seemed she would never be able to stop. She knew she had to pull herself together; it would soon be time to feed the twins. Cassie swore that "Weeping sours a mother's milk." Pandora wondered what she was going to do. How was she ever going to survive if Ward refused to understand? Her whole world seemed to be crashing down around her.

Finally, she dried her tears and rose from the bed, feeling drained and weak. She could not let this bring her down. She loved Ward and he loved her, nothing else mattered. He would return soon, after he'd cooled off. Then they would talk and make up.

She walked down the hallway to see if either of the babies was awake yet. Meraiah, the greedy one, always demanded her feeding first. Little Miriam would wait patiently, accepting gratefully whatever her sister left her.

Pandora lifted the netting over the cradle and peered down. There lay Miriam on her stomach, softly sucking her thumb. Meraiah, as usual, was under the tangled coverlet, completely hidden.

"When you marry, young lady, you're going to have to learn not to pull all the covers."

Pandora picked up the coverlet and froze. Meraiah was gone!

Her confusion quickly subsided. "Cassie, of course," she said with a smile. "She must have heard Meraiah wake up. She probably took her downstairs so she wouldn't disturb me."

Quickly, Pandora headed for the kitchen, expecting to find her missing baby in the down-lined basket beside the stove where she often slept while Cassie worked. She found only Cass and another of the servants sitting together over tall glasses of iced tea.

"Where's Meraiah?" Pandora asked lightly.

Cassie shot out of her chair. "Ma'am? She's sleeping still."

Panic seized Pandora like a cold flood. Suddenly, it seemed that all the evil in the universe had descended upon her. She felt the blood drain from her head. She reached out to steady herself, swallowing several times before she could find her voice.

"Quickly, Cass, send someone to locate Mr. Ward. My baby's been stolen!"

With a cry of alarm, Cassied rushed from the room, leaving her mistress near fainting.

Shaking off her dizziness after a few moments, Pandora realized that the phone was ringing off its hook. *Someone answer it!* a voice in her aching head screamed. She could not make herself move. She seemed rooted to the spot, turned to cold stone. Finally, she roused herself and ran to the hall.

"Yes!" she screamed hysterically into the receiver. "Ward, is that you?"

"Pandora? It's Jacob. Is Angelica there? She left early this morning and she hasn't come home yet. I'm worried. No one seems to have seen her all day."

Pandora's pounding head drooped. She leaned her forehead against the wall and closed her eyes. When she opened them again, she was staring directly into the waste basket near the phone, at two befeathered bags—Nettie's charms against evil.

"Pandora, are you all right? Are you there?"

"Yes, Jacob, I'm here," she replied tonelessly. "I don't know where Angelica is, but wherever she's gone, she's taken Meraiah with her. Jacob, we *must* find them. My baby is in grave danger!"

Chapter Twenty

Ward had been walking for hours, trying to sort out his feelings. Now, suddenly he found himself on the beach, a solitary figure in the darkness. He stood still for a time, gazing out at the phosphorescence of the restless waves. The night wind was hot and moist as if a storm was brewing somewhere out there beyond the horizon. He turned and walked on, his mind still churning.

Pandora! Pandora! he thought. *What are we going to do?*

It seemed plain to him what she planned to do. She would simply accept and believe whatever she happened to see—dreams, visions, or reality; they were one and the same to her. Ward worried that now her fantasies seemed to be replacing reality.

Ward's logical mind made Pandora's visions difficult to understand. However, there was no denying what his heart said: He loved Pandora! Nothing flesh and blood could change that, so certainly no phantom from beyond the grave should make any difference in the way he felt about her. He knew that and he kept repeating it to himself but the thought of Jean Laffite's ghost visiting his wife in her bed made him sick with fear—fear for his wife's sanity. If only Pandora didn't believe so firmly. But she did. He felt as if he'd just found out that his wife had taken a lover.

All this nonsense about reincarnation; he didn't believe it for an instant! Ward kicked at a shell on the beach in his frustration. If he had lived before, surely he would remember. Perhaps it wouldn't be a total, conscious memory, but some things would have stayed with him. Sights, sounds, feelings of another life. Then again, he could barely remember his early years in Galveston in this life, so how could he be expected to remember things from a previous life?

Ward glanced up. He was passing his old cottage. He'd never gotten around to selling it. Somehow, remembering that the little beach house was the first place he and Pandora had been together, he hadn't been able to part with it. So there it sat on its shaky stilts, the windows shuttered, giving it the appearance of peaceful slumber.

Suddenly, an idea struck Ward. He brightened, letting the troubling thoughts slip from his mind. He quickened his pace, hurrying toward the boarded-up cottage.

"Yes!" he said, smiling. "Yes, it might just work!"

Quickly, he mounted the stairs and unlocked the door. A rush of hot, musty air that smelled of mildew hit him in the face. He went from one window to the next, throwing them open and unlatching the wooden shutters. Soon the cozy cottage was filled with fresh sea air. He pulled the dustcovers from the furniture, then stood back, giving the place a quick once over. It looked just the same.

"Cassie can take care of the girls tonight," he said with a chuckle. "I have an appointment with my wife! I'll bring her back here, open a bottle of my best wine, and make love to that woman until I've exorcised every ghost in the place."

When he went back out on the porch, headed home to get Pandora, he saw it, there down the beach. His heart thudded loudly. He set out running—not to the castle on Broadway, but toward the eerie glow reflected in the sky.

* * *

Jacob whipped his horse to breakneck speed as he raced his buggy toward the Gabriel castle. What in hell was going on? Pandora had sounded hysterical on the phone.

It was bad enough that Angelica was missing—anything could have happened to her. She hadn't been herself for months. He'd hoped that the change in her was real, but he had guessed that it might be only the calm before the storm. Now Pandora said that Angelica had actually taken one of the twins—just as she had planned to do all along, he reminded himself. Why hadn't he watched her more carefully? Why hadn't he warned Pandora of this possibility? If anything happened to Meraiah, he would never forgive himself.

Jacob hitched the buggy out front, then took the front stairs two at a time. He had no chance to knock. The door flew open just as he raised his hand. Pandora stood before him—her face pale and drawn, her eyes red-rimmed from weeping.

"Pandora, what's happened?" he demanded.

"Jacob, have you seen Ward?" Her voice trembled and her tears were barely controlled.

"Don't tell me he's missing, too!"

She nodded. "We had a terrible row. He's been gone for hours. I didn't discover Meraiah's disappearance until long after he stormed out of the house. Oh, Jacob, I need him so. Where can he be? I have to find him and tell him about the baby. He'll know what to do."

"Pandora, I have an idea where he might be. Sometimes when he's troubled, he goes to the cottage."

"Oh, Jacob, of course!" she cried. "Why didn't I think of that?"

Quickly, Pandora dispatched one of the servants to the beach house. "I can't leave here," she explained to Jacob. "I've called the sheriff and he has men out searching already. He promised to telephone the moment there's any news. Oh, Jacob . . ."

"Try not to worry, Pandora," Jacob said softly. "Meraiah will be all right. We have to believe that."

She swiped angrily at her streaming eyes. "Why would

Forever, for Love

Angelica do such a thing?'' she demanded. ''The woman must be insane.''

Jacob took Pandora's trembling hand and held it, staring down at her wedding ring. ''Yes, Pandora, I'm afraid that's exactly it. I've known for a long time now that she was on the very brink. This is all my fault. I should have done something sooner. But I never guessed she would go this far.''

Pandora gasped and her hands flew to her face. ''You mean my baby is in the hands of a mad woman? Oh, Jacob!'' She lapsed into uncontrollable sobs.

Angelica hadn't meant to fall asleep. But Meraiah, after taking her bottle of milk, drifted off and the room grew so still that she found her eyelids growing heavy. The kerosene lamp burned on, lighting their cubbyhole hideout, the last place anyone would look even if they came searching for her. The lamp's flame made the room too warm and thick with dizzying fumes. Twice, Angelica caught herself nodding off. The third time, she slipped away completely. Relaxing in sleep, she stretched out next to the baby, until her crisp, black bombazine gown spread over the floor, one edge of it touching the hot, glowing lantern.

Coming awake with a jerk, Angelica screamed. The tiny pantry was thick with smoke and the hem of her skirt was afire. She kicked at the lantern as she scrambled up, beating her flaming gown. It tipped over, spilling its flammable contents across the floor. Angelica wrestled with the locked door, finally flinging it open before she and the baby suffocated. Her skirt was out, but now the fire spread across the heart-pine planks of the floor and up the dry walls. The pantry became an instant inferno the moment Angelica opened the door. She scooped up the baby and hurried out into the dark corridor.

''Hush now, Meraiah,'' she crooned. ''I'll take care of you. We'll be out of here soon. Don't cry, baby, don't cry!''

Thick smoke was boiling out of the room they'd just left. The weather had been hot and dry these past weeks and the wooden hotel was a tinderbox. Angelica looked back to see raging flames chasing her down the hallway. With a scream of sheer terror, she tried to quicken her pace. Her burned leg was throbbing painfully. The smoke was swirling around her now. The baby was screaming and squirming in her arms. She felt like she had opened the door to hell.

Pandora sat by the telephone, each moment crawling by as she stared at the clock on the wall. "Where is Ward?" she murmured. "What's happened?"

Cassie rushed in just then, her eyes wide. "Miss Pan, there's a big fire down to the beach. Come look!"

Pandora rose and hurried out to the porch. The night sky was lit up like a sunset. She stared at the brilliant, horrible sight for a long time. The dark shapes of frenzied seagulls soared against the backdrop of flames. Suddenly, the blazing hotel vanished. Pandora felt herself drift off, flying through the night sky with the gulls. When she looked down it was another Galveston Island she saw, another woman, another horror.

Flames lit this new scene as well. The woman below her choked on the thick, black smoke. The wild whoops of savages pierced Pandora's hazy consciousness.

"Isabel," she murmured. "You shouldn't have defied me."

Pandora tried to close her eyes against the awful scene, but it would not go away.

The woman was naked, tied to a post with burning driftwood piled all about her feet. The smoke from the smoldering wood grew thicker and blacker by the minute. She coughed and gagged, gasping for breath. Agony etched her beautiful face as she felt the flames licking about her ankles.

"No!" Isabel screamed. "Please! Have you no mercy? Kill me first!"

The chanting savages, their faces tattooed and their long hair braided and tipped with rattles from the island's snakes, danced around the pyre. Their women, dressed in skirts of Spanish moss, sat by complacently, watching as the Spanish woman screamed and pleaded, writhing on the stake.

Feeling the fire grow hotter, Isabel murmured prayers in her native tongue. She promised God, if He would save her from this Karankawa torture, she would forget Jean Laffite. She wanted him more than life itself, but she could not endure the pain.

"Save me from the flames, Father," she moaned, "and I swear I will never again lie with the man I love. I will leave him to his Nicolette."

The next moment, Pandora experienced a feeling of great relief. As if Isabel's prayer were given instant attention, the Indian braves, still whooping and dancing, brought buckets of water from the shore and doused the fire. Isabel sagged against her deerskin bonds. She murmured a prayer of thanks.

To Pandora's horror, she soon learned that Isabel's salvation was only a thing of the moment. The chief, a tall man with cane ornaments through the flesh of his lower lip and the skin of his chest, came to her. With one swift stroke of his knife he cut her bonds. Isabel sank down, burning her feet in the smoldering ashes. He grabbed her long hair and dragged her around the circle. Both men and women jeered at her screams and protests. When he was done with his shameful exhibition, he hauled her off to his tent and flung her down on a rug of skins.

Isabel—weak and bruised and aching all over—lay before him trembling. "Please," Pandora heard her whisper. But her plea went unanswered. The next moment, the strong chief fell upon her.

He was big and heavy and brutal. Pandora winced each time he thrust into the sobbing girl. Her nostrils flared. She could smell the evil of the man—shark oil and woodsmoke and unwashed flesh. He bruised Isabel's wrists as he held her down. He bloodied her lips and bit her breasts as he violated her. After a time, mercifully, Isabel lost consciousness, but for Pandora the agony of the scene continued.

Pandora saw ahead, to the days that followed. Others came to the tent, honored warriors invited by their chief to partake of his prize. Isabel seemed lost in some other world, her mind no longer capable of accepting the pain, the degradation.

Pandora was there, too, when Jean Laffite and his men slaughtered the band of savages and rescued the girl. Isabel was only a shell of the spirited woman she had been. Her once-bright eyes were dull and glazed with pain. Her body was tainted by the lust of many men. Pandora, to her horror, knew at last who Nicolette's murderer was. For, after her trial with the Indians, Isabel's soul knew only one emotion—hate.

As Pandora's terrifying vision was fading, Angelica roused from where she lay, overcome by smoke, slumped against one wall of the hotel's dining room. She clutched the baby so tightly to her bosom that Meraiah screamed in alarm.

"I have to get away," she moaned. "Far away!" The flames were closing in like a wall around her.

"Is anyone in there?" a voice yelled from somewhere beyond the inferno.

Angelica started to answer, but remembered that she had to slip away. No one must know that she had the baby. No one must keep her from boarding the train. She kept silent, inching across the floor to the doors on the opposite side of the dining room, praying that she could reach them before the flames engulfed her.

Angelica crawled another few feet across the floor. She could feel the heat intensifying. Smoke filled her lungs. Her burned leg throbbed painfully. "Just a little farther . . . get to the door . . . out where I can breathe . . ."

"Anybody there? Answer me, dammit!"

"Ward?" Angelica turned toward the sound of his voice. "Yes, Ward, yes! I'm here. Please, I can't go any farther. I can't breathe. The baby . . ."

Ward heard nothing. Angelica's dry, smoke-parched throat only managed a raspy whisper before she lasped into unconsciousness.

It was total madness to enter the blazing hotel. Ward didn't know why he was so sure, but he knew someone was inside. The flames, whipped by the rising wind, were through the dry roof now. Any moment the huge structure would collapse. Something was driving him. Something would not let him give up.

"Dammit, I'm going in there!" he said to the fire chief.

"That's crazy, Mr. Gabriel! If there is anybody inside, it's probably just some drifter who set the fire in the first place. Like as not, he's dead already from the smoke."

"Ward!" He turned, hearing Pandora's voice.

"Darling, what are you doing here?" he demanded.

"We could see the blaze from the house. Jacob drove me down. Ward, Angelica's missing and she's taken Meraiah!"

Ward didn't ask any questions or say another word. He turned from Pandora and rushed up the steps to the hotel. Her hysterical cry followed him into the inferno.

"I'm going with him," Jacob said.

"No!" Pandora screamed. "Come back, both of you!"

Inside, the two men found a sheet of flames before them. Covering their heads with their coats they fought through the thick smoke and flames, but found no one.

"It's no good, Ward!" Jacob yelled. "Nobody could have lived through this. We won't either, if we don't get out of here."

"You're right," Ward said, finally admitting defeat. "We'd better move fast!"

Just as they turned back toward the door, a baby's cry pierced through the crackling noise of the blaze.

"Meraiah!" Ward said, gripping Jacob's arm.

The two men dropped down on all fours, searching for clean air to breath near the floor. Crawling, they managed to make their way across the room. Moments later, Ward had his daughter in his arms and Jacob was carrying Angelica out of the doomed hotel. A cheer went up from the crowd when they saw the two men with their rescued burdens.

"Clear the way," Ward yelled. "We have to get them to the hospital. Fast!"

"Meraiah's going to be fine!" Jacob announced to the two worried parents who had been waiting in the chapel of St. Mary's Infirmary for word of their daughter.

Ward grabbed Pandora and hugged her soundly. "Thank God," she murmured.

"What about Angelica?" Ward asked.

Jacob shook his head. "I just don't know. She has some burns on her legs and feet. She's conscious now . . . has been for the past half hour. But she won't say a word; she just stares straight ahead and doesn't respond to anything. I've tried to get her to speak to me, but it's as if she can't hear a word I say. She's in deep shock, of course, but that can't account for everything."

"She'll live?" Pandora asked.

Jacob nodded. "Her body will. As for her mind . . ." He shrugged. "We'll just have to wait and see."

Pandora could find little sympathy in her heart for her cousin. She did feel sorry for Jacob, though. After all, what had he ever done to deserve such pain?

Life returned to normal at the Gabriel castle. Meraiah seemed none the worse for her dreadful experience. She remained listless for a few days after that horrible night. But soon she was her bright, aggressive self again, making sure that she received the lion's share of attention at all times.

Angelica did not fare as well. She remained in St. Mary's, until her outward injuries healed but some great, festering wound inside refused to give up its hold on her. Neither Jacob nor any of the other doctors could get through to her. She had locked herself away from the world. She neither spoke nor responded.

Finally, two months after the fire, when Angelica's mental state still showed no signs of improvement, Jacob was forced to go to her parents with his decision. The Sherwoods and their son-in-law sat in their parlor with Ward and Pandora. Jacob had begged their support in what he had to do, knowing that Angelica's parents would be against his plan.

Tabitha, her face pale and drawn, asked with feigned brightness, "So, Jacob, you've come to tell us you're bringing our little girl home? When?"

He shook his head sadly and Pandora noticed for the first time the sprinkling of silver at his temples. "No, Mother Sherwood. I'm afraid that's not why I'm here tonight."

"She's not worse?" Horace boomed.

"No, but she's no better either. I've decided to have her moved to another hospital. There's a good sanitarium in

New Orleans where they know how to deal with patients suffering from hysteria.''

Tabitha gasped and clutched her throat. "My God, Horace, he's sending her to a madhouse!"

"No," Jacob interjected. "Nothing of the kind, Mother Sherwood. The Ursaline Sisters in New Orleans take excellent care of their patients. I've been there; I've seen their institution. Angelica will have the best of everything, I assure you."

Tabitha Sherwood was sobbing now and clutching her husband's hand.

"Bring Madame's smelling salts at once!" Horace shouted to one of the servants. Then patting his wife's chubby hand, he said, "There, there, dear. We want what's best for Angelica. She won't be there long, I'm sure."

The weeping woman refused to be quieted. "Think of the talk, Horace. Why, everyone in Galveston will be whispering about us behind our backs."

"Is that all you care about—what people say?" Jacob asked in a cold voice. "I should think you'd be more concerned about Angelica's well-being."

Tabitha took a deep whiff of her smelling salts before she answered Jacob in a shrill, offended voice. "Of course I'm concerned about her. I'm her mother. No one could care more for her. But to send her so far away . . ."

"Mother's right, I think," Horace agreed. "Our little girl shouldn't be all alone now. Surely, the hospital here is adequate. No one will be the wiser that way. There'll be no gossip about her ailment. She'll be better off here, Jacob."

Horace Shewood rose and lit a cigar, signalling an end to the discussion.

Jacob sighed and looked at Ward. Both men had hoped they wouldn't have to resort to this, but there seemed no other way. The Sherwoods were being even more unreasonable than they had anticipated.

"Horace," Ward began, "I think you and I need to have a few words privately."

The older man turned a scowl on Ward. "Anything that's to be discussed concerning my daughter will be said in my wife's presence."

"Very well." Ward drew in a deep breath, dreading what he had to say. "There's still the matter of Angelica's crime, sir."

"Crime! What crime?" Tabitha was truly hysterical now. "You can't possibly suspect her of starting that fire on purpose. Why, she might have been killed!"

"And so might my daughter," Pandora reminded her aunt gently. "Arson is not the charge, Aunt Tabitha."

"What then?" Horace demanded.

"Angelica took our daughter, sir," Ward replied, avoiding the use of the ugly word *kidnapping*.

"Since when is it a crime for a relative to take a child for a stroll?" Tabitha demanded, trembling with outrage. "You should be grateful to my daughter for helping with the care of your children, Pandora, instead of accusing her this way."

Pandora bit her lower lip to stay her tongue. These two people had been like her own parents for most of her life. She did not want to cause them pain. But she would not have her own children threatened.

Ward, sensing her discomfort, quickly came to Pandora's rescue. "We know for a fact, Mrs. Sherwood, that Angelica planned to take our daughter away from Galveston, perhaps even out of the state. Jacob found train tickets to Houston hidden inside her bodice. Where she meant to take Meraiah from there, we have no idea. But had she not been caught in that fire, she would have left with our baby."

Tabitha Sherwood squirmed uneasily on the settee. "Wel-l-l," she whined defensively, "everyone knows that Angelica can't be blamed because of her *problem*."

"Exactly my point!" Jacob said. "Angelica *does* have a very serious problem. One we can't handle here. She needs the best professional care, care that she can get only in the proper institution. I'm doing this for her good, Mother Sherwood. For the good of everyone concerned, believe me."

"This is blackmail!" Horace blustered. "You dare come into my home and threaten to prosecute my daughter unless we agree to have her committed?"

"I don't need your agreement or even your approval,

336

sir," Jacob reminded his father-in-law. "I am her husband. But I did hope that you would both understand that this is the only way. There's no telling what Angelica might do next. Why, in her present state of depression, she might even try to harm herself."

The evening ended badly. But then, no one had expected it to be a family picnic. Pandora, Ward, and Jacob left Tabitha Sherwood in hysterics with her husband hovering over her, unable to help.

On that very night, Tabitha took to her bed with a migraine, never to rise from her feather mattress again. A month after Jacob turned Angelica over to the Ursalines in New Orleans, Mrs. Sherwood died of an acute attack of apoplexy. Before his daughter returned home, Horace would join his wife in the family plot after suffering a severe stroke.

Far away, across the Gulf, Angelica whiled away her days and nights in a white cell with the lyrical sounds of the French Market wafting in through her barred window. The "good gray sisters," as the Ursalines were called, were kind and gentle with their lovely, silver-haired, silent patient. But there seemed nothing they could do to draw the sad young woman out of herself. Sometimes in the night, they heard her scream out in terror or pain. Even those garbled, meaningless sounds gave them hope.

The beautiful Gabriel twins, with their thick chestnut curls and bright turquoise eyes, grew and prospered over the next months. On their first birthday, in April of 1899, their father bought them matched snow-white ponies. Pandora—her mother's instincts inflamed—protested to her husband.

"They're only *babies,* Ward. They can't ride ponies yet."

He laughed at his wife's fears and stole a kiss before he answered her. "And how old were you before you had a pony of your own, my love?"

Pandora blushed. She should never have told him. "My father gave me one at birth."

"Ah, and our poor, deprived little girls have had to go a whole year without ponies of their very own. A disgrace!"

"Very well," Pandora conceded. "But I hope you don't expect them to learn to ride yet. I didn't mount that pony until I was four."

"Come look, my darling." He took Pandora's hand and led her to the side garden where a shiny red cart upholstered in green leather stood in the shade of a tall palm. "We'll hitch those ponies to this fine carriage, and when their mother goes out for her morning drive, the girls can follow along with Cassie in proper equipage. The Gabriel ladies will be the talk of all Galveston."

Life was good at Pandora's castle. She had never been happier, more content, or better loved. Ward saw to all that. At least once a month, never telling her in advance, Ward would hurry home from his office early and hustle his blushing wife off through the streets of Galveston to the beach cottage for a night of unimaginable delights.

On one such evening in the late fall of 1899, as they lay naked in each other's arms before the driftwood fire, Pandora kissed Ward deeply, then said, "You know, darling, all Galveston is whispering about us. About how we run off to our own private love nest whenever we please."

Ward leaned up on one elbow and stared down into his wife's eyes—dancing and bright with the pleasure of having been well and thoroughly loved. "They're doing more than talking about us, my sweet. They're copying us. Three of my friends—Lowe, Swaggart, and Henning—have recently purchased small places here on the beach. They all claim that their love lives have never been better."

Pandora frowned. "How odd. I haven't heard any such things from their wives."

Ward roared, throwing his head back and laughing until he fell on his back. "I never said they bought the cottages for their *wives*, darling!"

"Oh, you." She gave him a shove. "That's a terrible thing to tell me. You'll have me acting guilty now whenever I see those women. I'd better not find out that you've bought a *second* beach house!"

Suddenly, Ward's face turned serious. He leaned down

over Pandora, forcing her shoulders to the soft, fur rug beneath them. "Why on earth would I ever need a mistress when I'm married to the most wanton and seductive woman in the world? I could spend the rest of my life making love to you every day—twice, three times a day. You're all I want, Pandora." His hands slipped down her body, caressing her skillfully, arousing her anew. "All I'll ever need!"

Meraiah and Miriam had just passed their second birthday when Pandora's calm waters began to stir with the threat of a storm. Ward was in Mexico, his annual tour of the silver mine. She felt desperately alone without him. Once again, although she hadn't dared mention it to Ward, she was having dreams and visions of Jean Laffite. Isabel also came to her in the most disturbing nightmares. Having seen the horrible visions of the Spanish woman and the Indians on the night of the fire, Pandora now feared some evil from the past more than ever before.

Nettie turned up on her doorstep one day in May of 1900. The woman looked weary and ill.

"Nettie, what's wrong?" Pandora asked.

The old woman shook her head and a tear dribbled down her cheek. "It's that Dan'l. I tell you, that damn old man's got no feelings for anyone 'sides hisself."

"What's he done now, Nettie?"

"Nothing yet, but he swears he's fixing to up and die on me. Won't eat, won't sleep, won't even talk to me no more. T'other day, he just took it into his head that his time had come. You got to talk to him, Miss Pan. Tell him what's what. He'd always listen to his mistress, good and proper like. You're the only one that can help."

Totally confused, but wanting to do what she could, Pandora hurried to the shack near the ruins of *Maison Rouge* with Nettie. They found Daniel lying on his cot, staring into space. Suddenly, looking down into the wizened old black face, it struck Pandora that she had not seen Daniel since she was a very young child. Nettie always talked about him so that Pandora felt as if she and the old man had never lost touch. But this was the first time in her adult life that she had actually seen Daniel in the flesh.

He turned his head when the two women entered, staring straight at Pandora. Slowly, a smile crept over his blank face. Twin tears oozed from the crinkled corners of his rheumy eyes. His withered, arthritic hand began to rise toward her.

"Go ahead, Miss Pan, tell this old fool he can't die on us," Nettie prompted.

Pandora looked from one to the other of them, then knelt down and took his gnarled hands in hers. "Hang on, Daniel. Don't let go. What would Nettie and I do without you?"

Daniel smiled and said in a weak voice, "If it wasn't for you, I'd of been dead a long time ago. I's tired now, ma'am but if you say I got to stay, I reckon I ain't got no other choice. You saved me once and now you come to save me again. Bless you!"

Pandora found herself cradling the old man's head and weeping. Daniel's words made little sense to her, but at least he had spoken. For whatever reason, it seemed important to her that old Daniel survive a little longer.

Only one thing bothered her as she headed home after seeing Daniel up and about again. Just before she left the shack, Nettie had pulled her aside and whispered a disturbing warning into her ear. Whatever could the woman have meant?

She was still wondering, when she returned to the house. Jacob Saenger, looking unusually grave, awaited her.

She hurried to him, still feeling the emotional impact of her visit with Daniel and Nettie's odd warning. "Jacob, what's happened? Is it Angelica?"

He nodded.

"Oh, no!"

Jacob took her hand. "You have it all wrong, Pandora. It's *good* news. Angelica is being released. She's coming home to Galveston." He paused and searched her face with pleading eyes. "That is, if you and Ward will allow her to return."

"*Allow her to?* Jacob, whatever are you talking about? Now that she's well, we'll be delighted to have her back. When is she coming?"

Jacob was smiling now. He'd been nervous about breaking the news to Pandora. As always, she had set him at ease. "I'm not sure. I have to go to New Orleans to bring her home. A week. Maybe two."

Pandora hugged him. "That's wonderful news, Jacob. I'm so happy for both of you."

After Jacob left, Nettie's words again began to prey on Pandora's mind. Over and over she heard the old woman saying, "You watch yourself, Missy. The snake ain't dead yet. It can still strike till its head's been lopped clean off!"

Chapter Twenty-one

Galveston was a busy place that summer and fall of 1900. Ships from all over clogged the harbor, handling more cotton than any other port in the whole United States. Real estate was booming, a sellers' market. Money seemed almost to wash up on the sunny shores of the Gulf.

"This city's jingling with more gold than Laffite and his pirates ever dreamed of," Ward told Pandora one bustling Saturday afternoon as they drove down the crowded Strand in their spanking new buggy.

"Just see all the people! Looks like all forty thousand of Galveston's citizens have turned out to take the air this afternoon," Ward said, waving his arm expansively. "Dressed to the nines, the lot of them, and with bankrolls in their pockets big enough to choke their fine horses. I tell you, Pan, Galveston is finally on the map. Nothing can stop us now. Yes sir, we've come a long way from back before the war when those scruffy drifters from Maine came down here with nothing more than dreams."

Pandora smiled under the wide brim of her latest Paris hat and nodded at her beaming husband, thinking, *We've come even farther from the days of Laffite and Nicolette*. She didn't share her thought with Ward; even now, as secure as she felt with her husband and her marriage, she hesitated to mention their former life on Galveston Island to Ward, the unbeliever.

They were on their way to meet Jacob and Angelica for a late lunch at the Tremont Hotel. Angelica had been back in Galveston for nearly two months. She seemed fine, better than she had been in years. She seldom ventured out in company, claiming her right to remain at home and mourn her parents in her own private way. However, Pandora had prevailed upon her cousin to come to lunch today since it was her birthday, the first of September.

"I hope Angelica likes her gift," Pandora said.

"Lord, she certainly should! That silver and onyx brooch is the finest piece of jewelry designed by my Italian craftsmen in years. I was hoping you'd keep it for yourself, darling."

Pandora squeezed her husband's hand and smiled up into his eyes. "Thank you for the thought, Ward. I'm just as happy with my new silver locket." She touched the small, delicately engraved heart at her throat. "Besides I wanted something special for Angelica after all she's been through."

' All heads turned as the Gabriels walked into the dining room of the Tremont. Pandora was reminded of another time when she had entered such a place on Ward's arm, greeted by admiring stares from all sides. How long ago that seemed.

The headwaiter fell over his feet in his rush to greet them. "Dr. and Mrs. Saenger are here already, Mr. Gabriel. I put them at our best table and served champagne immediately as you instructed."

"That's fine, John." Ward nodded to the man and pressed a bill into his waiting palm.

As they walked toward the other couple, Pandora appraised her cousin thoroughly. Angelica was dressed in a fine black silk gown embroidered with jet beads. Her silvery-blond hair was pulled back severely from her face under her wide-brimmed hat. She looked thinner and much older than her twenty-three years. Her emotional problems had left permanent scars. Most of all, Pandora realized, Angelica's pale eyes looked old. Pandora felt a sudden twinge of sympathy for her cousin. Nothing in life seemed to go right for her.

Jacob rose as they approached, smiling a bit nervously. "Well, there you are. We thought we might have to drink all this champagne ourselves."

"I'm sorry we're late," Pandora apologized, giving Angelica an especially warm gaze. "Ward got held up on a business call, something to do with the Emporium, I believe."

They took their seats and Jacob leaned toward Ward. "I've been meaning to thank you. If you hadn't agreed to help run things, I don't know what we'd have done. Angelica has no head for business and I'm simply too busy these days with my practice."

Angelica said nothing. All three of the others at the table began to grow uneasy. She simply sat there, her gaze focused on the locket around Pandora's neck.

To break the silence, Pandora lifted the silver heart and asked, "Do you like it, Angelica? Ward gave it to me for our anniversary." She clicked the hidden clasp and the locket sprang open. "I've been meaning to put locks of the girls' hair inside." She shrugged. "One of these days I'll get around to it."

Angelica's voice, when she finally spoke, was clear and wistful. "I've *always* wanted a locket like that."

Pandora felt deflated. Now, she was sure, their gift for Angelica would be a disappointment to her.

"Happy birthday, Angelica!" Pandora handed her cousin the beautifully wrapped package. "I hope you like it."

They all watched closely as she unwrapped her gift. For the barest instant, a small smile curved her pale lips. "It's lovely. Thank you both."

Jacob's eyes filled with tender emotion as he reached over to take his wife's hand in his. "What I have to give you, Angel, I couldn't wrap but I hope you'll like my surprise. I've had the old mansion on Broadway completely redecorated for you. I'm going to sell the house on 13th. We'll start moving back home this very afternoon."

Ward and Pandora smiled at each other. They knew this was what Angelica had wanted all along. Now, surely, she would be completely happy.

"Thank you, Jacob," Angelica said softly with tears in her eyes. "You can't know how much this means to me. But I have one request."

"You have only to name it," he assured her.

"I don't want you to sell the other house," she said emphatically.

Jacob looked puzzled, but agreed. "Whatever you wish, Angel."

The Gabriels and the Saengers shared a pleasant birthday lunch. By no means could it be termed a gay occasion, but at least it was a start, Pandora told herself. Angelica had hugged her with genuine warmth before they parted. Soon they would all grow comfortable with each other again, she was sure. Perhaps someday she would even come to trust Angelica around her daughters again; that would take time. Pandora still awoke occasionally in a cold sweat, crying Meraiah's name.

Not until she returned home and was undressing did Pandora realize she had lost her silver locket. "The chain must have broken," she told Ward, near tears.

"Don't fret, darling. I'll have another one made for you."

It was the hot, sultry Thursday evening of September 6 when the Gabriels next saw Jacob Saenger. They had just tucked the twins into bed and were about to go out for a stroll and a breath of air—if such a thing existed—when the front door knocker banged loudly.

"Jacob! This is a surprise," Pandora heard Ward say. "We thought you'd be spending your first evening at home. Weren't the movers supposed to finish up today?"

Pandora hurried into the hallway. "Is anything wrong, Jacob?"

"I suppose you might say that," he answered in a tone

edged with sarcasm. "Remember last Saturday at lunch when I told Angelica we were moving and she urged me not to sell the house on 13th Street?"

Ward and Pandora both nodded. "I figured the girl had a good business head on her shoulders after all," Ward said. "Property prices are going up every day. You could make a bundle on that place by keeping it a few more months."

"I didn't know what to think," Jacob confessed. "But I know now. She's just thrown me out."

"Jacob, no!" Pandora cried. "Whatever can she be thinking?"

Jacob slumped down in a chair, his head in his hands. "She's thinking that she doesn't want to live with me anymore. She just told me as much. I'm to go back to the old house. She wants the mansion all to herself."

"But that's crazy!" Ward blurted out.

Jacob gave him a pained look. "Oh, I sincerely hope not!"

"What did you argue about, if you don't mind discussing it?" Pandora asked.

"That's just it! *Nothing!* Angelica's been as sweet as can be ever since I brought her back from New Orleans. We've had no differences. I thought everything was perfect between us at last. As soon as the movers left this evening, she showed me to the front door and explained very politely but firmly that she had no intentions of sharing *her* house with me. *She kicked me out!*" Jacob let his head sink back down into his hands. "What the hell am I supposed to do now?"

Jacob left a short time later to go back to the empty house on 13th Street. The Gabriels tried to convince him to stay, but he refused. When he was gone, Pandora went into her husband's arms, trembling.

"Darling, what's wrong?" he asked.

Pandora could only shake her head. "I don't know, but I have this awful feeling."

That *awful feeling* manifested itself somtime after midnight in one of Pandora's nightmares—one of the same horrendous proportions as the dream she had had shortly before her parents were killed in the great hurricane of 1886.

She saw herself naked, being whipped by hard rain and thrashed by the raging sea. She screamed and cried for help, but the roar of the wind drowned out her voice. She was all alone, terrified, staring into the very face of death. When she saw three skeletal black hands reach out for her, she woke sobbing.

"Darling, darling, it's all right," Ward soothed. "I'm here. It was only a dream."

Pandora would not be quieted. "This was not just a dream," she told Ward between sobs. "It was *the* dream! There's a terrible storm coming."

"There, you see, darling!" Ward drew back the drapes at eight the next morning so that the bright sunshine filled their bedroom. "It's a beautiful day, not a cloud in the sky."

Pandora tried to smile to reassure herself but the nightmare retained its hold on her.

"I told Cass to bring our breakfast up since you had such a bad night," Ward told her. "You just stay put, darling."

Moments later, when Cassie placed the breakfast tray and the morning paper before her, Pandora's worst fears were realized. There was, indeed, a hurricane headed their way. According to the *Galveston Daily News,* the fierce storm had already ravaged Puerto Rico, the Windward Islands, Cuba, and the western coast of Florida. The U.S. Weather Service report stated that the West Indian cyclone was now gathering renewed strength over the Gulf, headed for the Texas coast.

Pandora's heart pounded with fear as she silently handed the paper to Ward.

He scanned the report quickly. She saw him frown, but when he turned to her his expression was pleasant again. "We might have a little blow," he confessed. "But look at that gorgeous morning out there, darling. Surely, we have nothing to worry about. The castle is built solid as a rock and we're over eight feet above sea level here—the highest point on the whole island." Pandora's worried expression never changed. "If you would feel better, I'll put you and the girls on the afternoon train to Houston."

"And leave you here alone?" she cried.

Later that morning, Ward went to his office, still sure that his wife was simply over-reacting to a bad dream. But when he passed the Levy Building on Market Street, he began to take her fears more seriously. Whipping high above his head, he spotted the two ominous weather flags—red squares with black centers—flying in tandem. Sometime earlier, Isaac Cline, the weather officer, had raised his hurricane warning over Galveston Island.

Pandora needed no flags to alert her to the coming danger. She was already preparing for the storm. She had the servants filling vats and jugs with rain water from the cisterns. She ordered the furniture from downstairs hauled up the wide mahogany staircase to the floor above. Only the massive, square piano remained in the front parlor, too heavy to be moved from its usual spot. Cassie was dispatched to the Emporium to purchase non-perishable food-stuffs. All day the household on Broadway was a flurry of activity even though the weather continued fine.

Pandora slept little that night. She lay awake, listening for the boom of the surf, the rise of the wind. But the night seemed inordinately still and silent. Ward, undisturbed, slept peacefully beside her.

Near dawn, she heard the first patter of rain against the windowpanes. Slipping out of bed, careful not to wake her husband, she dressed and pulled on her oilskin cloak. Moments later, she hurried out of the house. The stable boy hitched up the big wagon, as Pandora instructed, then she headed immediately for the beach. The light rain was becoming heavier and the wind was on the rise. Long before the beach house came into view, she heard the boom of the surf, like cannon fire out over the Gulf.

Dawn was just breaking as she drove up to the cottage. She'd meant to take care of this task earlier, but there had been too much to do at home.

The tide was higher than normal. The long, rolling swells broke on the beach with an ominous roar, sending a shiver down Pandora's spine. There wasn't much time. She would have to work quickly.

Hurrying into the cottage, she immediately began taking paintings down from the walls. Done with that chore, she took a sheet off the bed and gathered up everything else she valued in the cottage—books, shells, rugs, and Ward's antique coins. She was about to begin hauling the things out to the wagon when a knock came at the door. She answered it to find the slim, athletically built weather officer, Issac Cline, on her front porch.

"Morning, Mrs. Gabriel."

"Mr. Cline." She nodded, but neither smiled nor invited him in. There wasn't time for social amenities.

"I see you're packing things up. Good idea! I'm making the rounds now, warning everyone in the houses along the beach to take shelter on higher ground."

"It's going to be bad, isn't it?" Pandora knew the answer to her question already.

" 'Fraid so," he answered. "The barometer's dropping fast. Looks like we're in for a major overflow. There's water standing in the yards near the beach even now, and the storm's still out there a good piece. Let me help you with these things, ma'am. You need to get on home."

Pandora was grateful for Cline's assistance in loading the wagon. Already the wind was whipping the surf to flying foam that coated the telephone and power lines along the beach road. The ominous, whining song of the wet wires filled the air, making Pandora's skin crawl. Three bath-houses down the beach were swaying dangerously on their tall stilts. Any moment now, they would go crashing into the surf. Soon her own beloved cottage would follow.

Issac Cline waved Pandora off and wished her luck. At that moment, Pandora wondered if she would ever see the man again. The brickdust hue of the sky, the rising wind and surf, and her warning dream all promised a major disaster. Many would die before this storm was over.

Even as she headed for home and safety, the streets were clogged with sightseers off to the beach. Some were in buggies, some on foot, and many others crammed them-selves into the electric trolly that ran down from Broadway.

They all seemed in a holiday mood in spite of the high winds and driving rain.

"Hey, look at the size of those waves!" one young boy yelled to his friend. "Let's go swimmin'!"

"Go home to your mothers!" Pandora shouted to the pair of youngsters, alone together in the crowd. "It isn't safe at the beach."

They only laughed and waved to her, continuing on their early morning adventure.

Ward was coming down the front steps when Pandora drove up to the castle. "Where have you been?" he demanded. "I was worried sick!"

"To the cottage one last time," she answered sadly. "By tomorrow morning, it will be gone. I saved a few things. Mr. Cline is making rounds, telling people to evacuate the low-lying areas."

Ward's face turned solemn at his wife's words. "That bad, is it?"

Pandora nodded. "And bound to get much worse." She hugged him, clinging desperately. "Oh, Ward, I'm so frightened! Please don't leave me until it's over!"

"I won't, darling. I promise," he said gently. "Come inside now. You're soaking wet. Why didn't you wake me to go with you and help?"

Jacob Saenger received a frantic call at his office shortly before noon that Saturday. He was ordered to report to the hospital immediately. Cancelling the rest of his appointments, he headed directly to St. Mary's Infirmary. He'd been so busy most of the morning that he hadn't realized how quickly the weather had deteriorated. The light rain from earlier in the day was now coming down in torrents, and the wind had risen to a howling gale. There was no doubt now that a major storm was blowing in. The hospital would be inundated with injured. Already, he'd been told by his colleague on the phone, people were coming in with broken bones, gashes, and bruises inflicted by flying debris.

Even now, as he made his way on foot through the wind and rain, water was filling the streets. The wooden blocks of the sidewalk had floated loose and bobbed about his boots like so many oversized corks. He looked up at the wildly swaying palm trees just in time to save himself, dodging quickly when he spied a wind-driven slate shingle coming straight for his head.

He'd tried to ring up Angelica before he left the office. The telephones were still working, but the lines were jammed with frantic callers. He would have to try again from the hospital. He only hoped it wouldn't be too late by then. At the rate the wind was rising, the lines couldn't stay up much longer.

The hospital was a madhouse—everyone running this way and that. Many people had come in from low-lying sections of town seeking shelter. They got in the way of the doctors who were trying to care for the injured. The whole place was chaotic.

Before setting to work, Jacob hurried into one of the offices to use the telephone. Finally, the operator was able to ring through to Angelica's number.

"Thank God," he breathed into the receiver.

A moment later, he heard the operator's voice again. "I'm sorry, sir, but that telephone seems to be off the hook. It's not ringing."

Jacob gave an exasperated sigh. "Operator, try another number for me."

Ward hurried to the jangling telephone in the hallway. "Yes, who is it?" he demanded.

"Ward, it's Jacob. Thank goodness you're at home. I have to ask you a great favor. Angelica's all alone. I'm at the hospital. The injured are already pouring in and we're going to have to evacuate the old folks' home near the beach and bring them here somehow. I can't leave. Can you make it down to Angelica's house?"

"Yes, of course."

"Will you go down there and bring her back to the castle? She'll be terrified all by herself."

"I'm on my way, Jacob. Don't worry. I'll have her back here in no time. How bad is it there?"

A shattering of glass made Jacob duck quickly. "The

351

windows are all being smashed. Those damn slate roof tiles are flying through the air like shrapnel fired from a cannon. Be careful when you go out, Ward. A person could get decapitated.''

"I'll keep my head low, don't worry!"

Pandora had been standing near her husband as he talked to Jacob. When he hung up, she cried, "Ward, you're not going to leave?"

"Just for a few minutes, darling. Angelica's all alone down the street. Jacob asked me to bring her here." Already, he was pulling on his foul weather gear. "I'll be back before you know it, Pan."

Before she could protest further, Ward was out the door. The wind slammed it shut behind him. Pandora sank down in a chair, her head in her hands. She mustn't worry, she told herself. He *would* be back. The old Sherwood mansion was only a few doors down the street. Nothing could happen to him in that short distance.

"Oh, please, God, bring him home safely," she whispered in a deceptively calm voice.

A few doors down might have been a few miles in the driving wind and rain and the quickly rising water. The wind from the north was driving the bay waters into the city streets. Already, Broadway was a raging river. Ward could barely see his hand before his face in the torrents of rain. The black sky boiled with rage, making the early afternoon almost as dark as midnight. The air was filled with debris— branches, roof tiles, bits of wood from houses that had already been demolished. Inch by inch, gripping the iron railings of fences along the street, Ward made his way slowly toward the Sherwood mansion. For every step he took, the wind blew him back two paces.

By the time he got there, the bay had met with the Gulf. Water was waist-deep in the yard, flooding the Sherwood basement and washing under the front door. A furious gust of wind hurled him into the door and it flew open. He fell to the floor and stared up, unable to believe the bizarre scene before his eyes.

"You came. I knew you would." Angelica, dressed in her

finest purple satin gown—the one trimmed in silver lace to match the locket around her neck—swayed toward Ward to help him up.

"Angelica, we've got to get out of here. The place is flooding. The castle's on higher ground. You'll be safe there."

She smiled, then trilled a seductive laugh. "Darling, we can't be alone there and I have everything ready here. See?"

Taking Ward's arm, Angelica led him to the dining room. The table, covered with a spotless damask cloth, was set for two with gleaming silver and the sparkle of crystal. Candles glowed warmly. Angelica reached to the wine cooler and filled a champagne flute, handing it to Ward.

"We'll drink a toast and then we'll eat. And afterward, darling . . ." She went up on tiptoe to kiss his lips firmly.

Ward stood perfectly still, stunned, watching the water on the dining room floor climb up his boots.

"Stop it, Angelica! This is pure foolishness! You don't know what it's like out there. If we wait, we won't be able to get back to the castle at all."

Just then, Ward heard the giant oak in the yard crash against the side of the house; Angelica didn't seem to notice.

Slipping her arms around Ward's waist and leaning her head against his chest, she murmured, "Then, by all means, let's wait, love! We can forget about dinner, if you like. After all, we've both been dreaming a long, long time of this night. Come, we'll go upstairs."

Ward stared down at the woman clutching him. Her eyes were as glittery as if she were running a fever. The color in her cheeks was high. Her pretty mouth opened and she ran her tongue suggestively over her lips.

Suddenly, Ward scooped her up into his arms. She snuggled close, nibbling at his neck, and whispered, "That's more like it, darling. Let's go upstairs."

When Ward headed for the front door instead of the bedroom, Angelica fought him for all she was worth—screaming, hitting, biting. If she continued struggling against him like this, he knew they would both drown on the way home. Quickly, never letting go of her, Ward snatched loose a heavy curtain rope and tied it firmly about Angelica's waist. Moments later, amidst Angelica's screams and curses, they entered the storm.

Ward felt as if he'd stepped into a black, watery hell. Above the howl of the wind and the roar of the water, he could hear the screams of the dying off in the distance. Suddenly, to his horror, he realized that all of Galveston might be gone by the time the sun rose again.

Pandora! I've got to get home to Pandora, he kept telling himself as he groped his way through the rising flood waters.

Angelica stopped fighting so hard once she was faced with the killer hurricane as her major opponent. The going was rough. Ward tried to hold onto Angelica, but several times the swirling water swept her out of his arms. He used the curtain rope to tug her back.

Nothing looked real or familiar. Total darkness closed in. Broadway was now awash with all manner of debris—an angry river, uprooting trees, felling houses, smashing lives. He could no longer find the railings he had followed on his way to rescue Angelica. All he could do was cling to his charge and hope that he was going the right way. The swift current whirled them this way and that. Soon he lost all sense of direction.

Angelica let out an hysterical scream. "Ward, get him off me!"

Ward pulled her close and felt another man's hand clutching desperately at her arm. He tried to help the poor fellow, pulling as hard as he could to bring the victim's head above the surface of the foul water. When he finally managed, his blood turned suddenly cold. In a flash of lightning, he found himself staring into the glazed eyes of a dead man. Ward released the body and pushed on, not knowing where he was headed. All they could do now was hang on and hope that they could ride out the storm.

An hour later, Ward had still not returned. Pandora went about her duties as calmly as she could. Cassie was upstairs with Meraiah and Miriam, doing her best to entertain them and allay their fears. Meraiah considered the storm a great adventure, but even downstairs Pandora could hear her other daughter's terrified wails.

Pandora had ordered the horses turned out of the stable. Otherwise, at the rate the water was rising, they would be trapped inside to drown. The castle was quickly filling with strangers—people whose houses were gone or so badly damaged that they'd been forced to leave. The other servants helped their mistress cook a meal and distribute it, handing out dry clothing and blankets as well.

Two hours later, Pandora was at her wit's end. She went to the telephone for the dozenth time to try to ring Angelica's house. She put the receiver to her ear and gave a small cry. Only a dull silence issued from the instrument. The lines were down. She was cut off from the rest of the world.

When someone banged at the front door, Pandora dropped the useless phone and hurried to see who was there, praying that it would be Ward with Angelica. Instead, she found old Nettie and Daniel, standing in the water that now lapped onto her high porch. Both were drenched to the skin, and Nettie's hat had blown away. Their clothes were shredded, hanging in tatters on their wet, shivering bodies.

"Lord, Miss Pan, I ain't seen nothing like this since way back in 1818! Our shack got washed to kingdom come. Me and Dan'l just hung on to that old door and let it wash us right to you. We reckoned if we could make it here you'd take us in."

"Oh, Nettie!" Pandora hugged the old woman. "I'm so glad you're safe. Now if only Ward would get back here where he belongs!"

"You mean your man's out in that?" Nettie cried. "Well, me and Dan'l will just have to go fetch him."

"That's right!" Daniel agreed, turning back toward the door.

"You'll do no such thing!" Pandora scolded. "You're going to come right in here and get some dry clothes and some hot food."

The two bedraggled survivors did as Pandora ordered, blessing her all the while for her kind hospitality.

A dozen or so other survivors arrived and, in the crush, Pandora lost track of the pair. When she searched the house for Nettie and Daniel an hour later, they were nowhere to be found.

Everyone moved to the upper stories of the castle. The water was halfway up the stairs. Pandora made sure all the others were safe, then went to speak with Cassie in the nursery.

Several other babies had joined her own two children. Cassie was watching over all of them. The twins were both sound asleep at last. By the clock on the bureau, Pandora saw that it was after seven. Ward had been gone for almost six hours.

"Cassie," she whispered, not wanting to wake the children, "I have to go find him."

"No, Miss Pan!" The servant rose as if she meant to physically restrain her mistress. "Ain't no sense your going out there. You got to stay here with these babies."

Pandora glanced at her beautiful daughters and leaned down to kiss each in her turn. She knew what Cassie was saying. There was a chance that Ward was already dead. If she went out to search for him, their children, in all likelihood, would be orphaned. She couldn't bear to think about what life would be without Ward. Somehow, she felt sure she could find him. And when she did, they would both be safe.

"I have to go, Cassie. I can't explain it. But I have to!"

"You can't even get out," the servant argued. "The water's done up past all the doors."

Pandora didn't answer. Turning, she went to her bedroom and donned a pair of Ward's britches, rolling up the legs and cinching the waist with one of her own belts. She pulled on a warm sweater, then opened the door to the bedroom balcony. The black water swirled only inches below. Carefully, she eased herself over the railing, shivering as the water seeped through to her skin. She gripped a board that floated by and began paddling toward Angelica's house. She would go directly there, then back. Surely, she would find Ward along the way.

Only minutes had passed before she realized what a truly dreadful mistake she had made. Once she was out of the sheltering lee of the castle, she was lost. Rain pelted her like frozen bullets; the wind raged and howled. Pandora clung to her board, praying that she might live to see the morning as the wild currents drove her off course. Would she ever find Ward?

Between noon and eight-thirty that fateful Saturday, weatherman Issac Cline's barometer dropped from 29.48 to 28.48 inches. Early that day, the wind began blowing from the north, flooding the island with water from the bay. As it shifted throughout the day—northeast, east, and then from the southeast—the angry waves of the Gulf were picked up and hurled over Galveston. The storm tide, reaching fifteen feet, struck the island with full force between eight and nine o'clock that evening. By that time, Pandora's plank had carried her far beyond Broadway, beyond anything except her wildest nightmares; nightmares that now seemed all too real.

She felt perfectly alone in a world of death. Horses, cows, chickens floated by, and twice she was forced to shove human corpses out of her way. She wasn't sure where she was. Her hair, plastered by the wind and rain to her face, obscured what little vision she had in the black night. Three times she thought she spotted a light in the distance. Each time the wind and the pull of the current drew her in the other direction. Cold gripped her body. Her arms ached from hanging onto the rough board. Her hands were raw and filled with splinters. Only the glimmer of hope that she might find Ward kept her from giving up her hold on the plank and sinking into blessed oblivion.

Ward was clinging to his own piece of flotsam at the same time. Angelica was still tied to him by the curtain rope. He had no idea where they were or in which direction the raging waters were carrying them. There was little time to think of such things as they struggled to survive. Suddenly, the drag on the curtain tie lessened and Ward gave it a tug. To his horror, the rope flew toward him, wrapping about his shoulders.

"Angelica!" he yelled into the wind. "Can you hear me?"

No answer.

"Angelica, answer me!" He thrashed about in the water, searching wildly, but she was gone. When and how they had become separated, he had no way of knowing. Going back to look for her would be useless and deadly. The swift currents could have swept her in any direction. All Ward could do was hang on and hope that he was still alive when the storm blew itself out.

Concentrating on his vain attempt to find Angelica, Ward didn't see the huge shape moving toward him through the water. It struck him in the ribs, knocking the breath from him momentarily. He reached out with one hand to feel a large, solid object.

"Climb aboard, mate," some unseen figure called out in the darkness. "There's plenty of room on my roof."

Ward's heart pounded with relief. At least one other person was still alive in this nightmare. He pulled himself out of the water, inching up the slippery piece of shingled wood. "Where are we?" he asked the roof's captain.

"Damned if I know! When the storm surge came I was just climbing out of my upstairs window. Next thing I knew, I was off and sailing. That fearsome rush of water broke my house right smack in two."

"Where was your house?"

"10th Street, just off Broadway. But it sure ain't there no more! Thank the Lord my wife and kids are in Dallas visiting her mother! You got anybody missing, mister?"

Ward ground his teeth, trying not to think how close his own house was to the destruction. "I don't know," he answered. "I just don't know."

For several minutes the two men remained silent, fighting for a hold on the slippery roof. The water tossed them about like a toy boat in a whirlpool. Ward suddenly realized, as the rough shingles bit into his thighs, that he was completely naked. The water and wind had stripped his clothes from him. He heard a cry in the distance and shouted to the man with him, "There's someone calling for help. Maybe we can make it over to save them."

His companion didn't answer. Ward turned to look. The fellow who had rescued him was gone, swept off their shaky craft. Ward leaned his head down on his hands and offered up what seemed a futile prayer for the stranger's deliverance and for his own. It was unlikely that anyone would survive this storm. Pandora had been right.

"Help me, please!" came a pitiful moan from somewhere near.

Ward leaned off the roof as far as he dared, stretching his arm out toward the woman's voice. "Here, catch my hand!" he yelled.

"Ward?" The voice was stronger and familiar. It couldn't be, but it was.

Their fingers touched, sending a charge through their naked bodies. Ward gripped Pandora's hand, pulling her through the water. At last, they were lying side by side on the punishing shingles, but neither of them noticed the pain.

"Ward," Pandora sobbed. "I thought you were dead! I'd almost given up. I've been clinging to a board for hours. I was losing my hold; I couldn't have stayed up much longer."

"Hush now, darling," he whispered. "Save your strength to hold on. This can't last forever. The worst is over, I'm sure."

The long night stretched before them. As they clung to the roof and each other, the wind shifted, drawing the water back out into the Gulf and them with it. All night, the sea tossed them, the wind battered them, and the cold rain pelted their naked bodies.

"It's no use, Ward." Pandora's voice was only the hoarsest whisper. "I can't make it."

"Hang on, dammit!" he cried. "I don't mean to lose you now. Not after all we've been through. We survived the storm of '18, didn't we? It was worse than this! I won't let you die! You left me last time. I mean to live through this and you will, too!"

Pandora had closed her eyes, resigned to her own death. Now they shot open. By the angry, phosphorescent light in the sky, she saw his face, his green eyes glittering with love and determination. Both of them—Ward and Laffite—were here with her! A moment later, she spied the hands—black, skeletal fingers reaching out for them, the same beckoning hands she had seen so many times in her nightmares. Her dream was real and it was *now!*

She lay frozen on the hard roof, her whole body aching, but her heart still pumping, determined to live. She watched the hands reach out as their rooftop haven drew ever nearer. Suddenly, beyond the hands, she saw a ghostly figure beckoning. As the raging waters washed them closer, Pandora recognized the woman. It was Nicolette, urging them on. And then, Pandora saw a thin ray of light, a silvery lifeline flowing from Nicolette's upraised hand, attaching itself to Pandora's heart to draw them ever closer.

"Come, come, come!" the wind seemed to moan.

Their broken roof jolted to a halt while the waters swirled around them. For several moments, they both lay still, hanging on tightly, waiting to be washed away again, but nothing happened.

Ward gripped Pandora's arm. "We're caught firm!" he said excitedly. "We're saved, darling!"

For the rest of the night, they held each other, clinging together as if their very lives depended upon their closeness. The rain still beat at them, cold and vicious, but they shared their warmth and protected each other the best way they knew how.

At dawn, the winds died. The rain stopped. The Gulf waters drew back into their primeval bed. The sun rose— glorious, brilliant, all colors of a fire opal. The storm had passed.

Ward rose gingerly. Pandora gazed up at him, aching for every bruise and cut on his body.

"Would you look where we are!" he said.

Pandora glanced about. The rooftop that had saved them was lodged firmly in the top branches of the three oaks in Laffite's Grove. She smiled. Nicolette had saved them! Reaching out from beyond her grave below, she had brought them to safe anchor to keep her own love for Jean Liffite alive.

"Look out there." Ward's voice was somber now.

Pandora gazed out over the island—a scene of total destruction. A huge windrow of wreckage rose like a great rampart in the distance. Trees, houses, furniture, bodies!

"Oh, Ward!" she cried. "Oh, my God!"

He came to her and took her in his arms; he could think of no words to soothe her. At least they were alive. They would face whatever came together.

"Come, darling," Ward whispered. "Let's go home."

Epilogue

Pandora Gabriel, sat in a wicker rocking chair on the front veranda of the castle, the setting sun turning her bright hair to flame. A few late-blooming oleanders perfumed the air. Five white kittens frolicked about the folds of her lace skirt.

She was waiting . . . waiting for *him*.

Automobiles rumbled by on Broadway, widened now, the trolley tracks long gone.

"My, how Galveston's changed," Pandora mused aloud, remembering the bygone days when horses pranced up and down the avenue. Now, Pandora Gabriel was one of the few residents who still drove her matched team of white horses, riding behind in her open carriage.

"Ma'am, you want me to bring you some iced tea while you wait for Mr. Ward?"

Pandora turned and smiled at old Cassie. "No, thank you. But bring me my box, won't you?"

A moment later, Cassie shuffled back out. In her hands she held the antique box that Ward Gabriel had given

Pandora for her eighteenth birthday. The sunlight glinted on the bright lotus blossoms she had carefully painted so long ago—the *forever flowers,* as she always thought of them. "That sure is one fine picture, Miss Pan! I always liked it from the first time you painted it in Paris. Remember?"

"Ah, but this picture is different, Cass." She stared down at the two figures, embracing in the grove and said more to herself than to her servant, "This one never changes."

Cassie went back inside, leaving her mistress to her box of memories. Pandora rummaged through her treasures, finally locating the clippings about the great storm of twenty-five years ago this very day. She read them through, one by one, then leaned her head back and closed her eyes, thinking.

"Six thousand killed!" she murmured aloud, recalling that terrible night. "And Ward and I almost among that count. If it hadn't been for Nicolette . . ."

She'd seldom thought of Nicolette and Jean Laffite since the storm. They didn't come to her in visions anymore. By saving her and Ward their purposes had been fulfilled; the two ghosts could finally rest from their labors. Following the storm, she and Ward had grown too close to allow anyone else to intrude—even her beloved phantoms. Things were better that way.

"Let the past lay," Pandora told herself. "Live for now, for tomorrow, not for yesterday!"

Yesterday was much on her mind this afternoon. "Twenty-five years ago," she whispered. "It can't be that long."

There were so many things—good and bad—to be remembered about those days and weeks following the hurricane. Their reunion with Meraiah and Miriam had been joyous the morning after that horrible night. But not all had come home to be welcomed by loved ones.

She and Ward, picking their way through the rubble and the bloating bodies the next day, had found old Daniel more dead than alive.

She could still hear the poor old man sobbing, "I tried to save her, Madame Boss. Honest, I tried! But there wasn't nothing I could do. Now your baby girl's gone."

"My babies are fine," Pandora assured him, supporting Daniel's weight as Ward and Jacob dug through the pile of debris that the old servant had guarded all night and half the hot, steaming day.

Finally, near the bottom of the heap, they found a woman's near-naked body lying crushed and broken.

"Jeannette!" Daniel wailed. "Oh, poor little Jeannette!"

Pandora stared at the man, unable to believe her ears, but certain that he spoke the truth. "Nettie . . . Jeannette," she murmured. Then her tear-filled eyes focused on the sad, old man. " 'Gator-Bait?" she whispered, holding out her hand to him.

He nodded. "Ain't nobody called me that in many a year, ma'am. I reckon you know the truth now. Me and Nettie, we wanted to tell you all along but she said it wasn't our place. She said, when the time was right, you'd just naturally know."

'Gator-Bait lived for only a few days after the storm—just long enough to tell Pandora everything he remembered about Nicolette and Jean Laffite, and all about his life with Nettie.

A few nights after the storm, when Pandora went in to tell him good-night, he said, "Well, I reckon I've told it all, Madame Boss. I'm gonna take me a good, long rest now."

He never woke up again.

Pandora fished into the box to bring out two golden earrings. Their matched fire opals caught the flame of the sunset. She still had to look at them to believe it. "Crazy Nettie," as the island's citizens had called her, had been wearing the missing earring when her body was found. It still sent a shiver through Pandora to think that she had actually known Jeannette Laffite.

"My *other* daughter," Pandora sighed, thinking back over her relationship with the old woman, Nettie, and wondering why she never guessed until it was too late.

Searching the box again, her fingers touched a soft curl of hair. She drew it out, pressing it to her heart. Now she knew to whom it had belonged. The missing lock of Jean Laffite's hair had been found, amazingly enough, after the storm. It had been inside her silver locket where Angelica, who had stolen both, had placed it before the raging waters swept her out of Ward's protective grasp.

A chill touched Pandora's heart as she remembered those dreadful days after the storm. Burial was difficult. Six thousand dead lay tangled in the wreckage, and the weather was brutally hot. On Monday, the Central Relief Committee had decided that mass burials at sea were the only answer. Grimly, the men who had been pressed into service—some at bayonet point—loaded the three barges, their noses covered with camphor-soaked bandanas, a priest offering them slugs of whiskey to keep them going. The bodies were weighted and taken far out in the Gulf. It seemed the only solution even though families frantically dug through the piles of rubble trying to locate their missing loved ones before the funeral crews took the bodies away.

The burials at sea proved a useless effort. On Wednesday, the first of the corpses floated back to the beach. Others followed. For days, Ward and Jacob worked on the cleanup crews, hoping to find Angelica so that she might have a proper burial.

The two of them were working on the beach the Thursday after the storm, piling the decaying corpses into heaps to be burned. Had Ward not found her, Jacob would never have known his wife. Her head was gone from her naked body, sliced off by a flying piece of tin roof, but Ward noticed a gleam of silver still twisted about the neck. He recognized Pandora's locket—Angelica had been wearing it that night.

It was not until long after the storm's horrible aftermath that Ward told Pandora where he had found the locket, but she knew. She'd guessed the very day it happened. Angelica had broken the chain and stolen the coveted locket as they embraced after her birthday luncheon. Inside was the lock of hair tied with a faded scarlet ribbon.

Pandora did not wear the locket ever again. She gave it to Jacob, to place inside his wife's coffin. The lock of hair, she returned to the antique box.

Jacob Saenger, along with some two thousand other inhabitants of the island, left for good. He moved away to far off Boston in the late fall. Old Dr. Saenger was lost in the storm, washed away with his house to become part of the great windrow of wreckage that formed a barrier across the island, saving the houses on Broadway from total destruction.

"You always were one for remembering, darling." Ward's soft, husky voice brought Pandora out of her reverie.

She looked up at him, smiled, and closed the lid of her box. "Not so much anymore. But today, well, it just seems right to look back and give thanks." She paused and shook her head. "So much destroyed! So many lost!"

Ward reached out and took her hand, raising her gently from her chair. "I know what you're thinking—what might have been. Darling, what *is* is infinitely more pleasant."

She smiled and let him lead her inside. The castle was quiet with the girls away in Europe. She missed the constant flurry of activity most of the time. The late afternoon sun painted the Galveston sky in flaming hues. Pandora was wonderfully happy to be enjoying it here alone with her husband—her one and only love.

She looked up into Ward's eyes—warm silvery-gray touched with mystery.

"I wish we still had the beach cottage," he whispered. "I'd take you there this minute, darling."

His lips came down to cover hers. Not a spark of excitement had faded from his kisses through the years. He could still set her whole body tingling with his slightest touch.

When he drew away, Pandora took his hand and tugged him gently toward the stairs.

"I know a place . . ." she whispered.

The glowing sunset torched the scarlet damask walls and made the antique bed gleam with its patina of gold. The bedroom was warm and secret and locked away from the rest of the world. Only the scent of late-blooming oleander and the lazy hum of bees invaded their sanctuary.

Ward loved his wife slowly, but ardently, and all else fled

from her mind. There was no longer any room in the great, golden bed for a third party. No green-eyed lover intruded.

Afterward, when Pandora lay in her husband's arms—wonderfully warm, thoroughly loved, perfectly content—she knew, as she had always known, that they loved each other with a passion far beyond the here and now.

Far beyond all their yesterdays . . . all their tomorrows.

Author's Note

Galveston Island lay wrapped in thick, cottony fog the morning of February 13, 1987, when I saw it for the first time. I had been waiting for years to visit this place. As our car eased down Broadway, I strained to catch glimpses of stately palms and Victorian mansions through the enshrouding, gray mist. But the fog couldn't obscure the island's special aura—a certain haunted feeling, a sense of past and present coming together, a special mystery unique to this one spot on earth. I knew then that I would write this book.

My husband and I had flown from Georgia to Houston the day before, renting a car to take this side trip. We spent the day coming to know the island. I had no story as yet, only a setting. I needed to find my characters before I left the island.

Around noon, my heroine presented herself. As we toured Ashton Villa, the former home of the Brown family, the spirit of Bettie Brown seemed to hover about, begging me to take notes faster.

What a fascinating woman she was! Artist, world travel-
ler, collector, fashion plate, the belle of Galveston in her
day. Bettie never married, although she was beseiged by
suitors, even in her later years when any other lady of the
Victorian Age would have been considered an old maid.

Bettie Brown inspired the creation of Pandora Sherwood.

While browsing through the gift shop after our tour, I
came across a brief history of the family, "The Browns of
Ashton Villa," written by Suzanne Morris, author of the
intriguing novel, *Galveston*. In this booklet, Ms. Morris told
not only of the family, but of the mansion's miraculous
rescue from the wreckers' ball in 1971. At the last instant
before its demolition, the Galveston Historical Foundation
and several other local sources came up with $125,000 to
purchase Ashton Villa from the Shriners, who had used it
as their temple since they bought the mansion from the
Brown family back in 1927. Galveston was denied a new
filling station on the site, but retained a valuable piece of its
history.

Although Pandora's box exists only in my imagination, it,
too, was inspired by a story from Ms. Morris's booklet. In
1984, Bettie Brown's great niece, Mrs. Francoise Jumon-
ville Vosbein of Louisiana, found a hidden drawer in a
writing desk handed down to her from the Browns of Ashton
Villa. Inside the secret compartment, she discovered over
fifty mementos—letters, clippings, travel souvenirs—dating
back to the golden years of Galveston.

My story was taking shape. We wandered on, visiting the
Bishop's Palace, the Strand, the beach, the west end where
Laffite's Grove still stands. At that point, I remembered that
I'd come across an intriguing Galveston story about Jean
Laffite while doing research for *Tainted Lilies*, an earlier
novel about the gentleman smuggler's New Orleans years.
His wife had been killed in Galveston, the only casualty of
the forced evacuation of the island in 1821. Had her death
been an accident or murder? No one ever found out. She
died in Laffite's arms and was buried on the island.

I thought there must be some way to combine Laffite's
story with that of the Oleander City in its golden years. By

nightfall, I had my solution, and soon *Forever, for Love* began weaving its own tapestry in my mind.

The tragic hurricane that struck Galveston on Saturday, September 8, 1900, still stands on the record as the worst natural disaster ever to strike the United States. That anyone on the low-lying island survived seems miraculous.

The death toll is listed at six thousand, but we will never know the true figure. During the fifteen-hour seige, 3,600 houses were destroyed. After it was over, there was talk of abandoning the island altogether, and moving Galveston to the mainland. But some two thousand of the staunch survivors refused to leave. The funeral pyres on the island burned into mid-November, wrapping all of Galveston in a pall of black, evil-smelling smoke. The last body—the skeleton of a fourteen-year-old girl—was recovered on February 10, 1901. Many of the missing remain unaccounted for to this day.

For further reading on this great disaster, I recommend *A Weekend In September* by John Edward Weems, *Galveston, A History* by David G. McComb, and *Galveston* by Ray Miller.

Becky Lee Weyrich
Unicorn Dune
St. Simons Island, Georgia